Lost & Found

A Romance Anthology

A Collection of 9 Stories
by members of the
Grand Rapids Regional Writers Group
(GRRWG)

Edited by Diana Stout, Ph.D.
& Kay Springsteen

ABOUT GRRWG

The purpose of the Grand Rapids Region Writers Group (GRRWG) is to promote writing excellence of all genres, to help writers pursue publication and establish careers in their field(s), to provide continuing support for writers within the publishing industry, and to create a safe and nurturing environment.

GRRWG is a non-profit, equal opportunity, all-inclusive organization.

All profits from the sale of this anthology will benefit the Grand Rapids Region Writers Group.

DEDICATION

This anthology is dedicated to the memory of published author Judy Lieffers who wrote as Judith Marie Austin. A long-time, enthusiastic GRRWG member and a good friend, Judy is greatly missed.

CONTENTS

ACKNOWLEDGMENTS

The brainchild of this anthology was Diana Lloyd's idea born out of a GRRWG meeting and a discussion of ideas for raising money. She volunteered to chair it, collected stories from members, and created the cover. We'd like to give a special thanks Kay Springsteen, an editor for one of GRRWG's members, for her services performed during an extremely trying time, which we learned after the fact. Once Diana Stout joined forces with Lloyd, that's when this project grew legs. She edited, proofed, formatted, and performed the uploading. A special shout-out to Annie O'Rourke for her beta reading. And, a thank you to those members who contributed their stories for the good of the organization.

Lost & Found

A Romance Anthology

Diana Lloyd

Diana Stout

Jae Vel

K D Norris

Lisa Campeau

Martin L Shoemaker

Natalia Baird

Patricia Kiyono

Rosanne Bittner

Heat Index

Sweet—Hand-holding, no swearing, groping, or sex. Sweet short kisses only.

Spicy — Sensual kissing, thoughts of being in bed with the other, some swearing, minor groping, sexual innuendos, sex could happen but behind a close door, no graphic details.

Hot— Sex, intimate scenes between consenting adults, adult language (swearing included).

Introducing Diana Lloyd

 Thimbleful

Diana Lloyd writes history with heart and humor. "Thimbleful," set in Regency London, is a story of small gestures having a big impact for two stubborn people. Alice Ashdown's day progressed swimmingly until she lost her voucher to Almack's ballroom. Frank's day was an exercise in frustration from the crack of dawn until that evening when he catches a desperate woman rummaging through his carriage. Two people who have no need of each other discover a shared passion for life. Diana enjoys connecting with her readers through social media.

For more information about her books and social media links, please visit www.DianaLloydBooks.com

Heat Level: HOT

THIMBLEFUL
Diana Lloyd

Chapter One

London, 1812

Her cheeks red-hot with embarrassment, Alice Ashdown smiled tightly at the footman barring the door. Holding her head high, she turned away with as much dignity as she could muster. The crowd queued for entry parted like the Red Sea to let her pass. She considered herself a collector of experiences, but this was one experience she'd rather have missed.

Her one and only chance to attend a fabled Almack's Assembly Hall Wednesday night ball would remain an unticked box on her wish list. It was a crushing end to an otherwise grand day. The day evolved so perfectly she had no idea where she'd managed to lose her admission voucher. Fifteen minutes ago, she would have sworn against her father's life that it was in her reticule where it belonged.

Dodging carriages as she crossed King Street, Alice brightened her smile. She refused to be the dour old maid sulking outside the doors of the address to which everyone in London wanted an invitation. She didn't want pity; she wanted her voucher. Where had she last seen it?

How grand it would be to find it and return in triumph to wave it under the footman's nose. It must have taken quite of bit of persuasion for her friend Lucy to procure a personal invitation from the venerable Almack's patronesses for a near-spinster from the dusty edges of society such as herself. She had to find that voucher.

Standing out of the way of moving carriages a short distance from the crowd, but not so far as to risk a cutpurse, Alice scrutinized the events of her day. The only time she could recall removing the voucher from her purse was on the way home from an early afternoon shopping excursion. She and Lucy were admiring Lady Sefton's penmanship while the hack was stuck in mid-day traffic. Could she have somehow dropped the prized square of pasteboard thinking she was slipping it back into her reticule?

It was possible, but London was full of hacks for hire. There must be a hundred of them here on King Street. She'd never find it. That afternoon's coachman, she recalled, had been a jovial fellow with a red feather stuck in his hatband. With the smallest spark of hope, Alice walked up and down the street hoping against odds to spot the red feather.

Most of the coachmen were gathered in knots of loud conversation and cheap tobacco up and down the street. Others, anticipating a longer wait, had wandered off to the nearest pub. A pastime she'd resort to if she were more familiar with Town. And brave enough to walk into a London pub alone at night. She was a fish out of water looking for a red feather.

Like that one. Hardly able to believe her good fortune, Alice ran the last few yards to get a better look. Lamplight revealed a large red feather painted on the door of a carriage just down the way from Almack's.

Had their carriage this afternoon sported a red feather on its door as well? She couldn't recall, but it was too much of a coincidence to not investigate. Approaching timidly, she walked all around the carriage to make sure it wasn't occupied. God forbid she barge in on amorous liaison and ruin someone else's evening.

She dared to stroke the muzzles of the matched pair in harness who were already stomping their hooves with boredom. Cleveland Bays if she had to guess, and amiable ones too. If their coachman was about, he'd come running to shoo her away. Coachmen were funny about their horses, but she would be too if her livelihood depended upon them. When no alarm was called out and no one approached, she walked around and quietly turned the latch on the carriage door.

With a fortifying gulp of breath, Alice opened the door and crawled into the carriage. Keeping her head down, she first checked the seats. Running her hand along the seams and under the cushions all she found was a latch to a secret compartment. The metal ring was cold and tempting in her fingertips.

Too tempting. Biting her lip with anticipation, she pulled the ring and slipped her hand into the revealed space. A pistol, a fine one, but no voucher. When the carriage door creaked behind her, she closed her hand around the pistol. Not waiting to be accosted while in such a vulnerable position, she turned and aimed the pistol at the dark blot standing just outside the door.

"Back off," she barked out, hoping to sound much braver than she felt.

"I will not," a male voice replied. "It's my carriage!"

"I'm the one with the pistol." Alice straightened up as much as she could and waved the pistol a little to get his attention and disguise how much her hand was shaking. "I'm giving the orders, not you, sir."

"It's my bloody pistol and it isn't loaded. Now," he said, offering his arm, "Remove yourself from my carriage this instant."

Reluctant as she was to trust him, there was no ladylike way to eject herself from his carriage with him standing in the way. Keeping the pistol aimed in his general direction, she grabbed his arm and stumbled out into the street.

"Give me that," he said, snatching the pistol out of her hand. "And explain yourself."

He wasn't a large man, they were of equal height, but it was unlikely she could outrun him in dancing slippers. Fisticuffs might be an option, but it wasn't her first one. Resorting to a school-yard maneuver, Alice kicked him in the knee and pushed him out of her way as she ran into the street. He had his pistol and his coach; she needed witnesses. Surely, he would avoid shooting a woman in the back in front of a crowd.

Stopping to catch her breath and compose herself, Alice smiled at the nearby crowd and pretended she was searching for acquaintances. Her toes now throbbed from kicking his knee, and she was no closer to finding her voucher. This evening would be added to her list of experiences; not all of them had to be pleasant. The red feather coach would have to remain incompletely searched. She couldn't enter Almack's, and she couldn't stand here all night. There was nothing to do now but find a hack to hire to return to Lucy's house.

Alice froze with dread as someone's hand clamped down on her shoulder. Afraid she knew whose hand it was, she pasted on a blithe smile before turning around. Surrounded by witnesses, she was prepared to scream bloody murder in an instant if need be.

"We have unfinished business," the man said flatly. "Neither of us is going into that building," he said, nodding toward Almack's. You have nowhere to run and I mean you no harm. All I want is for you to tell me what you were looking for in my carriage."

"My voucher," she replied with a sigh. Even with witnesses, truth would serve her the best. "I lost it earlier today and the last place I remember seeing it was in a carriage like yours. The coachman had a red feather in his cap and when I

saw the red feather on the door I…I decided to give it a search."
She shrugged her shoulders. "Just in case."

"Feather? That's not a feather! It's a bloody nettle."

"Mind your tongue sir! I am a gentleman's daughter and
will not tolerate your continued incivility." It was embarrassing
to flout what little social standing she had, but any leverage she
might gain was worth it.

"Not…never mind, it's a literal nettle dripping with red
blood. A bloody nettle."

"Are you a doctor, a surgeon, or an anatomist?" she
asked, her curiosity piqued. "Why on earth a bloody nettle?"

"Family coat of arms," he replied with half a smile
playing around the edges of his mouth. "My father insists on
painting it on everything. Even my carriage."

"I suppose if my father had leave to use a coat of arms,
he would have done the same." Before she knew what she was
doing, they were walking together as they spoke, step by step
separating themselves from the crowd. There were many
reasons for her to fear this unknown man, but the one reason to
trust him won out.

"My coachman doesn't wear a feather in his cap and I
don't recall ever seeing one that does. As it appears both our
plans for the evening have been irrevocably altered by yonder
footman, I'll help you look for your red feather and then have
my coachman return you to your address."

"Did you lose your voucher too?" Whoever this man
was, his voice was persuasive and his manner mild. Each word
leaving his lips was pronounced with delicate precision as if to
disguise an accent or speech impediment. Rather than making
him sound pedantic or severe, it was oddly reassuring. It was as
if every word that left his mouth was nothing less than the
truth. He might be a fiend, a resurrectionist, or a common
murderer. Or, as his voice and manner suggested, he might be

the friend she needed in this moment.

"Trousers," he said, in answer to her question. "Almack's only admits gentlemen in breeches."

"I never knew that." Alice looked back at the crowd and noticed the other men's attire. "If I were you, I'd have been sore tempted to remove them and walk in with my stockings and garters enjoying the breeze."

"Oh, my," he said, stifling a laugh. "It was, indeed, tempting."

"You might have collected it as an experience."

"I don't follow…"

"I collect experiences. It is so much more rewarding than collecting teapots or, say, gambling debts." Alice shook her head at her folly. She was telling a complete stranger something she'd never admitted to anyone. Lucy knew, that's why she arranged for the voucher to Almack's, but Lucy was her oldest and dearest friend.

"I hope you add aiming a pistol at me to your list."

"Oh, I will." Turning away so he wouldn't see her smile, she scanned the street for any sign of a real red feather as another carriage rumbled by. Best not to get too friendly with a man who's name she didn't know, but she'd not turn away a fellow reject. The anonymous companionship he offered was worth a small risk.

"I bet I can guess your name." As if he'd read her thoughts, the man hit upon the very subject of her reticence. "You look like a…Mary."

"Alice. You weren't even close. Oh," she said, turning to him with a frown. "I see what you did there, you tricked me into telling you my name."

"Tricked?" He shook his head in mock innocence. "I said I could guess, and I did. It was a wrong guess but a guess all the same, Alice."

"I call corruption most foul, sir. I haven't given you leave to use my name. Besides, I don't know yours." If he was fair-minded, he'd tell her. When she recorded this experience in her journal, she should at least know what name to write.

"Frank. Well, more precisely, I am Franz Frederick Fitzjohn. I give you leave to call me Frank," he said with a bow.

"Pleased to meet you, Frank," she said with a curtsey. "I am Miss Alice Anne Ashdown. You may call me Miss Ashdown."

"We of boring monograms should be friends," he said, daring to wink at her and offering his hand to shake. "We could start a society of uni-alphabeters and meet at the corner of Cross and Crown every third Thursday."

"A society of twenty-six members, one for each letter of the alphabet," she chimed in as she shook his offered hand. The man was positively infectious with good humor. She doubted she would have had such casually pleasant conversation within the walls of the ballroom. An on-the-shelf country bumpkin would have been shuttled over to the wallflowers and promptly forgotten.

"I'm trying to decide if QQQ or XXX would be the more difficult monogram to find."

"Not if we look world-wide." As someone who'd never left England's shore, the notion of unfettered travel was her wildest wish. Mr. Fitzjohn had likely taken tea with maharajas and climbed mountains led by a troupe of dancing bears. Neither story would be doubted.

"Now that would be an experience for you to chalk up."

They had walked the length of the block back and forth by then with no sign of a red feather. Or any more bloody nettles for that matter. Frank Fitzjohn was a puzzle. Half an hour ago she was prepared to shoot him and now her hand rest on his arm as if they were any couple out for an evening stroll.

Her earlier embarrassment at being turned away faded into a crumb of irritation that would soon, with his continued company, float away into the evening air.

She'd forgotten what it was like to enjoy an evening with a bon vivant. To strip away a layer of armor and speak her mind about matters large, small, and absurd with no fear of accusations of impertinence or causing manly ire.

"What do you collect?" she asked, curious to learn more about him. Had they met under other circumstances, enjoying the company of such a man would merit a notable entry in her journal.

"Compliments."

Oh, the man had no shame at all! Alice envied the ability to be both ridiculous and confident at the same time. As an unmarried woman she had to carve out her own moments and measure them against society's expectations. This moment, with this man, might prove to be worth the experience.

"You probably have ten events you could be attending this evening; I shouldn't keep you any longer." If he insisted on keeping the air of mystery about him, she would abuse his good humor no more. Besides, she was curious to see if Lucy was still attending to the family emergency. Or if there'd been an emergency at all. "I'll accept the offer of your carriage and coachman now."

"I'll fetch my man," he said with what she hoped was a bit of reluctance. "He would not have anticipated such an early evening. Would you like to wait alone inside the coach or are you comfortable here beside the crowd?"

"Inside the coach, please." She'd rather be alone in a cold coach than an afterthought to the jovial crowd streaming into Almack's. Frank Frederick Fitzjohn, his bloody nettle, and his pistol would get an entire page in her experience journal.

Chapter Two

Secretly pleased with the smile she forgot to hide from him when he climbed into the carriage, Frank rapped on the roof to let the coachman know they were ready. His day had been one of the heretofore unnamed circles of hell. It started with a dull razor and nearly ended with taking a bullet outside of Almack's. The huntress attached to the shapely silk-draped arse found sticking out of his carriage was a puzzle. Whether she portended a further descent into hell or a way out, remained to be seen.

His charm was rusty with disuse, but he had twenty minutes to convince her to remain in his company before reaching her destination. A woman who collected experiences was too rare of a find. Moonlight had revealed an unconventionally beautiful visage in the seat across from him and he settled back to admire her. Fair of face, she appeared well-formed and was an obviously educated gentleman's daughter.

Perhaps it was a good omen that they were of equal station and temperament. Those who yoked themselves with gloom and doom were an anathema to him. They sucked all the air out of the room until he choked from want of a breath. Miss Ashdown was that breath of fresh air. He might even be able to convince her that some experiences were best shared.

"What experiences have you chalked up so far, Miss Ashdown?"

"Not the sort that would interest you, I'm sure."

"Are you already an expert judge of my nature?"

"It wasn't my intention to be judgmental, Mr. Fitzjohn. Most of my exploits would bore a man as he is able to do whatever he pleases when he pleases to do it. Women must grab at leftovers or keep their triumphs secret lest they be labeled lunatic."

"Fair enough," he said as he contemplated her words. "This coach, this small space containing but you and me, is sanctuary. Within these confines I will not judge you and ask that you return the favor. I speak to you as one human being to another."

She was quiet for so long, he began to fear she wouldn't speak for the remainder of their journey. He'd overstepped convention and now disappointment punched him in the gut for it. But, wait, her lips were curling into a sly smile.

"I swam quite naked in the sea at Land's End," she announced. "It was wonderful. Have you ever?"

"There's a spring-fed pond near our family estate," he replied, "When the weather cooperates, I enjoy a swim wearing naught but what I came into the world with. I've often thought it would make a grand place for a party. I'm thirty and five and haven't yet asked anyone."

"After I complete an experience of note, I often wish I might celebrate with a like-minded person. As a woman, it would be improper of me to inquire if anyone else enjoyed… invigorating experiences. I'd be labelled hysterical. But," she hesitated a moment and bit her lower lip as if contemplating her words, "I suppose I could ask you."

"Thank you. You could. I would have cheered you on at Land's End, applauded you, even thrown you a towel." More likely he'd have been in the surf with her, enjoying the joy and freedom of the swim. "The night is yet young. Let's have an adventure."

"Something to write in my journal besides lost my voucher, turned away at Almack's, and aimed a pistol at a stranger while rummaging through his carriage?"

"You forgot the part where you kicked me," he said, rubbing his knee for emphasis. "You should have gone for the nutmegs. That would have stopped any man. By the way," he had to wipe the smile off his face before continuing, "That pistol was loaded."

"Oh, my! Oh! I might have killed you! How horrible. Why are you laughing?"

"I just thought of the perfect adventure. Or, experience, as you prefer. It will be dashed difficult to top nearly murdering me, but I have a few things in mind if you're game."

"I'm always game for something new to write in my journal."

Frank rapped on the roof and shouted out the window to his coachman, "Number twenty-five Davies Street."

***

Alice wasn't sure if Mr. Fitzjohn had to bribe anyone to get her into Manton's shooting gallery, but she was the only female present this evening. Their assigned footman refused to meet her eyes as he presented a tray full of pistols for her to inspect and fire. There was a lovely pearl-handled flint-lock small enough to fit inside her reticule and a slightly larger ebony-handled percussion lock that she wanted to try.

Pointing to her selections, the footman bobbed his head and turned to her escort. Sighing, Alice knew that while she'd been granted admittance, she was still a second-class citizen within these walls. Every decision would be checked against the wishes of her escort. It would chafe more if she wasn't looking forward to having a go at the pistol she'd found in the carriage. From the short time she'd held it, she knew it was quality.

The footman returned with her selected pistols on a tray, presumably loaded and in good working order. There was also a length of combed wool and a small brass flask. Assuming the wool was for her ears, she had no idea what the flask might contain. Unsure of the room's protocol, she smiled and nodded her approval.

"Ready to begin?" Mr. Fitzjohn had removed his coat and was already making himself ready to fire at the targets posted at the far end of the gallery.

"I believe so, it's just that...I don't know what to do with this," she said, pointing to the tiny flask. Picking up the flask, he unstoppered the top and took a cautious whiff.

"I was hoping for a drop or two of good whiskey, but it smells like an unguent of some sort. You there," he called to the footman and held up the flask, "What's this for?"

"Burns, sir. Powder burns. I didn't want the lady to catch a blister from the spark."

"Excellent." Mr. Fitzjohn turned to her and smiled sheepishly. "I should have thought of that."

"I promise not to hold you responsible." Did Frank Fitzjohn have any idea what he was doing to her? He'd allowed her to choose her own pistols without hovering over her shoulder explaining the difference between each gun and offering his opinion. He didn't feel the need to stuff the wool in her ears for her as if she wasn't up to the task. He was treating her like a fellow human being, and it was becoming embarrassingly seductive.

The gallery lighting afforded her a chance to view him without hinderance of shadow or fickleness of moonlight for the first time. Fastidiously groomed except for a slight razor burn on his left cheek, he had a pleasant but unremarkable face. Eyes as brown as Turkish coffee suggested a seriousness his mouth didn't live up to. His smile was a wink between friends that transformed him. It nearly transformed her.

After multiple shots of the two smaller pistols, Alice allowed him to assist her with his pistol, the one from the carriage. It was one of the new tube-lock models, and she already knew she would later purchase one when she found the funds. Becoming a female marksman with a pistol was on her list of sought-after experiences.

Standing just behind her, Frank steadied her arm and cautioned her to mind the pistol's kick. She squeezed the trigger and hit the target a respectable distance from dead center. A ripple of excitement and triumph ran up her spine to be met by his warm breath on the back of her neck.

"We should go dancing next. What say you?"

"I'll smell of the gun-powder," she replied, knowing she should step out of his arms but not doing so. He was exactly as close as she wished him to be. Her initial plan for the evening was dancing—would it be so wrong to consider it now?

"You smell of lilacs."

Having him notice pleased her more than it should, and she lowered the pistol. She'd pinched a handful of the small blooms off a bush in Kensington Gardens yesterday just so she could sew them into the shoulder seams of her dress. It was frivolous to have done it on the off chance some desperate gentleman at Almack's would ask for a dance.

Frank was a pleasurable problem to have this evening, but that didn't make him more than he was. A bored man filling his hours with an amiable companion. But, she could hardly condemn him for it as she was doing the same. It didn't need to mean anything more than it was, she reminded herself. Tomorrow he'd forget all about her.

"Hanover Square," he shouted out to his coachman as he helped her back into his carriage.

"That is not my direction and you know it," she said, hoping he couldn't see her smile.

"I was just thinking it was bit of a shame to waste our evening dress on a shooting gallery and a closed carriage. It hadn't occurred to me until viewed in the well-lit gallery that your gown is exquisite. It was made for dancing and we should employ it to its purpose."

"I sewed it myself," she replied as she smoothed out the skirt. Fashioned from washed silk, the gown was a labor of love that expressed both her skill with a needle and her artistic taste. The blue fabric was reminiscent of a peacock feather, the delicate purple and gold embroidery around the hem and bodice meant to be an unpretentious embellishment befitting a woman her age. Society may consider twenty and seven a spinster, but her gown was fashioned to celebrate her age, not deny it.

"You're a skilled seamstress."

"Luckily, I enjoy the task. Between experiences, that is." Sewing was so relaxing to her, she sought out the solitude and silence of it when frustrated with everything else. Once upon a time, she contemplated becoming a seamstress for a dressmaker, but her thirst for experiences would make her an unreliable employee.

"Thimbles," he said quietly. "You once asked what I collected. My mother collected thimbles. Some came from as far away as the Orient. When she died," he stopped and swallowed hard as if still pained by her passing, "She left them to me, and I couldn't bring myself to sell them. To scatter them to the wind would be like erasing her life. She was a good mother."

"She must have been to raise a man like you. My condolences on the loss of her. Have you added to her collection?"

"I'm a bit embarrassed to admit that I have because I'm not sure why I do it."

"To honor her, I should think. It's sweet."

"Oh, dear," he said, hanging his head in mock despair. "I've gone twee."

"I won't tell anyone," she said, reaching across the way to lift his chin. "I wish I had gotten the chance to know my parents better so my mother and I might have collected thimbles together."

"You're an orphan, then?"

"My parents were elderly. I came along as a bit of a surprise. They had both passed by the time I was ten. Do not fret for me, they left me in fine fettle." She wasn't about to tell him about the property she inherited—it was a fact not tossed around casually. A female property owner was rare enough to invite scrutiny. Especially by cash poor men looking to make a quick gain through matrimony. "I hardly think the word *orphan* is appropriate at my age."

"So, about that dance," he said as he raised an eyebrow to her statement. "There's always a party somewhere in Hanover Square. I sent regrets to one for this very evening. Shall I rescind my regrets so you and I might take a turn about their dance floor?"

"Your hosts might not appreciate an unexpected guest." Here is where they must part. She was correct when she'd assumed he'd had other places to be tonight. She'd ask his coachman to transport her to Lucy's house after dropping Frank off in Hanover Square.

"We wouldn't trouble them much. For the… *experience*, we'll appear, dance one single dance, and then promptly leave. I am particularly fond of Scottish Reels."

"Then you should attend your party and I should return to my friend's house."

"I've been wondering why your friend wasn't with you at Almack's. Why were you left on your own? Your friend is a bit of a lout."

"My friend's name is Lucy and she's not any such thing. We planned on attending together when, at the last possible moment, her husband's family had some manner of emergency which required their presence."

"Bum fodder." He spoke the words with disdain. "Her husband was unhappy about her spending the evening with an unmarried woman. Probably the insecure, jealous sort." She wished she could call him a liar, but she'd suspected the same.

"He provided the only distraction that poor Lucy couldn't refuse—a sudden and mysterious family emergency. I chose not to let it spoil my evening."

"Good for you. We're here," he said, reaching for the door. "How about that dance?"

Chapter Three

Laughing and running back to his carriage like naughty children, Frank relished the feel of her hand clasping his and gave it a squeeze. He'd no idea whose party they'd just invaded, but the music was good, and his partner was light on her feet. With any luck their unwitting host was still shaking his head trying to place their names and faces.

Once inside the carriage, Alice dissolved into giggles. Her unabashed laughter was, to him, as precious as a chorus of angels singing *hallelujah*. The world was full of people who refused to see humor, who denied themselves full-throated laughter and enjoyment of the preposterous.

Could it be the peevish woman he'd found rummaging through his carriage was like-minded? If so, she was as rare as a unicorn. Being in the presence of such a woman was a time to be savored. There were still many hours before dawn, and he wanted to fill all the minutes with her.

"You didn't know them!" She wheezed out as the carriage jerked into motion. "You said you'd been invited." She put her hands over her mouth to hold in more laughter.

"I know I sent regrets to something this evening. I may have gotten my addresses mixed up."

"We might have been arrested or…something."

"We would have been quietly shown the door and suffered no more ill-effect than we did for being turned away at Almack's." Rapping against the roof, he called out their next destination to his coachman. "Vauxhall Pleasure Gardens."

"Again, not my direction."

"If you wish to be returned to your inconstant friend, I will do so immediately But," he added, "consider, if you will, an evening of adventures shared with me." If she asked to be returned, his evening would end as well. One did not encounter a unicorn twice in a day.

"Lucy is dear to me; I'll not listen to a rebuke of her."

"My apologies. I do not know the lady. If you've gifted her with your friendship, I should consider her worthy of it." He'd offended her with his blunt manner. Those who took offence at plain speaking were usually beneath his notice, but not Miss Ashdown. Her opinion mattered. "I have abused our sanctuary and I beg your forgiveness."

"On their face, her actions might appear cold, but I assure you she and I love one another as sisters. Life has gotten between us once or twice, but we always find our way back to forgiveness."

"I should hope then that we might do the same. I value your high opinion as I perceive it isn't given away frivolously. If you wish to remain in my company, I shall strive to be a man deserving of your friendship." He'd laid the stone-cold truth at her feet. Now, all he could do was wait for her decision. He was well and truly vexed with this woman. The ferocity of his feelings was in turns exhilarating and terrifying. And both extremes hinged on her next words.

"That is possibly the nicest thing a man has ever said to me." With her admission, she smiled and looked away as if embarrassed by it. Her next words were spoken into the void between them for him to interpret as he would. "Your company is most welcome this evening."

"I am relieved," he admitted, relaxing his shoulders a bit. "Perhaps you'd like to choose our next adventure. One of your more sought-after experiences would suffice. Although, I should mention that I am out of practice in tree climbing." Not only was she smiling and once again meeting his eyes, she leaned over and ever so briefly touched his knee while she laughed.

"I hardly came all the way to London just to climb trees.

I can do that back in Pudbury. On another evening Vauxhall might suit my mood. Tonight, however, I find myself enjoying our sanctuary too much to share it with a crowd."

"Pardon me, did you say Pudbury? Pudbury in Buckinghamshire?"

"It's such a small village, I'm surprised you've heard of it. Have you been there?"

"I spent a week there one afternoon." His joke was rewarded with her smile. "I once took the wrong road out of Buckingham and found myself quite lost. I had the further misfortune of asking a Mr. Hewitt for directions and if I might be allowed to spell my horse in his yard while I drew water. I was unaware at the time that he was the village idiot."

"Oh, dear." She stifled a laugh. "You must have encountered Old Mr. Hewitt. Young Mr. Hewitt would have done it for coin."

"Mr. Hewitt the elder chased me away with the sword he must have carried against the Romans. I had to wait until his mid-day nap to sneak back for my horse."

"Are you from Buckinghamshire?" She choked out the question trying to hold back her laughter. "My estate is just to the west of Pudbury."

"As I'm sure you've noticed, the King's English is not my first language. I was born in Bavaria. My father was an English ambassador and my mother the daughter of a burgher. They returned to my father's family estate near Aylesbury when Bavaria began to flirt with France."

"Do you think you'll ever return?"

"My home is here now." Could it be that the woman sitting across from him lived less than twenty miles from his own estate? Wait, she referred to her home as *my* estate. He was speaking to the owner of Ashdown House. A house with land his father spent ten years trying to purchase. How many times had they crossed paths?

"Surely I have found the only other soul in London who's been to Pudbury. It must be my lucky night after all." She spoke the words casually, as if it hadn't yet occurred to her they might share an acquaintance.

"We're both lucky." Lucky enough to find each other. She was right to want to savor their sanctuary. He didn't want to share her with a crowd either. Her bit of bad luck in losing her voucher was the best thing that happened to him all day. "Where would you like to go? My carriage is at your command."

"The weather is dry and the moon is full, let us enjoy the outdoors. How would a stroll through Hyde Park suit you?"

"Very well," he replied before shouting out their new direction to his coachman. While he knew the man would happily drive all evening long for the privilege of sleeping all the next day, Frank reminded himself to add a few coins to the man's pay for the day.

***

Even with the full moon, Hyde Park was a maze of shadowy nooks and crannies. If they stayed clear of the water's edge, they might manage a stroll without mishap. With the number of other carriages dotted alongside Rotten Row, she felt more at risk of tripping than being beset by a ruffian. She knew why the carriages were there and what was likely transpiring inside them. Assignations, liaisons, and all manner of lovemaking took place in every park in every town and village in the Kingdom after dark.

Whether Mr. Fitzjohn realized she knew that fact or that she'd purposely chosen this destination remained to be discovered. It was to his credit that he hadn't pounced upon her the minute they rolled past the gate.

The experience she craved was a delicate matter. Until

she was ready to translate her wishes into words, she was content to have him nearby. Mr. Fitzjohn might not know it, but this walk beneath the stars was part of the negotiation.

"Just so you know," he said, breaking the silence. "I haven't the sway to gain you access to White's or Brook's or any other gaming hell. Like yourself, while I enjoy the temporary excitement of games of chance, I have no desire to collect outstanding gambling markers." He paused then and placed his hand atop hers where it rested on his arm. "There is much you could persuade me to do for you, Miss Ashdown, but I refuse to be the man who leads you into danger."

"Thank you, Frank." They stood in the perfect convergence of shadow into inky darkness far enough from the road that they'd be neither seen nor heard. She hadn't intended to begin this way, but she was leaning over to give him a kiss on the cheek before she could check herself. He remained a perfect gentleman for almost ten seconds as she brushed light kisses across his cheek toward his mouth.

He lay his hand against her cheek, caressing her face as he brought his lips to hers. His kiss was tender but surprisingly brief before he drew himself away. She knew without any words that he was asking her permission to continue down both paths. Confirming her consent with a return to his lips, his arms slid around her waist to hold her near.

As their kiss deepened, she placed her hands on the lapels of his coat and began to spread them wide. She'd worked his shoulders free before he drew back with a question in his eyes. It was encouraging that he didn't immediately shrug back into his coat. The moon and stars revealed his shy smile. He might have looked boyish were it not for his beard.

"I'm asking for an experience."

His eyes widened at her words and one side of his coat was pulled back into place.

"Not my first, if that's what you're wondering."

"I was," he said at last. "I'd be lying if I said I hadn't also considered the possibility of such an encounter." He looked down to the ground for a moment as if collecting his thoughts. "This seems the appropriate time for me to confess that due to an illness suffered as a younger man, it is unlikely that I can father children."

"That doesn't make you any more or less desirable to me." She'd considered the possibility of a child when first considering this experience. Money and land insulated her from fear of being ostracized for a bastard child. She closed the space between them and slipped his jacket back off his shoulder. "Take it off."

He hesitated a moment but complied. Once removed he held it out to her like foreign cloth he had no idea what to do with. A nervous giggle escaped her lips as she relieved him of it and spread it out on the ground as their magic carpet.

"Lay down, if you will," she said, holding out her hand to him. Whether he retreated or complied she would remember the remainder of the evening for the rest of her life. One memory would recall her utter embarrassment and the other, if she convinced him, would bring a smile to her face on lonely nights.

Once he was settled on the ground, she hitched her skirt up to her hips and stepped over him. His sharp intake of breath convinced her that he understood her meaning. Quickly, so as not to give herself time to lose her courage, she lowered herself to her knees and straddled him. When he reached out to her, she pushed his hands away and shook her head.

"This is my experience," she said.

He nodded his acceptance. It was good that he understood her terms, but now was time for her plans to be put into action.

23

Freeing each breast from the confines of her bodice, she lowered the fabric as far as it would go. Ribs and nipples might be every man's dream, but she was proud of her ample breasts and rounded hips. Leaning over she rubbed her breasts against his beard, the prickly hairs awaking every nerve until her skin warmed and every touch radiated through her body.

Frank showed his appreciation by turning his head and sucking a dusky nipple into his mouth. On hands and knees, she hovered over him giving him his fill of her bosom. While his mouth kept her distracted, he grabbed her hips with his hands and crushed her against him.

His hardened cock strained against the fabric and she ground herself against him to see how he'd react. The strangled noise he let out could only be interpreted as appreciation. She was ready for him, already a pleasant tingling warmth was spreading between her legs.

Snaking one hand down between them she struggled with his trouser buttons until she held hard, heated, flesh in her hand. The impulse to sheath him had to be set aside for a moment. She wanted this experience to last until they both found the ultimate pleasure.

Lowering herself until she lay atop him, their lips found each other once again. Their kisses soon became frantic as they pulsed their hips against each other. Only when she thought she'd scream from want did she rise up and place her hand between them to guide him home.

Flooded with relief to finally have him where she needed him most, she bit her tongue to keep from calling out his name. She was in control and was determined to discover what felt best for her. Tensing her muscles around him, she rose back up to her hands and knees and flexed her hips. Slowly at first, but quickly building speed as arousal filled her senses, she began to ride him.

Remember this, she reminded herself before all thought turned to their connected bodies and the ecstasy that would soon be achieved. She was beyond coherent speech, content with the symphony of their bodies being employed to their manifest purpose. Somewhere far outside of herself, she heard Frank whispering her name over and over again.

Before she knew what he intended, his arms clamped around her and he rolled them over until he was now on top. There was no time to call foul as what he did with his body from the superior position was no less than heavenly. They were in a race now, a race to orgasm. When he slipped his hand between them and added his fingers to the race, her body bucked and pulsed with wave after wave of pure pleasure.

Somewhere in the back of her mind she was aware of his pleasure matching hers. But she pushed those thoughts aside for now. They were both still breathing hard from the exertion when he pushed himself aside and flopped back down on his back beside her. They didn't speak for a long while, but he inched his hand over to hers and held on tightly while their hearts slowed to a more normal rhythm.

"Make sure you spell my name correctly in your journal," he said at last.

Chapter Four

With the increasing sounds of life outside her bedroom window, Alice gave up any pretense of sleep. The sight of her ballgown carelessly tossed over the back of a chair brought a smile to her face. Unless Lucy and her husband had returned within the last few hours, there would be servants available to draw a bath. Impressions of certain events became clearer in hindsight. A long soak in lilac-scented water would be just the thing to help settle her mind enough to begin writing last night's experience.

Frank had asked so little of her. Was he content with her company as her true self, or did her nature not matter a whit to him? His kisses felt genuine enough. She smiled at the thought and brought her hand up to rub her thumb across her still whisker-chafed lips. She would have liked to experience what else his amazing mouth could do.

That would be an adventure for another time, most likely with another man. The odds of Frank Fitzjohn looking her up in Pudbury were slim. Wait, her property manager once told her of some persistent lout who kept making ridiculous offers on her property. Wasn't his name Fitz something? It couldn't be him. He dropped no hints. He asked for nothing.

Her mouth went dry and she swallowed hard to get the taste of doubt off her tongue. Those thoughts must be put aside so as to not shadow her recounting of the experience into her journal. With one last look at her beautiful gown still wrinkled and grass-stained from their lovemaking, she rang the bell for a servant to begin heating bath water.

While bucket after bucket of warm water slowly filled the small tub, the footmen hustled into her room, she rummaged through her things for a suitable day dress. She'd packed conservatively for her visit with Lucy. While the invite was for a fortnight, she knew she'd never last that long. It was becoming more and more difficult to pretend that she and Lucy's husband would ever see eye to eye.

Other than simply existing as an independent woman, she had no recollection of what she might have done to offend the man. No matter, Lucy was a faithful correspondent and the post held no grudges. Laying out her journal alongside sharpened pencils she waited anxiously while the servants vacated the room and left her to her bath.

Warm water hugged her body when she sat in the tub

and it rose almost to the brim even with her knees sticking out. There was a little purple bruise on her left knee and, unable to fight the inclination, she pressed her finger against it to gauge the damage. It was nothing and would fade away within a day or two. Just like her magic carpet ride.

Angry with herself for purposely spoiling the moment, she covered her knee with a washing flannel. Looking across the room at her open journal longingly, she wished it was possible to write in the bath without fear of waterlogged pages. As she began to wash and scrub it was easier to remember the feel of Frank's mouth and hands on her body.

Alone in the bath, pretending the warm flannel she dragged across her breasts was Frank's beard, she convinced herself his actions were earnest, his kindness genuine. It didn't matter what she wore later. It didn't matter that she'd be gone by the end of the day. She may not have achieved the experience she'd expected at Almack's, but she would never be disappointed in the experience she had.

She would take the unsullied memory and her updated journal back to Ashdown House before the end of the day. Frank was free to ask after her the next time he passed through Pudbury. It was all up to him.

***

Realizing he'd been staring at the same spot on the wall for the past half-hour, Frank gave up trying to talk himself out of the bold action he was about to take. If ever in his life he'd done something just for himself, this would be it.

His father, a hardnosed taskmaster in his best moments and befuddled elderly gruff in his worst, would have an apoplexy if he knew what his son was about to do. The thought shouldn't make him smile, perhaps it was the sight of his grass-stained clothes on the floor that tickled his humor this morning.

The clothes were most likely unsalvageable, but the

experience was worth it. Reminding himself to let his laundress know he didn't expect her to perform a miracle on them, he stuck his head out his bedroom door looking for a servant. Once instructions were dispatched, he stared at the open wardrobe cupboard trying to decide what he should wear.

Not that it mattered much, but he strove to always look presentable to any situation. And he was about to create a situation.

One did not let a unicorn walk by hoping to catch it on the next pass. If she was going to laugh him out of the room, he'd leave well dressed with his head held high. He'd relived every second of their time together over and over all morning. No doubt she'd already second-guessed her need for children. The possibility of being unable to give a woman a child had kept him a bachelor all these years.

It would be cruel to bind himself to someone who would always want what he couldn't provide. He'd be nothing more than a cuckhold with an estate. He'd no desire to be anybody's lifelong mistake. Now that he'd found a woman with a zest for life that matched his own, he'd ask the one question he never thought he would.

He needed a gift. Something that, no matter Alice's response, would make her think of him with a smile for the rest of her life. If he were home at Elm Park in Aylesbury, he'd find an appropriate token from his mother's things but the thought of waiting even one more day had already been dismissed.

The perfect idea got him dressed and in a carriage on the way to Covent Garden before noon. He'd playfully mocked friends who claimed to have fallen in love as if the act were akin to an unexpected tumble down a stairway. His argument that spontaneity of affection was more the result of swift calculation of monetary gain and societal advancement than epiphany, now sounded cold and misguided.

He began forming a notion as soon as she admitted to collecting experiences. If one must look for point of metaphorical falling, it was when she didn't flinch when he mentioned his likely shortcoming. Of course, her enjoyment of her own body didn't hurt matters. Her enjoyment of his body sealed the deal.

Aware that he was now smiling like a lunatic as he drove a leased gig across Town, Frank attempted to damper his expectations a bit. She was free to say no. It was all up to her.

***

Alice slathered a toast point with orange marmalade and was about to take a bite when she heard a commotion at the door. Judging from the way the servants hurried about, Lucy and her husband had returned from their emergency.

It was unusual for Lucy not to pop into the breakfast room to bid her a good day no matter how busy others might be. To Alice, it was further proof that no actual emergency ever existed. She finished her breakfast alone and in silence, making plans to be on a post chaise before nightfall.

Determined not to confront Lucy, especially in front of her husband, Alice used the servant's stairwell to return to her room. She'd already asked a footman to send a runner for the day's post chaise schedule even though she had no idea how she would explain her sudden departure to Lucy.

Their friendship would survive this hiccup, of that she was sure. To settle her mind and busy her hands, Alice grabbed her gown off the back of the chair and walked to the window to inspect it in the daylight. Much of the fabric could be salvaged and the embroidered bits used in future hats if she ever found matching ribbon.

Her travel sewing box was nestled at the bottom of her leather satchel and closing her hand around it was an act of comfort. Soon she'd be lost in the stitches and hours would pass by with barely a notice. Settled by the window, Alice opened the box to select the best tool for what she needed to do. A seam-ripper and a thimble should do the job nicely.

There, on top of her gold thimble and delicate ivory-handled embroidery scissors, lay her voucher to Almack's. Stunned recollection brought her hand to her mouth to keep from calling out Eureka and taking the news to Lucy. The memory came back from wherever it had been hiding all night and she could only shake her head at her own absent-mindedness.

She'd popped a stitch in her ballgown, a single stitch that no one would be aware of other than herself and pulled out her sewing box to quickly mend it. That's when Lucy rushed into the room to tell her about the family emergency. In the confusion, she must have placed the voucher in her sewing box rather than her reticule.

Frank would find it hilarious.

Only he'd never know. Even if she happened by chance to encounter him in Pudbury or Buckingham, she could hardly blurt out her discovery as if he'd remembered her or her dilemma and would know what she was talking about. She was likely the furthest thing from his mind this morning. She was content with thinking about him for a few days, his face would slowly fade from memory but the way she felt last night would be carried to her grave.

***

With the perfect gift tucked away in his pocket, Frank paced the length of the small sitting room where he'd been asked to wait. When the door finally opened, it was by the gentleman of the house—not the person he wanted to see. Still, he'd gotten in the door and for that he'd be cordial to the man.

"Frank Fitzjohn," he said, offering his hand.

"Lord Stephen Horsley."

His handshake was more of a question than an introduction and Frank knew he'd better answer quickly and satisfactorily if he had any chance of seeing Alice today. She would chafe at the thought that this man, the man responsible for leaving her alone on what should have been a lovely night of dancing, held her fate in his careless hands. If he was denied an audience with her, Frank was prepared to camp outside the doorstep until she left the house.

"Thank you for speaking to me, Lord Stephen." When the man nodded to a chair, they both took a seat. "I suppose you're wondering why I'm here today."

"Something about Alice?"

"Miss Ashdown. Yes, I made her acquaintance last evening at Almack's." With no idea how much of yesterday's events she'd related to her hosts, Frank chose his words carefully. "I was pleased to offer the use of my carriage to return her here."

"I'll bet."

"I beg your pardon, I'm afraid I don't understand your meaning. It was the gentlemanly thing to do." Damn it, he should have bought flowers. He'd been so pleased to find the perfect gift, he'd forgotten all about flowers. "All I seek is a few moments of conversation with the lady. We discovered we are nearly neighbors in Buckinghamshire, and I would like to offer the use of my carriage for her return trip."

"Ashdown House," the man replied with obvious derision. "If you think chumming up with her will smooth the way to a land transaction, you might as well turn around and leave now. She's the headstrong sort and won't listen to reason. Why on earth does a single woman need land?"

"Perhaps for the same reason single gentlemen do." He could tell by Lord Stephen's sour face that he hadn't liked Frank's answer and he tried to soften the effect of his words.

"Sentimentality would be my best guess. I understand she's an orphan, it might be all she has left of her parents."

"Her parents shipped her off to a girl's school the moment the child could walk on her own. I doubt she saw them more than a dozen times before they died. Their carriage accident was the best thing that ever happened to that girl."

"Carriage accident?" Frank couldn't help but do a little digging. She'd not revealed much of her life and curiosity got the better of him. "I don't believe she mentioned how they died."

"Her father was a stubborn old fool, that's where she gets it from. Ashdown went to great lengths to see that the property stayed in the family. I doubt he expected to have a female child. He tried to drive his carriage across a flooded stream and the only survivor was the damn horse."

"How unfortunate." Pity for the gloomy Lord Stephen's poor wife was the only emotion Frank could muster. If the man spoke too much longer, he'd suck all the air out of the room. "Is Miss Ashdown home to visitors?"

"She's a waste of a man's time, but I'll send someone up to let her know she has a caller."

Chapter Five

Keeping her expired voucher in her sewing box might serve as a reminder that her memory was fallible. She couldn't be angry. Other than nearly shooting the man who would now occupy her dreams, last evening was an experience beyond all expectations.

She was still staring at the voucher with a loopy smile on her face when a servant knocked on the door. She shoved the voucher back in her sewing box and so made sure her smile was replaced by nonchalance when she opened the door.

"You've a caller, Miss." The servant said as she curtsied. "A Mr. Fitzjohn is in the front sitting room. Will he be received?"

"Yes." Good lord, had she shouted that? While still not meeting her eyes, the servant girl jumped at her reply. "Please tell him I'll be down in just a moment."

"Yes, Miss."

With the servant dispatched, Alice rested her forehead against the door. He was here. Well, of course he was. He probably brought flowers or something and here she was in her drabbest dress ready for a night of travel. Running to the mirror, she checked her reflection, frowned, and tried repining her hair into submission.

She was a plump spinster in a mouse-gray gown today, not a daring temptress in silk. Frank would hand her some blooms, stay the required fifteen minutes, and walk out of her life forever. He was only here because he was a gentleman. There was no point in changing her gown or heating tongs to curl her hair. Like all unpleasant tasks, it was best just to get his departure over with.

If she would remember him always, he should remember her too. Her best thimble, the gold one with the black onyx top that she rarely used would make the perfect token of remembrance. He'd put it with his mother's collection but think of her and their night together every time he spied it. She slipped it into her pocket before making her way downstairs.

"Miss Ashdown," Frank greeted her as he rose from his chair. He was smiling like a man who had a secret and she wasn't sure she wanted to know what it was. Anything that would ruin last night could be kept to himself.

"Mr. Fitzjohn." She should probably have asked someone to bring them tea. This would be so much easier at her own home, but nobody ever called on her there.

Her hand went to her pocket and felt the thimble there. Was it foolish to gift a man a thimble? If he was a stranger perhaps, but Frank was no longer a stranger. After what they shared, she'd go so far as to say they knew each other intimately.

"There's your smile," Frank said, as he reached out his hands to hers. "You're looking well."

"That's very kind of you to say as I feel that I slept barely a wink last night." Blast. Why was she telling him? Might as well just blurt out that she was a love-sick puppy.

"I had trouble sleeping as well," he said before drawing closer to brush his lips across her cheek. "I could not stop thinking of you."

"Same." That was as much of an admission she was willing to make. The last man who called on her tried to trick her into signing over her property. If Frank mentioned her estate, she would shove a gold thimble up his left nostril and throw him out the door herself.

"Last night was…special. I don't make a habit of such behavior, I just wanted you to know I—"

"I absolve you of all responsibility, Mr. Fitzjohn. There is no need to bring your regrets. I'll be leaving town tonight. Have no fear, you won't accidentally run into me again." She didn't want his regrets, excuses, or explanations. "What happened is in the past now. I'll not trouble you."

"Your words shock and wound me, Alice. I didn't come here to discuss what was. I came here to explore what is and what could be. If you wish me to leave, please say so."

"I don't wish you to leave. I…I thought you came here for another reason. It was a poor guess at your motive, and I apologize for it. My mind is slow from lack of sleep. Please speak plainly to me."

"I didn't recognize your name until after we'd started

our adventure when you mentioned Pudbury. My father, bull nose that he is, has been trying to buy your land for years. While I knew of his plans, I paid little mind to it. I knew you'd recognize my name eventually so I thought I should confess that I have no ulterior motive and beg your pardon for my father's brutish methods."

"I wasn't sure until now. My major domo deals with those inquiries because they occur every single day. Some stubborn fool sent a solicitor to call every afternoon for a month. I refuse to speak to any of them. My land is not for sale, my house is not for sale. My heart is not for sale."

"Then you should keep your land and your house. I'm here to ask you to share your heart." Frank reached into his pocket and pulled out a single red feather. He brushed it against her cheek before speaking again. "I wanted to give you something that would help you remember me."

"I could never forget you." Alice pulled the thimble out of her pocket and presented it to him on her fingertip. "Something for your collection. For the same reason." Laughing as their unusual gifts were exchanged, Alice nearly fainted with relief and grabbed his arm for support.

"Steady there," he said as he led her to the sofa. "I believe it is customary for you to sit prettily while I heave myself down to my bruised knee."

"What on earth do you think you're doing?" He couldn't be proposing, he just couldn't be. They'd known each other less than a full day. Shaking her head to clear it, she stared down at him as her heart threatened to explode from her chest.

"Will you do me the honor of sharing experiences with me for the rest of our lives?"

"I…what?" She must be misunderstanding the situation. The only men who proposed to her were the ones who wanted her land, not her.

"Will you marry me, Alice Anne Ashdown?"

"I look terrible," she replied as she tried to smooth her hair down once again. "I haven't slept all night. I barely know you." And yet, she couldn't say no. The word wouldn't come out of her mouth. "It's not that simple."

"It could be. With one word from you it could be."

"Why? Why do you want to marry me?"

"Because I realized very early this morning that I cannot live without you. We'll draw up a marriage contract that specifies your estate will always belong to you. I'll sign it in blood if that's what you require. I can imagine no future without you in it."

"This is crazy." Just because it was crazy, didn't mean that it was wrong. "I want to say yes, more than you know, but I'm afraid."

"This much faith," he said, pulling the thimble from his pocket and turning it upside down so that it resembled a tiny goblet. "All I'm asking is this much faith in what your heart is already telling you is true. I love you, Alice."

"I think I love you too." She'd never spoken the words aloud before and they felt odd on her tongue. Those three words meant no turning back.

The poor, patient man was still down on one knee, so she slipped off the sofa to join him there. When he pulled her into his arms, she couldn't help but to seek out his mouth for a kiss. His lips would calm her nerves and satisfy her heart. If she were to get through this day, it would require many, many kisses.

"Say there," Lord Stephen, Lucy at his side, roared from the doorway. "What is the meaning of this? I gave you fifteen minutes and you repay the hospitality by making love in my sitting room?"

"Not to worry." Alice scrambled up to her feet. "Frank

proposed and I have accepted."

"He did what? Devil take you, woman. I offered you good coin for your land and you give it away after knowing this man for an evening?"

"My land, my decision, not yours to bluster and bully about. I'll abuse your generosity no longer. My bags are already packed. Lucy, I cannot thank you enough for arranging the voucher to Almack's and for attending to your family emergency. I mean that in all sincerity and I'll write you a long letter explaining everything once I'm home."

"Alice, please…" Lucy ran over to give her a hug. "I'm so happy for you my darling friend. You don't have to leave."

"Yes, I do," she replied, giving her friend's hand a squeeze. "Frank and I want to start our life together as quickly as possible. Upon hearing her words, Frank turned his head and winked at her. "It will be the experience of a lifetime."

***

Rocked back to sleep by the motion of the carriage, Alice awoke to Frank holding her hand. He was a man of both large and small gestures along with grand and humble declarations. And, he loved her.

"What are you smiling about?" Frank asked as he stretched his legs and rolled the muscles of his shoulders.

"I was thinking of you."

"Good. I was thinking of you too." He leaned over and kissed her cheek. "It's still some way to Elm Park, I think we have time for an experience. Or two. The way I'm feeling right now three isn't out of the question."

"Three? That would be something."

"Three in a moving carriage. What say you?"

"It might be experience enough watching you try to shimmy out of those trousers in this small space."

"My penchant for trousers helped fate throw us

together," he said as he began pulling on his shirttail. "Oh, ye of little faith."

"I've got at least a thimbleful."

THE END

Introducing Diana Stout

The Promise of Spring

An award-winning writer in multiple genres, Diana Stout, MFA, PhD is a screenwriter, author, blogger, editor, mentor, and former English professor, having served as a reviewer for academic journals, textbook publishers, and contest judge for multiple writing organizations.

In her short story, "A Promise of Spring," Patty escapes her best friend's party, seeking solitude when she's put into the company of John, whom she learns lives in her building and has been dealing with grief, too. Back home, a place that has given her joy recently is now gone. So, she seeks out the park bench she shared with her beloved husband and finds a lesson in nature.

Today Diana writes full-time and enjoys helping other writers. You can learn more about her work by visiting her website, Sharpened Pencils Productions.

Heat Level: SWEET

THE PROMISE OF SPRING
Diana Stout

"You can't go home, Patty. You just got here."

Janet's voice stopped my escape toward the door. Once again, my best friend had caught me sneaking away. How many times had I been caught in her plans of trying to match me up with some unlucky man?

With a sigh, I looked longingly at the door. So close, yet so far. With my coat draped over my arm, I turned to face my friend.

"Janet, this is a mistake. I just—"

"I know. You just wanted to go back home and paint another room, clean another closet. Patty, you can't stay behind those walls forever. You've got to get out."

Fred, Janet's husband, came up from behind and gave me a squeeze. "Don't let Janet rope you into anything you're not ready for. She just wants everyone to be as happy as she thinks we are."

Janet slugged Fred affectionately on the arm, laughing. "Stop saying that. Someday, somebody's actually going to believe you."

"Stay because you want to be with people, because you're enjoying yourself," Fred said.

I hated to disappoint my best friend and her husband, but the memories hurt. If I stayed any longer, the tears would come. Adam and I had shared so many good times with Janet and Fred.

I shrugged into my coat, buttoning it against the winter weather.

Janet grabbed the loose ends of my scarf and tugged at them, silently giving in. "I'm glad you came. Call me when you get home. It's been snowing ever since you got here."

"I'll call."

"How are you getting home?" Fred asked.

"Taxi."

"John!" Fred called out to someone behind me. I turned. A nice-looking man, his coat on, approached us.

"I was just coming to thank you for the party," John said.

Janet frowned. "You're leaving too?"

"Can you give Patty a lift home?" Fred asked him. To me he said, "You'll never find a cab now."

"I'd be happy too," John said.

"Really, it's not necessary," I protested.

"Where do you live?" John asked.

Patty gave him my address.

"Really? I just moved into the same apartment building last week. Still unpacking, as a matter of fact."

Minutes later, after we'd been properly introduced, we left the building and were nearly blown off the sidewalk by the harsh wind. Once in the car, blowing snow swirled around us as we waited for the car to warm up and the windows to defog.

"Would you mind terribly if we stopped to get something to eat?" John asked. "I came to the party straight from the airport, and while Janet's hors d'oeuvres were good, I need a meal. I know there's not much in the fridge at home. I need to go shopping."

I hesitated. A meal did sound good. And, Janet was right in one regard. I had been cooped up in my apartment for too long.

"Look if you don't want to, just say so," John continued. "I'll understand. With this storm we'd be safer going home right now, and you don't know me—"

41

"No. It's not that. Fred's told me about you. I know you work with him, and that he's quite fond of you." I hesitated, then responded. "Sure, why not." It *had* been a while since I'd gone out for a meal. Despite the storm and knowing we should be going home, I wanted to. For once, I was going to do what I wanted rather than what I should.

Soon, we were seated in a small Italian restaurant not far from our apartment building. Because of the weather, there were few diners. With the darkening sky outside, the lit candles gave the restaurant a warm and cozy atmosphere.

"I'm sorry to hear about your husband," John said. "Fred told me he died recently."

"Yes, six months ago. The expected wave of sorrow washed over me and I braced for the inevitable tsunami that would follow, surprised when the pain was more like a splash, instead. "He was my best friend." Even to my ears, my words sounded like a whisper.

John nodded, clasping my hand then letting go. "I lost my wife two years ago. She was my best friend, too. Everyone kept pushing me to get out, to meet someone new."

"Like Janet and Fred."

"They mean well."

"I know." I sighed. "It's just..."

"You don't have to explain. I understand. You'll know when you're ready."

I laughed. It felt good, especially considering I hadn't laughed in…six months to be exact.

The rest of the meal was pleasant. We talked about our families, past Christmases—something I'd been reluctant to talk about. John had a way of making me remember the good times, not to reflect on what I didn't have anymore. It was nice smiling again and knowing the gesture was genuine.

After our meal, John drove us back to our apartment

building. We parted ways at my door and I gave him a weak wave as I closed it, without inviting him in.

Once back in my apartment, however, the depression hit me again. Only this time instead of being warmed and comforted, I found the apartment strangely uncomfortable and a bit cold.

The next morning, I threw on my coat and went across the street to the park. It didn't matter that the wind gusted cold. At least, it wasn't snowing.

I dusted off the snow from the night before and sat on one of the benches, remembering the times Adam and I had spent here, throwing a Frisbee when we were younger, swinging and even playing in the sandbox with the neighbor children. The times we'd strolled through the park arm-in-arm, in love with the spring flowers and each other. The summer nights we'd escape from the droning sound of the air-conditioner, celebrating with an ice cream cone. We had loved this park. We had met here in fact, under that old maple that towered in front of me. It had become our tree.

I looked up at its bare branches. It looked forgotten, naked, and isolated. Pretty much reflecting how I felt. The tree was unsheltered from the weather, me unsheltered from life's tragedy.

A squirrel came out from a hole near the fork of the massive trunk. It must have been hungry to come out in this cold weather. I remembered the spring when we had watched baby squirrels emerge from that hole, their nest, for the first time.

The squirrel paused to sniff the air, then apparently feeling safe, came down the trunk and scampered across the snow, stopping in the middle of what seemed nowhere. She started digging. A minute later, she was eating a nut, one she'd obviously buried last fall.

I remembered something Adam had said. "Every friendship starts out as a seedling. Time, rain, and sunshine turns a seedling into a tree." We had talked about how our friendship had blossomed into love, binding us even deeper together as friends, much like the roots of a tree as they tunnel down into the soil.

Now, the squirrel and I were alone.

I looked up at our maple again. Once upon a time, it too had been a seedling. As it matured, it would lose branches, get diseased, and eventually die to be replaced by another seedling. It was the nature of things.

A huge sun beam broke through the clouds. The snow looked almost like fairy dust as the flakes reflected the rays.

As quickly as it had appeared, the sun was gone. It had been so pretty, a brief promise of the spring to come, the renewal of warmth and growth, in an otherwise cold, white sky. All I'd seen was a glimpse, but it had been a beautiful moment—just like my marriage to Adam. We'd had our moment of time together, and it had been beautiful.

I noticed for the first time, that there were other people in the park besides me. Where had they come from?

An old man, shuffled along the sidewalk, slouched, hands in his pockets, a scowl on his face. On another bench was a middle-aged woman, periodically digging her hand into a sack, sprinkling bird seed in front of her. Sparrows and doves rushed to pick up the meager droppings. I realized that I'd seen her in the park many times before, always alone.

And then, I noticed a couple walking through the park, just like Adam and I used to. Holding hands, smiling at each other, talking.

I wanted that feeling of being close to someone again. I didn't want to end up like the old man and the bird lady. I wanted to share my life with someone.

When I looked at the big tree again, I saw something I hadn't noticed before. There were other trees around it, other big trees. What I hadn't noticed, though, was how the upper branches, even though the trees were a good distance away from each other, touched and intertwined. Though they were all maples, none of the trees were alike ,and none were intertwined in quite the same way. I realized every relationship was like that, too.

While I had lost my husband, my best friend, that didn't mean I wouldn't have other best friends, possibly even another husband someday. Janet meant well in trying to set me up, hoping I'd pair off with someone, but first things first.

Feeling better than I had in months, I went back to my apartment.

Inside, I shed my coat, shucked off my boots, then went into the kitchen and grabbed the coffee cake Janet had dropped off yesterday morning on the pretext of making sure I would come to her party. I got the casserole I'd made yesterday, too—a casserole I hadn't been able to eat, carrying them out of the apartment, and up a flight of stairs.

Upstairs, at his door, I hesitated. I wasn't usually this forward, making the first move. But, I was older now, hopefully wiser. I've learned that life is too short to hesitate or have regrets, and I would regret it if I *didn't* knock. I raised my hand and knocked.

Seconds later, the door opened. John looked surprised to see me. Behind him were boxes, some opened, some not.

"I remember what it's like moving in, unable to find anything, getting hungry, wanting to unpack the pots and pans, yet not having the energy to cook."

I held out my offerings. He took the dishes.

"Enjoy and welcome to my neighborhood," I smiled and started to turn away.

"I'd enjoy it better if you'd join me."

I hesitated, wondering if he was just being polite. The look in his eyes told me he really wanted the company. "I will, but only on one condition. You let me help you unpack."

John let out a funny, but sincere sigh of relief. "Deal. Setting up a kitchen terrifies me. Knowing the best place for dishes and silverware. Never had to do it."

I smiled, feeling my spirits lifting. "Isn't that what friends are for?"

THE END

Introducing Jae Vel

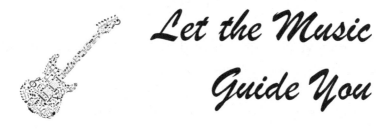

Let the Music Guide You

Jae Vel is an author, poet, registered nurse, and most important, she's a mom to an amazing daughter. Jae is a music enthusiast, exploring various genres and forms of expressing herself through song on a daily basis. Her fondest memories are singing with her mom and playing her guitar alongside her dad. Interact with Jae via Twitter @jvscribbles and feel free to share your favorite song to add to her ever-growing playlist.

Inspired by her own love of music and the people who have guided her on life's journey, Jae wrote this story. Discover how love helps Ava Fuentes find her way back to her passion after tragic loss and heartbreak crushed her dreams in "Let The Music Guide You."

Heat level: HOT

LET THE MUSIC GUIDE YOU
Jae Vel

With a weary sigh, I plop down on the floor of my spare bedroom. The laundry lay scattered on the floor around me, begging to be cleaned. Yet, I'm stuck staring at my ebony Gibson guitar covered in layers of dust, resting on its stand.

Damn you, Jared.

His phone call this afternoon had left me irate. Why did Jared call again after all this time? Talking to him had catapulted me back to a painful time in my life. The mess on the floor was the aftermath of my wrath.

I try to sort out the chaos of this room and my mind before Steve gets home or he'll think we were robbed.

But, I can't.

The memories of holding my guitar flood me.

How many years did I spend with it in my hands strumming the strings along to the melody in my head? I was chasing dreams of being a rockstar and touring the world with the man I loved. In the end, I was left with a heartbreak that I thought I had recovered from. Instead, I had just shoved it down deep where it disappeared from my feelings and thoughts.

At twenty-one, I had it all figured out. I was in a rock band and in love with the lead singer, Jared. We played all the local bars and festivals in the Midwest, rocking out with our fans. The adrenaline high made the long hours of practice and travel worth it. The exhaustion in my bones always remedied by the strum of my guitar.

At twenty-five, I'd been on the road when my world stopped and the music died. My parents and sister passed away; my grandma said a fire had started in the kitchen of our house. They never made it out. Only my little brother, Steve, survived.

Steve and I held each other tight during the funeral. The days passed in a fog. The funeral came and went, Steve clutched to my black dress the entire time while family and friends brought food and showered us with words of condolences.

None of it mattered.

It didn't bring our parents back or rid me of the guilt of not being here for them when my family was dying.

Steve asked me to stay, and I became a mom to a thirteen-year-old who had just lost the only home he'd ever known.

My future, my dream of traveling the world as the lead guitarist to Chaos Unbound was over.

It wasn't long before the band found a new guitarist and began playing without me. Jared slowly pulled away. He said he wasn't ready to settle down and raise a family. He was married to the band. Eventually, the money from the life insurance and house insurance came through, and Steve and I found a new home.

***

The conversation earlier today infuriated me; Jared hadn't listened to a word I said. He had called wanting to talk about the past. He missed me and wanted me to join a band he was putting together. But, the thought of playing again made me ache and filled my eyes with unshed tears.

I sit on the floor of my spare bedroom, the sleek ebony black body with devil horns calling to me. In the last five years, I had not picked up my once prized possession.

I'm tempted, but the passion I used to feel for music is gone.

I'm not a rockstar anymore. I work at the local bakery during the day. Occasionally, I bartend on the weekends at the local dive bar. Steve is a senior in high school and will be graduating this spring. I'm proud of my brother and his choice to go to the University of Michigan in the fall. Our parents had saved money for his studies and with the scholarships he earned, he'll be set. I'm not really sure what I'll do without him around.

"Ava, where the heck are you?"

"I'm upstairs, Steve."

His footsteps echo on the steps. I groan at the mess around me.

Steve leans against the door frame, and gestures at the mess with a flick of his hand.

"Whoa, what did you do?"

"Um, well, I had a fight with the clothes." I sigh at his exasperated look.

"I'm pretty sure my jeans and t-shirts won."

He rolls his eyes at me. "You're nuts. Get ready, we're eating out tonight. It's open mic night at The Fire Den, and Grace will be singing tonight." He paused. "You gotta come and cheer my girlfriend on. Please, will you come tonight...for me?"

I watch his lower lip jut out just like when he was little. What a brat.

"Why would you think I wouldn't go to support Grace?" I really didn't want to go, but he didn't need to know that. I love my brother and love to see him smile.

"Well, you refuse to play any music at home and even swat my hand when I turn on the car radio. He shrugs. "You're like anti-music now."

"Don't be ridiculous. Of course, I'll come and support Grace."

Truthfully, I couldn't remember the last time I had listened to music for fun. At my weekend job, music was always playing. I ignored it, keeping my focus on my customers and making drinks. A part of me hates music, the other wasn't sure what to think. I sigh. The brat is right.

Steve laughs as he looks around the room. "Think you can find something to wear in that mess?"

I throw a shirt at him as he starts to walk away.

"I'll be down in fifteen minutes."

I rummage through the mess to find my go-to wear of tattered jeans and a black tank top. In my room, I snag a pair of Converse sneakers, my cross necklace, and take a look in the mirror. The black eyeliner from earlier still looks decent. I shrug and spritz myself with the first scent I could grab and run fingers through my dark curly hair before walking downstairs.

The Fire Den is a short walk away. It's a dive bar with mouthwatering burgers and the best chocolate shake within one hundred miles. The place is crowded as expected on a Friday open mic night, but Steve's friends had found a table near the makeshift stage. I walk behind Steve toward the table fighting back the urge to cry. Being close to the stage again brings back memories of my unfilled dreams. My heart hurts. I take a deep breath. I'm here for my brother, for Grace.

I can get through this.

"You okay, Ava?"

"Yeah, why?"

He looks at the empty seat I was standing next to.

"Your hands are closed into tight fists and you still haven't sat down"

I unclench my fists and quickly sit.

"Sorry about that, it's been a while, you know. I'm good."

"Hey, Ava," Steve's friends say in unison.

I give a half-hearted smile. "Hey guys."

I glance around the bar and recognize most the faces in the crowd. My breathing slows, the noise of the patrons becoming more of a hum. A man in the corner catches my attention. Dressed in black, he stares directly at me. My heart pounds as we make eye contact. I want to stare back, but I turn back to my brother and focus on what he is saying. *My instincts tell me I know him. But where?*

Steve's voice is muffled beneath the pounding in my chest. He leans closer and shouts in my ear.

"Grace will be singing next. She's nervous as hell but determined to do this." He smiles. "I envy her bravery. She's gonna be great."

Watching how my brother lights up as he talks about Grace warms me. He's happy and that's what matters right now. My sole focus these past five years has been Steve. Seeing him excel and smile is worth the pain of the emptiness I feel inside.

"That's part of the thrill of performing," I say. "The anticipation of being on stage, the loud cheers from the crowd, the strum of that first note. It's quite a rush that's as addicting as getting high."

I close my eyes for a second to relive those moments from my past. Yeah, I missed it, but that life is done for me. I have no more love for music.

"I miss that part of you, " he says, barely above a whisper. "You came alive just then, your face lit up. I haven't seen that smile in years. When is that Ava I used to know coming back?" I pretend like didn't hear him, grateful the crowd is clapping and howling. Grace is on stage.

During the performance, I feel a heat boring into my back. I refuse the urge to turn around and look at the mystery man.

The crowd cheers for Grace as her sweet voice hits the final high note. The smile on her face is one I recognize. It's the look of satisfaction and the high of performing mixed in self-accomplishment. I miss that feeling. After every performance, the thrill would stay with me for hours.

I clap along with her fans and feel a hand on my shoulder. I know it's the man from the corner. Before I can turn around, I'm grabbed into a group hug by Grace and Steve.

"Eeeek, I did it!" Grace grins jumping up and down while not letting go.

"You sure did! You have a beautiful voice." I realize I mean what I say. "I'm glad I came to see you." I smile at her.

"I'm so proud of you, Baby." Steve takes over the hug and pulls Grace away for a kiss.

"Hi."

The husky voice comes from behind. I'm not sure I want to turn around. The baritone voice alone causes my breath to hitch and my anxiety to rise. It annoys me that a simple greeting creates such a reaction. I force a smile on my face and tell my hormonal system to take a chill pill. I've never been one to backdown from a challenge.

I turn around, ready to greet the mystery man. "Hi. Do I know you?"

"Noah Hill. No, uh, we don't know each other, but I've seen you before. Years ago, at a bar in Chicago. You play guitar for Chaos Unbound, right?"

Shaken at the mention of the band, I stutter. "Played. But y...yeah, but that was me. Years ago. I don't play anymore."

"Oh, well, I remember being mesmerized by the way your fingers danced across the strings of your SG." He pierces me with his slate-blue gaze and utters a self-depreciating laugh. "You were amazing. Even through the haze of my whisky brain, I couldn't forget such talent."

I stare back with mouth agape.

"Um, thanks?" I manage to utter.

I see his eyes move to the stage. "Will you be playing tonight?"

"No, I don't perform anymore."

"Oh? Why is that?" His smile crinkles the corner of his eyes. Damn, that just makes him more attractive. "Such talent shouldn't be hidden from the spotlight."

His words snap me back from my daydreams. It was just time for me to quit, that's all," I lie. He doesn't need to hear about the darkness and pain from my past. "Thanks for the compliments, though." I look around for Steve and Grace, who are no longer next to me. "I have to get going."

Yes, I was running away. Far, far away from this man. He's the first man to awaken my body in five years, and I'm not interested in heartbreaks.

"I didn't mean to spook you," he says, raising his arms in a placating gesture. He takes a step back. "Please stay and have a drink with me?"

"Hey Ava, I see you met Noah." I jump at the sound of Steve's voice. "He's Grace's cousin, in town for the next couple weeks to celebrate Grace's graduation and their grandma's ninetieth birthday. A family reunion for sure." Steve grins.

"Noah didn't mention that part." I say, looking at Noah.

"I would have given you that info while we had a drink together," Noah smiles. "I was hoping to win you with my charms and not because you know my cousin." He winks at me as he hugs Grace.

I roll my eyes at his cockiness. There would be no winning me over. I'm not up for grabs.

"Gracey, that was amazing like always," Noah continues. "Granny is hoping you'll sing for her birthday, and I can talk to Dave and Eddie about joining me with an impromptu band for you. What do you think? Want to put on a great show for Granny and the rest of the family?"

"Can we? That would be awesome!" Grace says.

"Ava, could be a great lead guitarist?" Noah says, his gaze pinning me to the spot. "You interested?"

Out of the corner of my eye, I see Steve's excited look on his face. How can I disappoint Steve and Grace? "Sure," slips out of my mouth.

"There you have it!" Noah claps his hands together. "We'll start practicing tomorrow."

"What you do play," I ask.

"We can practice in my parents' garage!" Grace chimes in, an eager smile on her face.

"Sure," I say again. For some reason *sure* is the only word I'm able to say.

Noah responds. "Drums." He turns as Grace hugs him.

Drums? I gulp. Jared played drums.

I excuse myself and walk to the bar, hoping a shot of tequila will calm my nerves.

Steve sneaks up behind me and whispers in my ear. "Sis, you sure about this?" I ignore both him and the crowd hollering at the next performer to come on stage as I order a double.

"No, which is why I came to the bar for a shot." I turn to Steve. Guilt rises at the worried look in his eyes. "I'm processing what I just agreed to do."

That's the truth. Being close to the stage again and feeling the energy of the crowd, I miss all that. I look over at Noah, I don't know if it's the feeling of being challenged by him or the nostalgia of playing in a band again with the yearning to pick up my guitar again. When did that urge to play disappear? Had I found my way back to my music? Maybe. Or, had it been there all along?

***

The rest of the night flies by and six a.m. arrives sooner than I like. The sound of the alarm jolts me awake; I groan knowing I barely slept. I have to get to work. I walk by the spare bedroom and peek at my guitar. This time, I smile as my fingers itch to touch the strings.

Maybe this is a good thing after all.

I skip down the steps to the kitchen, throw a random K-Cup in the Keurig while I reach for my favorite mug from the dishwasher. The mug was a gift my parents gave me as stocking stuffer one year. I stand by the counter tracing the mug's black music notes on the midnight blue background. My parents had always encouraged my dreams to be in a rock band, even after I decided I was not cut out for college life. No matter what, they cheered me on. But, the music took me away from my family We made up for it with phone calls while I was on the road. I know now that I missed a lot of their life and Steve's by chasing my dreams.

I wipe away a tear that attempts to escape. I don't want to cry anymore. It wouldn't bring them back.

At 6:30 a.m., my phone rings. I don't check to see who it is before I answer.

"Hi Lydia, I'm heading out the door right now," I lie. She doesn't have to know I'm just about to drink my coffee.

"Sorry to disappoint but I'm not Lydia." That voice does things to my body that it had no business doing. It's been five years since I've reacted to any man. I picture Noah's intense gaze and unruly cocoa dusted hair and instantly regret the image. "You running late to your morning errands?"

"Noah." I manage to groan out.

He laughs. "Happy to hear your voice, too. Not a morning person, are you?"

"How may I assist you this morning, Mr. Hill?" I can't keep the annoyance out of my tone. I sip my coffee to keep from saying more.

"In many ways, Miss Fuentes." Did he just flirt with me? His amusement bleeds through the phone and I shiver. "But, how about we start with setting a time to rehearse today?"

I'm so out of practice, but that sounded like an invitation to dangerous territory. He's leaving in two weeks; this is not the person that should be resurrecting my body from the crypt. The image that comes to mind makes me snort-giggle.

"What's so funny, Ava?" he questions. I picture the small dimple on his right cheek teasing me.

"Oh, nothing. Just an image that crossed my mind. I'm free after three today."

There's a pause; I'm torn between wanting to giggle again or daydreaming about feeling the fullness of his lips against mine.

"I hope you weren't imaging me naked and then laughing, because that would really cause my fragile ego to break." His laugh is an all-consuming hearty sound. I want to hear more.

"I confess. It was you with a pair of pineapple boxer-briefs, suspenders, and a bow-tie." This time the giggle comes out without resistance. My eyebrow arches in a challenge even though he can't see me.

"I could make that happen for you; all you have to do is ask." He chuckles.

Well, that backfired. I'm tempted to call his bluff, but I have a feeling he's not bluffing. I hear him breathing, patiently waiting for my response.

"I'll see you today at three."

I hang up quickly. His flirting is not what I'm looking for, and I didn't help much by flirting back. I'm not looking to fall for the trap of a good-looking man. He'll be gone soon. I don't need the complication in my life. I like my calm routine well enough. Just because I am attracted to the man doesn't mean I have to act on it. Right?

"Ugh, I'm late. Stop daydreaming, Ava." I do that a lot—talking to myself. I shake my head and quickly throw on clothes before heading out the door.

"Late again, Ava." Lydia hands me my apron and smiles. "You're lucky I love you."

Yeah, I'm not a morning person, but Lydia is my best friend and knows I need this job.

After a quick hug, I begin my day at the bakery.

It's a typical busy spring day and the time flies by. I'm only tempted about fifty-thousand times to sample all the delectable treats. By the end of the shift, my feet ache and I'm regretting having agreed to rehearse right after work. I pack a sample of cupcakes and say my goodbyes to Lydia. "See you tomorrow. I'll be on time."

She smiles. "You've only been saying the same thing to me for the last two years. I still have hope. Enjoy your day."

A quick stop at the house to pick up my guitar before driving to Grace's house has me rethinking this whole thing. I haven't played my guitar in years. Can I still play? Do I really want to? Not to mention my calluses are all gone. There's no way I can get them back in time for the party. Oh well, I guess we'll see. I grab the guitar and walk out the door.

On the drive over to Grace's, I turn on the radio. Before I know it, I start to sing to the music, then stop.

When was the last time I sang? It was the night I got the call. I had just finished a show and noticed the twenty missed calls from my grandma. That was the last time I allowed myself to be distracted by music.

My hand is shaking as I turn the radio off. I take a deep breath and keep driving. A part of me misses the music, and a part of me doesn't want to open old wounds. But, I'm already committed. I have no choice but to face this like any other challenge. Head on. I'll do this just once, and then store the guitar again.

I got this.

I'm barely out of my car when I hear Noah call out.

"I wasn't sure if you'd show up after you hung up on me.

"Aw, were you worried?" I tease, with a hand on my hip, watching him setup his drums. I try to ignore my nervousness and feeling like I'm repeating my life from years before. Noah makes me question myself. "I said I would come. I'm here, now what?"

Noah smiles. "I'm glad you came." He comes up to me and touches my face. "Looks like you missed a spot of flour." He brushes my cheek with his thumb.

I back up. His hand drops. "Um, I just finished with work." I hope he doesn't hear the tremor in my voice. Either I miss being touched or this man is Rayden from Mortal Kombat because the electric current that courses through me at that brief contact makes me wonder if I sound like an idiot.

There's that grin of his again. The dimple resurfaces and his slate blue eyes light up.

"I was thinking we could pick songs that we all know. We still need to wait on Eddie and Dave. Grace will be right out. We can brainstorm until they get here. Any ideas?"

Yeah. that I should go back home. "Are you looking to do Rock covers? It's been a while since I have played any but I'm sure I can figure it out again."

Where did this confidence arise from? I'm not even sure I want to do this and here I am, *all in.*

I can't lie to myself. I miss the music.

I'm afraid my heart wouldn't make it through the memories. Avoidance is a tactic I have been using the last five years. When I face challenges head on, a part of me avoids the emotions, terrified I will break.

I agreed to be part of this band because I don't want to disappoint Grace. Plus, Noah challenged me. I will just do what I always do—take deep breaths and talk myself through the moment. I can do this for Grace's grandma. Just this once.

"Ava, are you ok?" Noah asks. "You're shaking. Did you eat before you came?" I look down at my hands and see they're unsteady. He leads me to a wooden stool. "Here, sit down. Let me grab you a drink."

I watch him run inside the house for a drink. I close my eyes and take a few deep breaths. Quietly, I repeat my mantra. "I got this, just this once, I can do this."

"Hey, here you go." His voice is softer, and when I open my eyes, his face has changed from its usual look of mischief to one of genuine concern. He watches me closely without saying a word.

"I'm okay. It's just been a while since I have played my guitar—or any music for that matter." I take a sip of the ice water and feel my breathing slow down.

"Yeah, I heard the story from Grace. I'm sorry that happened to you and Steve." Noah looks down at his hands before he finds my gaze again. "You know, if this is too much, I understand. You're extremely talented, but the choice is yours. Do you just want to sit and listen today? Maybe decide afterward if you want to be part of this?"

His head tilts to the side, and he reaches for my hand, drawing circles on my wrist with his finger. I don't think the touch is meant to be sexual, yet it soothes me and thrills me just the same.

I don't pull away this time. Instead, I gaze into his eyes until there is a shift in the air. He moves closer, and I hold in a breath as I stare at his lips. "No, I said I would do this and I will. Just have some patience with me is all I ask."

"Okay."

He moves away and finishes setting up his drums. Was he coming in for a kiss? Wishful thinking on my part. I dip my fingers into my glass of water to splash a bit on my face. Setting the glass down, I get up to unpack my guitar. I need to focus on the reason I was here. A sexy man does not compute in those plans.

It isn't long before the other members of the band arrive. The conversation between the group is easy and makes me miss how much I used to love talking about music. After a few minutes of deciding which classic rock covers to play, the guys joke and tune up their instruments, ready to get rehearsal going. I'm on lead guitar and vocals with Grace, Eddie is on bass, Dan is rhythm, and Noah on drums.

"Ok let's take it from the top," Noah says. "One, two, three" He taps his drumsticks in rhythm and a surge flows through me. The black and red pick in my hand screams across the strings. I'm ready to play again.

With the first note of a Janis Joplin cover, the vibe in the garage fills me with a high I haven't felt in years. I can feel the smile on my face and the tapping of my foot. The love is back.

The chords come back to me the instant I splay my fingers and they glide across the fretboard. When my solo moments hit, I lose myself in the emotion. Each note, every bend of the string screams to be heard. My body moves in rhythm as my fingers dance over the strings. My mind goes silent, the pain, the chaos that I've lived with is buried under the euphoria of the song. The lyrics of *Pieces of My Heart* resonate within me. I get lost in my memories and let the pain seep out while Grace sings. I live every word.

I don't realize I'm crying until the song is over and I feel my wet face. The tears consume me.

"Everyone take five outside," Noah shouts. I want to tell him everything's okay, but the words are stuck in my throat.

The rest of the band glance at me. They quickly get up and walk outside.

"Ava, look at me. That was amazing," he says while gently touching my shoulder. "I'm actually at a loss of words to explain what just happened—but you belong to the music or the music belongs to you." He wipes the tears from my cheeks. "Are these happy tears?"

"Yes and no," I whisper. "I got lost in the moment, I miss this so damn much."

"You know what your tears tell me? They tell me that you're passionate about music, that you need this in your life, and that the talent you have shouldn't be hidden anymore."

I stare at him knowing he's speaking my truth. I haven't known him even twenty-four hours, and yet, he understands me.

He leans in, and I don't back away. Softly, his lips touch mine.

"That was beautiful," he whispers against my lips, and I kiss him back pressing a little harder. His lips are gentle, but his tongue slips through and grazes mine.

It dawns on me that I have not kissed anyone in over five years. I want more; he tastes like more. Our tongues entwine and caress one another. His arms pull me in close, my hands slip up to his neck and into his hair.

"Would you like another minute?" Eddie's voice penetrates the moment, and I jump back from Noah.

Noah clears his throat and looks at Eddie.

"Let's call it a day, back tomorrow same time. Let's plan to rehearse every day until Granny's birthday. Great job today."

I work on putting away my guitar as Eddie, Dave, and Grace leave in a hurry. I envy their quick movements. The haze

I'm in after that kiss makes it difficult to function. My fingers are all thumbs as I close my guitar case. I want to leave but a part of me also wants to stay.

"Ava." Noah's voice holds a question I'm not ready to answer. The thought of getting involved with someone who will be leaving in two weeks puts me on the edge. I was stupid to kiss him like that. I'm not looking for another heartbreak. I need to leave before I make another mistake.

"I can't, Noah."

I walk away and he lets me.

***

The blankets askew on the bed tell the story of a restless night. I didn't sleep much. The kiss is in constant replay in my mind with different endings to the reel. Sometime during the night, I decided I won't be kissing Noah again, no matter how much I desire him. He's leaving soon. I throw on burgundy jeans and a black t-shirt, slip into my favorite shoes, and toss a hand through my hair. After a cup of coffee, I'm ready to face the day.

Barely.

Lydia is decorating cupcakes when I walk in. The smell of freshly baked treats always makes me smile and my stomach grumble. I grab a cheese danish and work my shift. I manage to say a couple words to Lydia throughout the day, but I can't recall any of them.

I look up as the clock shows three minutes past three. For six hours, I worked until my feet ached, not once taking a break. Wow. I haven't done that in a long time. Lydia comes into the back and leans in the doorway as I'm getting ready to leave.

"I'm not sure what is going on in that head of yours, Ava," she says, "but tomorrow, can you add a smile and maybe try not to serve a peanut butter donut to Mrs. Davies? You know she's allergic. It's a good thing she noticed." The look of concern on Lydia's belies the stern talk.

She pins me with a motherly look. "Whatever it is that you have going on, snap out of it or take a day off tomorrow."

"Yeah, sorry, I have a lot on my mind today." I wipe my hands on my apron and take it off. I wave goodbye on my way out the door. Lydia shakes her head as she stands by the counter, watching me leave.

***

The drive to rehearsal doesn't take long. I get out of my car and start walking to the garage, but I want to turn around and go back home. I decide to do just that. I'll call with an excuse. I'm nearly back to the car when I hear Noah call my name from behind me.

"Running away again?"

Heat rises to my cheeks. Caught in the act. I quickly turn. He's closer that I expect.

"I. Am. Not. Running. Away," I say, as I jab him repeatedly in his chest. "You can save your jokes and sarcasm for someone else. I was grabbing something from my car. I'll be right in." I say it all without looking at him directly. I'm certain he'll read right through me.

I open the door and pretend to rummage for something. I can't let him get the upper hand today. Once upon a time, I was known for having a fierce attitude. Never afraid to try new things. That version of me still lives inside, at least when it comes to Steve. I won't let Noah trip me up today.

"Did you find what you are pretending to look for?" he asks. I glance at him. Even though he's not smiling, his eyes are twinkling, and it adds to my resolve.

"I was looking for when I cared about your opinion, but it seems like I lost it." I roll my eyes and strut into the garage to rehearse. I can hear Noah chuckling behind me. He circles his drum set and sits down.

I'm thankful for the space between us.

"'Sup, Ava?" Eddie looks up from setting up the microphones. His skinny jeans and charcoal t-shirt show off his great physique, but it does nothing for me.

"Hey Eddie," I say. "Sorry about yesterday It won't happen again."

"No biggie. Noah told us it's been a while for you. I know that music can bring out all kinds of emotions. Don't sweat it. We'll rock Granny's party." His grin makes it easy for me to relax and smile back. I walk by him and let my fingers brush his shoulder as a thank you. He nods and goes on about setting up the room.

"The best guitar player has arrived," Dave says as he enters the garage. "Uh, besides you, Ava, of course. You were amazing yesterday."

I chuckle when he hangs his head avoiding eye contact.

"Thanks, you rocked it out, too." We fist bump. "Let's do this."

I put my guitar strap on as Grace walks in with Steve. I falter for a moment, remembering why I quit music in the first place. Our parents. Our little sister. Gone. All while I was away.

I was supposed to call home that night, but I was too busy. I didn't get to tell them I loved them. The pain from that memory punches me in the gut.

Steve comes over to me and wraps me in a hug.

"They would want you to do what you love," he whispers. "Music lives in you, Sis. Play and sing. They would be so proud of you for raising me but it's your turn to go after your dream again."

A tear runs down my face before I can stop it. I pull Steve to me and hide my face in his chest.

"Thanks for that." I wipe my tears and smile at Steve. He really has grown up. I can't believe that he'll be leaving for college in a few months.

Noah clears his throat and my gaze snaps over to him. He winks at me as he speaks.

Ugh. The audacity of the man really gets under my skin. "Are we ready?" he asks.

Instead of answering, I play a C chord letting it ring out. My fingers begin to dance before the reverb kicks in. The others take their cue and jump in right on beat. The harmony is powerful.

The sounds flow through me, just like it used to. The beats hit, the rhythms race through my veins, my heart pumps faster, and the adrenaline surges. Grace and I belt out the songs of Joplin, Stevie Nicks, Meredith Brooks, Heart, and more. We make eye contact and feeling the moment. During the last song, I realize just how much I missed this. My emotions are running high again as I take it all in.

I feel my true self rising from the dead.

Music wasn't just part of what made me who I am.

It's my essence.

The rush I feel after rehearsal stays with me as I drive home. I walk into the house, drop my guitar on the couch, turn the stereo on and blast some Stevie Nicks and dance around. I belt out the song along with Stevie and I'm about to turn it to some Joplin when I hear clapping behind me.

I turn so fast I almost lose my balance. Noah's standing in the door frame, grinning from ear to ear. He is so sexy in his black leather jacket, grey t-shirt, and torn jeans.

"Steve let me in. He wants you to know that he's staying with Kyle tonight." Noah smiles nervously waiting for me to say something.

I should be angry at the intrusion, but the slight faltering in his usual cocky confidence catches me off guard. Instead of being angry at the intrusion, I walk up to him and kiss him. He

66

doesn't hesitate to pull me in closer and deepen the kiss. With the adrenaline high rushing through me, I let myself go. I kiss him hard, biting his lip and when he gasps, I dive in deeper running my fingers through his hair. The thrill that flows through me is a heady mix of lust and power. My hands roam under his grey t-shirt, my nails graze his back.

"Take off your jacket and shirt." I don't recognize the sultry voice that comes out of me, all I know is that I want this man. The intensity of this moment is new for me and I want to explore.

He peels his clothes off, but backs away before putting his lips on mine again.

"You sure about this, Ava?"

"Oh, yeah. Come with me." It's been too long, and I won't deny this moment, these feelings. I might regret this later, but I'll deal with those feeling then.

I grab his hand and walk him up the stairs to my room. He closes the door and tugs me toward him to yank my tank top over my head. The bra is next. In no time, all the barriers are gone and we are kissing again.

***

The sound of the alarm wakes me up, but an arm reaches it first.

Oh, shit, Noah!

"Um, hi," I mumble shyly at him. "I have to get ready for work."

I bolt from the bed and would have run into the bathroom but the clothes on the floor trip me on the way. I fall to the floor. Covering my face, I groan. *Oh, God.* I mentally slap my forehead. Such a smooth getaway.

"Running away again?" He laughs.

I want to punch him, but that means moving from the floor.

"No, I just don't want to be late to work." That's part of the truth.

"Need a hand?"

He leans over me and is gloriously naked. Thoughts of work flee my mind. He is one heck of a sexy man, and right now, I want more of him.

I grab his hand and pull him down on the floor with me and roll on top of him. I arch an eyebrow and lower a hand, reaching for him. "Mind if I have you for breakfast?"

***

An hour later and already five minutes late to work, I finally make it downstairs, and I text Steve to check in for the day. I leave Noah in my bed with the promise to see him at rehearsal. I cringe as I walk into Lydia's, waiting for the reprimand for being late yet again.

"Back to normal today?" she chuckles. "You know I love you, right? That doesn't mean I don't want to throttle you from time to time for always being late."

"Yeah, sorry I'm late. If you didn't love me, I would have been out of a job a long time ago. It's a good thing the customers like me too." I smile.

Lydia sighs. "I've known you and your family for years. I'll always be here for you. You look better today. I hope you solved whatever was bothering you."

"Um, I think so," I say, pushing away any unsure feelings I have.

I'm looking forward to band practice, like the old days when I was just starting out. The excitement of playing and seeing Noah are at the forefront of my mind while I work.

I walk out of the back room with a tray full of fresh-made donuts. The bell rings, signaling a new customer. I glance toward the door.

Jared.

"Hey Babe, long time no see," he says. "I've missed you."

He hasn't changed a bit—still wearing black t-shirts and skin tight jeans. His blonde hair falls over his forehead almost covering his hazel eyes. His crooked smile had always been my weakness, but today I feel nothing when I look at him.

"What are you doing here, Jared?" I ask. I set the tray on the counter. "I thought I was clear on the phone when we last spoke."

My clutched fists, hidden from view, shake at my sides. Anger and an emotion I can't describe flow through me.

"I missed you," he says. "I had to come see you. You didn't let me finish what I wanted to say to you on the phone."

"You mean when I hung up on you? Five years ago? You never were good with hints."

Seconds pass as my enraged stare stabs him, but as usual, he ignores my look and my words.

"Give this a chance. I know it's been years. But it was never the same without you. Spontaneous moments were kinda our thing, remember? I love you and I was stupid to leave you."

"Are you fucking insane?" I spit out through clenched teeth. "It's been five years and you think I'll just forgive you? How the hell did you find me, anyway?"

"I asked around." He shrugs. "I knew you were still living here, so, I stopped by your grandma's and she reluctantly told me where to find you. I had to beg her and promise her a kidney." He gives me a half-smile. "I figured she wouldn't tell you I had stopped by, so I came to find you."

"You're an idiot," I say.

"The band broke up after about a year after you left. They wanted you there. I found another band to play with for a while, but that fell through. I miss having you by my side. I was young and stupid, Ava. Can you ever forgive me?"

Incredulous bastard. The whooshing in my ears wouldn't stop. I hear him but can't comprehend his words. It doesn't matter anyway.

"Ava, are you okay?" Lydia asks from behind me.

I turn around and see her watching Jared. "Yes, Jared was just leaving."

"Ava, please just give me a few minutes outside." Jared pleads, his hazel eyes getting the best of me. That sad puppy-dog look was my weakness. How is it that Steve could get me that way, too?

I nod.

"Would you like the rest of the afternoon off, Ava?" Lydia asks.

"No, I'll be back in a minute. I'm so sorry about this." My face is flush.

I walk from behind the counter and follow Jared outside. He places his hand on my back.

"No." I twist away from him and feel Jared stumble.

"What?" His face is one of disappointment.

"No, you no longer have the right to touch me." I break through the red haze. "I forgave you for thinking the band was more important than me, Jared, but that doesn't mean I want you in my life."

"I was hoping you would give me another chance, maybe join the band I'm starting." Jared says while reaching for my hand, as if I didn't just reject him. Typical Jared. He never listens. I can't believe I didn't realize how selfish he was...and still is.

He doesn't love me; he loves the idea of me. I try to jerk my hand from his but he holds on. With the momentum he tries to hug me.

"No, Jared. I don't want any of this. You're five years too late. Please leave. "I put more space between us.

"I was an idiot, please forgive me," he says giving me a lost puppy look again.

"I forgive you, but I don't want any part of you in my life." I turn to go back to Lydia's.

"I had to try to get you back." He sighs. "Are you playing anywhere in town? Your grandma told me you had quit music, but I refuse to believe that. You loved music more than I did. You would eat, sleep, and breathe music when we were together."

"I did quit music, until just recently." As I say the words the excitement to be playing this weekend hits me. I grin widely. I think of Noah. Jared frowns seeing my grin.

I'm happy.

"Do you think I can come check it out?" He asks.

"No, it's not a good idea. Go home, Jared." He looks surprised at my rejection. "All right Ava, take care of yourself. Will you let me hug you one last time?"

I know I shouldn't, but I do. I give him a quick hug, and a sense of closure washes over me.

"Thank you, it was great to see you again. Be happy, Ava." He hops on his motorcycle and I turn, walking backing back into the bakery.

Lydia looks up from wiping down the counter. "You okay?"

"Yeah, I'm good. Just a blast from the past that needed closure."

Grinning, I get back to work. I feel Lydia staring at my back, probably hoping for more details, but I'm still processing everything. The last few days were intense, but good. Being in a band again feels right. I feel whole. And, I've met a wonderful person who gets me and believes in me.

Noah entering my life was definitely not expected.

***

The next few days of work and rehearsals go by in a blur. Our band has found our sound and we're ready to play Saturday.

Noah on the other hand has barely spoken to me. I'm not sure what changed his attitude, but I realize it's for the best. He was going to leave anyway. Better to end it now than later. Besides, I'm too engrossed in the music to analyze him...us right now.

Saturday morning arrives with Steve bursting into my room.

"Hey, Sis, I made breakfast."

"Huh? What time is it?" I open my eyes, blinking. The last few days had been a struggle in the sleep department, especially when I can still smell Noah on my sheets.

"It's nine a.m.," he says. "I'm heading out to help Grace and her family with the set up for Granny's party later today. Food is on the kitchen counter. Love ya! See you later." I hear his footfalls on the stairs and the door slam.

I groan thinking about today. A mixture of exhilaration and dread bubble up in my gut.

Maybe breakfast isn't such a good idea.

Nerves would always get to me the day of a performance, no matter how many times I took the stage, still, the rush was worth it. My jittery stomach always calmed down as soon as my feet hit the stage. That's where I belong, and I'm ready to be back.

I think about Noah. I admit I was hurt by his actions. Surprised more like it. I'd become attached to the man too quickly I'll survive this loss too.

I brush aside my feelings. I need to get ready.

My stomach lurches in protest as I get out of bed, but I push through and shower. For the first time in years, I sing in the shower. I belt out songs of love, heartache, and sex. I'm back and I'm loving every minute of it.

Black jeans, a red shirt, and black leather jacket is what I choose to wear today. I add my black and white chucks, silver skull jewelry, and make-up. Black eye liner, mascara—a bit of the goth look. Perfection. A quick spritz, and I grab my guitar from the stand.

I stare at it for a moment before caressing the strings of my ebony SG. My dad bought the guitar as my sixteenth birthday present. I had been eyeing it at the local music shop, and he made it happen for me. Both of my parents always believed in my dreams. It's time I played for them, as well. I pack up my gear and walk downstairs.

I'm supposed to meet up with the band two hours before our scheduled performance. Looking at the clock on the wall, I have one hour to kill. Coffee is on the list of things to do and maybe try to eat what Steve made for me. I think about Noah giving me the cold-shoulder yesterday. Was I just a conquest? He didn't seem the type .

I stab at the eggs on my plate and push around the sausage. By the time I have to leave, I've only eaten about three bites and drank half of my coffee.

Today is going to be interesting.

***

I arrive at the park and look out at the beach behind the gazebo where our band will play. Such a beautiful day for an outdoor event, not a cloud in sight.

I don't see Grace or Steve on the stage, so I set up and start to play a melody I had written years ago for Jared. My fingers remember the progression, and they readily flow up and down the neck of the guitar. My eyes are closed, engrossed in the memory of composing it for him.

We had made a good team back then, but I never finished the song because while writing it, I realized Jared was too engrossed in himself. I had put it away.

I'm no longer that girl who could only see being a rockstar as the end goal of her life. Raising Steve made me see things from a different perspective. Yeah, I gave up my dreams, but I gained so much by being there for Steve. I realize I can still love music, even if my dream of being a rock star will never come true. Meeting Noah and the rest of the band reminded me of who I truly am. I love this version of myself.

I keep playing, singing a sorrowful husky melody. Words I haven't yet written spilled out. I think of Noah as I sing.

"That was beautiful."

I startle at Noah's voice.

"You surprised me. I guess I was in a zone." I wish he wasn't leaving. "It's a melody I began to write for Jared years ago but didn't have lyrics for it back then. I guess I was inspired today to add some." I shrug and put my guitar back on the stand.

"Jared, huh? That the guy that you were with the other day?" Noah's face is solemn, his usual smile gone.

"Oh. That. Yeah, first time I've seen him in over five years When did you see him?" I ask.

"I came to see you at work the other day, and I saw you and him talking." Hurt is in his eyes.

"Is that the reason why you've been ignoring me?" I ask. I'm stunned.

"Maybe it was part of the reason." He watches me and moves in closer.

"Well, maybe you should have talked to me about it earlier," I mutter and move back. "Let's rehearse and get ready to play today." I see him flinch at my words.

He pauses. "Okay," he finally says. His one-word response fuels my shitty mood. I decide to lose myself in the music for now.

The rest of the band arrives and the rehearsal flies by. We're more than ready when the guests arrive. The turmoil about Noah disappears. I'm hyped and ready to play.

On the stage is where I belong. The adrenaline rush of performing, the music flowing out of me and connecting with the people.

I have found music again, my first love.

When our performance ends, the crowd hoots and hollers. The clapping brings me joy. Noah gives thanks on behalf of the band. I watch him closely as he turns from the crowd to pick up his gear. I refuse to go to him. I decide to pack up and walk over to the beach behind the gazebo.

I put my earbuds in and crank the rock music. I walk the sandy shore as the aggressive notes fill my ears. At the edge of the water, I bury my feet in the sand. The soft fluffy clouds in the sky as the sun sets are a contrast to the storm simmering internally. I turn the music up, and it beats in rhythm with the flow of tears. Mixed emotions soar through me. I dig my toes deeper in the sand until the cool water crashes against my bare feet. Over and over, the cold water soaks my skin and it helps to dissipate the rage, the pain, the chaos.

I'm hurt by Noah's actions and the joy from being back onstage swamp and confound me. I thought we had something special started, but instead, he's just like Jared, assuming he knows what's right. Tears build up again and flow down my cheeks. I had let Noah in when I had not let anyone else in for years. He brought me back to my love of music. He made me feel alive again. Yet, here I am.

Alone and brokenhearted once again. I let the tears flow.

Someone taps on my shoulder. I jump and turn around, taking out the earbuds. It's Noah.

He looks at me, then reaches up to wipe away my tears.

"Ava, I'm so sorry, I admit I got jealous when I saw you with Jared, but it's more than that."

I frown, waiting for him to explain.

"Ava, we just met two weeks ago and the intensity of what I feel scares me." He looks down and digs the sand with a toe. "You've been in the back of my mind for years. You and your music. Your voice touches a part of me that no one ever has. I know this sounds crazy, but the moment I first saw you years ago has stayed with me. And now? After getting to know you, I'm my best self around you. Playing music with you these past few days has been incredible." He stops. Now the only sounds that surrounds us is the lull of the waves, soothing, and consistent.

My heart leaps.

"Noah, it's not crazy," I whisper. "I've felt it, too. No matter how complicated this becomes, I want you in my life. You helped me find my love for music again."

He grins. "I'm happy I could do that for you. I promise to always help you find the things that bring you love and happiness, even if you're hellbent about avoiding them. I want to keep you around, too."

He grabs me and pulls me in for a kiss. Behind me, the sun disappears beneath the horizon, and the sky is kissed with clouds now colored in shades of orange, pink, and purple...just like the colors of our music.

THE END

Introducing K D Norris

An Affair of the Mind

"An Affair of the Mind" is an historical fiction that focuses on Lady Murasaki Shikibu, credited with 11th century writings generally called "The Tale of Genji" and often considered to be the oldest romance novel in existence. This story follows the relationship between Emperor Ichijō, who reigned from 986 to 1011, and a court poetess, the married Lady Murasaki, whose stories subtly reflect the Emperor's privileged, decadent but often dangerous world. Her works, however, shroud the identity of the Emperor while at the same time hinting of deeper passions. For more about K.D. Norris and his literary efforts, visit kdnorris.com.

Heat level: SWEET

AN AFFAIR OF THE MIND
(Lady Murasaki Shikibu and the tales of KoGenji)
K D Norris

"What is across that sea?" twenty-nine-year-old Emperor
Ichijō-*tennō* asked. Standing just outside the walls of Shitenno-ji
Temple, he spoke more to the sky and the setting sun than to
any particular member of the small entourage that had
accompanied him from the Imperial court, in Koyto, here to
Osaka, on sojourn in honor of the dead.

As Emperor, he obviously knew what land lay across the
Seto Sea to the west: The Island of Awaja. But, the question was
deeper than that, and everybody knew it. He turned to those
who stood the required two paces behind, looked to their faces,
one by one, inviting answers.

Saburo, his manservant, looked where his Emperor
looked and then back toward his master, dropping his face,
avoiding the Imperial eyes the servant had never—would
never—intentionally gaze into. "Your humble world, my god
and emperor." He bowed deeply as he spoke, keeping his gaze
focused on the ground at his master's feet until released by his
master's word.

"Of course."

He turned to the next person.

Akoguso, the latest in the Emperor's long line of *sensei*,
of his teachers, scratched his aged chin through his long, thin
beard and tried to sound as though he actually knew more than
his student. "The Imperial Island of Awaja, inhabited by
twelve-thousand of your subjects. Fishermen and farmers and
their families, and the various workers in their small villages,
and the Naruto lighthouse, of course."

After catching his Emperor's gaze in a brief glance, seeking approval, and receiving an expressionless and wordless response, Akoguso stepped back, startled, quickly looking at the ground at his master's feet, bowing deep until released by his master's word.

"Of course."

Finally, he turned to the woman, one of several Imperial court poets and a woman he thought was undoubtedly a Fujiwara spy, one of many loyal to the clan determined to rule him and usurp his empire. The poetess was older than he by a few years, and while possessing natural beauty, she chose to hide it with rather dull makeup and attire. He was told she was the overeducated daughter of a minor court administrator and the late-married wife of a man almost as old as her father. He knew little of the men in her life and even less about her.

As he looked toward the woman, she waved a small *hiogi*, a wood and paper fan, in front of her face, obscuring her gaze just as vain young women obscure the flaws of their faces with their painted fans. She then turned her face down, away from his gaze, but only after looking at him for a fleeting, flirtatious instant.

He knew why she did not immediately answer his invitation to speak, and he again turned his face west, to the setting sun.

"You, *hiogi*," he commanded, in his deep, practiced Imperial voice. "Remind me of your name."

"I am the Lady Murasaki Shikibu. My husband is Fujiwara no Nobutaka," she whispered.

He glanced back her way. Yes, yes. He now remembered. He returned his gaze to the sea.

"What do you see, Lady Murasaki?" he commanded.

The Lady furtively raised her eyes—he noticed without looking directly; he noticed much by pretending to look away.

She glanced to him, then to where he looked, across the sea, and then behind him, past the two other men, back towards the north, to the palace at Koyto.

Finally, she looked where her Emperor stood and unflinchingly gazed at his profile.

He still pretended not to notice her direct gaze.

"I know they say that from this place you can view paradise," she said, her words flowing as water in a fountain but her message as obscured as her face behind the painted fan. "But, I gaze to the west, to where the burning sun still shines, and to the east, to where the full moon rises and see nothing worth remembering other than your broad Imperial shoulders and your serene Imperial face."

Nodding, he smiled but held back a desired laugh; this was too sacred a place to disturb its quiet with laughter.

He nodded and wondered if this poet, this writer of masked histories, was the one to save his story.

Born Kanehito-*shinnō*, blessed now as Ichijō-*tennō*, Emperor of Japan, direct descendant of the Shinto sun-goddess Amaterasu—he accepted that his story would likely be lost, buried with him, only to be resurrected, rewritten by strangers if not enemies, dictated by the passing of time and evidence of treachery.

He lived life as the center of his own county's universe, which was only fitting, his being the first born and only son of God Emperor En'yū.

But, as he now knew, his universe was not infinite.

From the day of his birth, when given the name Kanehito, he was destined to either become emperor, another of the select few chosen by the gods to ascend to the Chrysanthemum Throne, or to be betrayed by the treacherous *Kugyō* in favor of another's ascension, to be held hostage in impotent Imperial luxury if not quietly murdered.

It had been the will of the gods that he was destined to reign, however, and had been named crown prince in his fourth year and become Emperor Ichijō mere days before his seventh birthday.

The first years of his reign were spent as a child playing as all children play, oblivious to any world outside his reach. In the years after he became a man, at age twelve, donning the clothes and hairstyle of a man as part of his *genbuku* ceremony, he lived a carefree life of leisure, luxury and learning. He witnessed his body mature, his mind blossom.

As long as he could remember, he had been handsome to the point of being beautiful in the eyes of men as well as women, educated and adept in the arts and sciences of his time, gentle in the games of love, and boisterous if not actually skilled in the games of war.

He learned quickly the artful lessons of Imperial influence and the playful games of the Imperial court, and his handsome looks and pleasant voice allowed him to mask his mischievous nature. He enjoyed the many women, the many experiences his young, carefree life allowed but knew he would never again believe in love after the cursed day he tearfully buried his first wife, Teishi, his chosen one, at the age of twenty-three. He had been just twenty-one. She had been thirteen when they married, he just eleven.

While he *enjoyed* his second wife, Shōshi, she had been chosen by others and he eventually grew suspicious of her. After all, she was part of the Fujiwara clan. And also, all the while, he continued the emotionless enjoyment of several Imperial consorts of his choosing and uncounted affairs with other women of no importance whatsoever.

He grew from boyhood into manhood knowing that every person in his universe adored him, respected him, prayed to him.

But, as eventually all men born and raised in isolated luxury learn, he came to understand how truly little he actually understood of his world—and the limits of his Imperial power. Some men are lucky enough to continue living with such knowledge.

As Emperor, Kanehito-*shinnō* continued to live with such knowledge.

Today, in the twenty-ninth year of life and the twenty-third year as Emperor, he knew his reign, if not his life, was coming to an end. His crime: beginning to question acts done in his name by the powerful clan Fujiwara *Kugyō*. The clan, and especially Uncle Fujiwara no Michinaga, who had been threatened by his questions, his independence. A clan that had always struck ruthlessly when threatened.

Blessed with Imperial power as a child and now, as a man, he thought he could simply possess and exercise that power fully. He did not understand the actual limits of power until his final, private words with his Imperial predecessor, the Emperor Kazan, his uncle who had abdicated the throne and became a Buddhist priest, and with whom he had been denied a meeting until now. The two had been purposefully kept apart, finally meeting last year. Even the Fujiwara could not—dared not—deny the current emperor a last private moment with his dying predecessor.

The former emperor-turned-priest welcomed his blessed, burdened nephew into the temple to which the older man fled his personal sorrow and the sorrowful state of Imperial affairs. At the modest country temple to which he had been exiled, in the simple but immaculate garden of that temple, Kazan spoke of Kanehito's unremembered father, Emperor En'yū, who had died an old man at the age of thirty-three, unable to withstand the weight of ruling in an unruly age, unable to exert any real power in the face of Fujiwara clan power. Kazan spoke of his own life and reign. He believed that the clan, then led by Kaneie, had caused the death of his beloved empress in childbirth so as to deny him a son, to prune the Imperial tree so as to bare the desired fruit for when the Emperor himself was eventually removed, cut away as deadwood in the winter.

In the end, Kazan offered simple words to guide his nephew through the labyrinth that was Imperial life.

"Trust nobody but those who love you," Kazan said, in the hushed voice of a man who trusted nobody, especially his servants. "But know that your Fujiwara woman will never love you more than she loves her father. Know in your heart that the people you rule will praise you, forever remember you, for the good deeds you do in their name. Know, too, that the people will forever curse your enemies for the evil deeds they do in your name. Trust the people to know the difference. Try to find the moment of truth with the next emperor that your father found with me, before he died. The moment that I have found with you today. Finally, if you can, leave behind a story they cannot bury with you."

Standing now on the precarious cliff's edge of Imperial power, Kanehito remembered the illuminating words of his uncle and the clouded story of his father, who, like himself, had been a gilded emperor siting on a golden throne that neither had ever wanted. Looking out, on a world that still revolved around him, he knew his story would soon exist only in flawed histories, and masked memories, and in the blind chants of the priests at the temple commemorating the day of his ascension to heaven.

But today, in the cool early spring, was not when his story would end. It was the day, he hoped, that his stories would remain alive, yet unnamed, as in the unmarked grave of a nameless poet whose poems remained.

"Will you write a poem of this place?" he asked Lady

Murasaki, looking back to her face.

"If you wish," she said, bowing, casting down her gaze, but then returning a furtive glance to meet his gaze.

"Bring your poem to me, and only me, when it is complete."

She bowed again, and once more, he noticed her expressionless face, only partially hidden behind her fluttering fan.

This woman amused him, and he was curious as to what she hid behind her mask. Prior to her arrival, he had little interest in the stories told by the royal court poets. Sei Shōnagon, the poet of his first wife, Empress Teishi—his beloved Sadako—wrote of mere pillow talk, and he had little interest in such foolishness but allowed her to remain in court. When Empress Teishi had died, his second Empress wife had brought this new poet into court.

This Lady Murasaki, and her writings, were different. Alluring in a way he'd never known.

He would enjoy knowing this woman. Pity she was already married.

***

Time passed. It was another day, in another place.

It was full spring, the cherry blossoms were in delicate splendor in Kyoto, but Kanehito*shinnō* was bored. The Empress was not speaking to him for the moment, as he recently flaunted a momentary infatuation with a new consort. He had intentionally picked one not of Shōshi's choosing, knowing it would anger her. It seemed as though anger was the only emotion he could rouse in his Empress these days.

This morning, he decided on a new way to anger the Empress and called for the Lady Murasaki. The Empress was a creature of habit, and her habit today would have been to spend some time with her poet; she would not like her habits being disturbed by his desires.

The Lady caught up with him as he walked in the garden among the pink-hued cherry trees. She moved in a quick step across the pebbled walkway, the delicate sound of her approach contrasting with the plodding steps of his manservant, who followed well behind the pair but within his calling distance.

"Was the Empress angry?" he inquired as her quick step slowed and she fell in stride a short distance behind, just off his right shoulder, where he could see her with a fleeting glance to his side.

She did not respond immediately, and so the two walked in silence — with his manservant falling farther behind as they walked — until they were beyond the distance of overheard whispers.

"The Empress said nothing to me, but as I left her, I was sent to her father — he asked what you wanted," the Lady whispered.

He glanced to her face, but continued to walk. "And what did you tell him?"

"I told him the truth, that I did not know."

"Do you always tell the truth about our moments together?"

"My Empress rules my life, but my Emperor rules the world."

They walked in silence, gaining more ground on the servant as they did so.

"The Fujiwara rule the world," he said, now in a whisper as well. "The Empress Shōshi is Fujiwara. There is no cleaving the child from the family. I rule what is placed before me."

The Lady said nothing, and they continued to walk.

He enjoyed the words of the Lady much more than any of the other poets. He had adored his beloved Sadako, but she had been a simple girl, and her simple mind assumed her

Imperial husband wanted certain amusements. Sei Shōnagon, at Sadako's request, created stories of affairs of the heart and of the flesh; stories intended to bring embarrassed laughter to the women of the court and sensual interest to the men. The Lady's words occasionally served the same purpose, but with a much more subtle hand.

As they walked, he lazily looked at the beauty of the pristine garden path and the colorful trees.

"So, you have been telling my Empress that I keep you around because of your pillow stories?"

"I tell her what she wishes me to tell her."

"Of course."

"Why do you not write me pillow stories; why must I think about the deeper meaning of your stories? Sometimes I simply want to be amused."

She said nothing, awaiting the invitation to actually answer his question—she always acted so when she was going to disagree with him. A quick glance offered the invite.

"Your world is filled with amusements," she said, looking at him directly.

"Yes, but not your amusements."

The Lady glanced away from his gaze for a moment then back to his face. "If you wish, my Emperor, I—"

"No. No, of course. Others keep me amused. But Sei Shōnagon did have a certain way with her words, her stories of concubines and conquest."

His voice trailed off, into his own memories of women of no importance. The Lady, not wishing to interrupt his memories, waited silently. After a few steps, he stopped and turned to her. She held her face down, appearing from the back to be avoiding his gaze, but her eyes looked up to meet his gaze.

"I have been told of her ways, her stories," the Lady whispered.

He stepped a pace closer.

She bowed deep. From a distance, where the manservant stopped and waited, it would appear as though she had displeased the Emperor.

"Excuse my words for causing displeasure," the Lady said.

"No displeasure. Your truth is welcome. I hear the truth so little these days."

The Lady then rose to face him. He was not of commanding Imperial height and the Lady was unusually tall, so they stood nearly eye-to-eye. He noticed, though, that she crouched slightly so as not be taller than he.

Yes, he thought, she is very subtle in all things. "Of Sei Shōnagon," she said. "I understand the Empress has arranged for her to take on the nun's life, to be locked away."

"Should I care?"

She once more bowed her head slightly, but again cast her gaze up.

"If your Imperial wisdom sees a better fate for her, should she be allowed to marry and live her life away from the court, surely the gods of beauty will favor such wisdom."

Was the Lady actually advocating for a rival poet? That amused him. "Some say she is your better in the art of poetry, yet you seek my mercy for her?"

"She is not without an eye for the human failings and a talent for remembering them," the Lady said. "I would hope my writing will survive me. I can hope no less for her."

He thought for a moment, weighing the consequences of overruling the Empress, and, therefore, her father and her family. "And who would make a good husband for Sei Shōnagon?"

"In my humble opinion, I know that the Empress' cousin, Fujiwara no Muneyo, has lost his wife..." She paused, awaiting his recognition.

He knew nothing of the man.

"He is the governor of Settsu province," she continued. "I understand he could use some culture and beauty in his life."

"Mmmm," he weighed the idea. "And what would the Empress think of such an act?"

"She will run to her father and protest at the insult, but he will ignore his daughter on this minor matter and allow your wishes to be so. Muneyo means little to him, and Sei Shōnagon means nothing."

She smiled a wide, and he sensed, mischievous smile. "He is a man. He understands that any man—even an Emperor—must respect women who are amusing."

He thought for a moment; only a moment. "I shall make it so."

The Lady bowed again, returning her gaze to the ground.

"So," he continued more loudly, so the servant would hear him seemingly angry with the Lady. "Your veins lack the black blood of ruthlessness."

"And so we might all be remembered," she whispered.

"Anyway, Sei Shōnagon's writing of *morning after* letters is far superior to mine," the Lady said, letting slip a brief laugh.

He had to agree and smiled to show his agreement. He had used Sei Shōnagon's advice on such delicate matters; a man must always respect the woman he takes to bed, even if she is of no importance.

But, he could not actually show agreement.

"I take no notice on such things," he said as he turned and walked.

The Lady paused a moment, then began to walk a short

distance behind; still farther behind them, the servant, too, began to walk.

The Emperor knew the servant's report to his Fujiwara master would be accurate and thoroughly confusing.

As they walked, he inhaled the sensual beauty of the brief life of the cherry blossoms.

***

Time passed. It was another day, in another place.

It was summer and the Emperor's entourage, which now regularly included The Lady Murasaki, escaped the oppressive heat and foul mood of the royal court to gain serenity in the country, at the ancestral home of his father's family. For years, he had been persuaded against any visit, but recently, after his first open clash with Michinaga, he decided to sojourn here to pray for his ancestors. Even the *Kugyō* would not openly oppose such an Imperial action without appearing to disrespect the gods and God Emperors.

It was a small, old estate on which nobody of importance lived anymore. There were a few house servants, but when he arrived, it was clear the servants barely kept the buildings in good standing. He had been assured the estate was being taken care of, but it clearly had suffered years of Fujiwara neglect if not malice.

He and The Lady walked around the estate while everybody else endeavored to make the place livable for an emperor. He witnessed the damage done by being ignored. The hedges leading to the main house were overgrown, the road uninviting. The gardens were unkempt and only wild flowers bloomed in their unremarkable color. The little pond behind the main house, the pond where he vaguely remembered sailing a boat as a small child, was filled with tangled reeds that clouded the beauty of its surface and choked life from its depths.

The estate was a reflection of his world, he thought, the

pond, his life.

"All days are chaos," he said. "All memories are faded glory."

"There was once beautiful order, there can be again," she said. She still cast her face down when she spoke, but now she rarely hid her face behind a painted fan, even if her words were still obscured. "Do you remember the beauty of the yugao?"

He looked at the soft white flowers of evening glory, growing on one of the building's walls. Years after they were last properly tended to, they still grew strong and carried a beautiful scent, but their blooms were faded from lack of the gardener's nourishment.

"They are pleasant in the evening of their life, true," he said. "But, they have sadly lost their full youthful glory."

"Beauty never fades as long as it is remembered," she said. "Order is always possible as long as it is desired."

Often, even in their private conversations—and always in the company of their Fujiwara masters—the Lady chose her words carefully, her meaning always open to interpretation. He enjoyed the game of looking for the layered meaning of her words, especially when it frustrated the Empress or her father. For that reason, and because he was often amused by the Lady and her words, he had arranged with the Empress for her poet to become part of his daily entourage. He knew the Lady would likely report back to Shōshi, if not directly to Michinaga, who had grown even more obsessed with control as his health began to decay. The Lady would tell them of her time with the Emperor, recalling all he said and did while they were together. But, he assumed the Lady skillfully waved her painted fan when she was with them, as well.

"I remember this as a place filled with beauty," he said, then turning to look around the estate.

When the Emperor made no effort to continue the

conversation and was, instead, now deep in thought, the Lady excused herself and left him to set up her quarters.

His entourage stayed at the estate for several days, during which he personally directed improvements and sent a letter to Michinaga, stating that he would visit this estate each year, on a date of his choosing, and expected it to be ready for his visit.

And then, on their last evening at the estate, the Lady brought to him a story. As with all her stories written for her Emperor, she read it aloud to him alone.

"It happened that when the beautiful young prince was driving about in the Rokjio quarter, he was informed that his *menoto*, whose name was Daini, was ill and had become a nun. Her residence was in Gojio. He wished to visit her and traveled to the house. The main gate was closed, so his carriage could not drive up; therefore, he sent in a servant to call out her son, whom he knew by name as Koremitz."

The Lady's voice, her words, were as soft and sweet as the recently fertilized and now vigorously blooming yugao flowers.

The story had the beautiful young prince, seventeen years old, going to visit the woman who had been his wet nurse in his infancy as well as a tender, protective handmaiden as a child explored his world. The young man grew strong and his *mento* was one of the reasons, so he respected her and treated her well from afar, and one day, after hearing of her illness, stopped by to pay his respect. But, as the young man sat outside her house, he saw a glimpse of a younger woman's face from a shuttered window of the house. He would learn that the younger woman was named Yugao and that she was new to the area. The young man inquired and found all to be known of the young woman—basically she was nobody, but she was beautiful and shy and had captured his attention. So, he would have her.

But, as the Emperor had come to expect from the Lady, the story was not simply pillow talk, not a story of moments spent in idle love games, and certainly not one of mere eroticism. Her stories stimulated the mind as well as the flesh. And, with this story, as with any affair of the flesh, there were consequences.

The young man in the story had other lovers in his life, including an older woman named Lady Rokujo. After paying his respects to his *mento*, and again glimpsing Yugao, he traveled on to visit Lady Rokujo, and, in secret, he was thinking of the younger woman while he was making love to the older woman. His older lover was wise, though, and somehow knew a younger rival had invaded her world. The young man recognized this but ignored the conflict. And later, he slipped away from his older lover and found a convenient time and place to take Yugao for his pleasure. While Lady Rokujo was refined, she was also flawed by jealousy, and that flaw made her evil spirit come to life one night and kill Yugao. The young man was heartbroken because he had caused the death of an innocent, gentle young woman. But, he was also frustrated because he now had to break off the affair with the older woman due to her evil spirit. He mourned for both of his losses for many days before he recovered and found other distractions.

"This young man has a soft heart," the Emperor said when the story was finished, when the Lady's words faded into the silence of a newly manicured garden. "He mourns as a woman would mourn, not as a man."

"He is but a boy, yet. He has not learned to hide his face behind the mask of a man," she said.

"The young man is of the royal house. Such a man is wise from a young age, and a wise man does not mourn for what his hand has not caused."

"Yes. I understand," she said.

"The man was probably sick for a time. The lady's evil spirit gave his spirit a drop of poison, as well. It was a lesson for him about the dangerous flaws of all women."

"Yes. That gives more truth to the story. I thank you."

"Of course."

Despite his critical words, he was moved by the story; he saw much to be learned. The prince was reckless in his affairs, coveting too much in too short a period of time, and his haste led to sadness. A fragile, older lover was left bitter while a naïve, young lover was left mournful. A wise man would have handled the situation differently; he would have understood the delicate nature of the evening flower.

"You name the younger woman for the evening flower," the Emperor said. "But it is the older woman who withers from lack of care. It is her beauty that fades, her soul that dies, when jealousy dries her roots."

"Yes."

"All women are as flowers," he said, "to be tended and appreciated and cut at their moment of perfection, for all flowers fade after their time is past."

"Yes."

"And, the beautiful young man, his face is familiar yet remains unknown."

"He is nobody, yet he is every beautiful young man," she said. "I put a false face on him, but you see a vague image in the mask..." she looked at him, questioning, "...of someone you know?"

As Emperor, he usually did not answer anybody's direct questions, and yet, he found himself more and more answering the Lady's thoughtful inquiries. She truly was gifted.

"I remember telling you of my mourning for Teishi, my

first empress, and of the nameless young woman who disappeared after my new Empress, Shōshi, found I had taken a lover. I hear echoes of my words in this story."

"All stories of the heart ring familiar. All stories give opportunity to see oneself in a character's mask, but it is still only a mask."

"Ah," he said, accepting her lie.

"So, in what mask do you see yourself in your stories?"

"I see no mask reflecting my face, not yet," she said. "I will see myself when I write the story that requires my face to show the truth."

"I would like to read such a story. When will you write that story?"

"When all other stories are written. How can one know the truth of one's life until one's life is lived?"

"Of course."

He then waved the Lady away and returned to the burgeoning beauty of the garden and to his memories of Teishi.

***

Time passed. It was another day, in another place.

It was fall and it was raining, and the Emperor was having tea with the Lady in one of the many tearooms of the Imperial palace in Koyto.

His days lately had been filled with the burdens of life as an emperor without Imperial power and without hope of ever gaining such power. He questioned every action, each motivation of every person around him. His hours with the Lady stood out as a rare escape from his burdens, but he sometimes suspected even her.

As a test of her allegiance, he had been telling her about his intimacy with women, sometimes falsely boasting but mostly telling the truth. She was very good at telling the difference between his tales and his truths. The Lady's allegiance seemed his, at least on these matters, as neither his Empress nor her father, were they to know, would resist the opportunity to subtly tease him on such matters.

The essence of many of the Lady's stories seemed to flow from his lips. Others probably came from other men of the Imperial house—those clearly less refined. Others simply from her imagination. Many stories flowed from the muddied water of the three rivers flowing together.

"Your words often flow as clear water from a mountain spring, yet you hide the source of this spring."

"You are the source of all that is good," she said. "All else is unworthy of your attention or my effort."

He laughed aloud. He laughed more in her presence than with any other person in his world.

Today, she read another story to him, her voice and her words melodic, the perfect voice of a singer in the night. As she began the story, the words came to life off her page.

"The beautiful young prince was still sleepless! 'Never have I been so badly treated. I have now discovered what the disappointment of the world means,' he murmured, while the boy Kokimi lay down beside him fast asleep. The smallness of the boy's stature and the graceful waving of his short hair could not but recall to the beautiful young prince the beautiful tresses of the boy's sister and bring her image vividly before him; and, long before the daylight appeared, he rose up and returned to his residence with all speed."

The poetic theme of the Lady's story, he came to understand, was that of the cycle of a cicada, a cycle echoed by a tale of a young woman whom the beautiful young prince desired but had to plot to seduce. In the story, the prince befriended the woman's brother and all but forced the young man to present his sister for the prince's pleasure. But, the prince ends frustrated in his effort and, vainly, angry at the brother.

As the story neared end, the Lady read two poems, the first from the young man to his desired.

> Where the cicada casts her shell
> In the shadows of
> the tree There is one
> whom I love well Though
> her heart is cold to me.

And, then, her response:

> Amidst dark shadows of the tree
> Cicada's wing with dew is wet
> So in mine eyes unknown to thee
> Spring sweet tears of fond regret.

The Lady's words faded as soft music into the air, but they also touched on painful memories—even an Emperor still felt pain. The truth of the story was clear: One should never betray one's family, nor ask another to do so. Both acts are condemned by the gods.

When the Lady had first come to his court, had started to write stories of his world if not his life, he was the Emperor and she avoided any hint that his decisions and deeds were anything but divinely perfect. But, as the days and the stories multiplied, the two had grown comfortable with each other. He was not perfect and her stories subtly exposed those flaws. He would also now ask her direct questions, and she knew he expected the truth in reply. She was, after all, possibly the only person in his life that spoke the truth to him.

"So *kirei hiogi*, you think I care too little for the women in my life?" he asked, using his private, intimate name for the Lady—his "pretty little fan"—inviting a private, intimate conversation.

"It is not my position to judge. It is my position to write stories that may reflect life in some small way then to accept judgment of the truth present or absent in my writing." She looked at him directly. In the security of their privacy, with her place in his world secure, her fan sat unopened at her side and she no longer hid the openness of their relationship. "Does my story lie, Kanehito-*shinnō*? If so, I will burn it."

He laughed, gazing back into her beautiful eyes. "No. But, the truth is not always a gentle lover."

Then he turned, silent. He sat a little taller, straightened his robe, and stalled for time and inspiration if not insight.

"I do care deeply for all the women in my life, even the ones I no longer remember," he said. "My wives, my concubines. The young and the old, the innocent and the well-trained. I care for all of them, but a man of my position is allowed to forget those persons that are forgettable, those of no importance, those…"

As he talked, the Lady glanced up from the tatami mat where she kneeled, the same mat where he sat cross-legged, the two of them facing each other. But now, her eyes stared at the center of his chest, avoiding his face. It was her signal that his actions, his words, were those of the Emperor, not a confidant or lover, and she would never question the infallible words of the Emperor, unless asked.

"Yes," he said, approving the question he knew she wished to ask.

"You, of course, care deeply for all your subjects," she said. "But ,do lesser men of power care for all their women, even the nameless whom they force themselves on?"

He never answered difficult questions, never acknowledged being ill at ease. He was too accustomed to the pleasures of a carefree life and a forgetful memory, but he witnessed the world around him and remembered.

"Men of a certain standing, of true power, need never force anything to gain their goals. All they desire comes to them freely given. Even if the desired woman does not understand her gift, at the time, she will come to know that she gave freely and justly. But, when a man desires a woman of a higher social standing than himself, then his simply taking what he wants is wrong. That man will be punished, either by the gods or, acting for the gods, by the woman's family. And, of course, even men of the highest social standing—a beautiful young prince—must choose wisely. An affair with a woman of much power but little social standing can bring ruin, even to an emperor."

He then paused, and watched as the Lady's gaze met his own. They smiled together. "Of course, it is more common that women seek power above their social standing. Women of beauty flaunted. Women of intelligence hidden."

The Lady laughed. It was a soft laugh. His was much more robust.

"Such a woman would be a boat adrift," The Lady said. "A boat lighted with lamps for celebration but without fixed purpose or destination."

"Yes," he said. "Yes. I remember your story on this matter."

The Lady nodded.

The story was one of the few which, he thought, did not echo his words. It was a story of a young crown prince whose boat drifted along empty water and empty life, falling in and out of love and lust, always seemingly unaware of his aimless, futile voyage. The young man's name was strange—*ukifune*—a term commonly used to express unpredictably or uncertainty, but which could also mean one whose fate is unknown, often due to a lack of morals. The main character of the story was a man, but the Emperor remembered thinking that the young prince was really a woman wearing a man's mask.

Empress Shōshi must have thought so, as well. Having obviously been read the story by the author, the Empress had used the story to mock the Lady during one of the rare occasions when the three of them were together. The Empress had called the Lady *ukifune*, joking that she was little more than a person of no matter on a common fishing boat, trying to entice an emperor to voyage. Kanehito, though, had wondered if it were really the Lady who was doing the mocking by reading the Empress the story. Did the Lady know the Empress would have never been so thoughtful as to see her own vain, ruthless face behind the mask?

In the end, however, the story had concluded without resolution, with the truth still deeply woven into the fabric of the Lady's words.

"This story, it ends without knowing what happens to the crown prince. Does his action betray his chosen path?"

"Only the gods can know if a man is destined for the throne. Only the gods can know the end of the story."

"Of course."

With that, she excused herself and the Emperor returned to thoughts of his many burdens.

***

Time passed. It was another day, in another place.

But, time and day had come to mean nothing to Emperor Ichijō, and place meant little.

This day, in early summer, the Emperor spent an unknown amount of time sitting in one of the many gardens reserved for him at the royal palace in Kyoto. He spent most of his days in such wasteful leisure, his thoughts filled with doubt and defeat. He called for the Lady Murasaki, and she came to him.

"I am buried alive," he said to the world as she

approached. "My story is written, and it is a tragedy."

"All stories are written before they are put to paper," she said. "The gods write them."

"The story you gave to me to read last night, is this my final story?" As he spoke, he touched the large roll of papers on the table before him.

"It is likely the final story I will write for you, Kanehito. My father has sent word that my husband has died and that I must retire from the court and return to my husband's house to mourn him. I will then return to my father's house."

"You cared nothing for your husband, nor he for you. You must mourn him, but why leave the court?"

"Because my father tells me to, just as he told me to marry."

"Of course," he said. "When will you go?"

"When you or Michinaga give me leave."

He thought for a moment. He would miss the Lady, but he would not give their master, the Fujiwara devil, the satisfaction of making this decision for him, of taking credit for sending her away.

"I will give you leave, Lady Murasaki. But first, read again the poem from your story. Let me remember your words and your voice."

He unrolled the papers on which the story was written, seeking the page with the poem that he wanted her to read. She closed her eyes, not needing to see the words on paper.

"If as my spirit yearns for thine, thine yearns for mine, why thus delay?
And yet, what answer might be mine if, pausing on her way, some gossip bade me tell
Whence the deep sighs that from my bosom swell?
And thy dear name my lips should pass, my blushes would

our love declare
No, no! I'll say my longing was
to see the moon appear o'er yonder darkling hill
Yet 'tis on thee mine eyes would gaze their fill"

As the beautiful words flowed from her beautiful lips, he remembered…

The story told of a beautiful young man gazing into the dark water of an unkempt pond, seeing his past and his future. The images in the pond showed a young prince who resisted the shackles carried by masked devils. The devils killed his father, his wife and child, yet, he still resisted. When all appeared lost, a golden sword formed in the water, made up of many pieces that flew together as leaves gathered on the surface of a pond. With that golden sword, he challenged the devils, and after he separated the head from the body of one devil, the rest faded into the darkness.

As Kanehito read the story, he thought of his own devils.

He had learned that, as Emperor, he could do what he wanted, when he wanted, as long as he did not directly challenge the *Kugyō* or interfere with their plans. Over the past year, he had attempted to rule as an Emperor should rule, but he was too weak, both in body and in spirit. His mood had been dark for many days as he considered the limits of his possible futures. But, he revealed his mood only to the Lady, in this place, in the garden where they met.

He had learned that only in the open, without walls to be listened behind, did he have true privacy with her. All that surrounded the Emperor, every person, every building, every room, listened to his words. And every word was heard by Empress Shōshi and her father Michinaga. Every person in his world waited to betray him, except, maybe, the Lady Murasaki, his *kirei hiogi*. With her, he risked the truth.

When they talked, he discussed his possible futures. There were those who loved and were loyal to the Emperor first and foremost; there were those among the *Kugyō* who hated the Fujiwara even more than he did; there were those, even among the Fujiwara house, who sought to control the Emperor as Michinaga controlled the Emperor. There were many who *said* they would rally to his side should he only ask.

But, he and the Lady knew there were other possible futures.

In the story, another image in the pond showed the young man as a god with wings, but his feet were held fast by the arms of the weeds that grew from beneath the dark water. In another image, people prayed over a grave, remembering a young man as a gentle soul, full of truth, and their tears warmed his heart in the afterlife.

At the end of the story, the young man saw a bright vision in the dark water. He stood in a garden full of violets surrounding a small pond. He gazed into deep, dark waters and spoke of his hopes and his fears, and a voice from the water spoke back to him as the wind sometimes whispers the god's response to prayers. The voice, the soft words of a gentle woman, told him that his end was coming; his death drew near.

When the Lady finished reading the poem, her eyes opened and met his.

"This story, I see reflection of your face in the waters," he said. "I see you as a flower, as true beauty in the darkness. Is this, finally, your mask Lady Murasaki?"

"I am in every story I write, just as you are in every story you tell me. The pond can have more than one ripple, interacting, building, and decreasing in size, but they all must eventually fade."

Kanehito understood the story now. From his day of ascension to the Throne of Heaven, he was living in a dark pool from which he could never escape, yet there was great beauty even in darkness.

"This is a true story, a fine story." He touched the corner of the first sheet of paper to the flame of a lantern. He set the burning paper into a stone bowl and, one by one, added the other sheets into the flame until the story lay in ashes.

"It is a story which cannot be written while I still live," the Emperor said. "For your own safety, it is a story that cannot be written while there are still spies for the Fujiwara."

The Lady said nothing.

"If I should ascend to heaven before you, I will wonder if this story will survive. Knowing my end, will you again write it? Will you use your skillful hand and your delicate fan to obscure its true nature?" he asked. "I wonder, too, if a thousand years from now, will they call your words the stories of Kanehito or KoGenji?"

"That depends on the thoroughness of the *Kugyō*, of the spies of the Fujiwara," the Lady said. "Only the gods can know what will be the truth in the future. You are a god even now, and your ascension to join the other gods will ensure you know the answer to all questions."

The Lady then fell to her knees and bowed deeply, so deeply that she showed the Emperor her still attractive figure tightly wrapped in her robe. "You are my Emperor," she said, as she rose and looked directly at him.at. "I am your humble servant, a widowed woman who writes simple stories."

He nodded. He understood. "Of course." Kanehito then waved the Lady away. What a fine world it is, he thought. What a fine world it is that the gods allow me to pretend to rule.

THE END

Author's Note:

It is often said that the stories compiled in the body of

words generally called The Tale of Genji and accredited to one Lady Murasaki Shikibu give the modern world its best glimpse into early eleventh century medieval Japanese culture. And while the Genji's tales are studied to death by students and repeatedly dissected by scholars, little is actually known of the author and even less about the sources and subjects of her tales.

What is clearly evident is that the author, whether Lady Murasaki or an even more deeply hidden personality, clearly had a good view through a royal window.

As I looked over my story of Ichijō-*Tennō*, the Lady Murasaki, and the possible fountain from which the *Tale of Genji* flowed, I realized my history may well be flawed. But, as the Emperor might say, my story may still be a story of truth.

It is believed that Lady Murasaki's book, *The Tale of Genji*, was written sometime in the first decade of the eleventh century in Japan, between, most say, the years 1000 and 1010 CE, in the last years of the reign of Emperor Ichijō. The lead character, Genji Monogatari provided a peephole into the refined if somewhat debased world of medieval Japan's upper-crust society. *Genji* is also often considered the first overtly fictional novel of romance.

It would be no surprise that in medieval Japan's Imperial court, a gifted female writer had to bury her skills, or at least cloak them in a shroud acceptable to the *Kugyō*, the patriarchal power-brokers of that time.

Such a reality may well be the true tale of Lady Murasaki: self-delusion, lust, and other traditionally male virtues make fine drama for the idle pleasure of the Medieval male ego, but a female dramatist needed to use a pseudonym, change the names to protect the guilty, and, above all, avoid any hint of the acts of those in actual control.

Whoever the Lady Murasaki Shikibu was, she was, almost without doubt, not named Murasaki Shikibu. All other details about her life, and the model for her created literary character Genji Monogatari, are little more than historical speculation and academic argument.

It is believed that the woman whom we now name Lady Murasaki Shikibu was probably born sometime in the 970s and died sometime after 1014, maybe as late as 1025. She clearly either had firsthand access to the last years of the Heian Dynasty Imperial court or she had extensive secondhand access, probably through more than one person, considering the range of her stories. There is some evidence that Lady Murasaki was a literary lady-in-waiting—a writer, a poet—in the Imperial court during the first decade of the 1000s, probably for Emperor Ichiro's second wife, Empress Shōshi and, maybe, for the Emperor himself. The Lady undoubtedly had a sound education and the most splendid of imaginations.

If there was ever a pseudonym, though, it is the name "Murasaki Shikibu." The first name means "violet" and is often used as a nickname, and it was also the name of a character in *The Tale of Genji*. The second name is believed to be the title of a royal court administrative position in a Bureau of Ceremony. Shikibu-shō would be a male position, however, so it is often assumed that The Lady was the daughter of governmental functionary.

Any biographical details about the author are, in the end, complete conjecture: unproven and unable to ever be proven beyond argument.

Her education and Imperial access could have had several sources. She could have been the educated daughter of a scholar and writer or the rare female scholar and writer herself. She could indeed have been the daughter of a Shikibu-shō and/or maybe even a minor member of the royal family—or an unimportant, if slightly rebellious, member of the powerful Fujiwara clan, the dominate family of that era in Japan. But, if she was either well-known in or a member of the Imperial court, she very purposefully hid her literary interests and intellectual skills behind the mask of a lesser person.

Lady Murasaki could have gained access to the royal court through marriage. There is one story that at age twenty-nine, she entered into a loveless marriage and became one of the several wives of a forty-six-year-old man—apparently at that time in Japan, a twenty-nine-year-old single woman had few long-term relationship prospects. If you believe the loveless marriage story, you can believe that the entire Genji tale was a fictional piece detailing her desired, fantasized male ideal. That idea makes sense except that Genji is not always much of a gentleman.

Anyway, Lady Murasaki somehow had access to the royal court.

My favorite story is that in the year 1005, an educated, well-respected married "elder woman" of thirty-five years of age, was appointed to the position of poet (and, hence, writer/chronicler) for Empress Shōshi. As part of the Empress' entourage, the Lady could easily fall under the spell of Emperor Ichijō, who for many years lived the privileged life of pampered crown prince and then bored Imperial figurehead. Or, possibly, the Lady could have been assigned to spy on the Emperor by the Empress or her manipulative father, Fujiwara no Michinaga, in whose diary a factoid of the Lady's presence is historically recorded.

Anyway, Lady Murasaki had some deep connections in the Imperial court as her original birthplace is now the location of the Roxan-ji Temple, a minor but well-respected religious site located just east of Kyoto's old Imperial Palace.

A final, possibly pertinent, point about Genji's source. One story says the woman's real name may have been Fujiwara no Takako because there is also written evidence of an educated, articulate, well-connected woman acting as lady-in-waiting to the court about that time. We will avoid detail and debate on this matter, and anyway, the story works better if we keep the author anonymous.

In the end, what we have is a diary of pseudo-fiction by one Lady Murasaki, and that document says she wrote the stories that became *The Tale of Genji*, and so that is where we will leave the authorship debate.

Additional conjecture surrounds the possible connection between the Lady and Emperor Ichijō, the most important figure present in the Lady's world during the time the stories were written. I choose to accept that there was a personal relationship, a strong connection, maybe a romantic connection, or maybe simply an affair of the mind.

Special note is given to Project Gutenberg for its free-use e-book of "Genji Monogarari" as well as the poems from the era. Online at www.gutenberg.org

Introducing Lisa Campeau

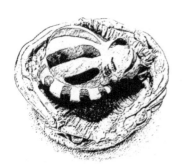

Long Lost Friend

Lisa Campeau enjoys writing sweet, small-town romances. Her first two novels, *Schoolmarm* and *Love Lessons*, are available as e-Books from Amazon.

In "Long Lost Friend," schoolteacher Bridget is unexpectedly reunited with Ryan, her best friend from elementary school, the boy who broke her heart by moving away at the end of fourth grade. The scrawny, often annoying kid she remembers has grown into a devoted attractive father. Their childhood friendship blossoms into a relationship that ignites both an adult love and the kid within both of them.

Heat level: SPICY

LONG LOST FRIEND
Lisa Campeau

Chapter One

Bridget glanced at the clock on the wall and squirmed restlessly in her seat. At the front of the classroom, her teacher was still droning on about long division—or maybe he had moved on to vocabulary by now. She honestly hadn't been paying attention the last half hour. And, judging by the whispers and giggles she was hearing around her, she wasn't the only one. She wondered why Mr. Stewart was even trying anymore.

Didn't he realize there were only two more hours of school left before summer vacation? He had promised she would finally have time to show and tell her new kitten figurines—as long as her presentation was educational. Now she was certain he had forgotten. She tried to meet his eyes and give him a pointed stare, but he didn't even notice. In fact, he seemed to be addressing the row of presidential portraits on the opposite wall.

Bridget slumped over her desk and let out a very audible sigh that immediately plunged the entire room into a humiliating silence. Even Mr. Stewart stopped his lecture and focused on her. She immediately clamped her mouth shut and stared down at her hands. As much as she had wanted to get her teacher's attention, the last thing she wanted to do was disrupt the class. She was really a teacher's pet at heart.

A loud snicker came from the desk next to her, and she glanced over just long enough to see her best friend, Ryan

Carter, grinning at her. His dark eyes were gleaming mischievously behind the chunky plastic glasses he had started wearing a few months earlier. She scowled at him, then returned to studying her desk. For the first time, she wished Mr. Stewart would return to his boring lesson.

"Miss Winters?"

At the sound of her name, Bridget raised her gaze reluctantly to the front of the room, but when she met her teacher's gaze, he was smiling kindly at her.

"Miss Winters, I'm very sorry. I almost forgot. There was something you wanted to share with the class, wasn't there? Why don't you do it now?"

Heart thumping with excitement, Bridget jumped out of her seat and raced across the room to the row of hooks where her backpack was hanging. Her anxious fingers fumbled with the zipper a minute, and when she finally managed to get it open, she reached inside and withdrew two small objects carefully cushioned in paper towels. She had gotten up extra early that morning so she would have time to wrap them over and over again so they would never break—and so her mom wouldn't see what she was doing. The only bit of information Bridget hadn't given her teacher about her precious ceramic kittens was that her mother had forbidden her from bringing them to school.

She hurried to the front of the classroom, where she unwrapped the figurines and set them on Mr. Stewart's desk before turning to face her expectant classmates. Ellie, one of the girls in the front row, caught sight of the kittens and gasped. A few other kids whispered and pointed. While Mr. Stewart shushed the class, Bridget beamed out at them proudly.

"I bought these from a catalog that came to our house one day. My mom said they were too expensive, but I just loved them so much I had to have them. I worked really, really hard to earn the money to buy them, and they just came last week!"

Gingerly, she picked up a ceramic orange kitten sleeping in a bed of colorful flowers while being watched by a bluebird. "I named this one Tiger. It's a boy."

"How can you tell?" Ryan smirked. Mr. Stewart frowned at him, then nodded for Bridget to continue.

Bridget lifted her nose in the air. "I just know." She set Tiger down on the desk and picked up the other, a gray tabby with white paws, standing on its hind legs in a patch of soft grass and pawing at a butterfly. "This one is Whiskers. She's a girl."

Ellie was now half out of her seat, straining to see it better. "Bridget, can I hold it? Please?"

Without thinking, Bridget pulled Whiskers closer to her chest, clutching her protectively. Then, at the disappointment on her friend's face, she loosened her hold on the kitten a little and looked to her teacher for help. "I-I don't know. I mean..."

"These are very breakable, and no one is going to touch them except Bridget," Mr. Stewart said firmly. "In fact, I think it's time to put them away before something happens to them. It's time for recess anyway."

Relieved, Bridget nodded and began winding the paper toweling around the kittens again. As eager as she had been to show them to her class, she would feel so much better once she knew they were safely inside her backpack. She took a step away from Mr. Stewart's desk when he spoke again, stopping her.

"Anything else to add before we go out for recess?" He gave her a significant look.

Bridget hesitated. "Uh..."

"Like, how this presentation was an educational one?"

Bridget stood there awkwardly silent, shifting her weight from one foot to the other. She had forgotten about that.

"Well...what I learned is..."

She paused again, her desperate eyes searching the room for an answer. When they landed on Ryan, he shot her a devious grin and flipped open the notebook on his desk. Bridget narrowed her eyes, watching as he quickly scribbled something in the notebook. She was almost afraid to find out what he was up to. But, when he turned it around so that she could see, she felt a smile cross her face. It was a hastily sketched dollar sign with the word "duh" scrawled next to it.

"What I learned is to work hard and save your money," she concluded quickly. She darted a hopeful glance at Mr. Stewart.

"Good advice for us all," Mr. Stewart replied. "Time for recess."

As the other kids scrambled out of the room, Bridget returned the figurines to her backpack. When she turned around, Ryan was still at his desk, waiting for her.

"I really saved your butt on that one, didn't I?" he teased as they walked out the door that led to the playground.

"No," she retorted. "I could have come up with it on my own."

"Oh, yeah. I'm sure you could've," he replied.

Bridget eyed him suspiciously, waiting for the inevitable clever insult. She had known him almost two years after all, and she knew him well. "Yeah? But..."

"But, it's the last day of school, and I thought we'd want to get out of there sometime before late July."

They were heading toward the swing set at the far end of the playground where they always spent their recess. It was a small metal set with two swings, almost forgotten by the other kids, who spent most of their time flying down the tall slides and clambering over the massive climbing structures. It gave them plenty of time for private talks, which Bridget loved —

even if she did find Ryan annoying sometimes.

Bridget dropped onto one of the swings and grasped the chains tightly. She kicked off with her feet and pumped her legs, gradually propelling herself higher into the air. Next to her, Ryan was doing the same, adjusting his speed until they were in perfect sync.

"Also, you didn't have to embarrass me in front of the whole class," Bridget said conversationally. She wasn't really angry with him. She had decided back in second grade that it was almost impossible to be upset about anything while swinging.

Ryan leaned back in his swing and tilted his head back so that he was staring up at the sky. "What?"

"You know. About how I know Tiger's a boy? Why would you do that? You're such a pain sometimes."

He sat up in his swing again and turned to look at her. "I just thought you could use the practice, you know? Someday when you're a teacher, you're going to be dealing with obnoxious kids like me every day."

"Don't remind me," Bridget moaned. "I just better have enough kids like me to even things out."

"Don't worry," Ryan said, his eyes following the trail of a jet flying overhead. "You're the smartest kid I know. You can deal with a class full of smart-mouthed boys."

Bridget turned to stare at him. Ryan was her best friend in the whole world despite the fact that he said or did something that drove her crazy nearly every day. Once in a while, he surprised her with a kind word or deed that was completely free from teasing and showed her just how much he really cared about her.

"You really think so?" she asked with a glow of pride. Her dream of becoming a teacher was one of the most important things in the world to her.

Ryan gave an awkward shrug. "Sure. You're Mr. Stewart's favorite, you know."

"No, I'm not!" she objected with a laugh.

"Oh, come on. You never forget your homework, you don't talk without raising your hand first, you never let me copy off your papers—"

She let out a horrified gasp. "Of course not! What could you possibly learn by cheating?"

Ryan chuckled loudly. "See. You're practically a teacher already."

"Yeah, well...you might want to pick up some of my habits if you want to do well next year. I've heard Mrs. Spencer is pretty strict. She won't let you get away with half the stuff Mr. Stewart does."

Ryan shrugged again. "Don't matter. I won't have Mrs. Spencer next year."

"What are you talking about? She's the only fifth grade teacher!"

She looked to him for an answer, but he had averted his face from hers and was watching the trees next to him as they rose and fell with the steady motion of his swing. The part of his face she could see had taken on an uncharacteristic reddish color. As the seconds ticked by, the silence between them intensified, punctuated only by the creaking of the ancient swing set.

"Ryan?" she said cautiously. "What are you talking about?"

When he turned to face her again, his face was as casual as ever though his cheeks remained a bit red. He pumped his legs harder and said in a matter-of-fact way, "We're moving."

"*What?*" Bridget reached out and grabbed the chain on his swing, sending him careening wildly in midair.

"Whoa! Hey, what are you doing?" he yelped, trying to

regain control of his swing. "Ow!" he cried as one leg struck the sloping metal pole next to him.

Bridget barely noticed. "You're moving? Why didn't you tell me?"

Ryan looked up from rubbing his bruised leg just long enough to glare at her. "I just did."

Too numb to move, Bridget sat motionless in her swing. As the back-and-forth motion gradually slowed, her thoughts were swirling madly. She was about to lose her best friend. Never again would they sit together like this, talking and teasing. As she dragged her feet on the dusty ground, tears were already coming to her eyes. What would she do without his devilish grin and exasperating whispered remarks in class? There had to be something she could do to stop this from happening.

"Can't you tell your parents you don't want to go?" she asked, already knowing how futile and childish the suggestion was.

He came to a stop beside her and frowned at the ground. "I tried. It didn't work. My dad got a new job out of state, and the money's too good to pass up. My mom's gonna find a new job when we get there. The factory she works at doesn't pay that much anyway."

Bridget was barely listening. "But...there has to be something we can do."

"There's not," Ryan said listlessly. "You'll just have to accept it."

A tear dripped down her cheek. "I don't want to accept it. Ryan...you're my best friend."

He shifted uncomfortably and looked away. "We'll make new friends, Bridget. By the time summer's over, you'll have forgotten all about me."

She stared at him in disbelief. "No, I won't," she declared

in a choked voice.

"Well...you're gonna have to," he mumbled, standing suddenly. "I have to go to the bathroom before class starts again. See you, Bridge."

Bridget watched open-mouthed as, without another word, her friend strode across the grassy playground and through the double doors into the school. Then, she sat another ten minutes, staring forlornly toward the fence at the end of the school yard, trying to control her tears. When the bell rang, she pulled herself off the swing and started back to the building, the ground beneath her feet little more than a blur to her downcast eyes.

She spent the remainder of the day cleaning out her desk amid the happy, last-day chatter of her classmates. She tried repeatedly to catch Ryan's eye, but he seemed intent on clearing his own desk. Whenever she tried to approach him, he quickly struck up a conversation with someone else, shutting her out completely. Bridget was devastated. This was their last day together. How could he not want to talk to her—to say goodbye?

At the end of the day, the students all took their seats again as Mr. Stewart gave them one last speech about how much he'd enjoyed having them in his class and wishing them good luck in fifth grade. Bridget examined the stray pencil marks on her desktop, too brokenhearted even to pay attention. The bell rang for the last time, and everyone raced out the door, scattering to catch their buses, meet their parents, or walk home. Bridget caught sight of Ryan just before he boarded his bus. He grinned and waved to her as if it were any other day. Swallowing down the hard lump in her throat, she raised her hand weakly in response.

When he had disappeared to the back of the bus, she turned and walked to the parking lot where she knew her mother would be waiting for her. She got to the car and climbed into the backseat, slamming the door irritably behind her.

"How was your day?" her mother asked brightly.

"Fine," Bridget answered. She didn't want to invite a lot of questions by revealing how miserable she really was.

While her oblivious mother carried on a mostly one-sided conversation in the front seat, Bridget sat quietly and stared out the window. As they neared home, she unzipped her backpack and began sifting through the papers inside until she found the thing she was looking for. It was a birthday card Ryan had made her when she turned ten. On the cover, he had drawn a picture of Bridget shoving a whole birthday cake into her mouth, candles, and all. Bridget had snorted with laughter when she saw it.

As she was setting the card carefully inside her backpack again, Bridget froze suddenly. Something was different. She reached her right hand inside again, digging through the papers to the very bottom of the bag. Her fingers traveled along, landing on one rather hard, paper-towel-wrapped object. Her fingers probed, more and more frantically, searching to no avail for the second one.

Desperately, she upturned her backpack and dumped the contents onto the seat beside her. Out came a flood of papers, which she brushed aside impatiently, and out came one—only one—of the kitten figurines. The paper towel was just beginning to unwind, and she could see the tip of one of Whiskers' ears poking out. She pulled her backpack close to her again and stared inside, her heart dropping for the second time that afternoon. It was gone. She knew she had put both kittens inside her backpack before going out to recess, and now one of them had vanished.

Without much hope, she unzipped and searched the outside pocket of her backpack. Finding nothing but a broken pencil and an old granola bar, she dropped the backpack on the floor and rummaged through the papers next to her, hoping...hoping by some miracle it was there.

"Bridget? What are you looking for?"

Bridget looked up suddenly. "Nothing!" she squeaked in a rather frightened voice.

She grabbed her one remaining kitten and dropped it into her bag, then gathered all the papers and shoved them inside with it. As they pulled into the driveway, she zipped her bag closed again, unbuckled her seat belt, and reached for the door handle.

"Well, you're off in a hurry, young lady," her mother chuckled as Bridget rushed past her into the house. "Anxious to start your summer vacation?"

Bridget turned to her mother, her face hot with guilt. "Um...yeah. I have to go unpack."

She darted down the hall to her bedroom, where she dropped her backpack on the carpet. She stared at it for a minute, wanting to search it again, just knowing that kitten had to be there. But, a more reasonable part of her knew there was no point. Tiger wasn't there. He was gone, just like Ryan. She flopped across her bed with a sob.

And so, Bridget spent the first afternoon of her summer vacation after fourth grade lying across her lacy, blue bedspread, drenching her pillow with tears.

Chapter Two

Twenty-two years later

Bridget sat at her classroom desk studying the book report in front of her when she felt someone watching her closely. Curious, she set the paper aside and looked up to see Jamie Anderson, her brightest student—though she wouldn't tell the rest of the class that—staring at her anxiously while nibbling on his fingernails like always.

"Can I help you, Jamie?" she asked, offering him a warm smile, which only seemed to frighten him more.

He removed his fingers from his mouth long enough to ask, "Did you grade my report yet, Miss Winters?"

"Yes, I have. And I can promise you have nothing to worry about."

"Did I...did I get an A?"

"You did."

Jamie emitted a low sigh of relief. "Thanks, Miss Winters."

Bridget shook her head. "Don't thank me, Jamie. You're the one who did all the work. You earned it." She gestured toward the window that was streaming with afternoon sunlight. "Now, don't you think it's time you went home and enjoyed this nice day? I dismissed class ten minutes ago."

Jamie's eyes grew wide with dismay. "The math test! I have to get home and study. 'Bye, Miss Winters!"

He raced from the room as Bridget's smile faded from her face. In the ten years she had been teaching, she had never run across a student more terrified of failure—or even mediocrity—than Jamie Anderson. And tonight, she would have to talk to his parents once again and explain that their son needed to know that it was all right to have fun and be a normal, imperfect kid. And like before, she knew they wouldn't listen.

With a sigh, she stood and turned to wipe clean the dry-erase board behind her desk. She loved being a teacher, especially at the very school she had attended as a child, but parent-teacher conference days could be long and exhausting. Although most of the parents she spoke with were pleasant and friendly, there were always a few that either didn't care or didn't believe what she had to tell them about their students' academics or behavior.

"Hey, Bridge." Alex Lane, music teacher and Bridget's best friend, pushed open her classroom door with a platter of sandwiches and two cans of cola. "Did you have time to eat lunch?"

Bridget set down her eraser and turned with a grateful smile. "No, I didn't. Thanks, Alex."

She sat down at her desk, grabbed a ham and Swiss sandwich from the platter, and bit into it hungrily. Alex sat on the edge of a desk in the front row with her own sandwich and studied Bridget critically through her large, dark eyes. Bridget squirmed a little in her chair and looked away, patting her hair self-consciously. Her looks usually didn't matter too much to her, but when she was with Alex, she felt a little plain in comparison. Alex always wore clothes that were stylish but not inappropriate for teaching, and her shoulder length black curls were always perfectly bouncy.

"You know, you should really add a little color to your wardrobe," Alex said, nodding toward Bridget's drab gray skirt and white blouse.

"I know," Bridget replied, snapping open her pop can and gulping down half of it.

"I have a friend who could perform wonders with your hair," Alex added, nodding toward the knot of light brown hair at the back of Bridget's head.

Bridget crammed the rest of her sandwich into her mouth, swallowed it, and stood up. "My first conference is starting in five minutes, Alex. I've got to prepare."

"All right, I can take a hint," Alex laughed as she left the room. "But, I'm not giving up on you, yet."

Bridget spent the next hour and a half in fifteen-minute sessions with parents, going over files that contained their children's report cards, standardized test scores, and some homework assignments. Jamie Anderson's parents came in, sat with her as she expressed her concerns with his fears of failure, and only left after asking if she had any extra credit opportunities for him to bump up his grades.

At five o'clock, she looked to see who her next appointment was with, then pulled up the file for Hector Carter. At the last conference in the fall, she had met with Hector's grandmother, a pleasant woman in her fifties. Bridget smiled as she flipped through Hector's file. He was one of her favorite students—smart, funny, and a little bit devious.

A minute later, there was a tap at the door. Bridget looked up to see a tall, rather handsome man at the door. He was wearing a button-down shirt and tie and had wavy dark hair and dark eyes behind wire-framed glasses.

"Hello. Come on in," she invited with a friendly smile.

"Hello, Miss Winters," he said with a grin. There was something familiar about that grin.

Bridget's eyes shot open wide. She had always wondered, just a little bit, if there were some relation—the last name was the same, after all, and there was definitely some resemblance in both appearance and personality but she hadn't dared to imagine, even in her wildest—

"Are you all right?"

His voice interrupted her runaway thoughts. Quickly, she took his outstretched hand in hers and shook it. He gave her hand a little squeeze before releasing it, and as soon as she was free, she retreated a step. "Would you like to have a seat?" she asked, gesturing toward one of the desks.

He had grown a lot since the last time she had seen him, of course, and the sight of him trying to fit his tall frame into a desk chair meant for a ten-year-old would have been comical if she weren't feeling so frazzled. It seemed unfair that he should be so relaxed while she was in a state of panic. Although she had imagined running into Ryan again many times over the years, she found his sudden appearance in her classroom a bit jarring. Unlike Ryan, she had had no time to prepare.

She sat in a chair across from him and quickly opened his son's file. "So," she said, tapping her pen over and over on the desktop. "Hector."

She heard him sigh and looked up to see him watching her carefully. "I hope this isn't awkward for you," he said. "I know it's been a long time, Bridget."

The sound of her name coming from his mouth after such a long time caught her unaware. She fumbled the pen in her hand, sending it flying across the room. They both turned to look as it landed on the floor and rolled beneath a nearby desk. As Bridget moved to retrieve it, he placed a hand on her arm, stopping her. "It's all right. I'll get it."

She looked away as he bent to pick up the pen, and when he returned to his desk, she was already pretending to be absorbed in Hector's file. She didn't like feeling surprised like this. She had so many questions but didn't know where to start. "He's doing quite well in most subjects," she said without looking up. "Talks out of turn on occasion, but we're working on it—"

"Well, he comes by that honestly, doesn't he?" Ryan asked lightly.

"Yes, he does," Bridget agreed. "But, it needs to stop."

Ryan held up a hand in mock defensiveness. "All right, all right. I'll talk to him."

"Thank you," Bridget said, shuffling the papers in her hands. "Now, like I said, his work is on par with most of the rest of the class. He's actually above average in reading, spelling, and vocabulary. He's struggling with multiplication a bit, though. Do you have flash cards?"

Ryan nodded.

"Okay. You can just quiz him on them or you can make them into a game. You each get a stack of cards and flip the top one. Whoever has the highest answer is the winner. Say I've got nine times six and you've got eight times seven. Who wins?"

Ryan shifted his gaze away from hers. "Uh..."

Bridget raised her eyebrows. "Really? You don't know?"

"It's been a while," Ryan said with a laugh. "And now, I'm allowed to use a calculator."

"You need to set a good example for Hector," Bridget told him. "In fact, he'll take more of an interest in math if you learn it together. You teach him, and he teaches you."

"Yes, Miss Winters," he said with a smile.

"Seriously, next year, they'll be working on long division, and if he doesn't know his multiplication tables by then, he's really going to struggle."

"Do you remember when we were in fourth grade? Mr. Stewart made us stand up in front of class and quizzed us on multiplication like we were in a spelling bee. You were always the last one standing."

Bridget sighed and rubbed her forehead, which was just starting to ache. She had forgotten how evasive Ryan could be sometimes. Whenever he was faced with an uncomfortable situation or conversation, he always managed to change the subject or turn it into a joke. No wonder he had left her twenty-two years earlier without so much as a goodbye.

She glanced at the clock and felt a rush of relief. Ryan Carter's fifteen minutes with her were over. She shut Hector's file and slid it across the desk. "Well, here you go, Mr. Carter. Please work with him on the items I mentioned."

Ryan picked up the file and got to his feet. "I will."

"Thank you. Have a nice day."

She stood and returned to her desk to find the file for

Candice Felcher, her next conference appointment. When she
turned around again, she was surprised to see Ryan still
standing there, watching her. Didn't he know he was supposed
to leave?

"Is there something else you need?" she asked, her voice
more formal than usual.

He shook his head slowly. "No. I just...want to tell you
how happy I am for you. When we were kids, you always said
you were gonna be a teacher someday. And now look at you."

Bridget felt her face flush with a strange mix of
embarrassment and pride. "Thank you."

There was a quiet tapping at the door, and she looked up
to see Mr. and Mrs. Felcher waiting there. Ryan cleared his
throat and turned to walk away. An absurd panic surged
through Bridget, and suddenly she was that ten-year-old girl
again, watching her best friend board the school bus on the
most devastating day of her life.

"Ryan!" she burst out suddenly.

He turned back to her with a curious expression. For
several seconds, she just stared back, her face hot with
mortification. From the doorway, the Felchers were observing
her with mild interest.

"Hector really is a great kid," she said truthfully.
"Just...keep up the good work."

Ryan just nodded, but the sudden light in his eyes
revealed to her just how much those words had meant to him.
Then, without another word, he was gone.

Chapter Three

As she went about her weekend, thoughts of Ryan
surfaced in Bridget's mind again and again. She was astounded

by the very fact that she had been teaching his son for the past several months without realizing it. And, she found herself replaying bits of their conversation and cringing a bit when she remembered her own aloofness. She hoped she had come across more as a teacher focused on her student's well-being than as a disgruntled former friend.

By Monday, she hoped that she had put the encounter out of her mind, but when Hector Carter walked into class, resembling his father even more than she had realized, the memory of their meeting immediately became a distraction in everything she tried to do. Grading four social studies tests before she realized she had the wrong answer key was one thing, but when she looked straight at Hector and called him Ryan, she knew she needed to get her head together.

Just before first recess, she announced a pop quiz in math. She passed out the papers and sat at her desk, listening to the quiet scratching of pencils and shuffling of papers. Her gaze traveled from one end of the room to the other, and when they rested on Hector, they remained there a moment, studying him as he applied himself diligently to his test. He had his father's tousled dark hair and eyes and exactly the same grin. Both were well liked by most of the other kids, although Hector had more friends than Ryan, who had spent most of his time with Bridget.

The bell rang, and Bridget realized that most of her class had finished their quizzes and had graduated from furtive whispers to the general mayhem that was inevitable in every fourth-grade classroom after several minutes of silence. She pried her gaze away from Hector, stood up, and clapped her hands together smartly. The chatter and laughter immediately died away.

"All right. It's time for recess," she told the class. "Please hand in your quizzes to me before you head outside."

They did as she asked, dropping their papers in a pile on

her desk. When they were gone, she fell into her chair again and buried her head in her hands. What was happening to her? She had never been the type to allow thoughts of a man to distract her from her work. Besides, she wasn't even interested in Ryan. In fact, it was kind of hard to think of him as a man at all. He had been her childhood friend for a couple of years in elementary school—nothing more.

To keep her mind off of Ryan, she pulled the stack of math quizzes closer and began to grade them. It was multiplication by sixes and sevens, and she knew them all by heart, so she plowed through them quickly, running down each problem and placing a red check mark by each incorrect answer. Most of the students had done quite well, although a few clearly hadn't been practicing at all. Jamie Anderson, of course, got them all right.

She was halfway through the pile when she ran across another perfect paper. She smiled as she reached the end without defiling the paper with a single red mark. She returned her pen to the top of the page and wrote A+ next to a smiley face. As she was placing it on top of the stack of graded tests, she glimpsed the name at the top and froze: Hector Carter.

She was still staring at the test and shaking her head in disbelief when the students traipsed back in after recess. Pushing aside the rest of the papers to work on later, she stood and walked to the dry-erase board, where she began writing a series of sentences, each with several punctuation errors.

"All right," she said, turning to her students again. "Who can tell me one mistake in the first sentence I wrote? 'I like cat's because there so playful.' Michael?"

Michael, a rather unenthusiastic boy who sat in the back row, looked up slowly as if she had just woken him from a very deep sleep. He squinted at the board a minute, then said, "Uh...the comma?"

Bridget turned and reread the sentence, her brow crinkling in confusion. "What comma?" she asked, gesturing toward the board.

"Uh...it needs a comma?"

Hector, who Bridget had noticed out of the corner of her eye fidgeting restlessly during this exchange, could keep quiet no longer. "It's the apostrophes!"

Ignoring him, Bridget scanned the rest of the class. No hands were raised, so she chose another victim. "Meredith?"

"The apostrophes?" Meredith ventured in a very quiet voice.

"Yes," Bridget said patiently. "But can you tell me what's wrong with them?"

Hector jumped in again, answering for Meredith, who was apparently taking too long. "Cats doesn't need an apostrophe because it's not possessive. And *there* is wrong, too. It should be a contraction—they are—with an apostrophe."

Bridget shot him a look of annoyance before returning her attention to Meredith, who pointed at Hector and mumbled, "What he said?"

Bridget smiled through gritted teeth. "Yes. Hector was correct. And now, unless he has something else to add—"

"Actually...there is one more thing," Hector cut in with a very familiar grin. "Everyone knows dogs are more playful than cats."

There was a round of giggles from the surrounding students which Bridget put a stop to with a single exasperated look. She approached Hector's desk and scowled down at him, watching his smile slowly fade away. "Please see me after school, Hector."

"Yes, Miss Winters," he replied meekly.

"Good," she said briskly. "Now...sentence two..."

***

After school, when Bridget had dismissed the class and sent Jamie home with the reassurance that he had aced his multiplication quiz, she called Hector to her desk. He looked so nervous as he drew near that she couldn't help but feel sorry for him, just as she had felt a little sorry for Ryan when he was sent to the office in third grade for drawing facial hair on the "Women of American History" photos pinned up on the classroom bulletin board. Actually, she had felt more guilty than sorry. After all, he still didn't know it, but she was the one who had told on him.

She smiled with the hopes of putting him at ease. "Do you know why I wanted to see you, Hector?"

"I think so," he said softly.

"I know it's hard for you, but you really need to learn to raise your hand when you want to speak in class."

He stared down at the floor. "Sorry."

"Everyone else in class raises their hand and waits to be called on. So, it's only fair that you do the same."

He lifted his shoulder in a little shrug. "That's what my dad told me."

Bridget tilted her head, trying to look merely interested. In actuality, the very mention of Ryan Carter had caused her pulse to quicken in a ridiculous way. "Your dad?" she asked in the most casual voice she could manage.

"Yeah. He talked to me after conferences. Said I had to raise my hand and wait my turn." He shrugged again. "It's just that it's hard for me to wait when I know the answer. I'm sorry."

Bridget smiled kindly. "I understand. But, please try to remember next time."

He raised his eyes to her and smiled back. "I will."

With a dramatic air, she reached into the stack of papers in front of her and pulled out Hector's math quiz. "Incidentally, you achieved a perfect score on your multiplication test. Well done!"

Hector pulled the paper close to him and nodded, looking pleased but not the least bit surprised. "My dad made me practice this weekend."

Bridget simply nodded, but inside she was delighted that someone—especially Ryan—had actually listened to her suggestions.

"He made me play this game with flash cards," Hector went on. "It was kind of boring, but I guess it paid off."

"That's the important thing," Bridget said, her face flushing a little. She glanced at the clock. "Oh, my. I didn't mean to keep you this long. You'd better go."

Hector folded the paper several times before dropping it in his backpack. "It's all right," he assured her as he slung the bag over one shoulder. "My dad's picking me up today, and he won't mind."

Bridget stood quickly. "Your dad is here?"

"He should be," Hector said, regarding her curiously. "He said you two were old friends. Is that why you called me Ryan today?"

Bridget's face burned with humiliation. "Probably. You do look an awful lot like him," she said mildly. What she really wanted to say was, *Please, please, please, don't tell your father I did that.*

"I better go, Miss Winters. See you tomorrow."

"Goodbye, Hector."

She waited until Hector had left the room before quickly throwing on her jacket and grabbing her purse. Then, she hurried after him, shutting off the classroom lights and closing the door on her way out. When she exited the double doors at the school's entrance, she blinked in the bright sunlight a minute while desperately searching the walkways in front of the school. In the distance, she could see Hector walking toward the parking lot on the side of the building. He suddenly waved to someone approaching and picked up his pace, and a second later, she saw Ryan coming to meet him. They stopped in the middle of the sidewalk and talked for a minute.

Bridget slowed her pace a little, hoping she would appear to be just another teacher heading to her car. When she caught up to them, she gave a little smile and skirted around them. "Have a good evening, Hector. Hi, Ryan."

"Bridget!" Ryan called out.

Biting back a smile, Bridget turned around. "So, Hector, did you tell your father about your multiplication test?"

Hector grinned. "I got an A+!"

"Awesome job, buddy," Ryan said, offering his son a fist to bump.

Bridget laughed. "Thanks for working with him, Ryan. And, keep it up. It really helps."

"I will. Thanks, Bridget...Miss Winters."

Bridget studied the ground as an awkward silence fell between them. She wondered if Ryan was as nervous about meeting again as she was. She looked toward the parking lot and took a reluctant step in that direction. "I suppose I should let you two go..."

"Wait a minute," Ryan said, stopping her abruptly. "Hector...why don't you go wait in the car. I just need to talk to your teacher a minute."

Hector gave them a slightly worried look. "All right."

When they were alone, Ryan touched her arm. Stunned, she looked up, into his unwavering gaze. "What—what did you want to—"

"Bridget, I think we should get together sometime."

Her heart raced. "You—you do?"

"Yeah. It's just...it's been such a long time. There's a lot we should talk about, don't you think?"

Bridget wasn't sure what to think. Was he asking her out? It seemed more like he was suggesting they catch up on old times. Unsure what else to do, she nodded.

"Great. I'll give you my number."

Without a word, Bridget reached into her purse and pulled out her cell phone. One surreal moment later, she was entering Ryan Carter's phone number into her contacts. When she was finished, she just stared at his name, listed alphabetically along with all her closest friends and family. Ryan Carter—the person she had thought she would never see again.

"Give me a call sometime," she heard Ryan saying, and she looked up to see him already heading down the sidewalk to where Hector was waiting. She gave a little wave with her phone before starting toward her own car. When she got there, she spent a minute fidgeting with her purse strap and straightening her seat belt.

She waved again as Ryan and Hector pulled away in a small, red pickup truck. Then, when they were out of sight, she got out of her car again and headed back to the school to retrieve all the books and papers she needed to prepare for the next day's assignments—the ones she had neglected to take with her when she raced out of the school with her crazy determination to run into Ryan again.

Chapter Four

Bridget waited a few days to get in touch with Ryan. On Thursday afternoon, she finally called him, and they set up a meeting for after school the next day. Hector would stay with his grandmother, allowing Ryan to get away for a couple of hours.

She spent an extra half hour Friday morning trying to assemble a look that would appear attractive but not as if she had spent a lot of effort. In the end, she chose a pair of ordinary black slacks and a floral blouse that was just flattering enough to have earned her a couple of compliments in the two years she had owned it. She packed a hairbrush and a little makeup for touch-ups in her purse before heading off to school.

It was the first relatively warm day of the year, and by last recess, she was feeling too happy to remain indoors catching up on her work. She slipped out to the playground to observe her students as they enjoyed the pleasant weather and general good vibes that Friday always brings. Loud, playful shouts drifted her way from every corner of the playground. Hector and his friends were playing a rambunctious game of tag that stretched from one end of the playground to the other. A group of girls were standing on the sidewalk with jump ropes, attempting a round of Double Dutch. Every swing was occupied along with the climbing structure and obstacle course.

She was about to head back inside when her gaze landed on a small figure sitting alone, leaning against the trunk of a nearby tree. Taking a few steps closer, she noticed that it was Jamie. He had a large, open book resting on his knees and was chewing on his fingernails, as usual.

Bridget squinted at the book he was reading and immediately recognized it as the social studies textbook she was using in class. She shook her head in disbelief. Ordinarily, she would never discourage a student from a little extra studying, but Jamie didn't need it. He needed play and exercise and friends.

The sound of the bell startled her out of her reverie. She returned to her classroom, her thoughts in chaos as they always were when she encountered a student with a special problem or need. Already, she found herself seeking out solutions in her mind.

The remaining two hours of school flew by. After dismissing class, Bridget quickly applied a coat of pink to her lips and a couple swipes of mascara to her eyelashes. Then, she spent a few minutes straightening and cleaning her classroom while she waited for Ryan to arrive. When a shadow appeared in the doorway a few minutes after three, she looked up with a smile. "Just a minute, Ryan—"

She stopped suddenly, her racing heart slowing to a crawl. It was Alex standing at the door, not Ryan.

"Who's Ryan?" Alex asked.

Bridget shrugged and busied herself with organizing a cluttered desk drawer. "Just an old friend."

"Oh." Alex came closer and leaned over the desk so that Bridget had to look at her. "I was going to ask about the practice schedule for the spring music program, but first I have to ask...are you going on a date? You're dressed up...at least, more than usual."

Bridget shut the drawer and looked up at her friend. "I don't know. He didn't say it was a date, but..." She glanced toward the open doorway and lowered her voice. "I kind of hope it is."

Alex scrutinized her a minute. "Do you want me to do something with your hair?"

Bridget pulled the pins out of her bun and let her hair fall free. "All right. But nothing too fancy. I don't want to be too obvious."

"Sure."

Alex brushed out Bridget's hair and pulled it up again into an updo that was far prettier than Bridget's usual style. Then she released a couple of tendrils to frame her face. Bridget pulled a small compact with a mirror from her purse and examined her reflection a minute, tilting her face from side to side. She looked and felt like a teenager getting ready for her first date.

At the sound of footsteps approaching from the hall, she quickly snapped shut her compact and shoved it in her purse. By the time Ryan appeared at the doorway, she was standing nonchalantly behind her desk, shuffling papers. She looked up with a smile. "Hi, Ryan."

Alex cleared her throat, drawing their attention. "Well, you two have a nice time. I'll see you tomorrow, Bridget."

"Wait!" Bridget exclaimed as Alex pushed herself away from the desk she had been leaning on. "I'm so sorry. Ryan, I'd like to introduce you to my best friend, Alex Lane. She's the music teacher here. And, Alex, this is Ryan Carter—my best friend from a very long time ago."

Alex stepped forward to take Ryan's hand. "Good to meet you. You're Hector's father?"

Ryan laughed. "I guess that depends on how he acts in music class."

"Don't worry," Alex replied with a smile. "He's a great kid—a natural on the recorder. I told him he should consider joining the school band when he's old enough."

"Really?"

She nodded and started to walk away again. "See you tomorrow, Bridge."

Bridget exchanged a look with Alex as she left that told her tomorrow would consist of a long discussion on the details of her evening. When Alex was gone, she turned to Ryan with a smile. "You ready to go?"

Ryan hesitated, looking a little embarrassed. "Actually..."

Bridget stared at him, suddenly mortified. It wasn't a date at all, was it? Not even close. It really was just a brief meeting at the school to set the past behind them. Or maybe to further discuss Hector's academic performance. Come to think of it, she hadn't even bothered to find out if he was single. It was entirely possible she had been primping and preening and getting herself worked up over a married man. She was attempting to hide her humiliation behind a professional smile when Ryan spoke again.

"I'm really sorry, but the restaurant I planned on taking you to is all booked up. Guess I waited too long to call for a reservation."

Bridget was so relieved she actually laughed. She didn't care where they went or what they ate as long as she was with Ryan. "That's all right," she told him. "Anywhere is fine."

"Thanks for understanding," Ryan said. "You sure you still want to be seen with a guy that's not intelligent enough to know you need a reservation to eat at the best restaurant in town on a Friday night?"

Bridget tapped a fingertip on her chin thoughtfully. "I suppose. After all, when we were kids, I didn't mind being seen with the boy who always finished his homework on the bus ride to school."

He smiled at the memory. "Guess I haven't changed much, have I?"

Bridget, who had found herself examining his body in what she hoped was a surreptitious way, had to disagree. But when she met his eyes again, she just shrugged. "I don't know. You went home and practiced multiplication when I asked, remember?"

"Well, yeah..."

She grinned. "Then I don't want to alarm you, but you—Ryan Carter—did your homework as assigned by a genuine, no-nonsense schoolteacher."

"I guess I did," he agreed. "But mostly, I did it for Hector. I want him to have a different attitude toward school than I did. I want an education to mean something to him."

Bridget's eyes widened. It was evident that parenting was one part of his life he took very seriously. As Hector's teacher and Ryan's friend, this revelation meant a lot to her.

She picked up her purse and turned to Ryan with a smile. "Ready to go?"

He grinned. "I've been ready."

They left the school and strode down the sidewalk to the parking lot, where Ryan had parked his truck. He let her in first, then climbed into the driver's seat. "So...what do you want to eat?" he asked. "There's a nice family restaurant just down the road. Or there's that Italian place downtown. I haven't been there, but I've heard they've got great pizza."

"Pizza," Bridget murmured.

"Really?" Ryan asked, looking at her questioningly.

"No. I was just thinking. Do you remember what they were serving for lunch the last day we ate together? It was pizza—that rectangle pizza that never had enough cheese and had those tiny squares of...I don't know...meat-like stuff on top."

"How do you remember that?" Ryan asked, looking both amused and impressed.

She shrugged. "I don't know. I remember a lot of things from that day."

Ryan smiled at her as he put the truck in gear. "Well, I think we can dine a little better than that today. Let's get out of here."

***

By five o'clock, they were sitting in a booth at a steakhouse in a neighboring town enjoying a basket of dinner rolls and waiting for their meals to arrive. They had started to catch up on the past twenty years of each other's lives, and Bridget could hardly believe how comfortable she still felt with him. She had told him about her years in college, her most memorable teaching experiences, and had reluctantly admitted that she had never really experienced a serious relationship.

Ryan, she learned, had attended college for a brief period before dropping out, but had, by that time, gleaned from the experience a real talent for computers. He had started his own business out of his home and was now tackling some of the trickiest, most frustrating issues a computer could throw at his customers. Although he started out serving mostly individual households, several large companies had recently signed on as clients.

"Look," he said proudly, handing over his phone. "This is my website."

Bridget put the last bit of buttered roll into her mouth and took his phone. On the screen was a beautifully designed web page dedicated to a business called Carter's Tech Magic. Along with a list of services and links was a series of testimonials to his skill and fast, friendly service.

"Did you write those yourself?" she teased.

"Nope," he said, taking his phone back. "Held their computers hostage 'til they wrote something nice about me. Nothing dishonest about that."

Bridget laughed. "Seriously, Ryan. It's really great. I'm proud of you."

"Thanks," he said, flushing a little. "I'm proud of you, too. Hector says you're the best teacher he's ever had."

"Really?" Bridget had never felt so touched.

"He did. And you've got some hefty competition there. The runner-up is his kindergarten teacher, and she used to let him look at picture books during nap time."

Their food arrived, and while the waiter was placing their plates in front of them, a question came to Bridget's mind that she had been wanting to ask Ryan for a while. When they were alone again, she gave Ryan a smile before digging into her eight-ounce steak. Mentally, she was rehearsing the question she needed to ask, rephrasing it a hundred times in her mind.

Finally, she set her fork down and blurted it out. "May I ask about Hector's mother?"

Ryan raised his eyes to meet hers. "What do you want to know about her?"

Bridget raised a shoulder slightly and stared down at her plate. "Well...were you two married?"

She looked up to see Ryan shaking his head. "No. I wanted to get married once I found out Hector was on the way, but...I guess she wasn't ready to commit—at least, not to me."

"Does she see Hector often?"

"She left when Hector was barely a year old. Signed over full custody to me, for which I was grateful. We haven't seen her since."

Bridget shivered a little. "I don't understand how someone can abandon their child like that."

"Me neither," Ryan said. "We were both pretty young, and we got ourselves into something we weren't ready for. She ran away from the challenge, and I guess there were times I wasn't sure if I could handle it either."

"But you did," Bridget said softly. "You're raising a wonderful child."

"Thank you," Ryan said with a smile. "But I didn't do it on my own. My mom's been there for us since the day he was born."

"She was the one who came to Hector's conference in the fall, right?" Bridget asked.

"Yeah. Sorry I couldn't make it that time, but we had just moved back to the area, and between getting settled and work—"

"I understand," Bridget assured him.

"Of course, if I'd known you were his teacher, I'd have made time."

Bridget smiled modestly. "Well...your mother was really sweet. I enjoyed talking with her. And...what about your father? Is he...?"

She knew that Ryan had not been raised in a single-family home the way she had. When they were in school together, he had talked often about his father, a driven man who worked most of the time and was, according to Ryan, probably the smartest man in the world.

Ryan looked away. "He passed away five years ago. Heart attack."

"Oh. I'm sorry."

His smile couldn't hide the hint of sadness in his eyes. "It was a long time ago."

They continued to eat in silence for a moment. The air was filled with the sound of country music, the incoherent buzz of conversation, and the clinks and clatters of forks on plates. The food was delicious, and the smells comforting. And just looking across the table and seeing her old friend munching away on his third roll filled Bridget with a warmth she had never experienced on a date before.

She finished half her food, and while their waiter was fetching her a container for her leftovers, she leaned back and slowly sipped her drink. Ryan had cleaned his plate, set it aside, and was watching her with a smile. "Would you like to order dessert?"

She shook her head. "I don't think I could eat another bite. But you go ahead, if you like."

He rubbed his belly. "I probably better not."

The waiter arrived entirely too soon with her container and the check. It had been such a pleasant evening that Bridget didn't want to leave. She looked at him, hoping desperately that he had enjoyed their time together as much as she had. She wasn't sure what she would do if he left her with a simple goodbye and no invitation to do it again.

Ryan paid the check, and they stood, pulling on their jackets. As he stepped up to her side, Ryan placed a hand gently on her back and left it there as they walked out of the restaurant side-by-side. Even as they stepped outside into the cool evening air, Bridget felt the warm sensation inside her growing. She smiled.

When they reached the truck and slipped inside, Ryan started the engine to begin warming the cab but did not move to drive away. He stared out the window a minute while Bridget sat on pins and needles, wondering if he would kiss her. Perhaps she should make the first move, she thought wildly. But no, that was too terrifying.

The silence was stretching out far too long, and she finally had to fill it. "It's such an amazing coincidence, us meeting again like this. And me being your son's teacher!" she marveled.

Ryan turned to her. "Or maybe not such a coincidence."

Bridget raised her eyebrows. "Are you talking about some kind of...divine intervention?"

He laughed. "Maybe a little. But what I was really talking about is that...it wasn't a coincidence me moving back here."

"What do you mean?"

"We moved around quite a bit after I left here. My dad was always chasing the next big work opportunity. But no matter where we ended up, I always found myself thinking about this place. My happiest memories are from here. Leaving that day was one of the hardest things I ever had to do."

"Really? You made it look so easy."

"It wasn't." Ryan hesitated a moment, then reached

under his seat and pulled out a small box. "I've got something for you."

Bridget's brow wrinkled. She took the box and opened it, pulling aside the tissue paper to reveal a small ceramic figurine of an orange kitten sleeping in a bed of flowers—Tiger. She gasped and quickly shut the box again. "I knew it!" she exclaimed. "I tried to tell myself it wasn't you, but deep down I always knew. Ryan, how could you?"

"I'm sorry, Bridget. But it was a long time ago. Are you really still angry?"

Bridget shot him a reproachful look and slid out of the truck. Seconds later, Ryan was by her side again, trying hard to get her to look at him.

"Come on, Bridge. I know it was wrong, but can't you forgive me?"

Bridget stared down at her feet trying to control her emotions. "It was the worst thing that ever happened to me, you telling me you were moving away. And then, you stole something that was important to me and made it even worse."

"I know. The reason I brought it back today was because I've always felt guilty. I didn't take it because I wanted to hurt you. It was because...that was the worst day of my life, too. I just really wanted to have something of yours...something to remember you by."

Bridget looked up again, her expression softening under his hopeful gaze. "I know," she said at last. "And...I do forgive you."

He exhaled loudly. "Thank you, Bridget. It turned out, I didn't need that kitten to remind me of you. I've—I've thought about you a lot over the years."

She felt her heartbeat quicken as he took her hand. A very different expression had crossed his face.

"I've thought a lot about you, too," she said quietly.

"Your friendship was one of the most important things in the world to me."

"Me, too," he murmured, stepping closer to her. "The last thing I want to do is to ruin *us* for you by doing something that makes you uncomfortable. But, the first thing I want to do..."

He placed his hands on her hips and pulled her toward him. He kissed her gently, softly, in a way that made her feel like he wanted her—and only her—desperately. It was a lingering kiss, and when he finally pulled away, he left her with a wonderful tingling sensation that made its way from her lips, through her entire body, down to the tips of her toes, and left her wishing he would pull her into his arms and do it all over again.

"So. What do you think?" he asked, gazing at her expectantly.

"Well..." she said when she was capable of speech again. "That was...very nice."

He smiled. "Good. It was supposed to be."

"Of course, we do have to consider the fact that I'm your child's teacher."

"Oh," he said, frowning, taking a step back. "Well...it's not illegal or anything is it? Does the school have some kind of rule—"

"No," she interrupted quickly. "Not that I know of. And it's not illegal. But—"

"Then what's the problem?"

She giggled and closed the distance between them again. "I guess there isn't one."

He put an arm around her again and smiled down at her. "Good. I've already broken the law once because of you, stealing that kitten, and I'd hate to have to do it again. But, I would if I had to."

Chapter Five

The following Monday, Bridget spent the morning trying to focus her attention on her students even though the kiss from Friday evening remained deliciously on her mind. All weekend, the memory of it had resurfaced over and over again, catching her when she least expected it.

As soon as she got home on Friday, she had immediately gone to her closet and began sorting through the totes that contained all the possessions she had taken with her when she moved out of her mother's house. Wrapped in newspaper at the very bottom of the third tote, she finally found Whiskers. She quickly cleared a space on her dresser and placed both kitten figurines there. As she stepped back to admire them, she had to smile. Tiger and Whiskers might not be suited to her current taste in decorating, but she really didn't care. They were another happy reminder of Ryan—not that she needed one. He was already always on her mind.

She hadn't seen Ryan since Friday, although they had talked on the phone for hours Saturday night. Their conversation had been a pleasant mix of remembering the two short years they had shared as children, catching up on their years apart, and revealing their plans and dreams for the future. On Sunday, Ryan spent the day exploring bike trails with Hector, but he called Bridget that evening and told her he missed her and would see her soon.

She missed him, too, and soon couldn't come fast enough as far as she was concerned. So, when she dismissed the class for morning recess and Hector came up to tell her his father wanted to see her after school, she was delighted. She was still grinning as he was leaving for the playground, but her smile faltered when she turned to see Jamie trudging out after him

143

with another textbook under one arm.

She reached out and touched his shoulder. "Jamie. Why don't you leave the book in here?"

"But...I need to study," he protested.

She shook her head and held out a hand to take the book. "I'm sorry Jamie, but these books are very expensive and aren't to be taken outside at recess."

"But, I'm really careful," he said, looking up at her in desperation.

"I know, Jamie. But, these are the rules, and we have to follow them."

A terrified, little noise came from the back of Jamie's throat. Bridget had a feeling that he had never been accused of breaking a rule before. She had to fight back a smile. In many ways, Jamie reminded her of herself at that age. In fact, without Ryan telling her to lighten up on occasion, she might have ended up the very same way.

Again, she held out her hand expectantly. Looking like he wanted to cry, Jamie dropped the book into her hand.

"Thank you," she said. "You may go out and play now."

These words, which would have most kids running ecstatically out the door, only made Jamie look more miserable. He started toward the door, then turned back to her. "Is it all right if I bring one of my own books out, Miss Winters?"

Bridget sighed and nodded. Looking relieved, Jamie hurried to his desk, pulled out a math workbook he had brought from home, and raced outside at last. Minutes later, he was under his tree, absorbed in his own world once again.

***

At the end of the day, Bridget caught Hector as he was leaving and asked if he would wait and walk out with her to meet his dad. She wanted to speak with him a few minutes first.

"Sure," Hector replied with a shrug. He waited

awkwardly by the door as she gathered her things.

As they were walking down the empty corridor a few minutes later, Bridget came to a sudden stop. "Hector, I was wondering if I could ask a favor of you."

Hector turned to look at her curiously. "I guess."

"Tomorrow at recess, would you invite Jamie Anderson to play with you and your friends?"

Hector couldn't have looked more disgusted if Bridget had asked him to eat dirt at recess tomorrow. "Jamie?"

Bridget sighed. "Yes, Jamie. I know he's not really a friend of yours, but all he does at recess is sit by himself and read. I was hoping maybe you could get him out there making friends and playing like a normal kid. You know...show him how."

Hector raised his eyebrows in disbelief. "You really expect me to hang out with a kid who has to be taught to have fun?"

"He's a fast learner," she added hopefully.

Hector let out a loud sigh and studied the floor for a minute, clearly searching for any excuse that would get him out of this. When he couldn't find one, he finally mumbled, "All right."

"Thank you," Bridget breathed, relieved.

"My dad said you and he are dating," Hector said conversationally as they started walking again.

Bridget's heart froze for a second.

"Yes. Yes, we are. What...what do you think about that?"

He raised one shoulder and kept staring at the ground. "My dad asked me that. I said I was okay with it."

She put out a hand and touched his arm, stopping him a minute. "Are you really?"

"Sure. You're a lot nicer than the last lady he dated. She didn't like kids much. But, you're a teacher. You have to like kids."

"That's true," Bridget said. "But, that's another thing. Does it bother you that I'm your teacher?"

He thought about that for a minute. "Nah, I guess not." Then, a rather panicked look came over his face. "Wait. You're not going to make an announcement about it in class or anything, are you?"

Bridget clamped her lips together in an attempt to contain a smile. "Don't worry, Hector. I promise I won't tell anybody."

They were outside by then, heading toward the parking lot. Up ahead, Bridget could see Ryan waiting there, leaning against the bed of his little, red truck. Already, she could feel her happiness growing, the memory of that kiss replaying in her mind and working its magic throughout her body.

"Hey, you two. How was school?" Ryan asked them as they drew near.

"It was all right," Hector answered. "Can I have chicken nuggets when we get home? I'm starving."

"We'll see," Ryan replied. He smiled at Bridget and gave her forearm a little squeeze.

Hector stared at them a moment, then retreated to the truck. When they were alone, Bridget stepped closer to Ryan and took his hand. "I've missed you."

"I've missed you so much," he replied, his voice a little husky, his eyes penetrating into hers. "What are you doing this weekend?"

"Not a thing," she said quickly.

"Good. I figure I still owe you a few more dinners for stealing Tiger from you."

"Absolutely," she agreed. "In case you don't remember, I worked really hard to earn the money for those."

Ryan chuckled. "I know."

"And when I went back to school in the fall, I spent the first month digging through piles of stuff in the lost and found searching for Tiger. I asked in the office, too, every day until they got sick of me and told me to stop."

"I'm sorry," Ryan said, his eyes twinkling in a very unapologetic way.

"Not only that...I asked Ellie if she took him. She was so mad I accused her, she didn't talk to me for weeks after that.

"I thought you said you knew I did it," Ryan pointed out.

"Shut up."

He laughed. "All right. I have a lot of making up to do. So...can I take you out again this weekend?"

She pretended to think about it a minute before nodding. "But only so you're not overwhelmed with guilt. That can really take a toll on a person."

"Thanks," he said dryly. "But, here's what I want to know. Haven't you ever done anything you've kept secret from me? Something you regret?"

Bridget looked away. "Well...remember that time you got sent to the office in third grade?"

"You're going to have to be more specific."

She rolled her eyes. "For drawing mustaches on all those historic women, remember?"

He laughed. "Oh, yeah! I had to stay in from recess for a week for that one. What about it?"

"I was the one who told on you." Her words poured out in a rush.

His laughter abruptly stopped. "What?"

"Sorry," she said with a smile. "But, they must have already suspected you, because they asked me straight out if you did it. And, you know me. I'm a terrible liar."

He lifted the corner of his mouth in a half smile. "Yeah,

you are."

"Forgive me?"

"Of course. Although, you might owe me a meal for that one."

"Deal," she said, shaking the hand she had already been holding the last five minutes.

"Any other deep, dark secrets about you I should know about?" Ryan asked, his eyes gleaming.

"Well...once in a while, after school lets out, I go out to the playground and swing when no one's around," she confided, her cheeks turning red with embarrassment.

"Interesting," he said mysteriously, giving her hand a squeeze.

A horn blared briefly as Hector made his impatience known. Bridget jumped and released Ryan's hand while Ryan turned to scowl at his son. Bridget gave Hector a wave, and he grinned mischievously back at her.

As she started to walk away, Ryan took her hand again, pulling her back to him. "Saturday?" he asked.

"Saturday," she agreed, her voice betraying her anticipation.

After one more beep of the horn, they separated at last. Bridget watched them take off, then headed to her car, already counting the days until she would be alone with Ryan again. Five days, she decided, was far too long.

Chapter Six

The next morning, Hector diligently avoided Bridget in a way that reminded her of Ryan on their last day of school together. When she finally managed to corner him just before recess, she reminded him of the promise he had made to her the day before. He squirmed and gazed longingly toward the door, where the other kids were filing out.

"Remember?" she asked. She pointed with a little tilt of her head to where Jamie was leaving the room with his math workbook.

Hector frowned. "Do I have to?"

"I can't make you do this, Hector," she said kindly. "But I'd really appreciate it if you'd at least try. Maybe you'll make a new friend!"

He exhaled loudly. "Fine."

After all the kids had left, she walked outside and crept down to the playground, close to where Jamie was sitting, lost in his work. He had a pencil out and was making marks in his workbook, completely oblivious to everything going on around him. A minute later, Hector slowly approached him. Bridget held her breath, watching carefully.

She was too far away to hear much, but she saw Hector say something to Jamie, who shook his head without a word and didn't even glance up from his book. Hector tried again, and this time Jamie seemed to ignore him entirely. He pulled the book up so it was directly in front of his face, blocking Hector from his view.

Bridget could see Hector's impatient sigh. He turned, caught sight of her, and stretched his arms wide as if to say, "What now?" Bridget made a vague circular motion with her hands, urging him to keep trying. He rolled his eyes and shook his head, but obeyed. Bridget moved a few steps closer so she could hear the interaction.

"Come on," she heard Hector say. "You can do schoolwork any time. It's recess!"

"No," Jamie repeated, his voice rising a little in frustration.

Hector had had enough. He stepped forward and pulled the book out of Jamie's hands. "Dude, relax. You don't need to study. You're already getting an A plus in everything."

"Hey!" Jamie stood up quickly and grabbed his book back. "Will you leave me alone?"

Hector turned to look at Bridget again. She bit her lip and wrung her hands, trying to conceal her disappointment. Hector might as well give up now before the situation turned really ugly.

Instead, Hector moved even closer to Jamie, took him by the shoulder and turned him around so their backs were to her. Once in a while, one or the other of the boys would turn and glance her way, and she knew they were discussing her. She could almost hear Hector saying, "Look, this is all Miss Winters' idea. Just indulge her this once and maybe she'll leave us alone." And, she could almost hear Jamie's reply: "Well...she is a teacher. Guess if that's what she wants, I better do it."

With obvious reluctance, Jamie dropped his book and pencil on the ground and took off after Hector. They headed toward the obstacle course, where a group of Hector's friends were gathered at the caterpillar, a climbing structure made up of a series of beams that resembled twin hills on a roller coaster. Kids climbed from beam to beam as if on a ladder, reached the top, crossed over and climbed down again, then repeated the process with the second hill.

Hector's friends seemed surprised to see Jamie with him at first. While Jamie stood awkwardly apart, Hector gathered them all into a huddle, apparently explaining the situation to them. Once again, Bridget received a few curious glances, and she stepped back and gazed around her, trying to look as if she wasn't spying on them.

A minute later, she looked over to see Hector and Jamie side by side on the caterpillar, climbing slowly up the first hill. They reached the top, where Hector easily slung his leg over the top beam to the other side and waited patiently for Jamie to catch up. After a few awkward seconds, Jamie was over the crest of the hill as well, and they raced down again, then started up the second hill. With a sudden burst of speed, Jamie passed by Hector, scrambled over the top and arrived at the bottom a split second before Hector. The boys gathered around and cheered, and Hector patted Jamie's back and offered his clenched hand for a fist bump. Jamie beamed.

Bridget dashed back inside, beaming as well. Jamie was a fast learner and quite competitive — traits that had served him well academically and were already working to his favor as he learned to navigate the playground with his new friends. She couldn't have been happier for him. As she prepared for her afternoon lessons, she found herself humming cheerfully and wondering if she should ask Ryan if she could treat Hector to ice cream sometime soon. He deserved it.

***

The week crawled by for Bridget, who was looking forward to Saturday more each day. She passed the time slipping outside at recess each day and watching Jamie play with the other kids. He had stopped bringing his math workbook outside and was beginning to look happier and more relaxed than she had ever seen him.

When Friday afternoon finally arrived, she walked down to the music room with a tote bag full of clothing options for her date on Saturday. She wanted Alex to look them over and help her choose what would be most appropriate. At the doorway, she stopped, and peered inside with a smile.

Alex was sitting at the piano, her long fingers sailing over the keys with a skill that completely mystified Bridget, who had never had a music lesson in her life. She closed her eyes and listened, not wanting to interrupt. Not until the music stopped did she venture into the room.

"That was beautiful," she told her friend.

Alex waved a hand dismissively. "Actually, it was full of mistakes, but thanks, Bridge."

Bridget carried her tote bag to the piano and set it down on the bench next to Alex. "Was that for the music program?"

"Yeah," Alex said. "Did you know that Hector volunteered to perform a solo on the recorder for the program?"

"Hector?" Bridget asked, surprised.

"Sure. I wasn't just talking when I said he's talented."

"Oh, I know he's talented. I'm just a little surprised that he volunteered. His dad never volunteered for anything when we were kids."

Alex raised her eyebrows. "Well, they're not the same person, you know."

Bridget blushed. "I know."

Alex nodded at the tote bag. "Speaking of Hector's dad, tomorrow is date number two, right? Are those the clothes you wanted me to look at?"

"Yeah." Bridget started pulling rumpled garments out of the bag and laying them out on the top of the piano. "What do you think?"

Alex cringed a little. "I hope you own an iron."

"I do," Bridget said defensively. "I just need to know what to wear. Don't worry, I'll get the wrinkles out before I leave the house. I promise."

Alex walked along the piano, glancing at the tops, skirts and dresses laying there. She dismissed some without a second glance, picked up others to examine more closely, and finally scooped up a rather short, low cut dress in deep purple. "Wear this," she said, holding it up. "But press it first."

"I know, I know," Bridget murmured impatiently. She tilted her head and eyed the dress uncertainly. She had bought it one day at a secondhand store on an impulse when shopping with some friends but had never gotten up the nerve to wear it. "Are you sure? I only threw it in there because it's the only dress I have that's less than five years old."

"Yes," Alex said without hesitation. "Ryan will love it, trust me."

"Are you sure it won't make me appear...you know. Too easy?"

Alex sighed. She crossed to Bridget and put her hands on her friend's shoulders. "Bridget...dear...you're a thirty-two-year-old woman who's never really had a serious relationship. Maybe it's time you wore something on a date that's a little more...enticing? Something to show him you're really interested?"

Bridget bit her lip thoughtfully. "I've never really dated a man before that I wanted to look enticing for. Can you believe that?"

Alex smiled. "And what about now?"

"Now...I want Ryan to look at me and forget about every other woman in the world."

"I think he already does," Alex assured her, handing over the dress. "And, this will seal it."

Bridget giggled and stuffed the purple dress in her bag. "Thanks, Alex. I owe you one."

"I'll cash in when I need help setting up for the music program," Alex said, pushing her gently toward the door. "For now, go home and get yourself ready for your date."

Chapter Seven

Bridget stared out her living room window toward the deserted driveway, waiting eagerly for Ryan to arrive. She had talked to him on the phone that morning, and he had told her he would pick her up at eleven for lunch. When she asked him where they were going after, he had become annoyingly secretive. But, a simmering anticipation she couldn't tamp down was increasing with each passing minute. She didn't really care where they went. They could eat cheese and cracker packets in the truck and then make out for an hour and she'd happily call their date a success.

When his truck pulled into the driveway, Bridget quickly tugged at her dress and gave her hair a pat. She was wearing the dress Alex had selected for her with her dressiest sandals and had decided to style her hair in loose curls and wear it down for a change. When she had looked in the mirror afterward, she had hardly recognized herself. It had been years since she had bothered to dress up so well.

Ryan rang the doorbell, and she rushed to the door to greet him. When she opened the door, the expression on his face was her immediate reward. His eyes traveled slowly up and down her body, to which the deep purple dress was clinging in all the right places, and up to her face, lightly enhanced with makeup and framed with soft, brown waves. Then he exhaled slowly. "Wow. Bridget...you look beautiful."

She smiled modestly down at her feet. "Thanks, Ryan. You look very handsome, too."

It was true. He wasn't dressed up as formally as she was, but he still looked great in a dark-blue polo shirt and jeans. His dark, wavy hair rippled a little in the breeze, and when she stepped closer, she could see a hint of shadow on his face—he had either forgotten or decided not to shave. Actually, she realized, he hadn't really dressed up at all. It was both exhilarating and a bit annoying the way he managed to make her heart stop with almost no effort at all.

He took her hand and walked her to the truck. "Where would you like to go for lunch?" he asked.

"Anywhere," she answered as she fastened her seat belt.

He turned and ran his eyes over her dress uncertainly. "Well...I was thinking about that pizza place in town, but if you'd like to go someplace a little fancier—"

"No!" she said quickly. "Pizza sounds great."

Fifteen minutes later, they were seated at a table with a red and white checked tablecloth, inhaling the tempting scents of a variety of Italian dishes. When their pizza arrived, Bridget ate carefully, trading her preferred method of eating pizza— with her fingers—for the more dignified, but far less natural to her, fork and knife method. Finished, she pushed her plate aside, resting her chin in her hand and giving Ryan her most alluring smile.

"So..." she began, playing with the tiny sapphire pendant that hung around her neck. "Are you finally going to tell me what we're doing next?"

He shook his head and picked at the food on his plate. "You don't want to know."

She squinted at him, puzzled by his behavior. "What do you mean? Aren't you going to tell me?"

He looked up with a sheepish smile. "I'll tell you what I had planned if you really want me to, but you're not going to want to do it."

"How do you know?"

"Trust me."

She reached across the table and took his hand. "Come on, Ryan. We've known each other forever. We've told each other our deepest, darkest secrets. Just tell me what you had planned, okay? I promise I won't laugh."

Ryan looked doubtful. He stalled for a moment, pulling out his wallet, extracting his credit card, leaving five dollars for a tip. When he had run out of distractions, he met her unwavering gaze again and let out a sigh of resignation. "All right. I-I was going to take you to the school."

"The school?" Bridget asked, trying to hide her bewilderment.

"Yeah. Remember how you told me you like to go out and swing when the kids aren't there? I was going to take you to the same swing set we always used when we were kids. And we'd swing together like the old days." His face was nearly red with humiliation, and he quickly added, "But, you're all dressed up and gorgeous, and it was...just a really stupid idea. We'll go somewhere nice. Anywhere you want."

"I want to go to the school," she stated promptly.

"What?" he asked, clearly startled.

"I want to go to the school playground, just like you planned."

He stared at her in disbelief. "But...what about your dress?"

Bridget shrugged. "It's just a dress." She grinned suddenly and rose from her chair, grabbing Ryan's hand and pulling him to his feet. "Come on. Let's go!"

***

"Are you sure you want to do this?"

"Will you stop asking me that?" Bridget asked with a laugh, as she strode toward the playground.

"All right," Ryan agreed at last. "But, you're officially not allowed to send me your dry-cleaning bill afterward."

"Deal," she said and started sprinting across the lawn. When she reached the swing set, she sat down and kicked off her sandals. Her feet were pale and sun-starved from being shoved into flats and sneakers and boots all winter. Beneath her, the ground was nothing but a dirt path, hard-packed by the trampling of children's feet day after day. She took several steps backward until she was on her tiptoes, then lifted her bare feet off the ground and let herself glide forward, then back again, in the exhilarating motion she had never outgrown.

Ryan was next to her, picking up speed, grinning like the kid she remembered from so many years ago. For a while, they swung in silence, hearing only the chirping of birds and the quiet hum of a distant lawn mower. Although it was barely spring, the sun was warm on Bridget's arms, the soft breeze gently massaging her toes and playing in her hair. She knew the soles of her feet were gradually turning brown with dirt, her dress was wrinkling, and her hair was tangling, but she didn't care. From the looks Ryan kept darting her way, she could tell he still thought she was beautiful.

"How are Tiger and Whiskers getting along?" Ryan asked.

Bridget looked over at him, overwhelmed with memories of their many conversations while swinging side-by-side. She smiled and said teasingly, "Well...they missed each other, of course. Tiger's still a little distraught over the whole ordeal. You know...being kitten-napped and all."

"Hey, I took good care of him," Ryan objected with a laugh. "Didn't have to glue him back together once, which is more than you can say for Whiskers."

Bridget frowned. "I never should have told you that. I fixed her tail so well, you never would have known I dropped her."

"I'll buy that," he said charitably. "You always were a bit of a perfectionist."

Bridget shook her head in amazement. "I still can't believe you held onto Tiger all these years. You moved so many times, I can't believe he never got thrown out or sold in a garage sale."

"Actually, he did end up in a yard sale once."

"Oh." Bridget looked over at him, trying to hide her disappointment. "So, what happened. He didn't sell?"

Lisa Campeau

Ryan chuckled. "No. And good thing, too. When I found out my mom put him in the sale with all our other junk, I was furious. I grabbed him and hid him in my closet where she'd never find him again."

A rush of warmth flooded through her, and when she spoke again, her voice trembled a little. "He-he meant a lot to you, huh?"

"You meant a lot to me."

They swung in silence a few minutes, Bridget relishing the last six words he had uttered as if they were a warm bubble bath or a bite of chocolate. Next to her, Ryan was gazing around at the playground. Although it was nothing new to her, she suddenly remembered that, to Ryan's eyes, this was probably like something out of a distant memory or a dream. Some things had changed, but many others remained the same.

"Remember when we used to race each other on the obstacle course?" she asked, nodding toward the tall humps of the caterpillar.

Ryan scratched his head and tried his best to appear perplexed. "I don't know if I recall that."

"That's because I used to beat you a lot. It bruised your ego, getting left in the dust by a girl."

Ryan gave her an appraising look. "Bet I could beat you now that you sit behind a desk all day."

"Unlike you, Mr. Computer geek?"

They narrowed their eyes contemptuously at each other until Ryan finally cracked a smile. "All right. I'm game if you are."

"You're on!"

Without waiting for it to stop, Bridget jumped off her swing, sticking a perfect landing several feet beyond the swing set. A second later, Ryan was next to her, staggering a little. She giggled at him. "Been a while, huh?"

158

He took her hand and together they ran to the start of the obstacle course. Along with the caterpillar, the course consisted of a set of four wooden hurdles a foot off the ground, a set of monkey bars ten feet long, and two series of connected balance beams running parallel to one another. Bridget stretched her arms and legs a minute, warming up her underutilized muscles.

They lined up between two nearby trees, just as they had as children. Ryan grinned at her and crouched down in a starting position, and, as best she could in her short dress, Bridget did the same.

"On your mark," Ryan began. "Get set...Go!"

Bridget took off and was instantly in the lead. She reached the caterpillar a split second before Ryan and started climbing. As she clambered over the top, she stopped to adjust her skirt, and Ryan breezed past her with a smirk. With a gasp of indignation, she dropped her skirt and raced after him, catching up with him halfway up the second hill. They were neck and neck when they climbed over the top, and Bridget managed to pass him only by dropping to the ground halfway down the ladder on the other side. Her bare feet hit the ground hard, and as she was wincing in agony, Ryan flew by her again.

"Should've kept your shoes on," he taunted as he raced toward the hurdles.

"Aargh!" Bridget turned and was on his tail again in seconds.

As she caught up with him, Ryan glanced over in surprise and bumped his shin on one of the low beams. He stumbled over the beam and landed on all fours, giving Bridget the opportunity to jump into the lead again.

The monkey bars were wide enough for two people to cross simultaneously, and when Bridget was halfway across and wondering if her shoulders would pop out of joint, Ryan was upon her again. As he started to pass her, she swung her legs, bumping him out of the way, and scurried the rest of the way across. At the end, she dropped to the ground and barely had time even to think about catching her breath when she heard Ryan drop down next to her.

Instinctively, she took off again for the side-by-side balance beams, jumping onto hers at the same instant Ryan reached his. She moved along the narrow beam, creeping along, one foot in front of the other, trying not to fall. Next to her, she could hear Ryan cursing quietly and tried not to laugh. The balance beam had always been his downfall.

She glanced over to see him, still holding his footing, but barely. As she landed on the final beam, she heard him shout "Whoa!" and saw him fall off, one-foot landing in the grass. This, in their old school days, meant he had to start over. But, before he even had the chance to return to the beginning of the balance beam, Bridget darted to the end of hers without falling and raised her hands in triumph.

She turned to gloat at Ryan, who was standing next to her. She was almost as tall as he was as she stood on the balance beam, which was six inches off the ground. As she moved to jump off, he caught her in his arms, swung her around, and pulled her to the ground. She let out a startled laugh as he landed on top of her.

"A little reward for your victory," he said and pressed his lips to hers.

She had been waiting so long to feel his kiss again that she had begun to wonder if it would live up to her memory. But, the second one was just as wonderful—sudden, sweet, and unexpected. When it was over, she lay there catching her breath, loving the feel of his warm, muscular body above her and the soft, lush grass beneath her. Without thinking, she raised her head, pulling his mouth down to meet hers again, and, as if he had been awaiting the invitation, he kissed her back with even more urgency than before.

A minute later, she remained contentedly beneath him, feeling the steady thump of his rapid heartbeat. She smiled up at him and reached up to touch his stubbly face. His glasses had gone askew, and she straightened them for him and then let her hand rest on his cheek. "You make me feel so—" She stopped herself suddenly. "Happy," she added quickly. "I'm so happy with you."

"I'm happy, too," he said, tracing a finger along her jawline.

She looked away a moment. What she had been about to say was "You make me feel so loved." But, Ryan hadn't told her he loved her. He seemed to show it in everything he said and did...but it was too soon. They had known each other forever, but those years in between didn't count. They were still just getting to know each other after more than twenty years apart.

He took her right hand in his and held it tightly while his left hand wandered somewhere out of her line of vision. A minute later, she could feel it on her thigh, slipping beneath the soft fabric of her skirt, and she gasped and brushed it away. "Ryan!" she said, trying to sound playful and not prudish. "What kind of girl do you think I am?"

Ryan immediately removed his hand and rolled off of her. "Sorry," he said quickly. "I guess I thought..." His voice trailed off awkwardly.

"Don't be sorry," she said, sitting up on her elbow and putting a finger to his lips with a smile. "It's just...we are in the middle of a school playground. At the school I teach at." Although she knew no one ever came by the playground on a Saturday, she found herself glancing around anxiously.

"I know. I'm sorry," he said again.

Hoping to let him know she still craved his touch, she took his hand again and settled it on her side. He ran his hand over her soft curves, along the dip of her slender waist and up the gentle rise to the top of her hip bone. Then, he stared into her eyes, not a hint of apology left in his intense gaze. "You're so sexy, Bridget," he said softly. "I can't believe no one has snatched you up before now."

She felt her breath catch in her throat. No one had ever called her sexy before. "I guess...I guess I've been waiting for the right one to come into my life...or back into my life," she said with a meaningful smile.

And then, he pulled her into his arms again and kissed her with a deep passion that pushed aside all her insecurities. For the first time, she honestly believed she was just as sexy and beautiful as he said she was.

Chapter Eight

Two more weeks flew by. Nearly every night, Bridget and Ryan spent hours talking on the phone or just texting each other, and on the weekend, when they both had time, they went out again. Ryan took her out to eat and to a movie, and then late in the evening, they returned to the school playground.

Two days before the school music program, Bridget asked Ryan if he would join her at it and was surprised to find out that Ryan didn't know a thing about it. She had spent the previous two evenings helping Alex set up for it and knew that she was counting on Hector being there.

"An invitation came home with the students last week," Bridget explained to him. "Are you sure you didn't get one?"

"If they sent it home with Hector, it's probably still crumpled up in his backpack," Ryan guessed. Then, he added affectionately, "Of course I'd love to go with you."

"Good," Bridget said. "It's a good thing I asked you about it, or you'd have missed Hector's big solo."

"Solo?"

"He's playing a solo on the recorder," Bridget laughed. "Alex told me. Didn't Hector—"

Ryan interrupted with a chuckle. "Hector's as absentminded as I was at that age. And, it's a really good thing you told me about it, or he wouldn't have been there either."

At five o'clock Friday evening, Ryan, Bridget, and Hector, along with Ryan's mother arrived at the high school auditorium. While Hector went to join his classmates, the others took their seats and waited for the show to begin. Bridget gave Ryan a smile and squeezed his hand. She had attended this concert every year since she'd been teaching there, but having someone she cared about to attend with made it far more special.

Ryan's phone dinged, and he reached into his jacket pocket and turned it on. As he checked it, Bridget watched him curiously. The light coming from his phone illuminated his features, and she could see his eyes widen for a moment as if in shock. Then he frowned, darkened his phone again, and stuffed it back in his pocket.

"Is everything all right?" Bridget whispered to him as the stage lights came on and a group of kindergartners were led onto the stage.

He gave her a quick smile. "Sure."

"You'd better shut your phone off," she murmured. "The program's about to start."

He nodded and gave her a distracted smile. As he switched his phone off, Bridget continued to stare at him, her brow furrowed with concern. Not until Alex appeared and began leading the children in a sweet song about friendship did she tear her gaze away from him.

The concert went on, grade by grade. When her class took the stage, Bridget sat up straight, a smile coming to her face as she surveyed the familiar faces of her students, most of whom had dressed up for the occasion. Next to her, Ryan was leaning forward, straining to see Hector, who was standing at the far left in the back row.

After the first song, Hector slipped out of the back row with his recorder and stepped to the front of the group. As he played, Bridget glanced at Ryan again to see him beaming down at his son with unmistakable pride. When the song ended, they applauded the performance louder and a little bit longer than the spectators around them.

When the program ended, Bridget excused herself a moment and went up to the stage to congratulate Alex. She was always amazed at how her friend managed to pull off such an elaborate production year after year. Then, she returned to the lobby to find Ryan again among the throngs of people milling around, looking for their children.

She found him standing with Hector, talking animatedly, and for a moment she just stood there, watching the father and son with a smile. Hector caught sight of her first and waved, prompting Ryan to look up and catch her gaze with a smile. When she walked over to them, Ryan put an arm around her waist and pulled her close.

"What did you think, Miss Winters?" Ryan asked, gesturing toward Hector. "Pretty expert recorder playing, right?"

"Absolutely! You were fantastic, Hector!" Bridget exclaimed.

Hector shrugged and offered her a humble smile in return. "Thanks."

When he turned to talk to his grandmother, Bridget looked up at Ryan. "You must be pretty proud, Ryan."

"I am," he agreed with a small smile—a smile that was a bit too tense for Bridget's liking.

"So...what's going on?" she asked. "That message you got just before the show...anything important?"

He slapped his hand to his jacket pocket as if afraid she could see through it into his phone. "It was...nothing."

"Oh," Bridget mumbled. "I know it's none of my business, but...it didn't look like nothing."

For a moment, Ryan studied her face, which she knew was giving away her feelings of hurt. He sighed. "All right. It wasn't." A small smile crossed his face. "I've been offered a job, actually."

"You...what?" Bridget asked slowly.

"Big company offered me a position in their IT department. Total surprise."

"Really?" she asked, trying to sound excited for him instead of terrified for herself. "Where-where at?"

He cleared his throat and averted his troubled eyes from hers. "Chicago."

"*Chicago*?" she cried. "They offered you a job in Chicago?"

He tightened his hold on her and met her eyes again. "Hey. I didn't say I'd take it."

"But, you're thinking about it?"

"I...I don't know."

Bridget felt the color drain from her face. That wasn't a no. She had so wanted him to say that no, he wouldn't take the job, that he'd never leave her again in a million years. But, he hadn't. She pulled out of his grasp and began brushing at the tears that were already stinging her eyes.

"Bridget—" Ryan began, taking her arm again.

"We should probably get home," she said, cutting him off. "I'm-I'm getting kind of tired."

He looked like he wanted to say something more, but then he glanced around the crowded room and seemed to think it best not to cause a scene. "Yeah. All right."

Bridget allowed Ryan to lead her gently by the arm out the door, followed by his mother and Hector. As he drove them home, not a word was spoken between them. In the backseat, Hector was entertaining his grandmother with knock-knock jokes, completely unaware that his life might soon be completely changed. Bridget felt a tear trickle down her cheek and was grateful for the darkness in the cab of the truck. Her class wouldn't be the same without Hector chiming in on every discussion whether he was called on or not.

And what would she do without Ryan? She had never had a man make her feel so happy, and she had the feeling she never would again. Her reunion with him had shown her how lonely and empty her life had become.

A moment of clarity broke through her misery, and she suddenly realized that Ryan was not driving her home. Instead, he took a side street that led out of town and five minutes later, pulled into a driveway in front of a little ranch house with gray siding and black shutters. As she was staring at the house in confusion, she could hear the two occupants of the backseat unbuckle their seat belts and open their doors.

Hector, who had started toward the house, paused, and turned around with a puzzled look. Still clutching his recorder, he looked smaller and more vulnerable than usual. Ryan rolled down his window and called, "It's all right. You two go on in. I'm going to take Miss Winters home, and I'll be back later."

When Hector and his grandmother were safely inside, Ryan rolled his window up and backed down the driveway again. Silence fell between them as they made the five-minute trip back to Bridget's house in town. When they arrived, Bridget immediately started to slip out of the truck.

Ryan reached out and took her arm. "Don't go yet," he pleaded when she turned to look at him. "Can we talk?"

Bridget paused, then nodded. "Would you like to come in?" she asked with exaggerated politeness.

"Yeah," he answered, pulling himself out of the driver's seat.

He followed her to the front porch and waited while she pulled out her keys and unlocked the door with shaky fingers. Without daring to look at him, she led him inside and through the living room to the kitchen. "Would you like something to drink?" she asked, pulling open the refrigerator and staring blankly inside.

"No. Thanks."

She shut the refrigerator again but didn't let go of the handle or turn around. A second later, she felt his hand on her arm and heard his voice next to her.

"I'm sorry, Bridget. I didn't mean to upset you."

"You really are thinking about moving to Chicago, aren't you?" she asked quietly.

Ryan sighed. "It's a great opportunity, Bridge. I applied for it over a month ago for kicks and never thought I'd hear from them again. The pay and benefits are outstanding, there's lots of room for promotion, it's one of the most reputable companies around...and just the fact that they even considered me makes me feel really...proud. I can't just...not consider it."

She turned to look at him with hurt-filled eyes. "You're leaving me again, aren't you? Just like before. Only it's not like before. Last time, you had no choice. This time, you do. You want to go."

She could see a flicker of frustration in his eyes. "All right. You're right, I do want this. I want a career where I can better myself and be challenged and maybe make a little more money. And, like you said, it's my decision. It's my life."

Deep down, Bridget knew she was being unfair and selfish. She couldn't expect Ryan to give up on a dream this huge in exchange for a relationship that was barely a month old. But at that moment, she didn't want to be fair or reasonable. She only wanted Ryan to stay with her.

"So...what?" she asked heatedly. "You're going to drag Hector away from his home and his friends just like your parents did to you? And, what then? Are you going to chase job after job and opportunity after opportunity, uprooting him every few years until you finally drop dead of a heart attack just like your father did?"

A terrible silence filled the air between them. As Bridget stopped to calm her breathing, she focused for the first time on Ryan's face and took two instinctive steps backward. She had never seen his face so tight, his eyes so cold and angry. He took a few deep breaths, and when he spoke again, he seemed to be trying hard to control his fury.

"You don't know anything about my father...or me. Everything he did was for his family. The fact that you would drag him into this—"

Bridget shook her head, her eyes suddenly streaming. "I'm sorry, Ryan—"

"And as for Hector...he's my son, not yours."

"I know," she said meekly.

"I'm a damn good father to him."

Bridget let out a sob. "I know,"

"And, if you really care about me, I would think you'd be happy for me," he went on. Although she knew he was still angry, she could hear his voice becoming slightly softer and gentler. "They've offered me something I've wanted for a really long time."

Bridget wiped her eyes and swallowed hard. "Ryan...I am happy for you," she managed through her tears. "It's just...it's hard to be happy for you when I'm so sad for myself. It's-it's been really...nice spending time with you again."

This was the greatest understatement she could ever remember speaking. Spending time with Ryan again had been the best experience of her life. The truth was, she was devastated by the mere thought of losing him again.

He gave her a small, sad smile and reached out, pulling her into his arms. He held her as close as possible, kissing the top of her head and running a hand up and down her back in a comforting way. "Hey. Let's not get ahead of ourselves, okay?"

Bridget nodded against his chest but didn't say a word. All she wanted to do was remain in his arms for as long as possible, because, in spite of what he had said, she had a feeling that his mind was already made up. She had seen in his eyes how much this opportunity meant to him. He would probably call that very night and accept the position—and then he would be gone.

Far too soon, Ryan pulled away again. "I better go. Hector will wonder where I'm at."

"Yeah," she said, running a hand over her eyes again.

She started walking him to the door, then thought of something and came to a halt. "Wait just a minute," she said. "I'll be right back."

She padded down the hallway to her bedroom and, with a pang of sadness, plucked Tiger off her dresser. Then, she headed back to where Ryan was waiting patiently in the living room.

"Is everything all right?" he asked her.

She nodded. Fighting back another surge of tears, she took his hand in hers and placed Tiger onto his open palm. As Ryan watched, open-mouthed, she closed his fingers over the little ceramic kitten. "Just in case," she said softly.

"Bridget...why—" he began.

"You'll need something to remember me by," she interrupted.

Before he could say another word, she ushered him to the door. She pulled him toward her, kissed him briefly, and held the door open as he stepped out. As he descended the porch steps, he turned to look back a moment, his expression bewildered. Bridget waved and shut the door without another word.

***

Two hours later, as she was preparing for bed, her phone rang. Bridget glanced at the screen, saw Ryan's name appear, and felt her heart plunge in despair. He was calling to tell her it was over, he was taking the job, he hoped they would still be friends and a hundred other painful platitudes. Tears filled her eyes at the thought. She just couldn't handle it right now. Maybe she never would.

It would be best if things just ended, she decided. Ryan had been right all those years ago—saying goodbye to someone who meant so much was the hardest thing in the world to do. And so, just like last time, there would be no goodbyes. She pressed the dismiss button, ending the call, then shut off her phone and dropped it into the cluttered depths of her purse.

Chapter Nine

Bridget spent the weekend trying to avoid thoughts of Ryan by staying busy and ignoring her phone. She spent hours at her mother's house, helping with spring yard work and sidestepping any questions about her personal life. She told her mother about her renewed friendship with Ryan but said nothing to her about his job offer. It would only disappoint her to learn that her only daughter's latest romance—and her only serious romance—had ended so abruptly.

It was hard for her to believe that she and Ryan had only reunited a few weeks before. Surely, she could forget about this brief fling and move on with her life. But everywhere she went, she was reminded of him. And, she knew that when she returned to school, it would be even more difficult, facing Hector and seeing the playground where they had shared the most wonderful, intimate moment she could remember.

On Monday, she went through the motions of teaching, greeted Hector like any other student, and spent recess at her desk, trying to focus on grading papers in the stillness of the classroom. When the day finally ended, she dismissed the class with a forced smile and turned to wipe the board clean as the chaotic sounds of twenty-five children packing up to leave hummed behind her. As she was setting the eraser down, she felt a tug on her sleeve and looked down to see Hector standing there with his backpack on.

"Hector!" she exclaimed. "Is everything all right?"

Hector scanned the classroom to make sure it was otherwise deserted, then mumbled, "My dad said he needs to see you after school."

"Oh." Bridget immediately began searching the room for an excuse to decline the invitation. "Well...can you tell him I have a project I need to get done? Maybe another day."

"All right." Hector turned around slowly, his eyes on the floor. He was almost to the door when he stopped and looked back at her. "Did you and my dad have a fight?"

Bridget felt a wave of guilt as she took in his despondent expression. "No, Hector," she said quickly. "We're just...taking a break, that's all. It's nothing you need to be concerned with. And I promise, I'll talk to him soon. Okay?"

"Okay," he said, walking morosely out of the room.

When he was gone, Bridget went to her supply cabinet to gather up the items she would need to create a springtime-themed display for her students' most recent book reports. She emerged with large sheets of blue and green construction paper, which she carried to the bulletin board hanging on one of the side walls of her classroom. As she was cutting the green paper into a series of rolling hills, Alex walked in.

"How was your weekend?" Alex asked, setting a stack of music books on the desk next to Bridget.

Bridget glanced up from where she was kneeling on the floor. "It was all right."

"Did you and Ryan have another rendezvous at the playground?" Alex asked, raising her eyebrows suggestively.

Bridget rolled her eyes. "I don't know why I confide in you sometimes."

"Come on, Bridge," Alex insisted, dropping to the floor next to her. "I'm just teasing. I think it's great you two found each other again."

Bridget jumped to her feet and began tacking up the hilly green meadows over the blue paper she was using to represent the sky. She scowled. The two sheets of green paper didn't line up neatly as she had planned—she hadn't cut them evenly.

"Let me help," Alex said, taking them from her and snipping away with the scissors. "So...is everything all right with you and Ryan?"

Bridget shook her head and sank to the floor as tears threatened to spill once again.

Alex dropped the scissors and quickly put an arm around her friend. "Oh, Bridge. What happened?"

"He's leaving me again," Bridget said, sniffling. "He's been offered a job in Chicago."

"Oh, Bridget. I'm so sorry."

"I know we haven't been seeing each other that long. I know it's ridiculous that I'm getting this upset, but..." she trailed off.

"You love him, don't you?" Alex asked keenly, her eyes searching Bridget's face.

"I do," she answered tearfully. "But, it doesn't matter, does it? Not if he doesn't feel the same way."

"Did he say he doesn't love you?"

"No. But he didn't say he does either."

"Well, Bridget," Alex said, pulling away just enough so she could meet her friend's eyes. "It sounds like you two need to have a conversation. I've seen the way he looks at you. He loves you, even if he isn't ready to say it yet."

"But, the job—"

"Bridget, I've never seen you happier that you've been the last few weeks. If you haven't already told him how you feel, you need to start. Maybe it won't change his mind about taking the job. But, if what you two have is as special as it seems, you need to do what you can to save it, not just give up on it."

Bridget stared down at the paper in her lap, her thoughts beginning to swirl. Alex was right. As soon as she heard about Ryan's job offer, she had immediately plummeted into despair. If she had thought about the situation rationally, she may have come up with a solution that didn't involve never seeing him again. They could have talked it over and come up with a plan together. Instead, overcome with fear and sorrow, she had chased him out of her life.

"I need to talk to him," she mumbled, jumping to her feet.

"Yeah...like I said," Alex said, gazing up at her perplexed.

Bridget knelt down and scooped the sheets of green paper off the floor. "I wonder if he's still out there," she muttered as she pinned the papers haphazardly onto the bulletin board.

"Out where?" Alex asked. She got off the floor and tugged at the papers out of Bridget's hands. Seconds later, the board consisted of seamless rolling hills against a deep blue sky.

"Hector said Ryan wanted to see me after school," Bridget answered as she quickly and randomly stuck the pretty, green meadow with thumbtacks.

"*What?*" Alex bellowed. "Bridget! He's probably still here! Go!"

Bridget gestured to the unfinished bulletin board display. "But, what about this? I want to get the kids' book reports up there by tomorrow."

"I'll do it," Alex said, pushing Bridget out the door.

"I was going to cut out some clouds and trees, too," Bridget added, turning back. "And maybe some tulips and daffodils. There's more paper in the—"

"Bridget! Go!"

Bridget turned and raced out the door, suddenly filled with fear. Ryan had been trying to reach her all weekend with no reply and had fruitlessly asked to see her after school. How much rejection would he be willing to take before he gave up and left town without another word?

As she emerged through the double doors onto the sidewalk, Bridget decided that she would do whatever it took to make Ryan know she still needed him. She would go to his house, and if he wasn't there, she would search all over town for his truck. If she needed to, she would go all the way to Chicago to find him.

Through the rows of cars in the parking lot, she looked for Ryan's truck. She spotted it at the very end of the lot. She picked up her pace, nearly tripping in her haste to reach it, but as she drew near, she saw that it was sitting empty. She slowed to a stop, frowning in confusion, then turned to scan the rest of the parking lot. And there, leaning against her car as if he owned it and watching her with amusement was Ryan.

Flooded with relief, she quickly strode his way. "Ryan! I'm so glad you're still here."

"Really?" he asked. "Because I was starting to think you never wanted to see me again."

"No!" Bridget shook her head adamantly. "Ryan, I'm so sorry! I really am happy for you, and I want the best for you and Hector. But maybe...maybe it doesn't have to be at the expense of our relationship. I know that Chicago is a few hours away, but we can still call and text and visit. And, they need teachers there, too, right? Maybe someday, if things go well, I can find a job there. All I know is, I love you, Ryan. I really do. And, I don't want to lose you again. You're the best thing that ever happened to me and—"

"Hey Dad," Hector broke in, having appeared from nowhere. "When are you going to tell her we're not moving to Chicago?"

"Quiet," Ryan stage whispered. "She hasn't finished telling me how wonderful I am yet!"

Astonished, Bridget jerked her hands out of his. She wasn't sure if she should feel relieved, outraged, or really stupid. "You're not *moving*?" she exclaimed loudly.

Ryan immediately took her hands again, warming her with his touch. "I was going to tell you, but you had so much to say, and it seemed rude to interrupt—"

"Right. Like that's stopped you so many times before."

He chuckled. "All right. You make a good point. But, I tried to call, too. Why didn't you answer?"

She looked away. "I don't know. I guess it was just too hard to talk to you when I knew you were disappearing from my life again. I guess you were right. Sometimes it is easier to leave without saying goodbye."

He pulled her into his arms, and she rested her head comfortably against his chest. "I guess we better stay together then, huh?"

"I'm getting out of here before you two do something even grosser than this," she heard Hector say as Ryan dropped a kiss into her hair.

When Hector had disappeared to the playground, Bridget looked up at Ryan. "I don't understand. I know you said you hadn't made any decisions yet, but you seemed so excited about the job. I could tell you really wanted it."

"I did," Ryan admitted. "In fact, I almost accepted it."

"What changed your mind?"

"A lot of things," Ryan replied. "Talking with you...talking with Hector. But mostly it was that...no matter where I go, I know I'll always be drawn back here, to this place...and especially to you." His voice was suddenly softer and huskier, revealing the depth of meaning in his words. "I love you, too, Bridget. I-I think I've loved you since we were ten years old. And I don't want to live without you again."

Happy, love-filled tears dampened Bridget's eyes. "I guess we're agreed then."

Ryan pulled back just far enough to reach a hand into his jacket pocket. "Guess we better give the kids the good news, huh?"

Bridget tilted her head, puzzled. "What do you mean?"

Ryan pulled out his hand and held out Tiger, the adorable orange kitten, sleeping in a bed of flowers. "You'd better take him home and put him back with Whiskers where he belongs."

"But he's yours," Bridget objected. "I gave him to you."

"And Whiskers is yours," Ryan said, his eyes twinkling. "But, it doesn't matter. They're like us. They're meant to be together."

"Then, let's never separate them again," Bridget agreed with a smile.

She opened her car door and set Tiger carefully in the passenger seat before turning to Ryan with a warm smile. He took her hand and kissed it, and together, like so many times before, they started across the grassy playground. In the distance, as always, their favorite swing set awaited them in the shimmering afternoon sunshine.

THE END

Introducing Martin L Shoemaker

The Duck Docket

Martin L. Shoemaker is a programmer who writes on the side...or maybe it's the other way around. A second-place story in the Baen Memorial Writing Contest won him lunch with Buzz Aldrin. Programming never did that! His novel *The Last Dance* (inspired by that lunch) was the #1 science fiction eBook on Amazon for October 2019.

Heat Level: SWEET

THE DUCK DOCKET
Martin L Shoemaker

Taking advantage of the frustrating halt in traffic, attorney Kate Voss leaned over and checked her makeup in the rearview mirror. Not a hair out of place. Her dark blonde hair was short and neat, perfect for Judge Bosscher's courtroom. He liked attorneys presentable but not flashy. The firm had briefed her well on the preferences of every family law judge in three counties.

Kate was glad she looked polished, ready for court. She wasn't the sort of woman to touch up her makeup while driving down the road.

Well...not when driving down a side road like Wilson between Walker and Grandville, so hilly and woodsy.

Well...not when traffic was heavy. But then, she avoided Wilson during rush hour, when it could become a parking lot in both directions, full of commuters who foolishly mistook it for a north-south shortcut. It was a *great* shortcut during the middle of the day but a lost half-hour or more in the morning or evening.

Kate's mistake today was not realizing that it was a half-day of school; and, Wilson at lunchtime today was almost as bad as at 8 a.m. on a Monday morning. Parents in minivans full of kids passed in both directions, along with delivery trucks, sportscars with their tops down in the beautiful spring weather, and occasionally a sedan. And, one damned school bus clogging up everything.

Kate's shortcut was turning into a long delay, exactly what she didn't need. She was already on Judge Bosscher's bad side (though rumors in the firm were that the judge didn't *have* a good side). Her only saving grace was that Lenny Johnson, the opposing counsel, was in just as much trouble. *VanTil vs. VanTil* was dragging on way too long for the judge's taste, and he had long since stopped hiding his disapproval.

If Kate were late, it would give Lenny an edge, and Kate owed Clara VanTil better than that. Kate tapped her earpiece. "Call Mrs. VanTil."

Clara answered. "Kate, is something wrong? I'm here at the courthouse."

"It's okay, Clara," Kate said in a calm voice that she really didn't feel. "We're not due in court yet."

"No, but we will be soon. And Henry...and Johnson...they want to discuss the property settlement again."

"No!" Kate said. Then she wondered, had Clara heard panic in her voice? She steadied herself. "Clara, don't look at it. Don't even talk to them. They're trying to hit you when you're weak."

"I know, but—"

"Clara, I'm doing this for you. *Please* don't talk to them. I'm on my way."

"Okay," Clara said. "Please...hurry..." She disconnected.

Damn! The firm had been abuzz all week with win-loss stats. In divorce cases, there were no real wins or losses, but the partners looked carefully at property settlements. Kate had in mind numbers that would make Clara very secure—and would look really good to the partners.

Kate worried that she had lied to her client. She wasn't really on her way, not fast enough, and it was all due to that damned bus. The driver was moving at a safe and legal speed over the hills and around the curves of Wilson—when the bus moved. But, all too often, it stopped to let off kids. First the yellow lights flashed to warn traffic to slow down as the bus pulled onto the narrow shoulder; and then, the red flashers started and the STOP sign swung out from the bus, stopping all traffic, north and south. Kids got off to the west. Others checked the road carefully and then crossed to the east.

Too many stops. Too much time wasted. Kate resisted the urge to shout.

After each stop, the driver turned off the flashers and waved a few cars around before signaling a merge back into the stream of traffic. That was as much courtesy as he could offer or that was legally required as Kate understood the law.

As the driver waved cars around, Kate could just make out the tan, muscular arm sticking out the window. Farmer's tan, no doubt. She wondered if the face inside had a left-side tan as well. Growing up, she'd seen that on herself: the pale right hand, the dark left, both strong like the one she saw here.

Kate got five cars closer before the bus signaled to pull back out into the lane.

Dumb, dumb, dumb. She should've checked traffic before taking the shortcut. Wilson was a beautiful country road — technically a numbered highway, but as a practical matter it was more of a scenic route: lots of woods, a few houses here and there. A few housing developments had built up over the years. It was a beautiful drive — if you weren't in a hurry, especially today.

As they crested a hill, Kate saw a long downhill slope ahead. She veered a little to the left to see if she could pass in this stretch, but no such luck. The oncoming traffic was almost as heavy. One car ahead snuck in, gunned it, and barely got around the bus before the oncoming traffic caught up to it. The bus driver slammed the brakes so the car could get back into the proper lane, but that only slowed the rest of the traffic. Kate was just going to have to wait her turn.

At the next stop, another four cars got past, putting Kate

directly behind the bus. She got a better view of the arm this time as it literally waved and let the traffic by. The driver held out a hand to stop as the bus signaled again to come in.

There couldn't be many kids left on the bus. Kate saw very few heads moving and not a lot of activity. Maybe the driver would be done soon and could get moving.

Then suddenly, the brake lights came on again. Kate barely stopped in time to avoid rear-ending the bus. She couldn't see any driveways or houses through here, just wetlands on either side of the road, so why was the bus stopping? Why the stop sign and the red flashers? Again, the hand came out the window, made an okay sign, and then pulled back in.

The driver couldn't be letting kids off here. There was nothing Kate could do except wait. As long as that stop sign was up and those lights were flashing, no traffic could pass in either direction, so Kate would have to wait. Several minutes passed. She checked the time on her dashboard. She was going to be late if this bus didn't get moving right now. She would have to break the speed limits just to get to the courthouse on time. Something she didn't want to do as an officer of the court.

Kate started thinking of three routes where she could edge over the limit and hope not to find any police around. That was when she realized how long they'd been sitting there. Way too long for a bus stop. Was there an emergency? Did the driver need help?

Kate turned on her flashers, opened her door, got out, and walked around the front of her care, over to the bus. As she approached the door, a man came around the front of the bus: tall, tan, and muscular in an attractive and noticeable way, with curly hair, big brown eyes, and a left arm full of ducklings. "Oh, here," he said. "Take these."

"What?" Kate couldn't formulate a better question. The

man held out three ducklings and dropped them into her arms. Without thinking, she took them.

"Thanks." The man pushed on the door and it folded, opening. He pushed the folds to the right.

A young teen girl stood just inside. "Did you find more, Mr. King?"

"Yeah, Tonya. Here, three more." The man took a duckling from Kate's arms and handed it to the girl. She passed it to someone behind her Mr. King did the same with the second and the third. "How many is that?"

"Um..." The girl looked back and called, "How many ducks?"

Someone shouted from inside, "Seven...No, eight."

"Eight," the man said. "How many did you see, Tonya?"

"I don't know, Mr. King. I didn't have a lot of time to count. I think...twelve?"

A little boy, all blond hair and braces, popped up behind her. "Thirteen Mr. King. Thirteen. I counted thirteen ducklings, plus Mama Duck. Thirteen."

Tonya added, "He counts everything, Mr. King. If he says thirteen, it's thirteen."

"All right, hold tight. I'll find them." The man closed the door again, returning to the front of the bus.

Kate grabbed his arm. "Mr. King, is it? Why did you stop the bus to pick up ducks?"

He appeared stressed. "I hit the mama duck."

"Oh, no."

"We've got to save the ducklings."

"But--"

"It's my fault. They're all alone, and it's my fault."

Kate had grown up on a farm around animals, and she had a pragmatic view of their welfare. Ducklings without a mother were easy targets for the road or for predators. There were plenty of coyotes around here. Snapping turtles, too. A snapper could take down a full-grown duck, much less a duckling.

So many times, Kate's dad had told her, "It's the way of things, Katie. Sometimes you can't fix it. It's just the animal's time." She had cried and she'd nodded. But, even though she'd known intellectually that her dad was right, in her heart she'd never given up easily. She had nursed injured birds, cats who'd gotten into scrapes, raccoons who'd lost their mother in the road, and a hundred other animals in trouble. Every time, Dad had given her *The Lecture*, and every time, she would nod and then go back to caring for her animals. Dad would shake his head, sigh, and do what he could to help her. He celebrated with her when she succeeded against the odds, and he held her on his lap and patted her back as she cried over each failure.

Unlike her dad, Mr. King reminded her of that little girl who wanted to save the animals. That girl, now a hard charging divorce attorney, looked at her watch and was now certain she'd be late for Judge Bosscher's court. But, it didn't matter. She recognized the look on King's face. He wasn't going to give up, just like she never had, so the only way to get this traffic moving was to help him.

"Five ducks, huh?" Kate said. "Let's find them, Mr. King."

"Tim," he said, smiling at her. "I appreciate the help. They got scared. I think they ran under the other cars."

Kate ran up to the nearest car in the northbound lane, bent down, and looked under it.

The driver rolled down his window. "Lady, what the hell is up with this guy and the ducks? I think we should just ignore his stop sign and get going here."

Kate shook her head. "I'm an attorney, an officer of the court. I don't think you want to do that. I'd have to report you.

And besides..." She crouched, reached an arm in behind the driver's front wheel, and pulled out a duckling. "...you might have hurt this little guy if you had."

"There's more of them?"

"Yeah, and he's not budging until we chase them down. There's four more after this one. If you want to get moving, get out and help."

"You're crazy, lady." But, the man got out and started walking down the line, peering under cars. Soon, he found another duckling, and Kate found two more. That made four. If the towheaded kid was right, there was one more. "Come on, maybe Tim has found our last lost duck."

They saw Tim crouched down by the side of the road. As they approached him, Kate saw he had his arm wrapped around a duckling, while his other arm reached out toward the ditch beside the road.

Kate found herself momentarily distracted by the sight of Tim leaning over in the reeds. *Nice butt,* she thought. But then, she remembered the time. "Tim? We've got them all, all five of them. Now let's get moving." She tried to check her watch, but she couldn't without losing a duckling. "I'm late for court. Judge Bosscher is going to find me in contempt."

Tim looked up at her. "I'm sorry, Miss..."

"Kate Voss."

"I'm sorry, Kate, but I think the mother is down in here. I thought I saw her hiding. She's still alive. I've got to get her to a vet."

"You hit her with a bus," Kate objected. "She can't—"

"I wasn't going that fast. She flew in front of me. She could have bounced off. She might be hurt. But—"

"All right. Here," she handed one of the ducklings to the man behind her so she had a free arm to balance herself, and then, she climbed down into the ditch beside Tim. She looked around through the tall grass. "I don't see any movement."

"You won't," Tim said. "She's scared and hurt, so she's hiding now. Maybe you can go make some noise. She's right in here somewhere." He pointed to shallows filled with reeds. "Maybe if you went a little farther down the road and made some noise in the bushes, you'd scare her into moving again, and I could find her."

Kate tried to answer, but at this point there was no way out of the mess except through it. She had to help Tim get his ducks in a row.

She started to climb back up the side of the ditch. Once Kate was back on the shoulder, she looked down at her shoes: her beautiful slate blue pumps, perfect for her slate blue dress, all designed to impress without being flashy. She didn't have to worry about flashy now. The shoes were splattered with mud.

Too late to worry about that. Kate walked ten feet to the south, and then she began to climb back down.

But, the ditch there was steeper, more slippery. Suddenly, her feet slid out from under her. Kate landed hard on her butt as she slid down into the ditch and splashed into the water. She barely kept her grip on the duckling. Her other hand slammed into the mud, splashing water all over her jacket. "Oh, shit!" she shouted.

"That did it," Tim said. "I got her!" He got the duck, while Kate got muddy and soaking wet...and looking down, a tear in her stockings.

At least, the ducks were all rounded up now. Kate looked around for a better way out. She had to walk through more mud to get to a spot where the ditch had a shallower slope.

When she got back up to the level, she saw Tim closing the bus door. He turned. When he saw her, he stared in horror. "Oh, I'm so sorry!"

"It's too late for sorry." Kate handed him the last duckling. "Now can we get moving? I'm going to get a huge fine."

"Yes, ma'am. I mean, yes, Kate." He opened the bus door again and slipped through with the last duckling.

By the time Kate was back in her car, Tim had turned off the flashers and was waving all traffic past. Four cars didn't even wait for Kate to get her own in motion, zipping by and pinning her in. A fifth one looked like it was about to go by as well, but the oncoming traffic stopped it.

As soon as Kate was in motion, she tapped her earpiece. "Call Donna."

Her assistant answered on the first ring. "Kate, you're in trouble now."

"I know. Tell Judge Bosscher I was unavoidably delayed by traffic, and then meet me in the women's room with my spare outfit." She looked down. "It'll make me later, but I can't go into court like this."

As Kate pulled past the bus, Tim waved and smiled. *Nice smile...If only they had an opportunity to talk more.*

***

Kate looked in her compact mirror as she approached the courtroom door. She had scrubbed off the mud as best she could. With copious hair spraying by Donna, she had managed to get her hair under control, but not nearly as well coiffed as she preferred for court. Her slate blue power outfit had become a simple white and brown skirt ensemble with matching brown shoes that needed a polish. She had scrubbed off her makeup. There'd been no time to fix it right. And, she had discovered that she had no pantyhose in her spare bag.

Kate took two big calming breaths, and she walked through the courtroom door.

"Well, Counselor Voss," Judge Bosscher said, his tone

brimming with acid. "Nice of you to join us."

Kate had enough experience to know: better to take the beating directly than to hide. She looked straight into Judge Bosscher's eyes. He was older, late fifties or early sixties, she wasn't sure. He had a shock of white hair on a mostly balding pate. He peered at her through wire rim glasses intently.

"My apologies to Your Honor and the court and to everyone here," Kate said. She walked briskly but calmly to the front. "I had unavoidable traffic delays. It won't happen again. I'll make sure to give myself a larger buffer next time."

"You will do that," Judge Bosscher said, "Or next time, I won't be so lenient. But this time, it will be a fine. Court costs plus Mr. Johnson's time."

"Yes, Your Honor. Again, I apologize to you and the court."

"Let's waste no more time. So here we are, Family Law Court 3, of the County of Kent, in the State of Michigan, already called to order in the matter of VanTil vs. VanTil. We are here to discuss property settlements, Ladies and Gentlemen. Have we made any progress since our last meeting?"

They hadn't, and that was a big part of why Judge Bosscher grew more and more annoyed with everyone in this case. He thought it was dragging on way too long. He had said as much in the last session.

No one spoke, so Judge Bosscher addressed Johnson directly. "Counselor Johnson."

Lenny Johnson rose. "If I may approach the bench, Your Honor."

Judge Bosscher raised his eyebrows and looked at Kate. "Any objections, Counselor Voss?"

"Forgive me, Your Honor, I'm not sure what this is about."

Bosscher said, "Perhaps if you would have arrived

earlier, you might know. Both counsels, approach the bench."
The lawyers did so. Judge Bosscher spoke in a low voice.
"Counselor Johnson, what is this in regard to?"

"Your Honor, my client and Mrs. VanTil and I were able
to reach an agreement on some of the outstanding issues, and I
am ready to introduce a document into records."

Oh, no! Kate looked over at Clara. Her client couldn't
meet her eyes. That was bad. "Your Honor, can I at least have a
moment to look it over?"

"One minute, counselor."

Kate looked the document over. It was just as she had
feared. Clara had folded on most of the outstanding issues. The
woman was tired, distraught. She just wanted the divorce over.
It was her decision, but Kate had really tried to keep her from
giving up too much that she would regret later.

But, Kate saw that Clara had initialed it, indicating she
agreed in principle to the settlement. There was nothing Kate
could do about that. "No objections, Your Honor."

"All right, Counselor Voss, you may return to your
table." Then, the Judge spoke up for the court recorder. "You
may proceed, Counselor Johnson."

"Yes, Your Honor," Lenny said. "I would like to
introduce into the record this preliminary settlement agreed
upon by Mr. and Mrs. VanTil regarding household property
and prenuptial property."

"I will take this under advisement," the Judge said, "and
I will consider it strongly in my final ruling. And, I would like
to thank you Mr. VanTil, and you Mrs. VanTil for working
together on this for the first time. Maybe we can finally get
things moving here."

"Thank you, Your Honor," Lenny said. As he walked
back to his table, he smiled a cat-and-canary smile at Kate.

Clara stared down at the table. It looked to Kate like she

was trying to keep her composure.

"All right," Judge Bosscher said. "We have household, we have prenuptial. We have no children—that's a relief—so we don't have to worry about child support." He paused and looked over his case file. "So that leaves only the business. Do we have any new information to bring on that matter?"

Kate sighed inadvertently, but not so loud so the Judge could notice. The business had become the crucial issue. Clara had given away too much too easily. Both VanTils were professionals with careers, so it was unlikely that there would be any spousal support. If Mr. VanTil fought for a stake in Clara's veterinary business, Clara was going to be squeezed but good.

Bosscher looked at Kate, "Since Counselor Johnson opened the discussion, let's hear from you on this one, Counselor Voss."

Kate stood again, stepped out in front of the table, and started to pace. "Your Honor, my client has seven years invested in veterinarian school plus another four years interning for various clinics before she opened up the VanTil Veterinary Clinic. This represents almost a third of her life invested in this business."

"I object, Your Honor," Lenny said.

"You object that it is a third of her life invested?" Bosscher asked.

"I object that it's not just *her* life Your Honor. My client helped pay for her veterinary school, and was the major breadwinner during her internship. He co-signed the note to launch the business."

"That all may be true counselor," Judge Bosscher said, "But, you are out of order presenting this now. I fully intend to let you make your counter arguments, but you don't get to interrupt Counselor Voss."

This time, it was Kate's turn to smile. Lenny had pushed too hard. Maybe he had undone some of the damage that Kate had done to herself today.

Then, Kate looked past Johnson to his client, Henry VanTil. The man was practically in tears. Nobody cried over a business interest, especially not when it wasn't lost yet. Johnson could still make a case that VanTil was entitled to a cut.

Kate frowned, looking more closely. Henry VanTil was trembling. If she had to guess, she believed that VanTil didn't want the business, didn't want to squeeze Clara like that, but Johnson had talked him into it.

Suddenly Kate realized where she had seen that look on VanTil's face before. It was the same look on Clara's face when Lenny had introduced the settlement agreement. Clara hadn't given up because she was tired; she had given up because she didn't want to take Henry for everything he had. Kate had talked her into taking a hard line, because she had seen them fight. Whatever residual feelings they might have had, they couldn't work together.

But now, Kate knew Henry had a weakness. If she could stall for time, she could figure out a way to play on it. Kate could get Clara what she needed, even if Clara didn't realize it for herself. Kate took another deep breath and thought about an angle she might try.

She paused. That was cold. When had the little girl nursing sick kittens become the cold strategist?

Just then, the courtroom door opened, and she heard an officer say, "Wait, you can't go in there with those."

Kate turned toward the door, recognizing muddy khakis, and those tanned toned arms holding a giant crate. Behind that crate could only be the face of Tim King.

"Your Honor," Tim said from behind the crate, "it's not Ms. Voss's fault. I'm the one who made her late. You should fine me."

Judge Bosscher banged his gavel. "Counselor Voss, what's the meaning of this?"

Kate looked from Tim back to the Judge. "Your Honor, I swear I have no idea."

"She doesn't, Your Honor," Tim said, lowering the crate slightly so he could peer over it and walk forward. "I would have been here sooner, but I had to find Papa Duck."

Judge Bosscher peered over his glasses. "Papa...Duck..."

"I knew he would be worried," Tim continued. "And then, I had to get the kids to school and figure out which court you were in."

Bang! The gavel fell down again. "Order in this court. Who are you?"

"Timothy King, Your Honor. I'm the bus driver who made Ms. Voss late."

"That's not the matter before this court today. Bailiff, remove this man."

"But, Your Honor, I can't let her get in trouble for my mistake."

The judge glared at Tim. "You are both going to be in a pile of trouble. Bailiff!"

Tim had almost reached the front of the gallery by the time the bailiff caught up with him and grabbed his arm.

"But, Your Honor," Tim insisted, "it's my fault."

The bailiff pulled on Tim's arm. The crate slipped, fell, and bounced off the gate between the gallery and the parties. It tumbled, hit the floor, and crashed open. In an instant, the courtroom was a cacophony of quacking, as thirteen fuzzy little ducklings and two adult mallards scattered.

"Order!" The gavel fell. "Order in my court!"

"Sorry, Your Honor." Tim pushed at the gate, but it was blocked by the crate. So, he stepped over, an easy task with his long legs. "I'll get them."

"Somebody get these ducks out of my courtroom!" Bosscher shouted.

For the second time that day, Kate found herself crouching down, looking for ducklings. Two had fled under her table; but, before Kate could bend down and get them, Clara was on her knees, cooing at them. "Come here babies. Come here. Come here. Yeah, I know you're scared. Come here."

Kate watched, fascinated, as Clara held out a hand and spoke in a low soft voice. The two ducklings came cautiously forward. Clara gently petted their heads and coaxed them until she could get a hand underneath them. Then, she got up and handed them to Kate. "Here, take these."

Kate stood, jaw slack, and took the ducklings. She turned to hand them to Tim, but he already had two of his own. "Lenny," Kate said to Johnson, "turn that crate back over."

"What?" Johnson said.

"Come on! We got a duck crisis here," she said. "You heard the judge. Turn that over, so we can put these in." Johnson turned the crate back right side up, found the lid, and leaned it against the crate. Kate put her two ducklings in, immediately followed by Tim's. Henry VanTil had another, and Clara was in pursuit of yet another.

Kate looked over at a bailiff, who had a distinct frown on his face as he held one duckling far out from his body, but too late; his uniform was already soiled.

Clara came up with another duckling. That gave them seven. Henry was on his knees in the gallery, trying to coax another out from under a seat.

"Counselor Voss," Judge Bosscher said, "I shall expect a full explanation."

"I'll try, Your Honor," Kate said, "but first we've got to clean these up." She looked around and saw another duckling had gotten into the gallery and was wandering towards the back.

At that moment, a bailiff opened the door. "Is there trouble in here, Your Honor?"

"No!" Kate shouted, but it was too late. The duckling had squeezed between the man's legs and out into the hallway beyond.

Kate pushed through the gate and ran down the aisle. "Let me through," she said to the bailiff, who barely got out of the way before she rushed through the door.

The duckling was waddling towards the front entrance. A number of people looked and laughed. Three of them combined forces to herd the duck into the hands of one, who stood up with the duckling and handed it to Kate just as she ran up.

"Thank you," Kate said, nearly breathless.

The man smiled at her. "It looks like a lot more fun in your courtroom today."

"Not at all," Kate said, hurrying away with the duckling.

When Kate got back into the courtroom, she saw Judge Bosscher slumped down behind his bench, shaking his head. His face was a shade of red she had never seen on him before.

When Kate got back to the crate, she put her duckling in. She counted eleven, including hers. Tim came up and smiled at her as he dropped in two more. "Now we just need Mama and Papa," he said.

Kate looked around, "Where?"

"Over there." Tim pointed towards the far corner, where the VanTils had blocked off Papa Duck. She saw the green head between their legs.

Clara crouched low, talking softly to the duck. His mouth opened and he hissed at her. Henry had taken off his jacket and was holding it out in front of him, sneaking forward while Clara kept the duck distracted.

Softly, Clara said, "Now Henry." Henry lunged forward, covering the duck with his jacket, wrapping it up so it couldn't get hurt. "Good job!" Clara smiled.

"You kept him busy," Henry answered. They brought Papa Duck over to the crate and dropped him in, jacket and all. Tim held the crate cover open as Henry pulled back, and then Tim closed the crate.

"Now where is Mama?" Kate said.

"Over here," Clara said looking up at the lights above. "She's scared. Come on, Henry, lift me up there."

Clara climbed onto a table. Henry moved beside her and hunched low so she could get on his shoulders. Then he straightened up. "Okay, careful," Clara continued. "Walk me over." They walked toward where Mama duck was crouched on the light.

"Awww..." Clara said. "She's injured."

"Yes, she is, Ma'am," Tim said. "She flew in front of my bus. I think she's more scared, but yeah."

Henry said, "My coat's still in the crate. Johnson, give me your coat."

"What?" Lenny looked indignant.

"Give me your coat," Henry insisted. "You heard the judge. We've got to get these ducks out of here."

"Your Honor," Johnson turned to the judge.

Judge Bosscher sat up in his chair, glared at Johnson, and said, "Counselor. Give him your coat."

Reluctantly, Johnson removed his suit coat and held it out to Henry. Henry said, "No, pass it up to Clara."

Clara took the coat and slung it over her left shoulder. Then the VanTils moved closer to Mama Duck. "Come here, Darling," Clara said. "I know you're hurt. You're scared, and you don't have your babies around. Come on. Let Clara take care of you and see what's wrong. Come here."

Clara held out her right hand, and Mama Duck carefully leaned forward and tapped it with her bill. When the duck didn't pull away, Clara reached her index finger out and stroked the duck's chin behind the bill. "I know, you're in a strange place with strange people. Everything is strange. Come here. Come on."

Mama duck waddled a little closer. Very gently, Clara lifted the jacket with her left hand as she continued to stroke the duck's chin. Then, she draped the jacket over the bird. Mama duck quacked in panic, but Clara just kept stroking. "You're okay. Come on. Come on down." She wrapped the jacket tighter with both hands and pulled the duck off the light. "I've got her, Henry. Let me down."

Henry carefully walked back to the table and bent down so Clara could step off. Then, he held out his arms in a cradle, and she sat in them as he lowered her to the courtroom floor. The whole time Clara looked down at the duck's head sticking out from the jacket. "It's okay, girl. It's okay." She turned and smiled up at Henry.

"It's okay." Henry petted the duck through the jacket. "We got you. You're safe."

Judge Bosscher banged his gavel, and Mama Duck's head jerked. "Your Honor," Clara said, "please, she's scared enough as it is."

Judge Bosscher stood and glared. "This is my courtroom, not hers, Mrs. VanTil. Can we put the duck away and get on with things?"

"No, we can't, Your Honor," Clara said.

"Excuse me?" The judge's eyes blazed.

Henry turned to the judge, his arms still wrapped around Clara. "The duck is hurt, Your Honor. The others are frightened. We need to get them all to our clinic to take care of her."

"You what?"

"Your Honor," Clara said, "I have a patient. That has to come first."

"Yes, Your Honor," Henry said. "We have to take care of some things."

Kate looked at the judge. "Your Honor, I move for a continuance."

Bosscher looked at her. "Whatever will get you all out of my courtroom the fastest. Clerk, set a new date for them to pick this back up again."

Kate said, "Your Honor?"

"Yes, Counselor."

"Let's not set a date until we know we need it." She nodded towards the VanTils, who had carefully set Mama Duck in the crate. They bent over to calm the ducks inside. Henry's arm was around Clara's waist.

"I see your point, Counselor," the judge said. "No new date until further notice." One more time he banged his gavel. "Court is adjourned."

Kate relaxed. She wasn't sure if this would count as a win or a loss in her stats with the firm. She didn't think she'd ever seen a reconciliation in a divorce case before.

And, she didn't care. She had gotten through this without landing in the county jail for contempt. Considering how the day had gone, she'd count that a win.

The VanTils handed Lenny his jacket back, and then they sealed the crate. Together, they gently lifted it and carried it out of the court. Lenny followed close behind them with a sour look on his face.

That left Kate suddenly standing in the front of the court, alone save for Tim. She looked at him again: hair disheveled, a sheen of sweat on his brow, still half covered in mud and duck feathers. Not really her type.

Well, not her type now. Back in high school, he would've been quite a catch. These days, she was likely to be seen with a fellow lawyer. Or, a business exec: someone from insurance, banking, something like that. Somebody moving up in the world, not driving a bus.

She looked at those eyes, big brown eyes that had been filled with concern at the plight of ducks and the fears of children. He had done what he had to do to make things right.

Maybe he was her type after all. Someone who cared.

Kate noticed he was gazing at her with the same interest as she was gazing at him. "You know, somebody made me miss lunch, and I'm hungry."

"I'm sorry," Tim said.

"I'm inviting you to lunch. Interested?"

Tim looked around the courtroom. "I am, but this place is full of feathers and duck poop. It's a mess. I need to clean it up."

"No, you don't, Tim," Kate assured him. "They have people who take care of that. Don't you, Your Honor?"

"Yes, yes," Judge Bosscher said. "Now go." Then, he leaned forward over the bench. "Don't worry, Counselor, we'll get the cleanup done." Then, with a slight smile and a twinkle in his eyes, he added, "I'll put it on your bill."

THE END

Introducing Natalia Baird

Decades of unfinished stories led Natalia Baird to develop her futuristic universe, Piodenverse, where magic and science coexist. Natalia's first published novella, "The Gift of Fire," is a science fantasy, romantic interlude involving two characters from a larger work. The story is set in our future, on an Earther-colony world that marries futuristic technology to a renaissance festival feel. Heroine Nic reincarnates into life after life with one goal: have children each time, and raise them to their mid-teens. Only this action will make amends for the tragedy to which she had contributed. Determined to continue earning redemption, Nic sets out in this latest life to find a parenting partner she can enjoy until she must leave for her next life. Then, Nic meets Damyl, and their instant connection challenges her resolve. Will true love prevail, or will Nic answer the call of duty and break both their hearts?

Check DracorvusArts.com for more information on Natalia's endeavors.

Heat Level: HOT

THE GIFT OF FIRE
Natalia Baird

20 March, Ostara, Vernal Equinox
314 years After Founding; 2705 Old Earth Common Era
Planet Verda, Earth Colony SG-05
Sethrenya Galaxy, Sector SG-372-VDE01

She had a body again. Pulsing blood woke newly formed flesh, distracting her as she adjusted to being corporeal once more, to the solid heaviness.

She shifted in her nest of hot ash, curled in a fetal position, cradling a smoldering inferno in her womb. Her bare skin brushed against the silky substance which woke the neurons of her new body to the feeling of touch.

I am here. Having thoughts was weird, but the woman's sense of self developed moment by moment along with awareness of her body.

But who am I? And where is here? Past lives emerged from the depths of her soul's memory until names and places whirled through her mind in a chaotic mess. The woman could feel her identity strain to a breaking point as it tried to accept them all. She teetered, searching for anything to steady herself, and she found a purpose all the lives had in common: the inferno in her womb was the center of her goal, her mission of atonement. She must pass that fire to three or four children. The woman clung to that duty, the need to make amends, using it to pull her sense of self into focus, and push away everything else until it was a muted clamor.

Eyes opened. Dark, but not dark. The fire within gifted

her colorless night vision. Familiar rough cave walls, streaked with multiple layers of soot, arched overhead like the inside of an egg. Her phoenix cave.

She rolled onto her back, stretching out arms, legs, and spinal column, sinuous movement introducing muscles, nerves, and tissues to the idea of coordinated motion. She was grateful she never had to reincarnate as other than human, never had to adjust to being alien.

Her mind tried to make comparisons to past bodies, starting with the most recent before careening off the receding memories of others. The woman exerted her will, settling the various images of herself into the past, distilling all physical comparisons to an acceptance of simple difference. Everything felt elongated. She must be larger than before.

A Tai Chi form rose from the depths of another life, and the woman put her new body through the dance-like movements, focusing on balance and fluid motion. During her performance of the martial art form, scenes from previous lives re-emerged. They were more orderly, this time, so the woman let them dart in and out of consciousness, gleaning what she needed before they settled into the past. Threads of deep sadness, and matching ones of hope and determination ran through all her lives. The loss of her children was tempered by the faint connections she could still feel with them, and a certainty that she would see them again. Releasing knowledge of her past parenting partners hurt, but she was soothed by a surety that it was all for a higher good. Bearing her children, as often as she was brought into being in her phoenix cave, was a duty she believed in with all her soul.

Details of past lives continued to blur as they were relegated to dreams and echoes of memories, and the woman did not resist the process. She would still be able to use previously learned skills and knowledge in her new life, but she would have no idea of their origins. For sanity, and to remain hidden, she needed to stay anchored in the present.

Using the motion of the Tai Chi form to enhance mindfulness, she watched her arms and hands as they passed before her, felt the shift and play of torso and legs, learning the new shape of bones, longer and broader than before.

The woman ended the form, pleased with the way her new body responded. Ashy fingers trailing over her skin discovered an oval face, defined cheeks, broad jaw and chin, a prominent but not beaky nose, wide full lips, a high forehead. Hair...silky, fine but thick, about shoulder length. Pulling a strand forward showed medium dark hair she assumed would be some shade of red in daylight.

She moved towards the cave's flame-shaped exit. On the ground nearby was a pile she knew contained provisions, and information defining her background for this time around. As she stared down at items that would be the starting point for who she'd become, a chill breeze snaked into the cave. Though she was naked, it did nothing to quench the heat radiating from the woman's womb, the heat that meant cold was never an issue.

A large static cleansing cloth was on top of the provisions pile, charged to attract dirt, allowing cleansing with no water. She wiped herself down, removing ash from body and hair. Next, she donned the clothing, including socks and low boots, custom fit to her long, broad feet.

Below the clothing, the woman found a rectangular, beautifully carved wooden box; a dark, fitted jacket; and a bag. The box she knew—it was present in each life and fit familiarly in one hand. She traced well-worn knotwork carved into a band around the edges of the lid, and a triple spiral of interconnected life around a stylized flame at the lid's center. The sides and bottom were satin smooth, cool, and comforting to her fingertips.

Within the box was her gold bangle, also present in every life, the metal twisted into a never ending Möbius strip. She could feel its etchings and knew the theme of knotwork and flames was continued. Absently, the woman pushed it onto her right wrist, working harder than expected to get it over her hand.

In the box, beneath the bangle, was a bio link disk that connected her to this life's computer, and accessed the Universal Datalinkers Web. Pressing it to the back of her neck just below her hairline, she flicked her fingertip across it five times, activating the molecular bonding, and it sealed itself to her flesh. Though she felt nothing, she knew the bio-disk was creating sensory neuro-connections between her and the computer that would allow her to experience sound and vision in her head.

Soon a light flashed, and a gender-neutral voice said, "Welcome to Rethuter's Artificial Intelligence systems. For a complete user experience, registration and full sensory calibration are recommended. Customizing user settings will also improve your AI experience."

The light and voice in her head appeared to surround her in the cave.

Curious about her voice, she spoke out loud, instead of silently forming the words. "Guest use to begin. Full set up later." Her voice sounded odd. Deeper, fuller, melodic. She liked it.

The computer's AI responded. "Guest account activated. You have a one-week trial use before registration is required."

"Activate Phoenix File." She was getting used to the way her new voice resonated in her head.

"Voice and neural imprint recognized. Accessing file."

An optical screen appeared, again visible only to her,

remaining in place no matter how she moved or turned her head. Currently, she could see the cave through it but could make it opaque if she chose.

A virtual file folder soon floated in front of her eyes, and the woman reached for it. The AI system followed her movements, translating them into actions in her computer. When she reached into the field, took the folder and opened it, it opened on the screen. There were several documents, and the file names began to give her the skeleton of her new life. Nicallea Brighe. Planet Verda. 2705 OECE. She opened the first document, Nicallea Brighe.

The woman scanned the document briefly, then her eyes stopped, trapped by the phrase, "Orphan of Athracian Aggression." Her throat and chest tightened when she read the words. Shoulders curled forward, hunching her over. She hugged her arms around her middle, driven by some impulse to protect the fire within.

Fractured images crashed through her brain, kaleidoscopic pieces of memories playing on the screen of her mind's eye, giving her a wild emotional ride. Trying to sort the chaos, the woman dropped to her knees and slumped forward, her crossed arms pressed between thighs and belly.

Ship-to-ship space battles. Hand-to-hand fights. Fleeting impressions showed beings from multiple races working together, fighting for their lives inside ships. Most were overwhelmed, losing to the vicious attackers.

She curved her back farther, pressing her forehead hard against her legs, grinding her teeth, ignoring the cave floor bruising her knees. A weight settled on her heart, and a growl rose in her throat. The woman recognized the enemy: aggressive, hive-minded Athracians. Their race ruthlessly attacked outsiders to prevent their own hives from decimating each other. Her heartrate doubled, laboring against the weight,

sending blood to pound in her temples. The growl burst free
and grew as her torso and gut tensed. Her hands clenched on
forearms pressed hard against her legs.

Only then did the woman identify the weight lying
heavily on her heart. In some unknown fashion, she'd been
responsible for those slaughtered. Her stomach twisted,
becoming leaden, and a vice-like grip tightened around her
chest. Heat flushed through her, then drained, taking her
strength with it. She rocked forward and back, huddled over
her knees, keening, and tears soaked the fabric of her pants.
Memories continued, cutting into her as they whirled like
broken mirror shards in a typhoon.

More death and destruction. Protections peeled away.
Sundered pieces of her soul. Having to run, to hide. Being
hunted.

The woman gritted her teeth, pushing her forehead
harder into her knees. Cutting off the keening, she gasped for
breath, squeezing her arms around herself. If she couldn't take
control, she couldn't succeed. The thought of her duty brought
a small measure of hope, and the woman clung to it. Her soul
was certain she was on her path to redemption. All she needed
to do in this life was stay hidden, and bear and raise her
children.

The weight on her heart lifted, the grip on her chest
eased, and the woman's breathing evened out. She was here
because she had agreed to it as her way of making amends.

The woman unfolded, sitting up, resting back on her
heels to consider what she had learned. The lack of details
made her brow wrinkle, but it smoothed back out when she
remembered the sense of being hunted, of hiding. Whoever was
doing this, sending her from life to life, had left her ignorant for
safety and secrecy. She would honor that and let these
memories go, just as she did her past lives.

As the memories receded, the ache in her soul eased. She didn't want it to ever fully go away, but she let the pain fade to the background for this interlude, this life she would gladly live, knowing she was in her proper place, doing all she could.

The woman uncrossed her arms, resting hands in patches of ash to either side of her thighs, realizing she would need to clean off, again. She stood and rolled shoulders and neck to release tension before retrieving the cloth. While she wiped herself down, she forced her eyes to continue scanning the optical screen, committing details from the document to memory. It was an unremarkable, easy to remember life they had created for her, as Nicallea Brighe. Being an orphan of Athracian Aggression meant she was one of millions. And while she wasn't actually an orphan, her memories of the Athracian attacks made her glad it was a status few beings were insensitive enough to poke at.

The woman considered the rest of the file's information. Nicallea Brighe had been created as a twenty-two-year-old human—a mixed bag genetically, but full human, no modifications. She didn't have magic controlling abilities, but she did have psychic genes—pyrogenetic and pyrokinetic. Nicallea Brighe, as with all of the woman's personas, was one of the rare humans who had the genetic code for creating and controlling fire.

The woman read further, finding that as Brighe, she'd recently arrived on an Earth-type planet, Verda, the fifth Earther colony settled in Sethrenya Galaxy. She'd recently completed general studies at Sethrenya Nexus University, after growing up in a Solist orphanage, dedicated to the Divine Energy Form Sol, where she and children of all races were trained in their pyro talents.

Her credit balance provided enough for six months of living, including setup of a modest home. She was on her own after that, but the file also contained links to apply for registration and licensing with the Compact of Enlightened Beings as a level seven pyrogen and level nine pyrokin. Once registered, she could earn a living working in any number of fields related to fire generating and controlling. Truly, she had everything needed to start her life and eventually see her children safely through their growth.

The woman closed her eyes a long moment, centering her breath, watching internal flames dancing on her eyelids. She let the information settle into her being, giving her formless self an outline. She would fill in details as she lived.

The woman addressed the first detail. Her name was Nicallea. She tried out short forms. Nic. Cally. Lea. No, she definitely felt like a Nic.

The Universal Datalinker's web showed the Universal date as 2705 Old Earth Common Era, OECE, and planet Verda's local time and date as 00:48, 21 March, 314 AF. It was Spring Equinox, 314 years after the founding of the colony.

A quick search through the file on Verda told her it had been terraformed, making it a copy of Earth in species and climate, with different land and water masses. Verda was also Earth-sized and had a yellow sun, so it had the same seasons and year as Old Earth. Nic looked forward to living on it. From faintly remaining impressions of her previous homes, it had been a while since she'd lived on an Earth norm planet.

She closed the files and optical screen, tucked the box and folded cloth into the bag, alongside necessities and a clothing change. Enough background was acquired, it was time for action. A final glance around her egg-shaped phoenix cave confirmed she had everything. Another chilly breeze came in, reminding her it was the Spring Equinox. She was not surprised she had reincarnated when day and night were balanced, before day tipped the scales. No matter where or when she ended up, she always regenerated in early spring, starting her lives in sync with the time of germination and the emergence from winter months.

Nic slung the bag over her shoulder and ran a hand through her hair, which made her realize that was a habit from an old life she probably wouldn't need. Her new hair, fine and straight, would rarely need smoothing, or adjusting. Settling on a head shake as her new hair motion, she faced the cave's exit. Though she was never cold, Nic pulled on the jacket to better blend in. A deep breath of the air brought in by wind flooded her nose with the sharp wet smell of land newly woken from winter, the promise of growing things and rain.

She squared her shoulders, settling feet firmly onto the ground. She was Nic. It was time to go see her new home and find out who Nic was.

***

30 April—1 May, Beltane, May Day, 314 AF / 2705 OECE
Planet Verda, Earth Colony SG-05
Sethrenya Galaxy, Sector SG-372-VDE01
Six Weeks Later

Damyl studied the chunk of wood, smoothing rough planes with fingers that sensed more than the surface, tracing lines of cell growth, patterns that begged him to incorporate them into design. Yet another soft chime triggered by a customer entering his store barely registered. Festival days, like today, brought tourists in droves to the original parts of cities on Verda, in search of an Old Earth-type experience. But even though there were more of them, they still wandered his store, checking out his unique carvings and seasonal offerings, and often never needed his assistance

He was proud of how he'd constructed his life. He'd chosen a storefront in Old Levrinton, the original medieval-style city, to allow himself to be creative, and earn a living at the same time. His choice really paid off, when tourists swarmed the planet, looking for Old Earth-style pagan celebrations.

As in other original cities on Verda, tourists were drawn to the novelty of the Old Earth-style buildings and twisting streets. Old Levrinton was one of many cities built early in Verda's development, when the colony charter held more sway. The charter required Old Earth-style architecture and city planning from Medieval or Renaissance periods, and Levrinton's sponsor, Arturo Levrin, had chosen a hodgepodge of Medieval European styles for his inspiration.

Old Levrinton's visual charm fed Damyl's muses far more than the modern city that had grown up around it, but he was glad the charter had only concerned itself with appearances. There were no restrictions on technology, as long as it was disguised, so he'd been able to use up-to-date technology to make his store simpler to manage. Customers could learn about him and his work by uploading holos and data sheets, and different tech made purchasing simply a matter of syncing AIs for credit transfer. His store included a workspace near the back where he could carve and still be present for those beings who wished to speak to him. It also let curious ones watch him work.

Comfortably ensconced at his workbench, with a trace awareness of a few beings who might be watching, Damyl turned the piece of wood once more, selected hand tools, and dug in without hesitation to free the statuette within. Two bodies—locked in passionate embrace. The familiar work did not prevent his mind from having other thoughts.

Beltane was today's festival. Bel Teine, bright fire. Halfway between Spring Equinox and Summer Solstice, it was also known as May Day. Beltane was one of his favorite holidays; he had always been drawn to fire.

All his life, he'd had dreams of fire, of being part of something much bigger than himself, and of being ripped from it. He would wake, feeling hunted, but determined not to give in to the terror. He was certain that if he stayed safe, he would make his way back to the fire at the end of his life. Whispered conversations with his siblings, instinctively kept secret, confirmed they all experienced the same thing, but none of them knew details.

Damyl rubbed a finger across the wood he carved, taking comfort in its smoothness. He'd had one of the dreams the night before, the first one in quite a while, and its echoes ricocheted, dredging up thoughts and memories he hadn't considered in ages. It also made him wonder if something was wrong with one of his sisters or his brother.

He focused on the carving, using it as a meditation to calm his mind before searching within for the glowing ember connections with his siblings. Relief bubbled out of him in a sigh when he felt all three of them. Then, confusion rose when he felt a strange energy flutter in his senses. It was hard to define, no matter how he approached it, and nothing he'd seen before, though it felt vaguely familiar.

He considered the familiar connections, again, and thought about the attenuated, nurturing connection he could find, if he were to look hard enough, if his mind was centered enough. When his mother was alive, it had been far more robust. He didn't even try to find it at this point, the store was enough of a subliminal distraction that he wouldn't be able to.

The new energy was different from any of them. Damyl wished it was a connection with his father, but no matter when he tried, he'd never felt an energetic connection with him, or anyone other than his siblings and mother, for that matter.

Damyl's father had loved his wife, giving his all to his

family, and when she died, he'd been grief-crazed. He was now out in the universe, somewhere. He checked in every once in a while, but he was effectively out of their lives.

More memories of Damyl's youth surfaced, driving away thoughts of the strange wispy energy. He selected another carving tool for a different detail, and let the memories come; if he didn't spend time reminiscing after one of those dreams, they'd haunt his subconscious for days.

He'd been fourteen when his soul had awoken as an independent being, and the dreams began to move into his waking consciousness as foggy memories. They'd never become very clear, just enough that he realized his fascination with fire had roots he could barely fathom, and that at the end of his life he would somehow rejoin the fire. The memories had also cleared enough that when his mother died shortly after his awakening, he'd hoped the faintly remaining connection with her meant they would see her again, when he and his siblings rejoined the fire.

He'd carried an extra burden when their mother died, because he couldn't shake the feeling that his awakening, as the youngest child, was what had made her leave them. Damyl looked blindly at the wood in his hand as guilt tried to settle on him again. He shook his head, taking a deep breath, loosening the tight ball that had appeared in his chest, reminding himself he truly believed it was all for a greater good.

His father's sister, who'd come to care for them when his father had broken down, had been instrumental in setting him on the path to self-forgiveness. Damyl smiled at the thought of Aunt Hannel. She'd done her best and had succeeded in giving them a loving, secure home. She'd known nothing of how they were different, just that their mother had died There was an unspoken pact between the siblings to keep it that way.

Even in ignorance, Aunt Hannel had been able to

counsel a grieving youth. She was the one who'd helped him understand that some things fit a pattern larger than a single being could see. Her perspective had triggered much soul searching and consideration of the dreams and foggy memories, allowing him to find the certainty he needed. He'd spent years sifting through information, letting it settle into pattern, and had finally felt secure in accepting that even if his maturation had triggered his mother's leaving, he was not at fault. It was simply part of a larger plan that he and his siblings had agreed to at some point.

Over the years he had speculated about what it all meant, he'd developed theories, which he had no way of proving or disproving, but which still felt right. The connection from his mother had fed a raging torrent of fire energy to him as a young child. To this day, fire made him feel loved, safe, and energized, all aspects that fed his flame fascination.

As a young teen, once his soul awoke, the energetic flow from his mother had dropped to a warm simmer, and then, when she died, to the faint trace it was now. Looking back, he figured the fire energy had nurtured what he now considered to be his soul's egg, a seed pod. He thought his soul might be a reincarnation, coiled within his child's body, fed by his mother, until it opened as he matured.

He was fairly confident on what he had theorized, but the how or why were more challenging. An extreme, visceral response to seeing a vid-report of an Athracian attack had been followed by a period of intense dreams, and he'd guessed the vicious hive race had been involved in his own history. But details remained frustratingly unknown. Eventually, the need for secrecy he and his siblings had long acknowledged overrode his desire for answers, and he stopped speculating, and just lived his life, knowing it would all come clear in the end.

Damyl turned the emerging statuette to get a better carving angle, and let the memories fade, glad they'd run their course. He lost himself in carving, determinedly ignoring the wistfulness that wished for someone with whom he could share the hidden part of his life.

A customer cleared their throat, and he reluctantly put the statuette aside, before swiveling toward them on his seat. Looking up, he was ensnared by vivid brown eyes. He could see the flames deep within irises set in the largest eyes he'd ever seen, but they were balanced by a broad strong face. Rich, deeply red hair, artfully cut in layers that shifted with her every movement, framed the face. Her tanned skin had a hint of brown common in the mixed genes so prevalent after humanity moved to the stars, and it covered lean muscle that shifted enticingly when she moved.

His soul perked up, and his fingers itched to touch. Surprised by the instant attraction, he tucked his hands into his apron pocket, setting them to playing with wood shavings found there. Right on the heels of that urge, he realized the weird energetic flutter within his soul, near the connections to his family, was stronger. Nothing solidified when he tried to pinpoint it, other than a surety that it was decidedly different than his other connections.

A moment later, he realized he was staring, and a flush rose to his cheeks. She seemed amused rather than offended, thankfully, a twist of her wide, lush lips revealing humor.

He coughed. "Ah. Sorry. Welcome to Tienecrann Crafts. What can I do for you?"

She tilted her head, "Is that how you say that?" She copied him, shaping the word carefully. "Tcheenakrahn. Hmm. What language is that, and what does it mean?"

Her throaty voice gave him goosebumps, and there was an exotic edge to her accent he couldn't place. Further interest

213

rose. He knew she could have retrieved the information from her computer AI but chose to ask him, instead.

He replied readily, intrigued, and more than willing to converse with her, though he kept his hands in his apron pocket, to be safe. "It's Old Earth Scots Gaelic. Tiene means fire, and crann means tree, among other things"

"Fire Tree Crafts. I like that. And your logo makes sense, now. I love the tree with fire tongues for leaves." She smiled, glancing around the store. "You definitely have fire's passion in your wood carving. You're very talented."

Her gaze swung back to him, and Damyl felt judged, then absurdly happy when she nodded approvingly. She held out an arm, decorated with a single gold bangle. He could see it twist in a Möbius strip, with tiny etchings. The bangle shifted as she turned her hand palm up, opening fingers to reveal a small pale wood carving of lovers consumed in flames nestled in her palm. It was one of a series made from a storm-culled batch of rowan wood he'd foraged.

He had loved working with the wood. For the series he'd carved lovers, freeing each pair from the branch's embrace. Then, he turned them into minuscule boxes. The joining between lid and base was concealed in folds of limbs carved from the rowan wood's outer tan and white layers. The inner chamber was dark with the deep red-brown heartwood, and just large enough to hold the smallest of love tokens. He liked that in Celtic tradition the rowan was a tree of protection and healing. He'd also used the wood for less provocative carvings.

Her fingers ran over the lovers' curves, bringing his mind back to her as she said, "I'm getting this one. You create exquisite detail, and based on your description, rowan wood is perfect for me." She paused, then asked, "Do you know where the best Beltane celebrations are for tonight? I'm new to this planet."

He looked at her consideringly. He was rarely forward, but this woman called to him, to his soul, and to his body. The flames in her eyes, the strange sense in the area usually reserved for his family, his frankly carnal response to her, it all made him frantic at the idea of letting her out of his store without knowing he could explore that more.

He hoped he kept his voice calm as he offered, "I usually go to a local festival behind Old Levrinton, within walking distance of here. Well, it's a bit of a long walk, about forty-five minutes at a leisurely pace. Our festival's not elaborate, but we have massive bonfires, and there are vendors, musicians, good beings of all sorts," he paused, leaving off mentioning the handy woods. They invited beings to slip away from the firelight and go A-Maying, celebrating fertility, love, and union in private.

Meeting her gaze with what he hoped was the proper level of interest and friendliness, he said, "You're welcome to join me."

He hoped the long walk wouldn't scare her off and considered offering to find transportation. But, the comfortable sandals and the muscles he'd noticed in her legs argued it wouldn't, and he decided it was better to know now, since he loved to hike.

She tipped her head to the side again, her silky hair sliding to echo the movement in a way that made him ache to run his fingers through it. She looked him up and down, considering him in the way he'd hoped she would. A slow smile, much more sensual, slid across her face, and he stifled a groan, hoping desperately his work apron would hide his body's approval.

The smile grew mischievous, and he figured she read his interest anyway. Damyl also guessed that interest was returned when she lowered her head a bit to watch him directly, and the flame in her eyes grew.

Her voice was deeper and huskier when she replied, "A forty-five-minute walk, with my own local guide to whatever parts of the old city we go through? Yes, I think I'd like that, if you promise to tell me what we're passing, and any interesting facts you know. I'm Nic, by the way, Nic Brighe." She glanced down at the sign on his counter. "You're Damyl Kinaed, proprietor?"

He laughed, shaking his head, standing to hold out his hand, relieved to have an excuse to touch her. "Yes, pardon my manners. It's good to meet you, Nic Brighe."

He was taller by several inches, but she didn't seem small to him. In fact, as she took his hand, her heat scalded beautifully into him, and the well-muscled grip was a comfort. This woman would be a partner in life.

When she touched him, the energy sharpened, making him realize it came from her. The heat from her hand triggered other memories. A frisson of concern shook him as his mother had burned that same way. He frantically compared the clarified energy connection to those with his family then let out a deep sigh, his shoulders relaxing. He was still certain of their difference. She only resembled his mother in the way she radiated heat.

He became aware of a look of concentration on her face as she held his hand, as if she were listening to something. A moment later, she shook her head, smiling, and eased her grip. Damyl reluctantly released her, thrilled when she trailed fingers across his palm as she let go.

He regathered thoughts scattered by her touch, then turned to the details of that evening, saying, "I live above my store, so I usually get ready and walk from here. If you want to go with me, I'll close up early, leave around five. We could get dinner at one of the vendors. And I would love to be your tour guide."

"Yes, dinner and your festival sound good, Damyl." His name on her tongue did nothing to calm his body.

He watched her look around the store, obviously in no hurry to leave. She wore a sleeveless V-neck green dress with a flowing skirt that hit just above her knees, embroidered in almost the same shade of green. The outfit seemed Beltane-celebration ready and showcased her slender strength well. Understated makeup highlighted strong cheeks, generous lips, and those stunning eyes.

The gold bangle was her only jewelry, but she had a wide, white scarf with embroidered flames and silver knotwork that looked like it could double as a wrap if it got cooler this evening. Of course, he'd love to help keep her warm, if she even got cold. He wondered about that, remembering that his mother never seemed to feel the cold.

He glanced at his watch, three o'clock, and mentally shrugged. She was enough to make him favor spending time with her rather than the wood that had held his interest moments before. "Would you like to sit? If you have nowhere you need to go, you're welcome to wait here."

He was rewarded with a wide smile. "That sounds lovely."

He invited her to sit in a space near his work bench, where he hosted friends, family, and customers alike. He made tea, and in between customers who needed him, he chatted with her. Their discourse flowed as easily as it did with his long-time friends, and laughter was frequent as they went through the verbal dance of getting to know each other.

Under the laughter, though, Damyl got a growing sense of seriousness, of drive and goals in life, and a tinge of something that made him think she'd experienced loss. He was frequently struck by how mature she seemed for her twenty-two years. When she told him she was an orphan, from an Athracian attack, he decided that was what he was seeing. His own response to the first vid he'd seen featuring an Athracian attack had been overwhelming, and that was just based on dreams and shadowy memories. He didn't want to think what it would be like for someone who'd experienced it this life.

Damyl finished helping a customer, glanced around to make sure no one else needed him, then turned back to his guest. The embroidered flames on her scarf caught his attention. He commented on them and the heat he'd felt from her handshake. Soon, he and a handful of customers were the recipient of a well-controlled fire show as she generated a small fire and made it dance.

Damyl sat back, watching the flame twist and turn through a hanging wooden mobile he'd spent weeks on, wondering at his utter confidence in her skill, that he had no worries at all. It probably stemmed from his mother's expert handling of flames, he mused. Long experience with his mother's talent meant he recognized Nic's skill and control from the beginning.

He was glad he'd dealt with his frustration about not being a pyro long ago. The gene was recessive, and though his mother had it, no one in his father's line did, so he and his siblings didn't. Although, if he and Nic were to have children— Damyl cut the thought off as premature. He urged his wandering mind to just enjoy her show and take things in the order they appeared.

A second flame joined the first, lean muscles in her arms tensing as she controlled the fire, hands swirling around each other, gold bangle shifting up and down her wrist. He applauded her performance, joined by the customers. "That is so beautiful! I am truly impressed. Nic, you are an artist!"

She dispersed the flames and dipped her torso in a half

bow from her seat. "Thank you, thank you, very much. I do festivals, weddings, funerals, and private parties." She laughed. "Well, not really, but I probably could."

He stood up to answer a customer question, and when he returned, she shrugged, saying, "And I might perform, if I get bored with my land management job. They send me out to make sure undergrowth in possible burn sections is properly cleared. I have a team of workers to coordinate, and they call me in if a burn is needed."

Damyl nodded. "That's good. I remember one year; a bit wasn't managed right. A lightning storm started a fire that took hours to get under control, even with top tech in play." He looked sideways at her. "You must be pretty strong, for them to have you doing that?"

She nodded, matter-of-factly. "Yeah. The Compact of Enlightened Beings rated my fire generation, and elimination, at level seven, and fire control at level nine."

He whistled. "Nice! So why are you here? You could have just about any job, any place you wanted. And you strike me as an adventurous sort."

She shook her head. "It's not what speaks to me." Shrugging, she continued, fingering her bracelet. "I'm only twenty-two, but I know I want a family—three or four children. A settled home, a place to explore from and return to. Any job I hold will be to support that, to keep me from being bored, and to help others, but it will always be secondary."

He smiled, nodding. "That sounds perfect. I'm already thirty, and I think it's about time for me, too."

They shared a speculative look. Damyl hid a grin at the idea he might actually find out whether their children would have pyro abilities. He also wondered again at the similarities to his mother but could find no way to introduce that topic. A moment later, he jumped as the alarm he'd set earlier spoke in his ear, telling him it was time to close up and get ready for the evening.

Nic laughed when he told her this, and he grinned sheepishly, shrugging. "I get lost in my carving, and I didn't want to miss out on tonight. I need to go upstairs, shower, change. You're welcome to wait for me here or up there."

She stood with alacrity, grinning. "Let's go up. I want to see your place."

He laughed, shaking his head. He herded the few remaining customers through their purchases, encouraging them to find the central square festivities and shop at the vendors there. He set security for evening, lights dimming, then headed to the back, followed by Nic.

"Up here." He gestured at a wooden staircase that rose along a side and back wall. She preceded him, fingers trailing sensually along the satin smooth wood of the railing he'd carved himself. Damyl watched her hand, his mind easily making the leap to wondering what it would feel like trailing over his flesh. His gaze moved down her back, appreciating its curves, settling on the bare backs of her legs. Her ankles, calves, knees, and lower thighs were visible beneath the loose skirt, moving in concert, muscles and tendons tightening and relaxing as she climbed. He kept his hands resolutely to himself, resisting the urge to touch her smooth flesh until she allowed it.

The top of the staircase opened into a wide room with exposed, rough-cut wooden beams crisscrossing the ceiling. He dragged his gaze from her legs, holding his breath as he watched her look around, hoping she'd find it agreeable. A chuckle almost escaped him at the thought that he was acting like the bird that invites a potential mate to view his nest.

He looked at the room, trying to see it as she would. One side held a low couch and two chairs, and windows overlooking the street below. A desk with shelves and cupboards to either side was midway down the long wall. The other side of the room had his dining table and chairs, china hutch, and galley kitchen. Scattered around were display cases, more shelves, and storage units. Much was wood carved by him, set off with deep jewel-tone colors, and a few strong patterns. It seemed a good space to him, and he hoped she'd appreciate it, too.

She walked around the room, touching, looking, spending time over a few items, and finally turned to him, nodding. "Yes, this is nice."

He tried to keep his deep sigh silent. She liked it.

She found his image frame, and flicked her eyes toward him for permission before flipping through pictures. "These are very good! Well-framed, and the detail is amazing."

"Thank you. I take them while hiking. Most are from within a few hours of here."

She glanced at him. "I hope you and I can go visit some of these places. I do enjoy hiking, too."

He grinned. "I would love to show you." Then, his stomach reminded him it had been a long time since lunch. He gestured to the only door in the room. "Do you need the facilities before I use them?"

She nodded. "Yes, that would be good."

"Through the door, to the right."

She vanished for a long moment, then re-emerged, looking more relaxed. "Your turn. I'll just watch the street until you're ready." Damyl watched her go to the windows and stare down, evidently drawn by the bustle of beings passing by below. He was caught, for a moment, by the beauty of sunlight glinting off her hair then shook himself free and went to get ready.

***

Nic heard Damyl go into the other room, but she kept staring down at the narrow, gently curving street in front of his store, letting her gaze drift with the colorful eddies and swirls of beings from all over the Universe moving along it. It created a restive backdrop while she thought.

She liked this city, Levrinton. There was a thriving commerce, and its citizens and visitors appeared to live in relative peace. She had only been here six weeks, but she had an apartment in the new, modern part of the city and a job working at something that was as easy and pleasant to her as breathing.

Her life was good, and now the drive to start her family was turning up the heat. Literally. The temperature of her body had crept up, notch by notch, as the weeks went on. Before today, though, she had met no one, no being who'd sparked more than a cursory interest—not man, woman, or other, human or alien. She'd even begun to wonder if she should just look for sperm donors. But she hadn't even met anyone she thought she could co-parent with, and she refused to do it alone.

Her thoughts turned to Damyl. He claimed thirty years. She let out a short laugh, thinking of the wood shavings and sawdust trapped in his shaggy brown curls and a round, cleanshaven face that kept him youthful looking. His age was evident, though, in his steady gaze. Whenever he looked at her with his hazel brown eyes, a pleasurable jolt ran through her, bringing her soul and nerves alive.

Nic gave a wolfish grin as she remembered the scrutiny with which he'd studied her in the store. Youthful he might look, but he definitely wasn't innocent. She anticipated exploring that interest.

When she'd taken his hand earlier, her soul had felt more complete, and the nebulous sensation that had drawn her into his store had clarified, becoming a faint energetic thread. Nic frowned at the thought of that energy. For a long moment, he'd reminded her of one of her children. She shook her head, resting her forehead against the window. Her relieved huff fogged the glass. Thankfully, a moment's concentration had shown her significant differences in detail. There was something about him her soul recognized, but the only similarity to her family consisted of a general energy feel, so she felt comfortable lusting after the man.

And. lust she did. Her vivid imagination had no problems supplying her with images of his preparations. She even knew what his bathroom looked like. She smiled and shook her head. Damyl seemed too good to be true.

He was fun to talk to, full of laughter, and there was some sort of recognition between them, already. She'd seen a look on his face when they'd grasped hands which made her certain he'd felt something, too. She briefly wondered if he sensed the same energy she did.

Their conversation, the flow of words and ideas, and laughter, had gone so naturally, so comfortably, it seemed like she already knew him. And, most importantly, he hadn't been scared off when she'd said she wanted children. And he was settled. The store below was proof of that.

Nic dampened her enthusiasm. She was almost convinced she'd found her partner in this life, but she shouldn't rush in without more facts. She set up a quick web search on her AI, requesting a background check to make sure he was as safe as he seemed. The search came back clean; Damyl looked eligible by report, as well. Beyond that, tonight would give her more information. Her pulse leapt at the thought, and the flame in her womb flared.

The bedroom door opened, and she turned from the window to see him emerge. His freshly scrubbed face, surrounded by wet hair that promised to spring into full curls as it dried, made her lips part, and cool air rush into her lungs. He'd gotten rid of the wood shavings. Her gaze traveled down his neck, and her eyes widened, the better with which to devour the sight of clinging fabric draped over muscular shoulders and upper arms.

He wasn't wearing a costume, like so many of those in the street. Given her simple dress, she was glad. His lightweight shirt was a patchwork of shades of green fabrics embroidered with silver Celtic knotwork. Her gaze traveled to well-corded forearms and broad, wood-roughened palms. Heat spread in a wave throughout her body, and her heartbeat increased as she thought about him touching her.

She ran her own palm up and down her arm, her eyes continuing their journey down his body, and pulled her lower lip between her teeth. He had tucked the shirt into dark green slacks with a black belt, setting off slim hips. Black sandals framed long feet with just a bit of hair. Her hand slid up her arm, and settled around the base of her neck, fingers rubbing the hollow behind her collar bone. Beneath her fingertips, her pulse beat strongly. Along with her sexual arousal, she still felt the flutter of energy she could almost recognize, the one that had drawn her into his store.

Something inside her solidified. Even if he wasn't the one for her full life here, he definitely seemed to be the one for the moment. Nic was confident they would deal more than well together, and she wanted to explore their connection—including whatever it was about him she recognized. She smirked. It also didn't hurt that he was alluring to look at, and her body liked him.

His hazel eyes were fixed on her, and as the intensity of his regard increased, she figured his body liked hers, too, and wondered if they would leave for the festival after all. Her breath hitched as she saw his tongue pass over his lips, leaving them glistening and parted. But, he simply held out his arm, and his voice remained light when he spoke. "Shall we go, My Lady? The festivities await our presence."

Nic laughed. "By all means, My Lord. I can't wait to see them!" Her body's arousal decreased to a low simmer. She could wait. Anticipation was good for intense sex.

She put her arm through his, automatically shifting the bangle so it rested comfortably between them. His skin was a lighter shade than hers, though it was obvious he spent time in the sun. Her high body temperature made him cool to the touch. She hugged his arm closely as they descended the staircase and left his store.

The narrow cobbled and bricked streets were noisy and chaotic, and she loved the festive mood and the finery she saw. Beings in Levrinton represented races from all over the Universe, of many shapes, sizes, and colors, and normally they were as varied in dress as the multitude of cultures they came from. While she was wandering before she found Damyl's store, the festival costumes she'd seen today had intrigued her enough that she'd done a web search. She'd found out most were inspired by various cultures from Old Earth's medieval and Renaissance periods, which made sense, considering Verda's colony charter. She was disappointed that she hadn't researched things well enough to get herself a costume. As they moved into streets full of beings in fantastic outfits, she was even more grateful Damyl had dressed simply, so she didn't feel like she'd made a faux pas.

Nic felt tension in the arm she held, but a sideways peek reassured her it was joyful. Damyl was looking around, a lift to his cheeks and eyebrows, and a twist to his mouth that make her think a grin was not far behind. He had almost a little boy air of anticipation to him. She liked that he seemed to enjoy being in the thick of the varied beings drawn to one of Verda's main pagan holiday celebrations.

Damyl cleared his throat, and she glanced toward him as they walked, daylight allowing her to see flecks of mossy green in the center of the greyish brown irises. Their sparkle exhilarated her, and she decided she couldn't have asked for her introduction to Old Levrinton to be with a better man.

He gestured at the intriguing mash-up of buildings around them. "Old Levrinton was sponsored by Arturo Levrin and was based on medieval towns of different countries from Old Earth's European continent."

Nic's world expanded as they walked. The immersive feel of being on the crowded streets, with the ancient looking buildings so near was totally different from her previous experiences on this planet. Levrinton's growth had happened after Verda's charter lost much of its power, and Nic's apartment was outside Old Levrinton's thick stone wall. The modern structures she saw near her home only showed the European cultures in touches reminiscent of medieval architecture, pagan details and carvings, and some tourist sites.

Damyl continued talking, and Nic enjoyed his patter. Even the bits she'd already learned were more interesting, coming from him. They traveled the maze of narrow, twisting streets, interconnected with small alleys, and he pointed out some of the famous, and infamous, storefronts, pubs, and homes. He shared legends and histories, and even a few ghost stories, as they passed through tunnel-like streets where buildings closely lined the roads, and only a limited amount of natural light entered.

Musicians and other performers created more texture for eyes and ears, with music and acts from many cultures. It was an enriching counterpoint to vendors and crowds. Individual buskers claimed spots along the way, and small groups held sway at squares. They paused their progress to enjoy a few, transferring credits to the buskers' accounts, and Damyl seemed to be right with her on appreciation of talents.

The so-called squares occupied junctions of multiple streets. Large, open, and broad, they were vastly different from the closed-in lanes and were rarely actually square. Restaurants and bars on the edges of squares took advantage of open space with outdoor seating, which was more often than not full. Fountains and statues with informative plaques could be seen beyond curious tourists, and more beings gathered in front of performers on temporary stages.

Smells filled the air as street vendors took advantage of festival permits to hawk Beltane wares and food. Mixed in among traditional Earther items, such as sweet breads and oatcakes, cheeses and yogurts, hearty soups, salads, nuts, and fruit, Nic could see vendors who catered to more exotic needs of beings from alien races unable to consume Earther foods.

She was drawn to several different vendors, sniffing the aromas, as her stomach growled, but he laughed and pulled her back on track.

When she snarled at him, he dodged in mock fear, then patted her arm. "No, really. These are probably decent, but I have a favorite vendor I want you to try. Trust me, you'll be glad you waited."

She shook her head, but gave up trying to steer him, and just enjoyed the walk. He explained Levrinton had a main festival in the massive new city government square and a smaller one in Old Levrinton's central square that drew most of the visitors. As they walked, the crowds thinned out, music faded away, and a few of the streets were actually empty. He turned down one of the empty streets, their footsteps echoing as they walked, and they soon came to a gated archway leading through a thick stone wall.

Nic had been tracking their progress on the mental map she'd created and knew they were at the back of Old Levrinton, looking at the city wall.

Damyl confirmed that. "Through this gate is a bit of land that was reserved to be garden plots for the original inhabitants. Beyond the gardens is Levrin Forest. Their protection is why modern Levrinton is a half-circle; the modern part grows in an arc away from here. These lands all have to be maintained, kept free of buildings, and there are even still gardens in some of the plots." He glanced at her. "I have a small one, mostly vegetables."

Nic tilted her head. Every new aspect he revealed made her appreciate him more. "Hmm. It's been a long time since I've tried to grow anything, but I'd be glad to give it a try." She was rewarded by his slow smile.

In her job managing land to minimize fires, she had been assigned a sweep on the far side of Levrin Forest but hadn't yet reached the city side. Damyl opened the gate in Old Levrinton's wall and waved her through into the full sunshine of a spring afternoon. After he closed the gate, she took his arm again, and said, "It's going to be nice to just be in a forest, in the country, and not have to work."

His hand rested solidly over hers on his arm. She enjoyed the coolness of his skin as they passed between the sunny fields and he pointed out his small patch of land, with about ten rows of produce. Soon, they moved into the shade of the forest, and she caught a hint of more music.

The music, and cheerful shouting and calling from celebrants, grew louder as they walked broad paths deeper into the forest. She heard mostly instrumental Celtic music, with some vocals, but there was a mix that came from generations of Earthers living and learning with races far different from their own. All of it was joyous, welcoming spring and new growth.

The sun was still hours from setting as the wheel of seasons turned towards the longest day of Midsommar, so she could see the gathering as they approached. It was held in a glade about a hundred meters long, a wide lane colorfully lined with booths and vendors down the middle, as he'd promised. And while there were more humans here, over half the beings were diverse races of aliens. They crowded the space, though not as thickly as in the city.

Damyl paused, waving an arm. "Welcome, to Levrin Glade Community Festival Site."

They entered the mowed, grassy lane, walking past beings stacking a pile of wood. It was carefully arranged to maximize air flow and burn creating a truly spectacular bonfire that reached to the heavens. Down the lane, several more bonfires were being built, on larger and smaller scales. Each fire had a carefully cleared ring around it to prevent spread.

Damyl must have seen her look. "The smaller fires are set up for those who wish to jump over the flames, to purify themselves, and get the blessing desired."

Nic nodded. "I read about that; it sounds good."

She drank in the sight of beings dressed in finery as provocative as it was beautiful. Nic also eyed some of the amazing crafts in the booths as they walked. She had very few decorations in her apartment. The carving she'd bought from Damyl would sit by itself on the nightstand near her bed. A tent with drums caught her eye, making her pause.

Damyl looked from her to the booth. "Yes, Ankiney's work is beyond compare. You like drums?" At her nod, he said, "Let's eat, and then we can come back. You'll want to spend some time here."

She let herself be guided onward, agreeing with his thought when she saw more of the drums as they passed.

He stopped at a booth, and a tall, middle-aged woman

with bright, suspiciously familiar hazel eyes looked at her. The eyes widened and the woman rushed around the counter to engulf Damyl in a hug. "Damyl! Merry meet, and blessed be! So good to see you, lad!"

Damyl hugged her back, just as fiercely. "Aunt Hannel, merry meet, and blessed be! It's good to see you, too." Nic recognized the name. When she'd mentioned being an orphan, he'd told her about his aunt raising him during his teen years.

The woman pushed him away, turning him to better see. "You look well. And so happy." She turned to Nic. "Who is this? The source of that happiness?"

Damyl smiled. "I can hope, can't I, Aunt Hannel? This is Nic. We actually just met today, but she took me up on my offer to come here."

Nic found herself at the business end of an inspection like none other she'd had. Aunt Hannel evidently liked what she saw, because she smiled, and wrapped Nic in her strong arms. The smell of herbs and life hovered about her. After a moment of surprise, Nic returned the hug.

As they released each other, Aunt Hannel said, "My goodness, you're warm! I haven't felt someone as warm as you in a long time." She paused, peering at Damyl but shook her head, turning back to Nic. "No matter. Welcome, Nic, merry meet, and blessed be. It's an honor to meet you. Call me Aunt Hannel. That's a beautiful bracelet."

Nic glanced down at her wrist, turning the bracelet, automatically feeling along its etchings. "Thank you, Aunt Hannel. I've had it a long time."

Aunt Hannel nodded. "I'll tell you, you won't find a man better than our Damyl. He's a catch that's slipped away from many another, but I've never seen him as happy as he is now."

Aunt Hannel captured Nic's hand, then pulled Damyl in, and looked at them. She grew misty-eyed and nodded. "Yes.

This is good." Then she released them and turned. "But you're hungry, are you not? You'd not dare eat elsewhere—not tonight of all nights, would you?" Aunt Hannel's joking threat showed Nic where Damyl got some of his humor, and she watched him as he watched his aunt bustle about, getting them food. She recognized the fond love in his eyes, and felt her soul settle further into the rightness of being with him.

A short while later, she and Damyl sat at tables in the center of the lane, bread bowls of thick barley chicken stew in hand, farls in a basket before them. The farls were new to her— herbed fried potato and oat patties, but they worked well with the stew.

Beings walked by on either side of their table, which was midway between two bonfire sites. Nic's stomach argued with her mouth about the speed of consumption, but she managed to eat slowly enough to enjoy the rich complexity of the stew— garlic and sage the only herbs she recognized.

She became aware that Damyl was watching her, with almost the same fondness he'd had for his aunt. She cleared her mouth long enough to say, "Wow. Yes, this is amazing. Your aunt is a such a good cook, and I felt so welcomed by her. Thank you for making me wait!"

He leaned back with a satisfied smile, chewing his own food, clearly appreciating it. "You're welcome. It's made with chicken, barley, and herbs from her farm."

Nic looked up, making the connection. "Her farm—was that your old home?"

Damyl nodded. "Yes. I mentioned Aunt Hannel earlier, that she came to live with us after my mother was gone, when my father left. Aunt Hannel used to live in Levrinton, but she moved to the farm to care for the two of us still at home. I was fourteen, and my sister, Geollie, was sixteen. Aunt Hennel being there allowed the other two come home when they wanted. Banna and Granton are twins, six years older than me, and they had gone to college before mother died."

He paused for a moment, but Nic thought it was more to order his thoughts than because of sadness. Damyl looked over at his aunt's booth and smiled. "Aunt Hannel decided she liked it better at the farm, and stayed on, keeping it going. Now, she makes the trip to Levrin Glade for the warm weather festivals, to see old friends, and me, once I moved here."

Nic processed that, more pieces of Damyl slipping into place. "So, you grew up on a farm, and that's why you have the garden here."

He grinned. "Right, again. Having fresh vegetables is very important to me, and I'm fussy about how they taste."

Nic laughed. "I look forward to tasting them, then, if they're anything like this food!"

After their meal, Damyl grabbed her hand and pulled her back over to his aunt's stall. His thumb rubbed across her knuckles as they chatted with Aunt Hannel while she waited on customers. The woman noticed their joined hands, and smiled, but she never commented on it.

Damyl seemed oblivious as he asked his aunt, "How was your trip?"

"It went well, no problems with the van or trailer," Aunt Hannel said. "And I had a few old friends help with set up—it's true many hands make light work. And lots of laughter helps, too. It's good to see them. And you, Damyl. There's just a few hours between your shop and my farm, but it's hard to find time, isn't it?"

Damyl grimaced but nodded. "I'm glad you still make it over here, or I wouldn't see you much, at all."

Aunt Hannel smiled at them. "Well, and that's the way life is, sometimes. Now, give me a hug, and go enjoy yourselves. If I don't see you again tonight, we can meet for breakfast at the May pole and talk more tomorrow before I head home."

Nic and Damyl dove back into throngs of beings filling the lane, and Nic was glad they ended up right back at the drum maker's stall. The drums were just as enticing up close. She tried several, her rhythms triggering dancers, then decided on two. A deep voiced one, as tall as her waist that they lugged down to Aunt Hannel's stand to store. The other was smaller, higher toned, but still resonant and singing, with a strap that allowed Nic to carry it. She set it on her left hip, the right being reserved for Damyl, and positioned it so she could drum as desired.

Then, they wandered. They took in the music, with Nic playing along at times. Damyl greeted friends and neighbors, introducing her. At some point, their fingers interlaced, and their sides pressed together as they walked with their arms around each other. A juggler had Nic's attention when Damyl stopped at the center square of the lane. He released her hand and took a thin sheet from his pocket, unfolding it to spread on an unclaimed bit of ground near the piled wood for the main bonfire. The central square, like the lane, was mowed grass, with a space cleared and deep trench dug surrounding the fire.

Others were also staking spots near a small stage to one side between booths. Nic and Damyl settled down, the material providing a barrier between dampness and dirt and their finery. Nic put the drum to one side and gladly snuggled against Damyl when he held out an arm. They had a clear view of the stage, which had carvings so clever and detailed, Nic wanted to see them closer.

"Did you do those carvings? I'd love to go look at them."

Nic had to smother a grin when Damyl reminded her of a shy little boy as he admitted, "Yes. Those were some of my earlier pieces, but I am still happy with them, and everyone else seems to be, too. Go ahead, look. I hope you don't mind if I stay here?"

"Of course not." She got up, glad the material he'd laid down meant she didn't need to brush herself off.

She wasn't the only one inspecting the progression of carvings along the front of the stage. They followed a progression, left to right, through the seasons. She could see Samhain, or Halloween, themes on the left, winter, then spring, and summer holidays, ending with Mabon, or Autumn Equinox, on the right. The animals, fruits, people, gods and goddesses, and seasonal cues, all told a clearly seen story. Nic was once again drawn to the technical and artistic skill displayed.

At the front corners were two posts carved with female and male elements, and she figured these would be changed out for each specific holiday. This one, Beltane, featured spring, fertility, life. The post depicting the current male aspect of Divine Energy Force, had a shaggy-haired man with horns, and greenery curving all over. There was a stylized sun corona behind the man's head, and forest animals parading along the edges in with Celtic knotwork and more greenery. She saw lovers peeping out from leaves as well, and barely disguised phallus symbols.

She walked back to the other corner to see the female representation of Divine Energy Force, pausing on the way to watch beings erecting a tall May pole in the glade outside the line of booths, behind the stage. There was a ring of greenery and flowers at the pole's top, and long red and white ribbons were carefully controlled while they planted it deep in the ground. She looked forward to the morning dance around it, winding ribbons into a symbolic womb. When she'd researched Beltane earlier, that tradition had spoken to her.

She continued on to the stage corner post representing

Beltane's Female Divine Energy Force. It caught her attention, fascinating her. In stunning detail, the carved relief showed a woman, slender and beautiful. She looked commandingly, lovingly, out, and Nic found her gaze caught by the carved one. The woman had one arm curved, palm out, as if beckoning, and Nic had to stop herself to not reach back. She blinked, breaking the spell, bemusedly looking at the rest of the corner piece.

A wheel of stars hovered behind the woman, in front of a tree and massive moon. An owl perched on the branches of the tree, birch, she thought, and Nic recognized the patterns from Old Earth's moon. A wolf sat at the woman's feet, protective and submissive, and the drape of the woman's flowing robe was caught between the wolf's front and hind legs. There was a sensuality implicit in the woman's body, yet it was hers to give, not to be taken. Nic stood and stared, lost in the carving.

A cool hand rested lightly on her shoulder, and she jumped, turning to meet Damyl's eyes. He smiled, but she saw concern in them. "You alright? You've been standing here a while."

She smiled back but was sure he saw her slight confusion. "Yes. I mean, I think so. Just," she motioned to the carving. "There's something here that's calling to me, and I don't know why."

Damyl nodded slowly. "It's Arianrhod."

"Arianrhod?" Nic's fingers found her bracelet, and she began to slowly turn it on her wrist.

He nodded again. "She's the Star Goddess, the Silver Wheel. She rules fertility and childbirth, because she is the Celtic goddess of reincarnation."

Nic was sure he could see the light go on in her mind, but she didn't explain and was glad when he didn't ask; now was not the time. "Reincarnation, fertility, and childbirth. Hmm. We'll have to talk about that sometime, but it now makes sense to me." She laughed and saw him relaxing as she did. "I think I have some more research to do."

He offered her his arm again, leading her back to their seats. "I can fill you in a bit, if you want."

She nodded, as they sat, and he continued. "She's from Welsh mythology, and was a very powerful goddess, a woman complete in herself. That was the original description of a virgin, actually, just a woman who's complete in herself. She needed no man's protection and lived in her castle with her female attendants. She was sexually active, choosing her mates as they appealed to her." He glanced sideways at Nic, a smile twisting his lips. "You do strike me as having similar characteristics. Except, where you're fire and gold, she is water and silver. Her mythology ends poorly, she was tricked, stripped of power by men. But, I like to think she was reborn, like the reincarnation goddess she is, and took back her power."

Nic nodded, thoughts crashing through her head. She turned to him, and Damyl leaned forward, pressing a light kiss to her mouth. Nic's scattered thoughts coalesced, brought into focus by the silky smoothness of his lips, their slight coolness reminding her of the wooden treasures he carved so skillfully. Except, his lips were living wood.

She enjoyed the brief caress and followed it up with one of her own, longer and deeper. Damyl's lips parted as hers did, and his hand reached up, cupping her jaw, fingers in her hair. Skin slid past skin. Goosebumps crept up Nic's back, and heat flared inside. She nipped hungrily at his lips, then paused, taking a deep breath, resting her forehead against his. They breathed each other's breath for a long moment, and Damyl lightly stroked her neck, his hand cool on her jaw. Hazel, heavily lidded eyes with giant pupils filled her sight when Nic finally lifted her eyelids.

She reached up to hold his hand to her cheek as they

slowly separated. "Wow. That was a wonderful kiss."

He nodded, and Nic turned to press a kiss into his palm before dropping their joined hands to her lap. He had to clear his throat before he could speak. "Wonderful. Yes, and so much more."

She sat back, watching him consideringly. When she didn't say anything else, his brow creased, and uncertainty flashed in his eyes.

She lightly squeezed his hand as she said, "I've enjoyed this afternoon far more than I thought possible. I think you're a fabulous being. You speak to my soul, and I hear you, loud and clear. In fact, so loudly, that I need to step away for a bit, so I can make sure I'm hearing myself, too."

She brushed curls back from his forehead, glad the frown had smoothed away. "Are you alright with that?" Nic looked around and decided what she'd do. "I'll go walk the festival, look at things, and listen to myself. And I'll use the facilities." She chuckled briefly before framing his face with her hands and leaning in for a light kiss. He caressed her lips with his, and her eyes closed as sensation drew her in. She backed up placing a finger on his mouth. "And then I'll come back, and we'll see what comes next. I want to make sure I feel the same when I'm not right next to you — that I'm not just caught up in the moment."

He kissed her finger, then shook his head, smiling wryly. "So wise for a young one." He continued. "Yes, I'm alright with that. In fact, I could use some thinking space, too; I've never felt such an instant connection with anyone." After a moment's consideration, he said, "I'll be by Aunt Hannel's booth when you're ready."

They stood, and Damyl gathered the sheet they'd sat on, folding it as he walked away. They were like combatants returning to their corners for a rest. She frowned lightly. It wasn't as if they were fighting—not yet at least. They had the potential for some spectacular blowouts, since they each held strong opinions, but the respect was there. He looked at her, talked to her, treated her as a partner, an equal.

She continued to watch him, appreciating the flow of muscle as he moved. He wasn't totally smooth; she could see some awkwardness, but only as he walked. His hands and arms, though, it was as if he'd focused all his coordination into them. She looked forward to him touching her, knowing it would feel amazing.

The certainty astounded her and unnerved her. Especially as, when he disappeared from view, her soul cried out at his loss. This man made her wish she could choose her own needs over the mission, and guilt careened over her, that she'd even consider such a thing. She gathered her drum, and turned resolutely away, severing the final physical connection to begin her own wanderings. Contents of booths, beings she passed, the details flowed in and out of her consciousness, barely imprinting as she thought.

She was used to having certainty, and being able to categorize the unknown, and deal with things logically. But, she had no context for the intensity of her bond with Damyl. And, she feared losing herself in him to the point that she could no longer deny her own needs, could not stay focused on her mission. She feared failing, again.

Her previous lives were mostly packed away deep in her subconscious, even more so now that she'd been living this life. She knew she'd never felt an instant connection like this. Most of her partnerships had resulted in love—or at least fondness— and she'd never had a problem putting her mission first. Surely, she would be able to stay strong, and not lose herself, even with Damyl.

She waited in line for the facilities, staring off into space, thoughts tumbling in her head. Afterwards, she stopped before reentering the festivities, and looked around. She was at one end of the lane, where they'd entered, and Aunt Hannel's booth was near the opposite end. A young busker fiddled madly nearby. She stood, enjoying his tune, and transferred some credits to his account in appreciation of the break his music gave her madly circling thoughts.

Then, she turned away from the lane and wandered into the surrounding forest. She followed a path that grew less well-trodden, the forest encroaching closer as she went. The sun was about an hour from the horizon, glinting through spring green leaves, and even with muted festival sounds in the background, the peace of the forest settled into her.

Nearby, a male cardinal foraged, his red feathers fire bright amidst the green. It took a moment, but she found the brown female, standing guard while the male hopped along the forest floor, looking for food. Then, the male returned to her side, taking his turn at watch while she searched. The pair resonated deeply with Nic, and she remembered her earlier thought. The respect was there. Damyl treated her as a partner, an equal, and that would help her maintain who she was, keeping her true to her duty.

A deep breath filled her lungs with the fresh air, and she exhaled her fear and unhappiness, tension flowing from her body. She smiled, lifted a hand to the birds, and went back to the fair. This time, as she moved through the beings crowding the lane, she saw everything, and the flames in her sight seemed brighter, illuminating, and bringing life to it all. A flash of light caught her eye, and she turned to stare at a jeweler's stand. Her gaze landed on a pair of rings, gold and silver twisted together, with a carved flame seated centrally.

Moments later, she had them wrapped in a black velvet bag, tucked into the small pouch at her waist, and was striding towards Aunt Hannel's booth. As she moved, she felt the rings' presence with each step as the drum bumped rhythmically against them.

Damyl chatted with his Aunt while she whirled about, serving hungry festival goers. When the sun was almost down, she'd put out self-serve kettles of the stew and packages of bread, leaving an honor-system payment option. It was considered inappropriate to give away fire or food today, so she usually made a profit. Damyl had even paid for their own meal earlier.

He caught himself looking down the lane, hoping for a flash of bright hair, and resolutely turned his gaze to Aunt Hannel. She was talking about a problem they'd had at the farm, and how her old farmhand, Mo, who'd been there since Damyl was a child, had fixed it. Then she broke off. Damyl followed her gaze, and his heart leapt.

Nic moved down the lane, looking confident, beautiful, ageless, and focused on him. He stood, meeting her gaze, his own heat rising to match hers. She came to him, stepping in close, looking intently into his eyes, and he caught his breath at the flames swirling in the depths of hers.

They called to him.

"Damyl Kinaed, will you handfast to me, tonight, for a year and a day?" she asked, in a voice deep and rough,

He swallowed, barely registering his Aunt's pleased gasp. What else could he say? "Yes. Nic Brighe, I will handfast to you, tonight, for a year and a day."

His carefully wrought control over life disintegrated beneath the onslaught of her passion, and he was happy about it. He took her in his arms, as she wrapped him in hers. They kissed, and Damyl was oblivious to the applause that started with Aunt Hannel and spread to all nearby.

Damyl came up for air, his lips and arms, hands,

everything that had touched her, wonderfully hot from her heat. He knew in some way Nic was similar to his mother and also knew it didn't matter. If Nic was like his mother, if she had to leave, he'd deal with it—they'd deal with it. In the meantime, he wanted Nic in his life, for as long as possible.

A silly grin spread across his face, but he couldn't care. "How do you want to go about this?"

Uncertainty finally appeared in the woman before him. "Um, well, I'm not really sure. How does one actually do this? I know it happens. I know Beltane is a good time to do it, and the general custom, but how do you folks do it here?"

Damyl's grin faded to a fond smile as the ageless woman was replaced with a young one. His Nic was evidently impetuous. No surprise, really, with flames riding her. He looked around. "Aunt Hannel, I haven't kept track of things that closely, is there still a Levrin Glade Registry?"

She nodded, hand flipping around as she interacted with her AI. "Yes...and you two are now registered for a year-and-a-day binding." She considered the space before her a moment. "There are eight handfastings registered. And, blessed be, Aitane and Erensia are doing a formal wedding ceremony. They're finally doing a life pledge!"

Damyl's eyebrows rose. "That's great! They've been short terming it a long time. I remember them from over a decade ago."

Damyl turned back to Nic, relieved to see a pleased smile as she watched them.

She said, "I figured you'd be able to get this going. When do the handfastings happen, and what is your ceremony?" Damyl rattled off a description of the events that would happen that evening, then looked at his aunt who was chuckling. "Did I miss anything?"

She shook her head. "No, I think that was it, and a more

succinct description I have yet to hear. I didn't think you paid that much attention."

Damyl shrugged. "It happens every year. I have friends who have done it, and I've thought of what it would be like to take part in it." He looked at Nic, his tone warming and deepening. "And, now I will."

Aunt Hannel shook her hands at them, playfully. "Begone with you now. I'll see you at the fire." She turned, then grabbed something and whirled back. "Wait!"

Damyl looked back, surprised, then he grinned. His aunt had a flower wreath in her hands, red, white, green, and silver ribbons trailing.

She stepped forward, placing it on Nic's head, and kissed her cheek. "A bride should have a crown. These are from my own fields. Blessed be, my dear, and welcome to the family."

Damyl thought he saw a tear in Nic's eye. She squeezed his hand, and her voice was suspiciously throaty as she said, "Thank you, Aunt Hannel. This means a lot to me."

They wandered the lane, and at one point, he started to pull them towards a jeweler. "We should get tokens to exchange."

She pulled back, and he looked at her, surprised. She let go of his hand to push the drum back and dig in a small pouch at her waist, retrieving a black bag. "Actually, I found these earlier. Wasn't sure when to show you."

He held out his palm automatically as she tipped the bag, and two rings landed heavily. He ran fingers over them, turning them to catch the evening light. His carver's sensibilities appreciated the quality of the knotwork, and the tiny central flame. He automatically tried on the larger one, not really surprised when it fit. His Nic was very tactile.

He glanced up to see her watching him, slight

apprehension visible. He let his approval color his voice as he said, "These are beautiful. And perfect."

She grinned, reminding him that, as mature as she seemed most of the time, she was still a young woman. Aunt Hannel was always talking about old souls and he figured Nic was one of them. Especially with as fascinated as she'd been by Arianrhod. Damyl guessed her soul had been around a few times.

She held out the bag, and he slipped the rings back in, watching her tuck them away for safe keeping. Silver catching fire in the westering sun made him look back over at the jeweler's stand. "Let's go over there, anyway."

She trailed after him as he approached the wares, and he smiled when he saw what lay in shining silver glory on a black velvet bed, silver chain spilled around it.

"Arianrhod, the Lady of Stars' silver wheel." The wonder in Nic's voice was clear to him, and he motioned to the pendant when the artisan came over.

He was familiar with the woman. She'd had a stall there as long as he'd been attending festivals, and her work had inspired some of his own designs. "Brenny, we'd like to see Arianrhod's Wheel."

It was small, only two of Nic's fingers wide, but the detail was amazing. The inspiration for the design was obviously stars in a time-lapsed image, with points dragged out into silver swirls. In the empty spaces between swirls, a background glowed, like an iridescent Aurora Borealis. It was also mobile, the silver stars turning in front of the iridescence when spun. An outer wheel with triangular Celtic knots at the compass points, and a central star pin framed the whole thing.

He ran the pendant through his fingers, feeling the disc's smooth turning, the individual tooling of each star's streak, and he loved the effect. When he was satisfied, he handed it to Nic.

"You feel such a strong connection to Arianrhod, this feels right. Will you accept this Silver Wheel as a Handfasting gift?" He peripherally noticed Brenny look up sharply and grin, but he was focused on Nic.

Nic nodded, apparently at a loss for words. He leaned forward, brushing her silky hair out of the way as he clasped the silver chain around her neck. He ran his fingers over the necklace, loving the contrast of her hot skin against the cool metal, knowing soon they would be indistinguishable. He tapped the wheel where it rested at the top of her breasts. "I look forward to our discussions about why this wheel calls to you so strongly."

Fleeting sorrow crossed her face, followed by acceptance. She took a deep breath and nodded. "I do, too."

Damyl touched her arm. "Are you alright?"

Nic's smile was weak, but he thought it was genuine, and her voice was even as she said, "I am. And I love that you're so attuned to me." She took a deep breath and let it out slowly before continuing. "It's just that the reincarnation discussion will not be an easy one, and it may be a large part of our decision to continue beyond a year and a day, or not."

Damyl's heart twisted then eased when she took his hand, lacing her fingers into his, and leaned against him. "I am looking forward to our year, and I truly hope we can continue beyond it. We will have our discussions, share our truths, and go from there. For now, let's enjoy the time we have together and not worry about the future."

Since that echoed his own philosophy, he didn't fight the tingling that rushed through his body when she stroked his cheek and pressed her lips against his, scalding heat into him. He tightened his fingers around hers and slid his free hand around her waist, losing track of his surroundings for a long moment. Gradually, they broke apart, lips nuzzling a few last times, and the noise of the festival came back in. He became aware of Brenny, standing behind her display case, grinning at them.

Nic's heat surrounded Damyl as she slid her arm around his waist, and he draped his arm over her shoulders. He looked down at her, seeing her grin back at the artisan as she rolled her pendant between her fingers. "Brenny, this is beautiful; you do excellent work."

The woman beamed. "Thank you, and congratulations. About time this one jumped the broom."

Damyl wanted Nic to be near the central bonfire for its lighting, and the sun was near the horizon, sky painted with salmon, orange, and pink, so they bid goodbye to Brenny, and he urged Nic along. Their earlier spot was taken, but he found them a spot almost as good, and spread out the sheet once more.

They sank to the ground as the sky darkened, and a couple who appeared fully human stepped forward onto the stage. They were stately in robes of white and silver that had branches with green leaves, and bright flames embroidered along hems. The crowds quieted, and Damyl shifted, entwining himself around Nic's heat, whispering in her ear, telling her they were the local high priestess and priest. She rested against him, hugging his arms. He stroked his hand over her wrist, encountering her bracelet, and idly ran his fingers along it. He was amused, realizing it was a soothing action, and wasn't surprised he saw her do it often.

The High Priestess, short and delicate, but full of flowing energy, spoke. Her voice was amplified so it sounded as if it came naturally from all over the glade. "Arianrhod, Crown of the North, Lady of Stars, Mother goddess of reincarnation, fertility and childbirth, welcomes you to Beltane."

The man, tall and thin, had a deep voice that belied his

appearance. "Cernunnos, Lord of Wild Things, Horned One, god of the hunt, of fertility, of sunlight, welcomes you to Beltane."

They put a call out for fire starters for the central Beltane fire. Damyl grinned. This was the main reason he'd wanted Nic here. Her hair slid across his face as she looked up, but she hesitated.

Damyl nudged her.

She looked back, and he stole a quick kiss. She nuzzled back, then asked, "Are you sure I won't be taking someone's spot?"

He shook his head. "Go ahead, they'll love it. You can join with the others and have fun." He nodded towards an older man, who had flames bright in his hands. "Watch Wenn there, he'll show you when to light the wood."

Reticence gone, Nic laughed and stood, calling fire. She and three others moved to cardinal points around the central fire. A woman with a fiddle stepped forward and started a wild tune, and scattered drums joined in. Nic started to move to the rhythms, and Damyl grinned as she set her fire to dancing. After a moment, the other three joined in, less surely, but game.

Their flames became clearer in the gathering dusk, and as the music and drumming crescendoed, voices started chanting, "Bel-Teine Fire! Bel-Teine Fire!"

Nic watched Wenn who held his hands up high, flames tight to skin. Nic and the others did likewise. The music ended in a flurry, and Wenn's arms dropped, pointing to the wood pile. Nic also dropped her arms, and Damyl was sure she was being careful, because her fire levels stayed even with the others. Deep in the heart of the pile, flames grew, gathering strength as the fire fed on well-dried wood.

A great cheer went up, and the music started again. This time, it was multiple musicians, obviously used to playing

together. Nic came back to Damyl, sinking down with a
satisfied sigh.

She seemed flushed, grinning, and he guessed her blood
raced from using fire.

"That was fun!" she said, breathlessly.

He shared her grin and held out his arms, welcoming her
back into his embrace. She shifted so he could hug her close. He
trailed his lips over her ear deciding she was not at all adverse
to the idea as she snuggled closer.

The fellow fire starters came over and chatted for a
while. They loved her fire dance, and Damyl figured they
would practice what they'd seen her do and that the next fire
lighting would be a spectacular show.

When they were alone again, full night had settled, and
all the bonfires along the lane had been lit from the central one.
Aunt Hannel joined them, spreading her own sheet next to
them. Nic showed her the rings, and Aunt Hannel nodded in
approval. However, Nic didn't share the Silver Wheel. It hung
at the vee neckline of her dress, just barely visible between her
breasts as she slouched against him.

They watched as the May Queen and May King, chosen
by common accord from locals, put on a small play, enacting
the meeting and falling in love of the god and goddess. The
couple sank down in simulation of a loving embrace for a long
moment, then rose, hand in hand to the cheers and applause of
their audience.

After the play, it was their turn. The High Priestess stood
on the stage again, High Priest nearby, and called for those to
be handfasted. Nic glanced at Damyl, and he thought he saw
some nerves, but she rose steadily enough, and firmly grasped
his hand.

The Priestess called the names of the couples, and Damyl
moved forward, in unison with Nic, to join others in a line in

front of the stage. The bonfire blazed at his back, and Nic was just as hot at his side while they waited their turn.

Finally, the High Priestess reached them. "Nicallea Brighe, Damyl Kinaed. Do you have tokens of your troth?"

She blessed the rings Nic held out, then continued. "On this Beltane night, in Verda's three hundred and fourteenth year after founding, do you agree to handfast to each other, forsaking all other unions for one year and a day? Do you troth to honor and respect each other, to share your lives of your own free will, yet remain separate individuals? Nicallea, what is your response?"

Nic's eyes practically glowed as she turned to look deep into his, and her voice caressed places deep within him. "I do so troth my honor and respect to you, Damyl Kinaed, forsaking all other unions for one year and a day." Nic slipped his ring onto his hand, her fingers hot and the band close to the same. She handed him the smaller ring.

"Damyl, what is your response?" Caught up in Nic's eyes, he barely heard the Priestess but managed to get out, "I do so troth my honor and respect to you, Nicallea Brighe, forsaking all other unions for one year and a day." And he put Nic's ring onto her finger.

They turned to the waiting High Priest, and he held up his hand, three cords dangling from it, two red and one silver. Together, Damyl and Nic braided them into a single strand. Then, as they held hands, arms entwined, the priest wrapped the cord around their wrists, tying it into a knot. It settled next to Nic's bracelet, and Damyl thought they looked good together.

The High Priest said, "As this cord binds your wrists, let your troth bind your lives, and may you live in mutual honor and respect.

The priestess and priest repeated the rituals with the last

two couples. Then, all the couples paraded around the fire to a strong heartbeat drum rhythm, before ending up in a line again. The Priest stepped forward and talked briefly about commitment, honor, and respect among partners. Most of it went over Damyl's head, so focused was he on the woman he was bound to. When the Priestess unbound them, laying the cord across their freed wrists, it was all he could do to resist pulling Nic into the forest. Heat pounded through him.

He glanced sideways, and the look on Nic's face as she stared at him made him groan. She grinned wickedly. Finally, the last couple was unbound. Nic's hand was hot on his arm as they joined the others in walking around the bonfire again, unbound, but together. At the end of the circle, each pair jumped over the broomstick lying in the path. When it was their turn, Damyl's heart beat faster, and his breath came quicker. He looked to Nic, meeting her eyes. They shared a quick kiss then laced fingers together and jumped.

When they landed, they'd passed the threshold into their new life together. The High Priestess offered them each a ceremonial sip of mead, and the High Priest a piece of honey cake.

Aunt Hannel joined them, carrying handmade clay mugs full of liquid. Damyl recognized the work of a local potter as she handed one to Nic, and one to him. "Now, here's your mead, don't spill a drop." She winked, and added, "It's good for fertility, you know. Made with honey from my own bees."

Nic sniffed at the mug and took a sip. She smiled delightedly. "Oh, that's what the Priestess gave us. It's lovely! Mead, you called it? And it's made with honey?" Closing her eyes, she drew the scent into her nose again, then took another swig, lips and jaw moving as she swirled it slowly around her mouth, concentrating on the flavor.

Damyl's groin tightened at the sight, and he turned

gratefully when Aunt Hannel pressed a ribbon-wrapped, halfmoon-shaped package into his hand. "And sweet-bread, baked and broken with my own hands." She engulfed them in a hug that was thorough without spilling the mead.

"You two look so radiant. You have my blessing, and may your year together be all you wish it to be." She was smiling, but her eyes glistened, and she sniffed, wiping her nose.

Damyl guessed she was remembering her brother and his bride.

Aunt Hannel shook her head sharply and handed him a matching clay liter bottle with cork along with a strap contraption, allowing it to be worn over a shoulder or around a waist. "And here's the bottle with more mead. I have your drum, Nic, do you want me to store it for you?"

Nic nodded, eyes widening as she realized she'd forgotten her new prize. "Yes, please—thank you for taking it with you! I got so caught up in Damyl and the ceremony, I didn't even think about it!"

Damyl couldn't help but be pleased he'd been the reason she'd forgotten and smothered a grin.

Aunt Hannel shook her head, "No worries, at all, my dear. Glad to help." She turned to Damyl, handing him some folded fabric. "And here's your ground sheet." She brushed her hands together. "Now. Blessed be, and begone with you. I don't want to see hide nor hair of you 'til the sun rises. But, be here for the Maypole dance."

Damyl kissed her cheek, Nic hugged her one more time, and then Damyl took Nic's hand leading her down the lane.

***

Nic followed Damyl, as he clearly had a destination in mind, and she was pretty sure his goal matched her own. As they passed the main bonfire, she tilted her head back, following sparks rising from the flames, spiraling upwards to a sky full of stars. She felt her soul rise with them, and just barely stopped herself from releasing her own sparks and flames to dance with them.

She'd had her turn with fire. Now, it was the bonfire's chance to shine. She shouldn't detract from that. Tonight, she was one of many in the flickering shadows, sheltered by night, celebrating growing day, life, spring, renewal, and fertility.

Breath tickled her neck, then cool lips. She closed her eyes and leaned into the caress, shivering responsively as Damyl chuckled. She realized she'd stopped while watching the sparks, halting him with her.

His voice stoked the heat deep within her. "Tempting, isn't it? I can feel your fire rising. I can see your draw to it. Shall I give you something to replace that urge?" He nudged her to one side of the lane, off the main path, into the shadows between booths. He retrieved her mug and set both mugs near the base of a booth, sheltered, where they wouldn't spill.

Nic gladly turned to Damyl when he stood. He couldn't give fire form, as she could, but he had his own connection and seemed to understand the hunger it woke deep within her. It was more than understanding. Her flames fascinated and drew him, not as a moth, but as a hunter to a campfire.

She stared deeply into his olive-brown eyes, loving the tiny spark of flame she saw reflected in their mossy green centers. This man called to her soul like no other, and she was so willing to answer, she'd trothed her life to him for a year, and a day, despite the fear her feelings for him would make her forsake her duty.

She pulled his head down to press her forehead against his, then rolled hers until their lips met. Soft, at first, exploring, still learning each other. The kiss deepened. The connection between their souls almost overwhelmed her, it was like nothing she'd ever experienced—not in any of her lives.

Her few decades here would feel short if she spent them with him.

The surety of that thought and the accompanying sadness broke the spell their lips were weaving. Nic pulled back, looking at him, flames in her vision letting her see even the shadowed parts of him. Again, truth washed over her, leaving concern that she would betray her mission in its wake. Never had she felt this way at the start of a relationship, and she didn't even really know him. He returned the look, eyes dilated from more than darkness. He turned his head inquisitively.

She reached out, stroking back his dark curls, running her fingers around his skull, smiling as his eyes slid shut and he leaned into her touch. She would not be able to be with him for long if doubt kept appearing. She closed her eyes, calling on her certainty that her duty was essential, not only to her redemption, but to the unseen overall plan. She would not betray their trust. Calm settled over her, and she made the decision to trust her dedication to her duty and allow herself to answer the call of her heart, for however long she could. Pushing away the future with an ease learned from pushing away the past, she focused on the flesh before her.

She leaned forward and set her mouth to learning how to call heat from him to match her own. Both their hands soon joined the dance, unbuttoning, touching, stroking skin bared by shifting fabric. Heat rose.

Nic took a deep breath, awareness of others nearby intruding. "Mmmm. You were bringing me somewhere, I believe?"

Damyl's nostrils flared. He bent, retrieving their mugs, pressing one into her hand. He grabbed her other hand, leading her back into the throng of beings. They walked closely entwined. Nic enjoyed the feel of his body—firm, cool, muscles pressing against hers as their movements bumped them together. Soon they reached the end of the lane, opposite the direction she'd gone before. He held her hand, thumb running over her flesh, keeping the fires fresh as the path plowed deeper into the forest, taking them farther from Levrinton.

She hadn't noticed, surrounded by fires as she'd been earlier, but it was very dark. Modern path lights that lined the way were unlit, replaced by infrequent fire torches. She looked back. Levrinton had also extinguished exterior lights, eliminating light pollution, allowing the stars overhead to multiply. No artificial lights on this night, only fire. She could smell bonfire smoke, even as fresh wind diluted it.

Nic let herself be steered; Damyl was the native here. She had just come into being six weeks ago and was still learning her new home. He turned them down what had to be an animal trail, a tiny track that led to a small clearing, deep within the woods. Water trickled over rocks, a small fall into a natural pool. Rocks and moss surrounded the edges.

Nic looked around, enjoying the peace and beauty, knowing she saw more than he did, though the two rising crescent moons had to give him some sight. They drank deeply from the mead then placed mugs on a rock ledge and Damyl hung the bottle, so it rested in the cool water. She helped him drape their sheet over thick moss, then they sank to the ground, lips meeting, hands clutching eagerly as all thought burned away.

They discarded clothes, and Nic's crown ended up tangled in her dress. Nic pushed Damyl back, straddling him to control his entrance. This was her first time in this life, and she intended to enjoy it. Her fingers wrapped around flesh just slightly less warm than her own, stroking gently to not over stimulate him. She welcomed his hands, cool digits exploring the hot flesh between her legs, feathering along her breast, stoking her fires. Soon, she was ready to accept him.

She guided his member to her opening, feeling his blood throb under her hand, and settled onto him, gradually letting herself stretch and open until she felt him deep within. His coolness was a sharp contrast to her internal heat. She lifted and settled a few more times, growing bolder and more intense as she adapted, pleasure building.

When he shifted, turning them, she gasped, his thrusts calling forth a volcano. The heat in her womb built, reaching outward, towards something she couldn't sense, and she knew they were in the process of creating her first child. Her chest tightened at the reminder she would eventually be called onward, and she gave in to a single moment of desire that she would not have to leave Damyl.

Nic wrapped arms and legs around him, shifting in counterpoint to his movements, making sure he stroked the right spots. Damyl forearms were under her, and he braced himself on his elbows, pressing his face into her shoulder so he could nip lightly at the bed of muscle while he slid out and back in with a twist.

She overflowed, clutching him to her, orgasm extended by his coolness as he continued to thrust. Moments later, he came, then collapsed onto her, lips unerringly finding her neck. She tipped her head to place a kiss on his ear, feeling as if she'd come home.

Nic looked over his shoulder, attention caught by a shuttle lifting from the nearest space port, engine glow showing more clearly than usual in the dark sky. She tracked its path to the stars as she stroked her hands up and down Damyl's back. He growled, bit her neck, and she felt him stir within her. The spaceship was driven from her mind. She gave an answering growl and curved her fingers to claw lightly down his back as she tensed internal and external muscles in encouragement.

They continued to celebrate life and fertility until dawn began graying the sky, and each other's flesh was no longer new. As pre-dawn light grew, Nic raised up on her elbow, trailing her fingers across his features, now very well known to her.

He smiled up at her and reached up to tuck strands of her hair behind her ear. "Good morning."

"Good morning." Nic leaned down, claiming a long kiss that said everything she wasn't ready to articulate. She raised up, searching his closed eyes.

They opened, hope clear in them, as he said softly, "Yeah, me, too. I'm hoping this continues."

Nic smiled. "If I have anything to say about it, it will. At the least for a year and a day. Happy May Day."

She laced her fingers into his and sat up, staring into a forest she thought he could probably see, by now. The moons were well on their way down the sky and faded as day rose. Contentment filled her. The place now truly felt like home to her, especially if the man next to her was included in the bargain.

Nic considered her reluctance at her inevitable departure. She acknowledged it but pushed it to the side, bringing her will to bear. True, it would be harder than ever before, leaving this man, but she was duty bound, and must continue to atone. She truly wanted to do what she could to repair what she'd had a part in breaking. Even if this time around, it wrenched her soul in two.

Damyl rolled over, shifting so he sprawled across her lap, and kissed her hip, bringing her attention back to his physical form. He wound an arm around her, and she draped hers around him, then leaned down, pressing a return kiss to his shoulder. The Silver Wheel he'd given her fell forward to land against his back.

"You seem troubled." His breath wafted across her belly, and his fingers stroked her bracelet.

She loved that he knew there was something amiss and decided it was time to explain. Their connection was too intense for her to be anything but honest. She needed him to know the truth before they got in any deeper, needed to know he accepted all of her. At the least, she hoped they could enjoy this year together, but it needed to be his decision.

She took a breath, then paused, not sure how to put it. It was a mark in his favor that he waited, not pressing while she gathered her thoughts. She realized she was nervous—an emotion she hadn't felt in a long time. But, she'd never before needed a parenting partner to totally accept who she was.

She took another deep breath, held it a moment, turning the wheel in her fingers, then decided on an indirect approach. "You know I can call fire, that I have a connection with it." He nodded, his hair brushing against her skin, fanning embers of her desire. "It's more than that."

She was silent for a bit, wrestling with the tension in her gut that showed her how much she hoped he would take this well. Then she remembered the connection she felt with this man and plowed on. "You know how I felt an instant affinity for Arianrhod? I'm not sure how many times it's happened, but I've lived through several lives. This life began at Spring Equinox."

Damyl was silent long enough for her to feel the first stirring of doubt. Then he commented lightly, "So, when you said you were new to this region, you were really serious."

She smacked his shoulder. "Ha. Funny. But, yes. And, I'm not even sure if I've been on this planet before. I remember vague bits and pieces of my previous lives, not enough to be able to identify where they were. I try not to recall them, in all honesty."

His arm tightened around her hips, as he pressed his head against her middle. She felt his lips move against her belly. "How long are you here? If you were born six weeks ago, was that fully formed?"

"Yes, I come into being fully formed, with consciousness, and dim memories of past lives. I don't know how it happens, or who makes it happen, or much of why. But, there is always a life set up for me to step into. I determine what I do with whatever identity they've given me. Mostly, I go from where I am, who I encounter. I'll be here a couple of decades, long enough to have a family, and see my children mostly grown..." She trailed off.

"You don't know why? How do you know when your time here is done? Will you just vanish? Do you have to go?" Damyl's voice broke on the last question, and Nic hugged him hard as he lay across her lap.

"I don't fully know why, but I do have to go. It's my duty, something I have to do, to make amends for a terrible mistake. I have to move on, and have more children, until the end, when I can rejoin the fire." His grip tightened around her waist, squeezing almost hard enough to hurt. Then, he relaxed.

His voice was muffled, but she could understand him. "Rejoin the fire? Remind me to tell you about my dreams, sometime." He was silent a moment, then asked, "How does it happen?"

She shrugged. "When my children are old enough, there's a spot that appears in every life I've had. I call it my phoenix cave. I go there, and...well, I use the term phoenix for a reason. It's where I'm reborn, too."

"Hmm. Phoenix, huh?" His voice was calm.

It could have been the calm of disbelief, but, willing to give him the benefit of the doubt, she said, "Yes." Then she fell silent and let him think, as he'd let her.

It wasn't long before he asked, "You were serious, earlier, about wanting a family?"

Nic nodded, her hope rising at the definite interest in his voice. "Yes. That part I'm sure of. In every life, I need to have children—three or four of them." His other arm wrapped around her waist, too, his head tucking in against her stomach as he hugged her. The tension in his arms belied the calm in his voice. He took a deep breath, and exhaled slowly, the cool air blowing across her belly and stirring her pubic hair, as he relaxed into her. Her patience and candor were rewarded by lips nuzzling with intent, and his hands moving around her hips, caressing.

She barely heard his words, but his quiet "I accept," sang in her heart. His calm presence and intense focus on her body soothed her sorrow, helping her push away thought of an unchangeable future. By staying in the here and now of sensation as they celebrated the sun's rising, and the turning of the seasons, in the age-old dance of life, she quelled the frantic sense of not wanting to lose this man.

She knew they would be together far longer than a year and a day.

***

30 April- 1 May, Beltane, May Day, 334 AF, 2725, OECE
Planet Verda, Earth Colony SG-05
Sethrenya Galaxy, Sector SG-372-VDE01
Twenty Years Later

Nic and Damyl walked the path from the Levrin Glade Beltane bonfires, dark trees arching overhead. Damyl nudged Nic's shoulder, guiding her down the faint track.

She glanced around as they entered the clearing. "It's barely changed." The small falls, rocks, and moss still framed the pool.

He didn't say a word, hanging the refilled clay bottle of mead so it rested in the pool, then spreading out the sheet on moss that was just as thick as it had been the first time they were here. She held out a mug to him, and they drank deeply of Aunt Hannel's latest batch of mead, eyeing each other over the rims. Clothes were abandoned as easily as they had been twenty years before. But this time, there was no learning period, no easing into it. Instead, they used their years of experience to bring heat until it exploded.

Nic lay back, gasping, loving the feel of Damyl collapsed next to her. He had definitely kept his vigor—not bad for an old man. She enjoyed teasing him about turning fifty this year. True, he was young by Universal standards, but half a century still was a landmark birthday for humans, and that gave her lots of leverage. He usually didn't retaliate by contemplating how many years she'd accrued over all her lives.

She chuckled as a shuttle lifted off, pointing it out to Damyl. "Our first night, there was a shuttle lift off, too. It caught my attention for all of a second before you recaptured it." She rolled over, resting her cheek on his chest. "It doesn't feel like twenty years since we handfasted. How are we old enough to have been married nineteen years? To have a nineteen-year-old Beltane baby?"

She shifted to her back, staring up at the night sky as he rested an arm over her waist. Out of habit, he found her gold bangle with his other hand. She smiled. "I'm really glad we made the trip back here. Lots of good memories, and Levrin Glade does a good celebration." She craned her neck to look at him. "Happy anniversary, Love."

He did a partial crunch, hand wrapping around her ribs to roll her towards him, and they kissed. She still enjoyed the cool slide of his lips against hers. That contrast never got old.

They lay together, delighting in cool night breezes on heated skin. There was no rush, and they planned to spend all night again. Annaly, their Beltane baby, was off with her own friends at a different celebration. She was their one pyro child, and Nic had helped her gain mastery over her gifts. Their daughter helped light festival fires, wherever she was. Coleth, seventeen, was here, somewhere, with his friends. The two younger children were here, too. Chellea at twelve and Adren at thirteen needed more supervision, but they'd driven in with Aunt Hannel. She'd taken charge of them, ordering away Nic and Damyl, much like she had their first year.

Nic rolled again, settling her chin on Damyl's chest. "It's weird, not needing to worry about anyone. It seems over this last year Chellea has matured, and there's an independent person behind those eyes."

Damyl's chest grew stiff under her chin, and his arms tightened around Nic. She knew what he was thinking. They'd had this discussion, many times, and it never got easier.

They'd compared her knowledge to his experience of what had happened with his mother. They'd always come to the same conclusion—that once their children were grown, and self-aware, she would have to move on. Neither of them liked it, and they were no closer to knowing exactly why, but neither was willing to break the contract she had, to let her renege on her duty.

She rested her cheek against him, winding her arms around his torso to hug him back. "I know, me too." She was quiet a long moment. "I'm having more fire dreams. It's getting closer."

They were quiet a long time, then by mutual accord, they tabled the topic and returned to enjoying each other, living in the moments of love they had.

Long hours later, stars faded from view, and birds began

to wake. Nic sat up and hugged her knees, watching the colors of morning, enjoying the show, trying to store the moments in a memory she could retrieve later. She wondered if this was how people who knew they were going to die felt. She might not die as a normal person did, but this life would be gone as surely as if she had.

She turned to Damyl again. Large, strong hands, calloused with years of woodworking, framed her face, and Damyl pulled her down for a long kiss. She focused with intensity beyond even her usual, giving and receiving touch, using knowledge to stir Damyl's fires as much as he stirred hers. As the sun rose, they gathered their clothes, dressing with lingering touches, then returned along the path, to join with their family, and participate in the Maypole dance.

**

19 September, Mabon, Autumn Equinox, 334 AF, 2725, OECE
Planet Verda, Earth Colony SG-05
Sethrenya Galaxy, Sector SG-372-VDE01
Four and a Half Months Later

Damyl shut the door after looking in on Coleth, their oldest boy. Their youngest son and daughter, Adren and Chellea, were also sleeping soundly. They'd all exhausted themselves at the Connamay Valley Community Autumn Equinox festival earlier this evening. Annaly was out with her girlfriends for the evening, enjoying her last free time of the summer, and he didn't expect her back until late. She'd start her second year at university soon.

He and Nic had moved to a home not far from Aunt Hannel's farm near Connamay Valley when Coleth was still inside Nic. They'd lived in Damyl's apartment above his store with Annaly but knew more beings in the space would be impossible. Since then, he'd hired a string of artisan students to run the shop, diversifying to sell some of their best offerings along with his, and he only went into the shop to drop off his carvings and to check on things every other week.

Their new home was in a spread-out suburb, neighbors only shouting distance away. Their side of the street had backyards carved from a nearby forest. There were several neighborhood children who'd grown up with theirs. It had been a good life.

Damyl slowly took the stairs leading down from the upper hall, wending around the open living room which was dimly lit by candles. Flames danced and glinted, bouncing off the glass-front display cases he'd built. They'd filled them with his wood carvings and many stones and other treasures they'd collected on hikes or travels. As he descended, Nic came into view, sitting on the couch.

There was a stillness to her body he recognized. When he could see her face, he wasn't surprised it was vacant, with motionless eyes caught by the flame she'd coaxed into her hand. The nearby candle's wick sat empty, waiting, and the fire in her palm reflected brightly on her gold bangle. He tried calling to her, resting his hands on her shoulder, leaning to kiss her ear, but there was no response.

He sat on the edge of the chair by the couch, so he almost faced her, knee to knee. Desolation filled him as he watched her face, usually so mobile, now still, and he spoke, knowing she wouldn't hear him. "Nic, love, where are you? You've always been fascinated by flames, but lately you're...lost more and more." He sighed, his breath causing her tamed fire to flicker.

He could remember his mother getting lost like this near the end. Annaly, then Coleth, then Adren, and now, Chellea had all gone through the awakening. Just as he and his siblings had.

Damyl knew soon he'd be without Nic. They held out

hope their souls would be reunited in the fire, but that was a lifetime away. Thinking of not having her physical presence ever again ripped at his soul. He no longer questioned why his father had left, he just hoped he would cope better when Nic was gone, especially for Adren and Chellea.

He wondered if it would hurt any less if they knew why. If they knew exactly what it was all for. Damyl's teeth ground together, and his fists clenched as he fought to regain surety that Nic leaving was important, crucial, even, to a much larger plan they both supported.

He squeezed his eyes shut a long moment, forcing himself to stop thinking about losing Nic. The fire pooled in her hand made his eyelids glow red and was bright when he opened his eyes. Damyl passed his hand over hers, feeling his palm singe slightly as he broke her visual connection.

She blinked, looking dazed. He leaned in, one hand on the couch's arm, the other cupping her face, and kissed her fiercely, calling up her body's responses to him to win her back from the flames. She responded, lips clinging to his gratifyingly. They were even hotter than usual. She'd gotten gradually cooler over the years as their children grew—never to his temperature, but closer. Then, during this past year, her body temperature had skyrocketed, again.

She shuddered, and he pulled back. When she turned to him, he watched her eyes. They widened slightly, then a fleeting look passed through them, despair, he thought. He wasn't able to see clearly in the candle-lit room, and then it was gone.

She blinked, again, a poignant smile curving her lips as her eyes met his. "Hi," she said softly, and her voice sent shivers down his spine, dissipating the question forming on his lips. She stared into his eyes, as intensely as she had at the flame, but then Nic felt everything intensely. She glanced away and slid the fire back onto its wick. He felt heat rising from her other hand, near where his held onto her leg.

She stared at the flame long enough he feared he'd lost her again. Then he was caught in the fiery depths of her eyes as she turned to him, asking, "Damyl, the children are in bed?"

He nodded, feeling her ardor spill into him.

Their gaze held, and she reached up to his face, cupping it in both hands, winding fingers into brown ringlets just starting to be shot with gray, pulling his mouth to hers. Her kiss was even more passionate than usual—desperate. The thought surfaced and scattered almost before it formed, lost in the maelstrom of feeling Nic left in her wake. They had become very skilled at living in the present, and he fell eagerly into habit.

They moved together in a dance of need to their room, falling into bed, tensions building when practiced lips and fingers roved over much loved, well-known flesh. Damyl felt Nic's heat increase, engulfing him, and he groaned, striving to give back to her as much as she gave. His Fire-Queen.

***

After their loving, Nic leaned on her elbow, staring down at Damyl's sleeping face. Flames danced in her vision, almost obscuring him, but she ignored their call and pushed them to the corners as she studied him. Her hand, long, strong, and darkly kissed by the sun, traced delicate lines around his features.

She smiled dejectedly as he shifted in his sleep, burrowing further into the pillows and blankets. A long moment later, she sighed, and climbed out of the bed, tucking the feather comforter around him so he wouldn't miss her heat as much. The flames were insistent, and the heat bubbled within her, reaching a critical point. Her time was up. She had to leave, tonight.

She stood, looking blindly down at him, turning her bangle around her wrist as she remembered their years together. Even if she could take nothing with her, she would try to fix memories into her mind. They'd had a last night of love to hold, maybe it would keep him warm when he woke to finally find her gone.

He also had the children to remember her by. She would have nothing, unless these memories stayed clear, unlike the others. Even the thought that she was doing her chosen duty brought no comfort. Her soul wept. She wanted to stay with Damyl, her love. He made her soul sing.

Nic forced herself to dress in a simple tunic, pants and walking shoes. She took off the Silver Wheel necklace he'd given her that first night, setting it on the nightstand where he would see it when he woke. She couldn't take it with her. Anything other than the box and her gold bangle would vanish in transition.

At the door, holding her carved wooden box, she paused again to stare back at Damyl. He wouldn't wake; the loving they'd shared ensured that. She ran fingers over the Möbius strip of her gold bangle, taking comfort in the familiar textures.

He was the best of them all. She found herself fighting not to resent the duty she'd bound herself to. Shame engulfed her, that she could be so selfish as to put her own desires over the need to make amends. The flames were a gift, not a curse. They allowed her to fix whatever horrible mistake she'd made.

Though going felt like ripping her soul from her body, she turned, and pulled the door softly closed behind her. She crossed the living room, set the box on a step, and climbed the rest to look in on her children.

Coleth, Adren, and Chellea were sleeping soundly and didn't even stir when she pressed a hot kiss to their foreheads. Annaly was still out with her friends, and Nic left her a small note. She and her daughter had talked, and Annaly was old enough, and practical. She'd be able to help the others.

Annaly knew most of what her parents did, as well as what her own awakening told her. She also knew Nic couldn't bear to tell Damyl when she had to leave. The good-bye would be too painful, the loss too heart-wrenching. Nic grimaced, thinking he probably knew her well enough to realize she'd just said goodbye.

Nic closed Annaly's door, then swiftly ran down the stairs, reclaimed the box, and left their house with barely a second glance. The surrounding countryside was mostly blurred by tongues of flames. She really must hurry. Her goodbyes had taken too long. She closed her eyes and concentrated on the heat within, turning until she faced the direction in which it drew her.

It was a moonless night, but she jogged down the two-track leading away from their back yard, toward the forest. Her night vision had improved along with the resurgence of internal heat. Now, it let her easily avoid ruts and holes. Some ways down the two-track, the fire led her onto a little used path, barely a trail. The haloes of flame grew, as always before, fascinating her, making it hard to think of anything except following their lead. Images of Damyl kept springing to mind, briefly quelling the flames each time.

Her trail reached tangles no being had entered for years, and she looked around, plotting a path through the mess that would get her where she needed to be. Shortly, she came upon two boulders that were always the entrance to her phoenix cave. While nowhere near her birthplace, some agency always brought the boulders near her when needed.

She squeezed between them, felt a ripple of energy and was standing in the flame-shaped entrance she had walked out of twenty short years ago. The warmth of the cave engulfed her as she entered, pushing back an image of a laughing Damyl.

She could sense fire waiting for her, as if she was surrounded by urgently licking tongues of flame, welcoming her, urging her onward to the blackened and charred circle of piled ash. She put the box near the entrance, and pulled off her bangle, setting it carefully within. Discarded clothes and shoes landed carelessly next to it.

She could almost see the waiting flames she sensed crowding closer, and she stretched out her hands. But, thoughts of Damyl kept interfering with the ritual, and she didn't feel the flames' draw as much as usual. She stepped into the circle, not surprised the ash was still warm when she wiggled her bare feet into it. She concentrated on the physical sensations to banish the tears that threatened. Momentarily gaining control of herself, her arms flew upwards, almost of their own volition, and her head fell back. That was the signal the flames were waiting for.

Her hands formed a funnel above, arms leading down to her body, and the flames poured through, burning their way down to join the heat rising from her womb. They engulfed her in their caresses, from the inside and out. She let out a shuddering breath as the tongues surrounded her, and agony grew, but she kept her stance. This was the worst and the best of it.

Normal fire didn't hurt her. But this fire burned away the old incarnation, setting the ground for the new, cleansing and purifying her spirit, so she could rise and take on her new life. While her senses retained a layer of protection that dulled the edges of her suffering, the intensity could only be embraced as an experience of life. At least the searing sensation took all her attention, keeping images of Damyl at bay. Shortly, all directed thought ended, and she gave herself over to the burning of her physical self, and glimpses of past lives that always accompanied the change.

Heat, licking tongues caressing, blistering...charring...
PAIN

"Nic? Let's go down to the beach today, okay? The sun is absolutely wonderful, and I'll pack a lunch for us. We can sit, or run in the sand, do whatever we want—just the two of us." Damyl's face is so sweet, lit up like an eager little boy's, a touch of pleading in his beautiful eyes. His hands clasping mine, thumbs running along my skin, sending a message echoed by the tenor of his voice. How can I not give in? There really is no contest.

Scorching flames searing flesh, devouring...

"Caryn, love, you must stop pacing like that—it's not good for your ankle. Katryn will be fine, it's just a little bump!" Cool hands catch and hold mine, earnest brown eyes look deep into mine, and I look back at Ran—I'm sure the pleading in my eyes, the panicked fear I feel is very visible. It must be, for he shakes his head slowly, then pulls me into his cool arms, and I collapse into his shoulder, biting back the sobs.

Hunger, deep lust for life, savoring the dissolution of body...

"Annaly! Get your father, quick!" Damyl comes running around the last corner of the path, concern written all over his face, and contractions start again, deep inside me. "It's time, Damyl. He wants to be born."

Damyl takes my hand tenderly, helps me into the bed. After sending Annaly for the midwife, he mops my forehead with cool water. I'm hot, as usual. I smile up at his loving face, feel the caring in his touch, such sensitive hands, a carver's touch.

Suffocating heat. No breath left. HOT! Hot! Hot!

"You're it!" The little girl who tagged my daughter, Fait, runs, shrieking with laughter. The other children also scatter before the new "it" can tag them. Pride wells up in me as my little girl shrugs, gamely accepting her defeat, then turns to coolly scan the rest of the children. She targets one and streaks after the child. I smile and turn my head to rub the hand that touches my shoulder as Zet steps up behind me. He watches with me for a moment, then breathes a suggestion into my ear, and I readily let the curtain fall back into place as he draws me towards the bedroom.

Inferno deep within me, raking at bone, tasting marrow...molten heat at my core.

Damyl shifts, moving closer to my body as we cuddle in front of the hearth. Silence, comfort. Here's a sane pocket of warmth and security while the winds and snow howl around us. I lean my head into his neck, his arm cradling me, and we sit, secure in each other's love.

Shuddering wracked what was left of her physical self, and Nic embraced the final assault of the conflagration, welcoming the climactic moment when agony finally ended as the firestorm consumed the last of her body. Her soul lifted above the circle of ash, and she watched, as always, until the last of the flames surrounding the ashes of this incarnation died down to nothing.

Only this time, she also felt anguish, loss, a pull to stay here, in this time, with Damyl. A voice within her cried out against the deprivation. She had done so much. Was it not enough? Was there not another way she could make amends that would let her stay with Damyl?

She was drawn up, pulled out of the cave, into the Netherlands of disembodiment, where nothing was real. She expected no sensations, nothing that told her she was a being, nothing at all. She'd always welcomed the cessation of sensation, it helped distance herself from the life she had to put behind her, helped her truly be reborn.

This time, though, she was haunted by flashes of Damyl. She writhed about, trying to escape his memory; he belonged to the past. But, he followed her inexorably, until she despaired of escaping, and just allowed him to accompany her in the nothingness where they drifted. Timeless.

***

A growing ball of fire roused Nic. She focused on it, unsure if it was beneath, above, or next to her. She had no sense of direction.

Fire? That's odd. And I still think of myself as Nic...

And then, the fire had a voice, licking along her ears, tracing a molten pathway into her mind, bringing her alive with sensation.

Fireborn. Daughter. Sister. Phoenix Mother.

The words, especially the title, opened her mind. She saw memories, safely stored behind a screen, waiting for the proper time to emerge. And she knew the voice belonged to the fire she and Damyl remembered and both hoped to rejoin. It was an entity she trusted as much as she trusted herself.

The fire seemed to hear her thoughts or sense her recognition. *Yessssss. Beloved Mother, one of the brave nine. You have done well by us. We will do well by you.*

A memory emerged from behind the screen. Her soul recognized Damyl's soul in another body, remembered decades spent together, physically, and then much longer, in the fire. They had formed a bond that was evidently as strong as they'd believed it was. Misery welled up and spilled out of her. How she missed him.

The comforting voice of the fire filled her. *Be at peace, beloved Mother. We are offering you a choice, to continue on, or to stay.*

Hope began to rise, but she crushed it. *How can I stay? How can I betray those who put their trust in me?*

Beloved Mother, do as seems needful to heal your soul. There is another who would serve as you have.

Nic could barely grasp the notion. *I could stay, and another would take my place?*

Yes, Beloved Mother.

Lifetimes of focusing on other's needs, and fear of dishonor for abandoning her task prompted Nic to deny the hope, yet again. *But, what of my duty to make reparation?*

You have done enough, Beloved Mother. If you wish, another will take up the burden.

Nic finally heard what the fire was telling her and began to believe. She considered her soul, her lives, all the times she'd negated her own desires. A new determination filled her. This could be her time, and she and Damyl could be together again, physically. Euphoria flickered, then flared to life. *Yes, if there is another, I choose to stay.*

Darkness swirled around Nic, shutting off consciousness, but the fire's words followed her into oblivion. *Rest, Beloved Mother, and enjoy your life. You have three more decades together. We will contact you when it is done, and you and he may do your parts then.*

***

Slowly, the woman once more became aware she existed. Aware there was another life waiting for her. Aware of an unusual lightness in her soul.

Then, she could see again, hovering over the pile of ash,

over the lump that would be her new body, her new incarnation. She realized she still thought of herself as Nic, and memories of Damyl washed over her, bringing desolation at the thought of a life without him. Then confusion rose as she tried to reconcile her anguish with the lightness in her soul. It felt like hope.

The ash-covered lump resolved itself into a being, and she watched with no eyes, removed from the act as only one who has no flesh can be, distracted by the ache from Damyl's absence. More of herself returned, and Nic had a sense her time in the nothingness had been different.

The fire was there.

When the new body was ready, she was drawn down, fitting each portion of her consciousness into it, being sure all of herself was there. The flesh felt disturbingly familiar, disrupting her dejection. Usually, there was a period of adjustment.

She opened her eyes, and wiped ashy grit from them. She looked at her fingers, turning her hand slowly, studying the shape and color, the texture. She lightly traced a faint scar running from thumb to elbow as her heart beat more rapidly.

She pushed down emotion, afraid to hope. New bodies were usually blemish-free. That scar had been on Nic's body, and those were Nic's hands. She ran inquisitive fingers over her face, feeling the skin stretched over high cheek bones that Damyl had brushed his fingers over, pulling at full lips he had kissed, stroking her hair back from her high forehead as he had thousands of times. She was back in the body she'd had as Nic, at the same stage of life she had just left.

Illusive memories from the nothingness swirled in her mind, sparks from a bonfire, most of it frustratingly just out of reach.

But, the fire was there; it called me Beloved Mother. And, something gave me hope. And now, I've returned to the same body.

Energized by the thought that Damyl might not be lost to her, she stood, scrubbing her fingers to remove ash. The flame-shaped exit and walls of her egg were harder to see than usual. She still had flames for night vision, but they simmered on low. There was a pile next to the opening, and when she lifted the first article, it tipped her world further. The tunic she'd discarded upon entering hung from her fingers.

She dropped it again, brushing ash from her body and hair best she could, then she turned the top inside out, using it to clean herself a bit more. She shook it to remove loose ash, turned it right side out and pulled it over her head. A chill breeze entering the cave flowed around her, and she shivered. Shock made her stand stock still, head tipped towards the opening.

Cold? Shiver? I'm never cold.

And yet, when another blast of wind hit her, she found herself scrambling for her pants, socks, and shoes, wishing she'd grabbed a jacket. She paused, turning her attention inward. The molten burning she'd always felt in her womb wasn't there. She was still warm, but the burning heat was absent, more easily overcome with external chill.

She called Flame, relieved when it responded as usual, and just as strongly, but it felt more remote. She hesitated over the conclusion she wanted to reach, not wanting to delude herself. *I need to see what's outside the cave. Then, maybe, I'll know.*

Fear froze her for a moment. *Oh, Goddess, how long has it been?*

Desperate now to find out the truth, she picked up the box that was also waiting for her and slipped outside without even pulling on her bangle. It was dark, and she couldn't see well, but it looked the same. She tried accessing her AI, but the disc had evidently not made the transition. *I should have taken it off before I burned.*

Nic forced her way through the overgrowth surrounding the cave, thankful when she stumbled onto the faint trail. She tried to speed up but had to slow back down as unseen branches and thorns caught at her. She ignored the scratches they gave her.

As soon as the trail spilled onto the two-track, she started jogging, reversing her course along the path she'd taken a—long? short?—time ago. Her heart battered at her chest from more than exertion. Here, the forest was back a respectful distance, so she could see further, but the moons were still absent, and cloud cover obscured the night sky, so she still had no notion of time. She kept running. Jogging not only got her home faster, it helped stave off the chill in the air.

She watched the horizon through the trees, eager for a glimpse of their home, speeding up when she saw the rooflines of their house and the neighbors to either side. The sky was just starting to lighten, so at least now, she had a rough time estimate. *Just before dawn. Damyl may be waking soon. He's an early riser.*

Chest heaving as her body struggled for oxygen, she stopped at the edge of the forest. The windows of her house were dark, and a quick perusal showed her it looked the same as when she'd left. The hoe Damyl had used in the garden yesterday was even in the same place. Her pulse slowed its frantic pace until it just beat strongly from effort. She wiped rapidly-cooling sweat from her eyes and hoped Damyl was not awake to miss her, yet. A light turned on in the house, drawing Nic's attention. She hesitated, inexplicably nervous, taking a moment to pull out her gold bangle and push it onto her wrist. She twisted the bangle back and forth, running fingers over the etchings, finally remembering that each marking represented one of her children. Her memories from the nothingness also came flooding back, dreamlike, but complete. She remembered

274

that another had been willing to take her place, that she'd been allowed to choose staying here.

She shivered in a chill wind. She'd been standing long enough to lose the heat from her run, and there was frost on the ground. But, uncertainty still held her prisoner. *I've lost much of my fire. What if I've changed too much?* Then, more memories rose, of who Damyl had been to her both in this life and before, filling her with belonging. Her fears were unfounded. *Damyl loves me, not my fire. He was my partner long before this all started.* The thought released her, and she ran towards the house and the man she thought she'd lost. The back door opened quietly to her touch, letting her in to the welcome warmth.

The kitchen was dark, and she had an odd sense of disconnect with her home. But, her way was gently lit by a single lamp in the living room, and familiarity slowly woke. The soft yellow light, their favorite for relaxing in the evenings, showed Damyl slumped on the couch, face in his hands. His shoulders were shaking, and she could see her silver wheel dangling from his fingers.

Glad she had the remedy, Nic felt her heart break for his sorrow. She shivered with residual cold from outside, set her box on the counter and called softly. "Damyl?"

Damyl's head snapped up and around, eyes red and swollen. He'd been awake a while then, she realized. As soon as he saw her, he pushed off the couch, stumbling across the room to gather her into the warmest hug she'd had in eternity.

She squeezed him back, feeling her soul knit back together. Her hair and neck were getting wet from his tears, but she didn't mind, her tears were watering his nightshirt, too.

Damyl pushed back from her and cradled her face in his hands. She kept her arms around his waist, not willing to give up the feel of his warm body, and his touch filled her with a sense of rightness.

He had a frantic edge to his features as he searched her face, and a desperate tinge to his voice. "Nic? Nic, you're here? Did it not happen yet? Your skin is cool." She felt him rub a finger wonderingly at some of the ash on her face, his other hand moving to caress her shoulder.

She reached up, clasping his hands, pressing them to her face, turning to plant a kiss in his palm. "I'm here, love, and it did happen, but differently."

He barely seemed to hear her, and his words tumbled out with a sob. "I woke up, found your wheel. You were gone. Not in the house, not in the neighborhood."

Nic reached up and put a finger on his lips. "Damyl, Love. I'm here." She pulled his head down for a lingering kiss, before staring earnestly into his eyes. "I'm here, here to stay. I won't leave you."

Damyl stared at her, and she saw him wanting to believe, fighting disbelief, afraid to hope. He noticed he still held the silver wheel and put it back around her neck.

Nic smiled, fingers finding and turning the star wheel, more of her life settling back in. "Join me in a warm shower. I can tell you what happened while I clean this ash off and get warm."

Confusion filled his face. "Warm?"

Nic nodded. "Yes. Not only is my skin cooler to touch, but I actually feel the cold now. Maybe not as much as you, but..." She shivered.

Damyl pulled her to their bathroom without further questions. He turned on the shower, then paused, looking to her to set the temperature. Soon, clothing littered the floor, and they stood under the warm stream, as they had many times before. Damyl used a washcloth on her, gently, almost reverently scrubbing off the ash.

She kept to the basics with her explanation—there would

be time to describe everything more fully later. "I burned, like before. But this time, you stayed with me. Well, at least your memory did. And then, the fire was there." She looked at him, seeing belief start in his eyes, as his hands told him she was really there.

He frowned. "The fire? Oh, you mean our fire?"

She nodded. "Yes, our fire. The one we came from and hope to return to. And, we will, I am certain. So many memories are still locked away, for security, but at least that much, I remember." She closed her eyes, letting the water run over her head, feeling her body warm from the heat, and Damyl's touch. "The fire also let me remember why we need to be together."

She felt his lips nudge at her neck, and she smiled as they moved on her skin when he prompted, "Why we need to be together?"

She tilted her head to allow him better access, the warm spray creating an intoxicating slickness. "Yes. Evidently, our souls have been together for a long time, both before the fire and in it."

He slid his hands down her back, cupping her buttocks, pulling her to him. "That sounds right, to me. I felt a soul-deep recognition from the very beginning."

Nic wiped water drops from her eyes, wrapped her arms around him, her breasts pressed tightly between them, and kissed him. His lips clung to hers, and he followed her, not letting her end the kiss right away.

She gently disengaged, placing one hand on his chest, touching his face with the other. "The fire gave me a choice. It said there is another, and that if I wanted to, I could choose to stay with you, and the other would finish my task. I am here."

"Another?" Damyl's voice held equal parts disbelief and hope.

Nic ran hands over his wet skin. Now that the relevant parts were told, she was interested in something else. She shrugged. "It just said another. I have no more knowledge, and I don't think that is by accident." She kissed his neck, licking at the moisture, then stopped, as a memory from the very end came back. "Oh, wait. I do have more. The fire said we have three decades. They would let us know when it was done, and we could then do our parts."

She finally saw soul-deep acceptance in Damyl. He ran the back of his fingers through the water on her cheek. Contentment filled his voice when he said, "So, we have three decades? And then, some unknown jobs to do? I say we make the most of our time now."

He turned off the shower. They'd barely toweled off before reaching for each other and moving to the bed. Nic saw a new level of awareness in his eyes that matched her own, brought on by the memory of their fear they'd never again be together in physical bodies. His lips and flesh were unusually warm against her skin, and his touch stirred the embers of her fire to a blaze that nearly matched its previous vigor. A thought occurred to her, and she grinned.

"What's the grin for?" Damyl had covered her body with his and was resting on his elbows, looking down at her.

Nic gave a deep chuckle, and Damyl dipped to claim her mouth in a long kiss. When he released her, Nic said, innocently, "I was just thinking that my cooler body temperature is going to take some getting used to. I keep noticing that your skin feels different. It's almost warm." She looked at him through her eyelashes. "Almost like a different lover."

Damyl growled, running his hands over her body, finding the heat between her legs, and bringing her to fever pitch. "We *are* different lovers. Ones who have more than twice as long together, to discover each other all over again."

Nic welcomed him into her body, the dichotomy of similarity and difference driving her rapidly to the edge.

After their loving, she wound herself tightly around him, and he held her just as close. She looked forward to learning Damyl as a new lover as thoroughly as she'd learned the old one and to being with him forever, no matter what form. She knew, deep in her soul, she'd finally found her home.

THE END

Introducing Patricia Kiyono

WHITTLED PROMISES

Patricia Kiyono writes sweet contemporary and historical romance. *Whittled Promises* is set in New York City and rural Michigan during the middle of the nineteenth century. Ellie and Vinnie meet as children in a New York orphanage but were separated when the Orphan Trains sent them to different cities in the west. Before they part, Vinnie carves a talisman for Ellie—a replica of the one he wears—and promises that its special power will help her whenever she needs it. For more information about Patricia Kiyono, please visit her website at https://www.patriciakiyono.com/

Heat Level: SWEET

WHITTLED PROMISES
Patricia Kiyono

Preface

During the first half of the nineteenth century, the United States experienced a massive influx of immigrants from Europe. They came for various reasons: poverty, military oppression, and a desire to achieve their dreams. Cities like New York grew exponentially, and the overcrowded conditions and lack of resources resulted in many children being left on their own. Organizations such as The Orphan Asylum Society, The Roman Catholic Orphan Asylum, and the Hebrew Orphan Asylum took care of many, but the sheer volume of children needing their services filled them to overflowing.

Charles Loring Brace believed these children would be better served by placing them with families, especially in rural areas, where they could benefit from fresh air and hard work. Working with the Children's Aid Society, he began to send them to farms in northern New York State, and when that proved successful, he expanded the plan to locations farther west. In September 1854, he sent 46 children by train to Dowagiac, Michigan, beginning a "placing out" program later known as the Orphan Trains. Some resources specify that all of the children on this first train were boys, but I ask you to allow me literary license for Ellie, my female protagonist, to be among them.

I thought about what life for these poor children must have been like and imagined two of them meeting again by chance after being relocated. I hope you enjoy my story.

Prologue
The Orphan Asylum, New York City, April 1854

Vinnie Martinelli never understood what made him stop. Crying girls were normally a good reason to put his head down and keep moving—far away from the tears. It was dinnertime, and he'd worked all day, weeding the courtyard. At fourteen, he was one of the older boys in the orphanage and was expected to work harder and longer than the younger ones. He was hungry, and the thin soup in his bowl wasn't going to go far toward easing that hunger.

The girl's long braids, the color of wheat, had started to come free from its ties, and her dress hung loosely. She was dressed like any other girl living in the orphanage, but there was something about this girl that made him want to make her feel better. He'd seen her in the classes held in the orphanage and knew she was about his age. The chatter of hundreds of other children faded as he focused on the girl, and before he could change his mind, he walked over and sat on the bench across the table from her.

"What's the matter?" He kept his voice low to avoid drawing attention from the others.

The girl looked up and peered at him through watery eyes, and he felt himself drowning in pools of blue. All coherent thought left him, and he wondered if he'd caught that brain fever he'd heard about. The sadness turned to wariness, and she leaned back, away from him.

"I won't hurt you, I promise. I just thought you might need some help. Are you sick? Should I call the matron?"

She shook her head. "I was so hungry, but those—those awful boys ate my supper. They just took my bowl and passed it around, and they all ate from it until it was empty. Then they put it back and said, 'Here, now you don't have to eat it.'"

Vinnie's own stomach growled. But, even greater was the feeling of anger. How could anyone take advantage of her?

"I found a half a loaf of bread in the trash earlier," he lied. "So I'm not all that hungry."

He scraped most of his meal into her bowl. "Might as well let someone else eat this."

Her eyes opened wide. "But—"

"I don't really like this stuff anyway. You're doing me a favor, eating it for me." He picked up his dry biscuit and chewed. "Better eat that before someone else takes it away."

***

Hours later, as he tossed on his narrow bunk in the boy's dormitory, his thoughts went back to his odd behavior. Why did he care about whether or not the girl got something to eat? It wouldn't be the first time someone had to go hungry because some bully had taken more than his or her share. Until now, he'd minded his own business. That was how he'd survived.

He'd been on his own for almost three years now. His father had disappeared one day, and his mother hadn't been able to carry on. He'd watched her slowly fade away, even though he'd done everything in his eleven-year-old power to help her. He'd done odd jobs to help keep them fed, but in the end, she'd given up.

The only thing he had left of her was a pendant. A little charm his father, a carpenter, had made when courting his mother so long ago. An oval-shaped pendant, carved from wood, with a single rose etched on it. She'd strung it on a piece of coarse twine and put it around his neck. "Keep this near your heart, Vinnie," she'd told him as she gasped for breath. "It'll guide you and tell you what you need to do."

He fingered the pendant, as he did each night and whenever he was troubled. Did the little girl remind him of his mother? Was that what drew him to her? She didn't look anything like his raven-haired, dark-eyed mother. Maybe it was the fragility, the vulnerability, the hopelessness he saw in her eyes.

***

For the next several days, he kept an eye out for the girl, spending what time he could getting to know her. Her name was Ellie Brown, and she was a recent arrival at the home. At each meal, at each inspection, each outing, he'd look for her, ready to step in if she needed help. But, she seemed to have gained confidence since that day. A larger girl started to push her around, and he'd nearly run over to help, but he'd stopped worrying when Nellie landed a punch to the larger girl's gut, sending her to the ground. Of course, Ellie had been punished, but the bully hadn't bothered her again.

He'd been aware of her in the school room, too. She was a serious student, reading even when the teacher allowed them to do other things. He didn't have much use for the stories and poems they learned, but she appeared to love them. Not like math, where numbers didn't have to be interpreted to find the meaning. They were solid, unchanging. They made sense. They were useful.

He found her one day, engrossed in a book. She'd made a cozy nook for herself under the staircase. The sight made him wish he could enjoy it with her. "What are you reading?" he asked.

She looked up and rewarded him with a shy smile. "Hi, Vinnie. I loved that story Miss Gobles read to us today—the one called *The Rose and the Ring*. I asked the teacher if I could borrow her book to read it again."

He nodded. "That was a good story. You're lucky you can read all those long words. I'd have trouble with it."

"Reading is easy. Numbers are hard."

"For you, maybe. Not for me."

"Okay, when I have trouble understanding arithmetic, I'll ask you for help. When you have trouble reading, you can ask me. Deal?"

He grinned and stuck out his hand. "Deal."

***

A week later, his ears tuned in to her sobs again. This time he found her behind a post, sobbing into her apron. He looked around for someone who might have hurt her, but she seemed to be alone.

"What's wrong, Ellie? Did someone hurt you?"

She sniffed. "They're sending me away."

He stepped back, as if he'd been hit. "What happened? Are you in trouble?"

She shook her head.

"Were you adopted?"

Another shake.

"Where are they sending you?"

"I don't know. Somewhere out west, I think. They gave me a sack and just said for me to have everything packed in this bag and be ready to go tomorrow."

"Better than being here, I'll bet."

"But, I don't know anyone out west. And, I don't know what it'll be like. What if there are wild animals? Aren't there savage people who cut all your hair off?"

"But, if you get adopted by a family out there, they'll protect you."

She gazed up at him. "Really?"

He nodded, hoping he'd told her the truth.

***

The next day, Vinnie arose early and waited in the dining hall until he saw her. He carried his lukewarm oatmeal and sat down opposite her, and she smiled as he settled on the bench.

He'd spent most of the night working on a special gift. Needing to give her something to reassure her, he'd taken a small piece of wood and carved a replica of the pendant his mother had given him. He'd carved, and sanded it until it was smooth, even tracing and etching the rose in the middle. He'd pulled several strings from a burlap bag and braided them together to make a necklace to hang it on.

When they finished eating, they stood, and he motioned for her to follow him to a quiet corner. He pulled the pendant from his pocket. "I'm glad I found you before you left. I want you to have this. It's a special necklace. It'll keep you safe and tell you what to do. When you're worried, or don't know what to do, just touch it—even through your shirt—and the answer will come to you."

She made no move to take it. "This is yours, Vinnie. I've seen you touching it, when you're having trouble reading. I couldn't take it from you."

"Sure you can. I have my own." He pulled his pendant out of his shirt. "See? My ma gave it to me before she died. My pa made it for her, so I made one just like it for you. I've had it since I was six or seven, and it always worked for me. Even when things were bad, it always told me what to do so that things would get better."

He looped the cord around her neck and sucked in a breath when her arms wrapped around him. "Thank you, Vinnie. You've been so good to me." She stepped back and gave him a wide smile. "I'll take really good care of it," she promised.

He watched her walk away, knowing she took a part of his heart with her.

"Take care of her, Ma," he whispered.

Chapter One

Dowagiac, Michigan, March 1866

Bud picked up his satchel and descended from the train. He'd been riding for several hours and needed something to eat and drink. The train would pause here for a short time before continuing on to Kalamazoo, where he would transfer to the line taking him north to the Traverse Bay Area. He picked up the worn satchel containing all his worldly goods and made his way toward the general store across the street from the station.

It seemed fitting to be taking the train to his new life. Twelve years earlier, it had been a train that had brought him from the crowded streets of New York City to the vast plains of Nebraska. When he'd been put on the Orphan Train, he hadn't really expected to find a family to adopt him, but he'd been eager to go somewhere new. New York held nothing but bitter memories for him, and he'd heard wonderful things about the wide-open spaces in the West.

Nebraska was nothing like New York, and he'd quickly learned to make adjustments. In New York, he'd been accustomed to people dismissing him because of his social standing, or lack of one. But farther west, his name sometimes caused people's brows to raise and distrust him. So he'd taken to shortening his last name and using the nickname his fellow farmhands had called him. Though his legal papers said otherwise, he thought of himself as Bud Martin. As far as he was concerned, Vincent Martinelli was part of his past.

And now, Nebraska would be another part of his past. He was, he figured, about two-thirds of the way through his journey to a place called Homestead Township, in the northern part of Lower Michigan. Thanks to the Homestead Act, he could purchase land for a mere $1.25 per acre, and after five years of living on it, the land would be his. He'd saved more than enough money to make the trip, purchase several acres of land, and purchase supplies for building his home. He'd need to pay for room and board until he'd built something habitable. Starting over was always hard. He knew, because he'd done it several times already. But this time, he was determined to make his dream come true.

He would be a landowner.

The idea had come to him late at night, after he'd sunk into his bedroll at the end of a hard day on the Nebraska farm where he'd spent almost half his life. For the most part, the experience had been worth the long, grueling trip. The Simmons family hadn't been warm, but they hadn't been cruel, either. They hadn't adopted him or any of the other boys, but simply took them on as cheap farm hands. He'd learned to ride a horse and care for animals. To a fourteen-year-old from New York City, it had been a rough transition. At first, the other field hands had been cruel, mocking him for everything from his name to his accent to his lack of knowledge about animals. He'd learned when to let their taunts go, and when to fight back. But, the thing that he'd observed was this: owning land was power. The more land one owned, the more power he wielded, and the more people would listen to him.

He wanted some of that power for himself, so he'd saved his money. The War Between the States had stalled those dreams for a few years. Although Nebraska was still a territory, soldiers from Fort Kearny were often sent to battle states, but their main purpose had been to protect the settlers. During his time in the army, he'd spent a lot of time building everything from furniture to buildings. Perhaps it was due to his father's influence that he was happiest when working with wood. He'd heard there was lots of forest land in Michigan. After serving in the Union Army at Fort Kearny, he'd collected his pay and headed east.

The general store in Dowagiac was like countless others he'd shopped in, except this one was prepared for the passengers coming through. A sizable portion of the counter held several small burlap sacks. A chalkboard next to them divulged the contents: one beef sandwich, one pickle, and one piece of gingerbread. The price was reasonable, and the fact that the items were prepared and packed, ready to eat, was a plus. Most of the other passengers thought so, too. By the time he'd paid for his meal, very few sacks were left. Since it was a pleasant spring day, he took his meal outdoors to eat. He didn't particularly want to go back on the train, but sat on the edge of the porch. A few others did the same, and some wandered toward a distant copse of trees. He dug into his lunch sack and pulled out a hefty sandwich and dug in. Whoever had put this meal together sure knew what they were doing. The meat was perfect and tender and seasoned just right. The bread was fresher than anything he'd eaten since he'd begun his trip.

He'd finished half of his sandwich when he heard a whine. Turning his head, he came face to face with a mangy dog with bright red fur. He'd seen animals like this, accompanying their masters on a hunt. It was a spaniel, if he remembered correctly. This one seemed friendly enough, sitting calmly beside him. But, those huge, sad eyes called to him, begging for a bite to eat. Bud couldn't help tearing off a corner of his sandwich and sharing it with his new companion, who wasted no time consuming it. Thankful for the generous portions of food, he and the dog shared the rest of his meal. When they'd finished every bite, Bud stood, wanting to walk a bit before getting back on the train. The lunch had been so good and so reasonably priced, perhaps he should purchase another of those meals in a sack for later on. He'd have a hard time finding such an affordable meal again. He unhooked his wallet from his belt. The train's whistle blew, warning passengers to get back on, and it distracted him. He felt the leather wallet slide out of his hand, and spun his gaze back to see his lunch companion running off with it.

"Hey!" he yelled. "Get back here with my money!" He ran after the mutt, who dashed into the store. The dog ran up one aisle and down another, and customers leaped out of the way as Bud weaved his way through the merchandise. When the thief ducked under a display table, Bud skirted around it, planning to nab him as he came out, but the dog tricked him, coming out another side. Bud heard a crash as his foot caught one of the table legs, knocking the display to the floor, but his focus was on the money as it left the building and ran around the side to the back. Once outdoors, it was easier to run, and with his long legs Bud nearly had the dog. He leaped into the air, ready to pound on the culprit when the world suddenly turned black.

***

When Bud next opened his eyes, he was lying on a bed — one with no lumps. His vision was fuzzy, but the ceiling above him told him he was in a place far nicer than anyplace he'd slept in a long time. The smell of something delicious — beef stew, perhaps — tickled his senses, and someone pressed a soft cloth on his head. He couldn't remember the last time someone had done that for him.

"How are you feeling? Does your head hurt?"

The words, though spoken softly, hit him like a douse of water. His head began to pound, and he closed his eyes, bringing his hand up to his forehead.

"Of course his head hurts. What would you expect? You knocked the man unconscious, throwing that door open." The raspy voice came from farther away.

"I heard the yelling and crashing and needed to investigate."

"There wouldn't-a been anything to investigate if it hadn't been for that wily mongrel of yours," the man returned. "That critter has been nothin' but trouble from the day you started feeding him. He grabbed that wallet right outa this man's hand, he did, and then raced around the store with it. Of course this fella had to chase after him, but then you came along and knocked him senseless."

"I didn't mean to! I was just going to call Duke and tell him to bring me whatever he'd stolen. I didn't realize this man was so close when I opened the door."

Keeping his hand on his forehead, Bud opened one eye. The speaker was as lovely as her voice. Not beautiful in the primped-up manner of the women in the saloon he'd visited a few times, but a natural, approachable beauty.

"And, this man here missed his train," the man continued. "Probably got a wife and kids wondering why he hasn't come home."

"Oh, dear. When he wakes up again, I'll get his information and let his family know."

"You do that. Maybe they'll send someone for him. In the meantime, since he's in your bed, you're gonna need to sleep down in the storage room."

The hand at his brow stilled. "Yes, Sir."

The girl's response brought out his protective instinct, and he opened his mouth to reassure her that he was fine, but the words wouldn't come. He could tell that the raspy sounds coming from his throat weren't discernible to anyone.

"Please help me raise him up so he can drink."

The man shuffled over from the corner. He was just as Bud had imagined. Craggy, world-worn features in his face, tall and gangly. He came to the other side and placed a hand behind Bud's right shoulder, while the girl took his left side, and together they raised him so that he was sitting. The girl brought a glass to his lips, and he drank greedily. While he drank, the girl propped the pillow up against the headboard. When the cup was empty, he scooted back, sank into it, sighing.

"Thank you," he murmured.

"Glad you're back among the living," the old man muttered. "It woulda been a shame to have a body to bury with no name for the headstone."

Bud turned toward the man. "You didn't look at my identification papers?"

The man shook his head. "Around here, we respect a man's personal property. If you hadn't made it, we might have looked to see if we could locate your next of kin. Your things are all right here, except the wallet that fool dog ran off with. Did you have any luggage on the train?"

Bud shook his head, then wished he hadn't. He closed his eyes again, willing the dizziness to go away. "No. Everything I own—other than my money—is in that satchel." He waited a few moments, then opened his eyes again. Thankfully, the world had stopped spinning. He held his hand out to the man. "I'm Buddy Martin. Sorry about the mess in the store. And, I'm sure your customers didn't appreciate me running through."

The man took his hand and shook it. "Earl Cannon." He nodded at the girl on the other side of the bed. "That over there is Nellie. And, I can't say you didn't do anything any man would do if a dog ran off with all his money."

Mindful of his aching head, Bud turned to his left and gave the girl a careful nod. Looking back at Earl, he asked, "Did anyone happen to see what the dog did with my wallet?"

His heart sank when Earl shook his head. "No sign of it anywhere. That no-account Duke probably buried it or dropped it in the river. I'm sorry."

Bud closed his eyes. Five years of savings, gone in an

instant. Opening them again, he met Earl's eyes. "Since it looks like I'll be staying in town for some time, I'd like to replace whatever I destroyed. I have no more money, but I'm pretty handy. If you could use some help fixing things up, I'll be glad to do that. And, if you know where I could get some honest work and a place to stay until I save enough to finish my trip, I'd be much obliged."

Earl nodded. "Sounds like a fair trade. The doc said you should probably stay where you are for the rest of the day, but once you're back on your feet, we'll talk about it."

Bud wanted to insist he start today, but reason ruled. It wouldn't hurt to rest a little longer. He turned to the girl, who'd already risen and had moved her chair aside.

"Thank you for taking care of me."

Her cheeks took on a rosy hue. "It's the least I could do, seein' I was the one who knocked you unconscious."

"Still, it was nice of you to get me to a real bed, rather than leave me on the ground, where people could trip over me."

A ghost of a smile tilted her lips. "You were kind enough to get hit *behind* the store, so there was no danger of that." She stood and smoothed her apron. "I'll finish cooking supper and bring you some. You just rest."

"Yes, Ma'am." He couldn't remember the last time someone had taken care of him. Not since his mama. And that was so long ago he had trouble seeing her face clearly in his mind. All he could remember was the overall feeling of peace, of being cared for. The feeling he had now.

The woods of Northern Michigan could wait a bit longer.

Chapter Two

Nellie Cannon folded two extra blankets and spread

293

them out over a low shelf in the storage room. She could have unfolded the old camp bed her father had taken in trade, but she was too tired to figure out how to assemble it. Still, she couldn't bear the thought of sleeping directly on the floor. With all the food in the room, there was no telling what four or six-legged creatures she'd be sharing the space with. Instead, she'd emptied the entire shelf and wiped it down thoroughly before laying the blankets on it.

At least, the shelves weren't full. In past years, when Mother Cannon was alive, the storage room had been full to overflowing, and she would have had to sleep on top of supplies. But for the past few years, ever since Mother had passed away, Father had been particularly stingy about ordering for the store, and there was plenty of room. Nellie often wondered why he'd become such a penny-pincher. How could he expect the store to make a profit if he let supplies run out?

She understood the need for her to sleep down here, but it brought back bitter memories. In her previous life, as Ellie Smith, she and her mother had slept in alleys, on park benches, or wherever they could find a place to lie down. After Ma died, she'd been sent to the orphanage, where she'd had to worry about predators of the two-legged kind. When she'd come to Michigan, she'd been one of two girls taken in by Earl and Muriel Cannon. She and the other girl had shared a room and a bed, but the other girl had run away less than a year later. Since then, she'd had the luxury of having her own room, her own retreat. Mother Cannon insisted on calling her Nellie rather than Ellie, saying the name was prettier with an N at the front, and eventually she stopped correcting her.

But for now, a stranger rested in her room. As her adoptive father had pointed out, it was her fault that he'd been knocked unconscious and missed his train. Giving up her bed was the least she could do. Other than a nasty bruise high on his forehead, he hadn't seemed to be any the worse for wear. She wondered where he was headed, and where he'd been. Did he have someone waiting for him? He hadn't responded when Pa had mentioned notifying next of kin.

Once settled in, she realized her thoughts wouldn't allow her to sleep. She might as well get some work done, something that didn't require a lot of thought. Perhaps it was time to do a thorough inventory of the storage room. She relit her lamp, found a notebook and pencil, and began to catalog each item on the shelves. The familiarity of the task calmed her.

When she got to the shelf with medicinal supplies, she paused. How could there be only one bottle of laudanum? Normally, she was careful to keep it in stock. She made a note to order more.

The cooking supplies presented another puzzle. The bag of flax seed she'd placed on the shelf just a few days ago was nearly empty. The canister in the shop was full, so she hadn't yet opened the bag. When had it been opened? Who would have needed so much of it? It seemed odd for a thief to take the time to open the bag, take half the contents out, and leave the rest. She needed to remember to ask Father the next day. In the meantime, she made a note to order more.

She worked steadily, until the wick in her lantern burned down and started to dim. She put down her pencil and crawled back onto her makeshift bunk. By the time the light went out, she'd completed her inventory and she sank into a deep sleep.

***

The next day, Nellie was up early. She supposed it was due to sleeping on the hard wooden shelf rather than her bed. But, she reminded herself that the stranger needed it more than she did. Buddy Martin, from what she'd seen and heard, was a nice man. His hands were rough and calloused, so he was used

295

to hard work. He'd brushed off her apologies, instead thanking her for not leaving him on the ground. As if anyone with an ounce of humanity would do that!

When she'd brought him a tray, he'd gobbled down his dinner the previous night and then thanked her profusely. Apparently, he hadn't learned polite table manners, yet he wasn't totally uncivilized. And, he had the kindest eyes. The kind of eyes that drew her in like a hypnotic melody.

But she couldn't, wouldn't give in. Every woman she'd ever known who'd given her heart to a man had ended up settling for a life she would never want. She'd watched her own mother—her real mother—give everything she'd had to a tyrant who'd eventually beat her to death. In the orphanage, it had been women who'd done most of the work, while men made the decisions. And then, the train had taken her to Michigan, where her life had changed completely. The Cannons had been nice enough, but it was clear that the only reason they'd taken her in was to help with cooking, cleaning, and minding the store. They'd seen to all her needs. She'd had food, clothing and shelter. She'd even been able to go to school for a few years. Earl had grumbled about the time wasted, but Muriel insisted that they needed people they could trust to help with the bookkeeping. Nellie had loved school, so they'd let her continue, at least until she'd learned enough to deal with ledgers and ordering supplies. She would have loved to learn more, but Earl decreed that five years was more than enough. Fortunately, the teacher, Miss Barker, still visited, loaning her books to read and encouraging her.

When Muriel died, Nellie had considered leaving, but as she'd packed her things, she realized she had more to gain by staying. Because Earl had no other children, the store would eventually go to her. There had been a son, she'd discovered. She'd never seen him, and no one talked about him, at least not to her.

Soon after she'd arrived, she'd found a photo tucked away in a bookcase. It was a young man, perhaps in his early twenties. He had Earl's cleft chin, and Muriel's eyes. The photograph had been torn in half, and then glued back together. Knowing that photographs were expensive and precious, she'd gone to Muriel to ask who it was. Her adoptive mother had gone white and hustled her back up the stairs, glancing back to make sure her husband hadn't seen.

"Child, I'm sure you can tell by looking at this picture that this is Earl's son. His name is Lucas, and he inherited his father's stubborn nature. It was only a matter of time before they clashed so badly that the boy left to find his fortune. Earl was so angry that he ripped the picture in half and threw it out the window. He told me I was never to speak his name again. I went out later on and found the pieces and hid them."

"Muriel, come down here and help this woman get what she needs," Earl's command from below had her glancing down and then reaching out to put a hand on Nellie's shoulder. "Put that photograph back where you found it, and don't ever mention it."

Lucas had never returned, and Nellie assumed he'd either died or had made his fortune elsewhere. She'd stayed on, working hard to keep the store profitable.

As she did whenever faced with a problem, she felt through the fabric of her nightgown, gently stroking the pendant that a kind boy at the orphanage had given her years ago. She'd often wondered what happened to him. Had he also been sent to a new life, far away from New York? Was he happy? Did he still wear and use the magic power of his pendant?

In the years following, she'd come to depend on her talisman to get her through troubling times. Maybe now, she hoped, it would help her overcome her bothersome interest in the handsome stranger. She had to keep her eye on the prize. The store.

Chapter Three

Bud arose early the next morning. He dressed and washed up, marveling at how a filling, nutritious meal and a solid night of sleep had revived him. What a difference it made, sleeping in a real bed, inside a quiet home. He spared a thought to revising his plan to head north. Or perhaps adding to it. Once he purchased his land, he'd build a nice home on it. He'd fill it with good, sturdy furniture. Maybe once he was established, he'd look for a wife. One who could make the place look more comfortable, more civilized. But, he had no patience for women who were silly and vain. He needed a partner, someone who was willing to work beside him. Who wasn't afraid to get her hands dirty if needed.

Someone like Nellie?

Maybe. Someday. At the moment, he was in no position to think of such things. He was still nothing. A nobody, as his foreman used to say. But, that was going to change someday. He'd save his money and…

Money. Earl had told him his things were in the satchel, but the dog had run away with his wallet. So he was broke again. Blast. That wallet had contained five years of saving and doing without. He had no choice but to stay in… what was the name of this town again? He needed to find out.

Maybe that wouldn't be such a hardship. He'd have to find a job and a place to stay so that Nellie could have her room back. But first, he needed to help Earl to clean and fix up his general store. The train's whistle interrupted his thoughts, and he moved toward the window. He was on the second floor of the building, and the train station was across the street. The window faced the street, and he observed the train slowing down as it pulled into the station.

Apparently, Earl and his daughter lived above the general store. He hoped she hadn't been uncomfortable. The girl was one fabulous cook. The previous night, she'd apologized for the simple food, but the beef stew, chock full of vegetables, and the fresh sourdough bread were more than he'd eaten in a long time. He couldn't remember the last time he'd been so full.

*****

He did his best to rearrange the bed linens so that they looked the way he'd seen bedrooms in the boss' house done up. It had been a long time, but he thought his effort looked close. He stepped out of the room, looking for the staircase. In the kitchen, he found a tray set with a plate piled high with eggs, fried potatoes, and a muffin. A note on the tray indicated that the food was for him, and that there was coffee in the pot on the stove. Gratefully, he sat and polished off every bite. He'd make darned sure Earl got his money's worth of work from him.

He brought his plate and fork to the counter, then made his way down the stairs. At the bottom of the stairway, a worn curtain partially hid the contents of what he presumed was a storage room at the back of the store. He pushed the curtain aside, finding merchandise stacked on sagging shelves. The lowest shelf held a stack of thin blankets. Was this where the girl had spent the night? He'd make sure she slept in her own bed tonight. He wasn't sure he could fit his tall frame on that shelf, but he'd make do. Then again, they'd probably want him to find other accommodations, now that he was recovered. Closing the curtain, he opened the door into the store. Earl waited on customers at the counter while Nellie restocked shelves. She looked up as he entered and bestowed him with a friendly smile as she nodded. He nodded back as he approached, then paused when she seemed to shrink away. Did he frighten her? He spoke quietly, but didn't move any closer.

"Thank you for the breakfast."

She nodded but kept working.

He frowned. Was she afraid of him? She'd been so solicitous the previous day. Perhaps her father had warned her against getting too friendly with him. Suppressing his disappointment, he turned toward Earl. He waited until the man finished helping his customer, then stepped forward.

"Good morning. What would you like me to start on today?"

Earl regarded him thoughtfully. "You look a lot better this morning than you did yesterday. How's the head?"

"Good as new. I'm ready to work."

"Glad to hear it." He stepped around the counter and led Bud toward the display table that had been a victim of the previous day's chase. "I'm gonna need this repaired, if you're handy with wood."

Bud bent and inspected the broken table. No wonder it had been smashed. The thin boards used for its top had been no match for his weight. The legs hadn't fared much better.

"If it's all the same to you, I'd rather start from scratch. This top is too thin to support anything with any weight. Do you have any wood I can use? Something more sturdy than this?"

Earl scratched his chin. "Okay, I'll go with new. If you do a decent job on it, I'll have more work for you. If you want it." He went over to the counter and dug out a notebook and stubby pencil. He wrote a short note on it and tore the page out and handed it to Bud. "Judd's Lumberyard is about a quarter of a mile from here. Give him this note. I want quality, but if he can't set you up for a dollar, then just get what you need for the top and use what's left here for the base." He pointed toward the back of the store. "If you go out the back door past the storeroom, you'll be on Front Street. Head east, and the lumberyard is on the north side of the road."

Bud nodded, but decided he'd do whatever it took to replace the entire table.

"Where are your tools?"

"Nellie keeps a hammer and nails in the storeroom, and there's a shed in back. I'm sure we've got everything you need."

As he walked through the storage room to exit the store, a soft hand stopped him.

"Mr. Martin."

He couldn't remember ever being addressed as Mister anything, and he turned to hear what she had to say.

"I know my father didn't give you very much money for the lumber. His penny pinching is a sore spot between us. With things falling to pieces around here, it'll be a miracle if there's anything left." She reached in her apron pocket and brought out a handful of coins. "I did some mending and earned my own money. Someday, I'm hoping this store will be mine. I want there to be something left here when that time comes. So please, get what you need to make that table sturdy." She turned and dashed back in as Earl called her from the front of the store.

Well, at least he'd be able to make a better table, he thought. It appeared there was more to the young lady than good looks and good cooking. She had a solid plan for her future. Unlike most women he'd known, that plan didn't rely entirely on having a husband. He tucked that bit of curious information away as he took in the sights of the Michigan town.

The main road through the city ran along the back of the store. Walking through the town, he took in the neat shops, the cheerful shoppers, the happy children. This was so unlike anywhere he'd lived before. In New York, people didn't smile, didn't wave hello, and didn't acknowledge strangers. And then, when he'd been sent west, there were no neighbors to speak of. Other than the people on the farm, one could go for weeks without seeing someone new.

He reached the lumberyard and spoke to the owner, who read Earl's note and shook his head. "Earl is a good man, but he's a skinflint. How big is the table he wants you to build?"

"About six feet long, and two feet wide." He reached in his pocket and brought out the coins Nellie had given him. "Earl's daughter gave me this to put with it."

The man nodded. "Nellie's got a good head on her shoulders. If Earl had any sense, he'd put her in charge." He took the extra coins and the note and led Bud to the cut lumber. In just a few minutes, he'd made his selection and arranged for delivery. By the time he headed back to the general store, he'd found a boarding house, where Miss Lydia, the owner, agreed to let him stay in exchange for maintenance work on the property. Nellie would not have to sleep in the storage room again.

Chapter Four

After Bud left, Nellie set about clearing away the broken table. She'd already moved the merchandise to another part of the store. Earl watched her work but made no move to help.

"Don't throw away that wood. Bud can probably use it."

Nellie bit her lip and nodded. She moved the pieces through the back storeroom and placed them on a pile behind the store. Then she swept the floor clean.

It was time to package up the sandwiches for the passengers on the afternoon train.

Remembering the fiasco from the previous day, she stood outside and whistled. Duke came bounding toward her.

She'd found the friendly mongrel digging through the trash one day, and he'd stayed ever since.

"I'm sorry about this, Duke," she told the sad-eyed dog. "But, until you learn to behave yourself, you're going to have to stay in the back while we have extra customers." She led him to the hen house, currently unoccupied. Earl continued to balk at getting new hens when the last bunch died. She opened the door and tossed a piece of jerky inside. When Duke ran after it, she closed the door and tied a rope to secure it. She cringed as the dog's howls of protest followed her back into the store, but she knew he'd settle down eventually. Going in the back door, she trudged upstairs and got to work.

She was just in time. The whistle blew across the street, signaling the arrival of passengers. She stationed herself at the counter, ready to greet them.

Soon, the store filled as passengers poured inside. Gentlemen, in tailored suits and tall hats. Ladies, dressed in summer finery. Nellie wondered how they managed the long train ride while coping with their bustles and corsets. The thought made her thankful for her circumstances. No one expected a little nobody like her to subject herself to such torture.

Within minutes, almost all of her meal sacks had sold, and the train continued on its way east. She kept the remaining sacks next to the register, knowing that the locals occasionally enjoyed them as well. Then, she went around to the back to let Duke out of the chicken coop. To her surprise, Duke was out of the coop, playing a game of fetch with Bud. He chased after a small stick and obediently brought it back. She thought about how much time had elapsed since the howls had stopped. How long had they been playing?

"Thanks for keeping Duke occupied. I know he wasn't happy in there, but I didn't want him bothering the passengers and running off with their things—again."

"You're welcome. The farm where I worked had a dog. It was bigger than this one, but I remembered how much fun we had, so I thought maybe he'd behave himself if I played a game with him."

She laughed. "Do you plan to play with him every time the train comes?"

He grinned. "Well, no. The chicken coop was a good idea. Especially if you're not going to have chickens in there."

Her smile disappeared. "I've been begging Father to buy some more chickens. If we had our own eggs, we wouldn't have to depend on local farmers to bring them here. Sometimes they forget, or we get them after they're old. The farmers prefer selling directly to their customers and making a greater profit. I can't blame them for that."

"I take it your father doesn't like to take advice from you."

She snorted and turned away. "No, he doesn't," she agreed. "He tends to not listen to anyone who's...female."

"Ah. I've known a few men like that." Hugh Simmons, the man who'd owned the farm he'd worked on, had been especially indifferent to women. Bud had always felt sorry for Simmons' wife and daughters. "Well, I think he's mighty lucky to have you around." He paused as a wagon drew up beside them, bringing the lumber he'd purchased. "Guess I'd better get to work on that table."

Nellie went inside, partly to start cooking supper and baking for the next day, and partly to keep herself from staring at the man. She couldn't resist peeking out the kitchen window to watch as he worked.

She'd just finished mixing the dough for the next day's bread when Earl called her to come downstairs. She couldn't imagine why he couldn't deal with any customer's needs, but she wiped her hands on her apron and went down.

Mrs. Adelaide Winston, wife of the pastor at the Harmony Baptist Church, stood near the front counter with two other women. The frowns on their faces indicated they weren't on a friendly social call. She took a deep breath, pasted on her most pleasant smile, and approached the women. "Good afternoon, ladies. How can I help you?"

Mrs. Winston's frown deepened. "Miss Cannon, I understand that you have been housing a man unrelated to you here in your living quarters. This is not the behavior I would expect from an unmarried woman in our congregation."

Nellie took a step back, as if physically struck. For a moment, she was transported to the orphanage, and the women became the older girls, taunting and teasing her. She'd felt so helpless then, until she'd found a friend in Vinnie. Knowing that she had someone who believed in her had given her the strength to stand up and fight for herself. Her hand went to her throat, and her fingers wrapped around the pendant Vinnie had carved. Strength coursed through her, and the tension eased. She could deal with this.

Straightening, she faced the woman squarely. "Mr. Martin was injured on our property. He was knocked unconscious. Surely you didn't expect us to simply leave him there, when The Good Book teaches us to have charity?"

The woman's eyes narrowed. "I see you've adopted your father's impudent nature. Of course, you would need to tend to him, but you also allowed him to remain here the entire night."

"Yes. I recall learning a verse from Hebrews: 'Do not neglect to show hospitality to strangers, for thereby some have entertained angels unawares.'"

"Two men carried him upstairs. To *your* room. That is entirely inappropriate."

"He was unconscious! Were the men supposed to carry

him to the boarding house? His money was stolen. Even if he'd been awake, he wouldn't have been able to pay."

"Nevertheless—"

"Miss Cannon?"

The women turned as one. Bud held a piece of paper out to Nellie. He held his hat in his other hand. "I truly appreciate you letting me stay in your storage room last night to recover from my injury. Here's my address at the boarding house. If Duke ever digs up my wallet, I'd appreciate you sending it to me there." He pivoted and left before she could respond.

Mrs. Winston recovered first. "Well, I suppose if he was sleeping in the storage room, that's not quite as bad. But how do we know that he was? You don't keep a bed in there, do you?"

"Actually, we do." Earl's gruff voice cut in. "If you ladies would like to see for yourselves…" He gestured toward the back.

"I would like to see how a man that tall could possibly sleep in a storage room." Mrs. Winston marched toward him, and Earl held the curtain aside so that she could peer in. One by one, the other ladies followed suit. Hearing them whispering to each other, Nellie wondered what they saw. Aside from the blankets she'd left folded on the bottom shelf, there was nothing to indicate that a person had slept there.

Nellie peeked in. And, held back a gasp. The cot was set up, and the blankets she'd folded and placed on the shelf lay in a pile on it.

Mrs. Winston seemed a bit subdued, but she quickly recovered. She drew herself up. "In light of what we've seen and heard, I am recommending to the pastor that your membership, as well as your father's, be reinstated. Your charity toward your fellow man is duly noted." Lifting her nose into the air, she breezed out, her entourage following.

As soon as the door closed, Earl grunted. "Well, wasn't that nice of them to reinstate my membership in a place I have no intention of going."

Chapter Five

Bud trudged toward the general store. In the month he'd spent in the small Michigan town, his reputation as a carpenter/handyman had grown. Thanks to recommendations from Nellie and Miss Lydia at the boarding house, he'd secured plenty of work, and had been able to save some money. He showed his appreciation by helping them in any way he could. He especially enjoyed it when Miss Lydia sent him to the general store for supplies, because he could visit with the pretty proprietor.

The previous day, he'd received a contract from the owner of the stables to build a series of troughs. The numbers on the contract added up, but there were several words on the document that he couldn't figure out. He'd noticed several thick books in Nellie's room during the one night he'd spent there. If the books were hers, that meant she was a good reader, and he trusted her, more than anyone else, to help him.

He'd timed his visit after the morning train. Hopefully, she'd have time to look at the contract for him. Perhaps he could offer to do some work for her in exchange.

He found her outside, weeding her garden. The little plot behind the store had begun to sprout with neat rows of vegetables. Around the outside edge of the garden, a series of stakes created a short fence, as well as a ring of marigolds to discourage unwanted scavengers. She looked up as she approached, as if she could sense him. Her smile encouraged him, and he came closer.

"Good afternoon, Mister Martin."

"Afternoon, Miss Cannon. Your garden's looking mighty healthy. Are these crops for your own table, or will you sell them in the store?"

"They're for us, mainly. In the store, we sell what local farmers bring us. That makes bookkeeping easier."

He nodded. Numbers were something he understood. He'd always envied the bookkeeper on the Simmons' farm. "That makes sense. But, what doesn't make sense to me are words. If I help you out here, would you help me with some reading?"

"Of course. What do you have?"

"I've got a contract for some work, but since I've never dealt with this person before, I want to make sure I understand his terms." He looked around and saw she had several rows to finish weeding. "How about I trade my weeding services in exchange for your reading? If we both work on it, we'll get this done in no time."

She laughed. "You've got a deal."

Happiness washed over him. He'd happily weed the garden every day just to see her smile.

He walked to the opposite side from her and bent to work. Soon, he'd worked into a rhythm, and they worked in companionable silence. He remembered how he'd felt when he'd first arrived in what he'd felt was a foreign land, with such wide-open spaces, no place to hide. So many smelly animals. Somehow, he'd come to appreciate the land and the animals. Just as he was coming to appreciate the town of Dowagiac.

His hands worked, and his mind wandered, just as it had in the Nebraska fields. Another row, and another.

His thoughts ended abruptly when he backed into something—someone. He straightened and spun around, seeing Nellie do the same. She rubbed her hip, and he felt a moment of panic. Had he hurt her?

"Oh! Beggin' your pardon, Miss Cannon. I wasn't paying attention." He noticed her cheeks were pink—was it from embarrassment, or was it from the sun?

"No apology necessary, Mister Martin. I wasn't paying attention, either." She looked around the garden. "Looks like we're finished. Thank you for your help. It would have taken me so much longer by myself." She wiped her hands on her apron. "Now, let's go inside and have something to drink, and I'll look at your contract." She led him into the store, and since there were no customers, they went upstairs. She poured them each a glass of lemonade then sat. She took a long draw from her glass, then reached for the paper.

She read silently, frowning a bit. Did she find problems in it? Or were the words too difficult? He itched to ask, but knew better than to interrupt. Finally, she set the paper down. "Most of it seems straightforward, but there are a few sentences that concern me. I hope I'm mistaken. Shall I read it aloud?"

"Yes, please. That is, if you have time. I know you have the afternoon train arriving in a little while."

She straightened. "Oh, goodness, I'd lost track of the time! I need to get those sack meals ready."

"I'll help you, if you like."

Her smile was back, and his heart lifted as it always did.

"Thank you!" She jumped up and pulled a pile of small canvas bags off a low shelf.

"Count out twenty of these and put an apple in each one." She pointed to a bushel of fresh apples in the corner. While he did that, she sliced two loaves of bread, laying them out neatly on her rolling board. Noticing that Bud had finished his task, she pulled a chunk of roast beef from the icebox and handed him a board and knife. "Would you slice this? Keep the slices kind of thin—it's all I have today." He nodded and went to work while she buttered the bread slices. He'd helped out in a kitchen enough times to know what to do—not to mention, he'd eaten enough of Nellie's sack lunches to know what she expected.

Working in a kitchen, side-by-side with Nellie, it felt right. It felt… like home.

In no time, twenty sandwiches had been prepared, wrapped, and put in the meal sacks, along with an apple and a cookie in each. He helped her carry them downstairs just as the train's whistle blew. By the time the first passenger disembarked, the sacks were neatly lined up on the counter.

Bud held back, not wanting to get in her way. She was so efficient, so intelligent, and yet so open and friendly. She'd read his contract, and found something amiss, so he'd stay until she was able to explain, and if she needed help, he'd step in.

"Young man, could you help me find the laudanum?" A tiny, graying woman blinked up at him. Her pallor and the cloudiness in her eyes reminded him of the pain in his mother's face as she lay dying.

"Yes, Ma'am. Let me get it for you." Thanks to Nellie's organized system, he found it quickly and brought her a small bottle. She thanked him and dropped several coins in his hand before returning to the train.

He stepped out toward the platform to make sure she made it back on, and his worry eased when a young man helped her climb the steps into the passenger car. Hopefully, the laudanum would help her endure the rest of the journey.

"Thanks again for your help," Nellie said. "I have two meal sacks left. Would you like one for your dinner? Or perhaps tomorrow's lunch? It's the least I can do after all you've done today." Nellie's melodic voice made him forget his worries.

"You don't owe me anything. I came to you for help with my contract. What was it that you found concerning?"

310

Her lips rounded in an O. "I forgot! Let's go back upstairs and we can eat while I show you what I found."

He followed her up the stairs and helped her set out plates as she poured water for them to drink. They munched companionably for a few minutes, and after he'd helped her clear the table, she picked up the document and pointed at a paragraph in the middle.

"Right here, it says that the cost of the materials will be deducted from the amount you are paid. Is that your understanding?"

Bud's jaw dropped. "N-no." He gulped. He thought back to his conversation with the businessman. "I remember he said he would have the materials delivered by next week, and I could start working after that. So, I assumed he would purchase them, and would pay me the amount on the contract."

She nodded. "I assumed as much. He was sneaky, putting that in the middle, where he hoped you wouldn't look."

His face darkened. "I guess I'll have a discussion with Mr. Arnold. I'm glad I didn't sign the contract yet." He stood. "I'd best be going, unless there's something else I can help you with."

She shook her head and stood. "Thanks to you, the garden is weeded, and you sliced so much beef I have almost enough for tomorrow's sandwiches. I hope you're able to work things out with Mr. Arnold at the stables. He's not known as the most honest businessman, but if he likes your work, he'll recommend you to others."

As he trudged back to the boarding house, he thought about how his focus had changed since he'd gotten off that train just a few weeks earlier. For the past five years, he'd been working toward a goal—moving to the north, buying his own land, and building a life for himself in the woods. But, in the last month, he'd become a part of this town, and a certain young woman filled more of his thoughts than he'd realized.

Was it time to change those plans?

Chapter Six

Nellie sighed as the last of the morning train's customers left. The day had been busy since she'd opened, with local customers and vendors arriving even before the train, but she'd had no help. She'd barely had time to prepare the sack meals. Thank goodness the morning meals were easy—a muffin, which she'd baked the previous day, and a piece of beef jerky. Still, she'd barely got them packed before the train pulled into the station.

Where was Father, anyway? She hadn't seen him all morning. Had he left? Where would he go? He didn't have any friends that she knew of. Normally, he was up long before she was and greeted her with an admonition that she'd slept the morning away. But today, he wasn't up, and it was nearly ten o'clock. She would have gone upstairs to check, but every time she thought about it, another customer or vendor came in.

Well, she didn't have time to worry about him. She checked the store shelves, noting what needed to be restocked, and making a mental note of what needed to be ordered. She heard the front door open and turned to greet the customer. Her smile widened when Bud entered.

"Good morning, Mr. Martin. What can I get for you today?"

"I was hoping you had one of those sack meals left from the morning train. I've been working hard, and Miss Lydia's breakfast has worn out."

She laughed. "You're in luck. I have one left." She handed it to him and collected his money. She searched for a topic of conversation as she put the coins in the till. "What are you working on today?" she asked.

"No projects for the rest of the day, but Miss Lydia needed a few things, so I volunteered to get them for her. He took out a scrap of paper and handed it over. "I'm afraid her handwriting isn't the best, so I hope you can make sense of this."

She peered at the list. "I can fill most of this, but I'm not sure we have a kettle. I sold our last one a week ago, and Pop talked to the salesman with the cooking utensils."

"Where is Earl? I can ask him while you're getting the rest."

"I haven't seen him all morning. It's not like him, but I guess he slept in." She frowned. "I've been so busy since I came down here that I haven't had a chance to check on him."

Bud's brows drew together. "I hope he's not sick. Would you like me to check on him?"

"That would be nice. Thank you."

Bud headed up the stairs while Nellie collected the items on the list and set them in a wooden crate. She'd gotten about halfway done when she heard his quick footsteps coming down the stairs. Bud poked his head around the curtain. "I'm getting the doctor." He disappeared before she could ask.

Twenty minutes later, Doctor Knapp removed his stethoscope from his ears. "I'm sorry, Nellie." He put his supplies back in his bag and stood. "As far as I can tell, he's been gone for several hours."

"I had no idea he was sick!" Nellie cried. "I thought he was just tired. If I'd known, I would have sent for you sooner."

The elderly gentleman placed a comforting hand on her arm. "No one is blaming you, young lady. Earl's been unhealthy for a long time. I'm amazed he lasted this long."

"He has? I knew his back bothered him, because it hurt to walk, and he couldn't lift things. What was wrong with him?"

"He had heart disease, and a host of other ailments but refused to let me treat him. He insisted he could keep it under control on his own, by using his grandmother's flaxseed poultice." He waved a hand toward the empty gin bottles scattered across the floor. "I suspect he used alcohol to forget the pain."

Flaxseed poultice. Pop had been using the flaxseed to treat himself, and when the laudanum didn't do enough to ease the pain he'd turned to alcohol.

"Doctor, is there something I can do to help?" Bud asked. "Shall I send for... someone? I think Nellie—er , Miss Cannon— could use someone to help her."

Bud's question brought her out of her stupor. "I can do this."

The doctor shook his head. "Mr. Martin is right, young lady. I know you're bright and capable, but there are arrangements to be made, and you have a store to run." He turned back to Bud. "If you don't mind, would you please run back to my home and ask my wife to come? She'll understand."

Bud nodded and disappeared.

Nellie's hand went to her pendant. What would she do? Looking around, she decided to tidy the room before anyone else came. She gathered up the gin bottles and used one of Earl's discarded shirts to wipe dust and cobwebs away.

Dr. Knapp stood. "Perhaps I can help—er, clothe Mr. Cannon before he's taken away?"

Nellie felt her face heat. She had no desire to see what her adoptive father wore, or didn't wear, under the sheet. "Thank you, Doctor. I—"

"Anyone here?" An impatient voice rose from the store, and Nellie ran downstairs. Father was beyond help. The doctor would take care of Father's body. And the doctor's wife would know what to do after that. Right now, she had a store to run.

Chapter Seven

Bud lowered the handles of his wheelbarrow down and wiped his arm across his forehead. When he'd come north, he'd thought he'd be able to escape the stifling heat he'd experienced on the plains. But, the mugginess here was just as draining.

At the moment, business was slow, so he'd completed a bench he'd promised Nellie. The bench was too bulky to carry, but not so big that he needed to borrow a horse and wagon, so he'd used the rusty wheelbarrow in his landlady's work shed to transport the finished bench to the store.

Now that Nellie was in charge, several changes had taken place and the store was busier than ever. Her sack lunches were becoming so popular that she'd hired some women to help her prepare, pack, and sell them. Even locals purchased the meals, but they needed a place to sit down and eat. So she'd asked him to build a bench or two and set them on the side of the store. If that went well, maybe she'd put up an awning. And if business continued to grow, Nellie planned to have Bud build an entire covered dining area, with tables. The girl definitely had business sense.

As he approached the store, Duke came bounding toward him. Bud was tempted to pick up a stick and throw it but knew if he started playing the dog would never want to stop. They'd both have to settle for a pat on the head and a promise to play later on.

He carried the bench over to the side of the store. But when he set it up, he noticed several tall weeds sprouting up against the wall. The bench would certainly look more inviting without the weeds behind it. A recent rain had softened the ground, so he grabbed the tallest one and pulled. It came up fairly easily, so he continued along the wall.

Every now and then, something unexpected would come up with the roots of the weed—a spoon, a train ticket, a belt buckle. He'd apparently found one of Duke's hiding places. He imagined the owners wondered what had happened to the items buried there. The last weed was the largest. Grabbing it with both hands, he gave a mighty pull, falling backward when it finally came out of the ground. He stood and shook the dirt loose from the roots. A brown, rectangular object dropped into the hole, and he froze.

Could it be?

He set the weed down and reached into the hole with a trembling hand. The tooling on the wallet identified it as the one he'd had on his belt when he'd first arrived in Dowagiac, a lifetime ago. When his plans for traveling north had been so close. How much of the wallet's contents would still be inside?

To his shock, it was all there. Every bit of money that he'd had when he'd stepped off the train. He wiped the dirt off the wallet and attached it to his belt. After almost two months without it, the additional weight on his belt seemed odd. But he didn't dare set it down, in case Duke decided to find another hiding place for it.

He gathered up all the weeds and took them to Nellie's compost pile. Then, he set the bench next to the store, where the overhanging roof gave it shade from the afternoon sun.

He had some decisions to make, but first, he had a job to finish. And then, he needed to find Nellie.

Chapter Eight

The day after Earl's funeral, Nellie served the last customer from the morning train. She wiped down the counter then climbed the stairs to prepare lunches for the afternoon train. Once that was finished, she turned her attention to Earl's room. It was time to take care of a chore she'd been putting off. She'd already taken care of the messy things—the alcohol bottles were gone, trash thrown away, and the floor swept. Now it was time to go through his personal effects. If she was going to run the store and continue to live there, she would need proof of ownership. Surely, he had a copy of the deed stored in his room.

While tidying up, she'd discovered a wooden box with a keyhole under his bed. She'd likely find what she needed inside, but she either needed to find the key or damage the box. A quick perusal of his usual hiding places proved unfruitful, and she spent some time wondering if she should simply smash the box with a hammer. But, something told her the key was in his room.

Earl's worn clothing had been stuffed into a bag. Everything had been so threadbare she didn't think the cotton shirts and trousers would be of use to anyone, yet she hadn't tossed them out. Was it possible that Earl had kept the key in one of his pockets? It would be in his nature to carry it with him at all times. She held her breath and dumped the sack's contents onto the floor. Ever since his wife died, hygiene hadn't been high on Earl's list of priorities, and the odor wafting from his clothes sent Nellie to the open window to avoid retching. Not wanting to handle the clothing them any more than necessary, she nipped over to the kitchen for a spoon for digging into the pockets.

The right-side pocket had a hole in it, so the spoon went through. But when she pushed the spoon into the left side pocket, her heart sped up when she heard a clink. Carefully, she angled the spoon and pulled out the metal object.

A small key, about an inch long, fell out. She cradled it in her hand for a moment then took the lockbox to the kitchen table. She held her breath as she brought the key to the lock.

A perfect fit.

With a quick turn of her wrist, she loosened the lock and slid it off the hook. She set the lock and the key in her apron pocket and opened the box.

She wrinkled her nose as the aroma of sweat and tobacco rose from the contents. She gingerly lifted things out. Several items were of questionable importance, such as receipts for goods purchased. She put those aside to put with the store's ledgers. There were other documents, past due notices that she hadn't seen. She took those out to study. A bit farther down, she found Muriel's death certificate. The wrinkled condition of the document told her that Earl had probably crumbled it at some point, intending to toss it, and then thought better of it.

Below the death certificate, the contents were much neater, and more organized. As Nellie expected, Muriel had taken care of the paperwork of the business as well as the home.

Farther down, she found treasures she hadn't expected. A love letter, a photograph of a much younger Earl and Muriel, standing in front of the store. They both wore serious expressions, but Earl didn't have the hard, unyielding countenance she remembered, and Muriel seemed content. Setting the photo aside, she picked up the next document.

The large letters of the word DEED took up most of the top of the folded sheet. Careful not to harm the faded sheets, she scanned it. There at the bottom the beneficiaries were named. Muriel, and… Lucas Cannon. Her heart sank. Her name didn't appear anywhere. She turned the page over to make sure. Nothing.

Why would they not name her as a beneficiary? She'd been with them twelve years. She'd worked hard with them to ensure the store remained profitable. Why would they not acknowledge her as their daughter? Her disappointment hurt as much as a physical blow, and she dropped down to sit on the bed. Tears blurred her vision and lost track of time. A stranger now owned the store. What would she do? Where could she go?

"Anybody here?" Bud's deep voice boomed from the bottom of the stairs, bringing her out of her stupor. and she dashed down the stairs, wiping her wet cheeks with her apron. Forcing a smile, she faced him.

"Hello, Mister Martin. How are you today?"

"I'm fine, thank you." He frowned. "But, I get the feeling you could use a friend. Is there a way I can help?" He nodded at the paper she still clutched. "Did you receive more bad news?"

She bit her lip. "I always assumed the store would eventually belong to me, but looks like the store is going to be owned by someone else."

Bud's eyes opened wide as he took that in. "Someone else? Did Earl have other relatives no one knew about?"

"He had a son who left years ago, before I came. According to the deed I just found, everything goes to him."

Bud groaned. "And, if they can't find him, or if he's dead, the store will be sold to the highest bidder." When Nellie stared at him, he explained, "One of the farmers near the place I worked passed away with no heirs. All his neighbors were speculating on who'd be able to bid the highest."

She closed her eyes. "If it goes to auction, I don't have the money to purchase it."

***

Nellie sank into her favorite chair. Her baking and cooking for the following day was done, and she'd closed the store for the night. She'd spent nearly an hour combing Earl's room for adoption papers, without success. Now she had some decisions to make.

Bud had assured her that even if Earl's son was not found, and if she had no legal claim, it would be some time before she'd be expected to turn the store over to whoever inherited or purchased it. A visit to the constable confirmed this. She could remain in her quarters and keep the store running. Perhaps, he'd told her, the new owner would agree to hire her, letting her run the store and continue living there as part of her wages. There was no urgency for her to leave.

Still, she couldn't ignore the fact that she couldn't stay indefinitely. She would need a plan, including a place to go and a way to make a living, if she had to turn the store over and leave. Her hand wrapped around her pendant and she closed her eyes.

She'd been only eight years old when her biological mother died, but she remembered a tiny, fragile woman, huddled in a corner of the tiny apartment they'd shared with her abusive father and an assortment of aunts and uncles. After a particularly violent beating, she'd waited until her father had left and gone to her mother, who lay there fingering her rosary.

"Mama, what can I do to help you?" she'd asked.

Her mother had handed her a worn book. "Read to me, Ellie," she'd begged. "I can't see the words clearly right now, but the words always help me feel better. Start on the page where the little piece of ribbon is, at the part I marked with a pencil."

And so little Ellie sat close to her mother and read, "The Lord is my Shepherd…"

Nellie's eyes opened, and she sat up. Although the memory of her mother had been painful, it had given her an idea. Muriel had kept a Bible that she'd carried with her to church each week. Earl had put it in a box of things to sell or give away after his wife died, but Nellie had retrieved it before the box had been sold at the auction. She went to her bookshelf and found it, looking for the passage that had always comforted her mother—her biological mother.

She found it, near the middle of the worn volume. To her surprise, an envelope nested there, addressed to her. Shame washed over her. Muriel, who'd been gone nearly three years, had left this personal message for her in a book she should have opened long before this. She opened the flap and pulled out two neatly folded pieces of paper.

The first was a letter:

> *Dear Nellie,*
>
> *I always knew you were a bright young girl. I was so pleased when Earl agreed to have you come and live with us. I know he wasn't kind to you, but he respected your ability to use what you learned. I've begged him to go to the court and make your adoption legal, but he keeps holding out hope that our son will return and take over the store. I know that's not going to happen, because my sister back East sent me a notice in the paper that Lucas was killed at Antietam. Earl refuses to believe it.*
>
> *For once in my life, I've gone against him. I filled out the papers and got Earl to sign them when I told him it was an order for the store. I'm praying God will forgive me for this, but it's the right thing to do. I know you'll take care of Earl, even though he hasn't been a good father to you. And I know you'll take good care of the store.*
>
> *With much love,*
> *Mother Cannon*

Behind the letter was a Certificate of Adoption, dated just two months before Muriel's death, and the newspaper notice of Lucas' death.

She replaced the pages in the envelope, shaking her head at this turn of events. All this time, Nellie had thought Muriel hadn't regarded her as anything but an unpaid employee. But, one of the last things she'd done on this earth was to take care of this on her own. She'd signed the letter "With much love." Had she really felt love, or had she simply written the words without much thought?

Energized, Nellie rose and put the envelope in her purse. In the morning, she would find out what to do with these documents. If Lucas died in the war, there should be a death certificate somewhere. And with the signed adoption papers, the store would be hers.

Chapter Nine

Bud strode into the general store, his tension increasing with each step. He had a plan and he needed to put it into action before he lost his nerve.

Leroy Jones, one of the oldest residents of Dowagiac, kept Nellie busy. Apparently, Leroy needed help to find every item on his list. Nellie fetched each item one by one. When he'd gone through his entire list, he reached for his worn money bag, fumbled to get it open, and counted his change. One penny, then another, then another.

Bud gritted his teeth. His hand went to his throat, as it always did when faced with frustration. Almost immediately, his mind's eye went to his mother, struggling through her illness to carry on with daily tasks. She'd needed his help and compassion, not his disdain for things she could no longer do. And, Leroy needed the same.

Finally, the man completed his purchase, and Bud stepped forward. "Morning, Mr. Jones. Let me help you with those." He picked up the man's purchases with one hand and held the door open while the elderly gentleman shuffled slowly toward the door. Then, he placed the sack in the broken-down wagon outside and helped the man get up into the seat. He was rewarded with a toothless grin.

"Thanks for your help, young man. I know I don't move as fast as I used to, and I appreciate you being patient. Miss Nellie's got a keeper in you." He touched his hat and drove off.

He stepped back into the store, eager to complete his mission. Nellie greeted him with a smile. "Thank you for helping Mister Jones. He's such a dear man, but I know it can be difficult waiting for him. What can I do for you?"

"Marry me." He'd had a speech all rehearsed, but the words poured out of his mouth before he could stop them.

She paled, and the cloth she'd been using to wipe the counter fell to the floor. Her hand went to her chest, and he wondered if he'd caused her to have something he'd heard women call the vapors.

"Are you hurting?" he asked.

She stared at him in confusion. "Of course not. Do I seem unwell?"

"Your hand went to your chest. I thought perhaps you were in pain and I ought to run for the doctor."

Her expression cleared. "Oh. No, I'm fine. It's just..." She blushed becomingly. "Whenever I have a—an unexpected situation, and I don't know what to say or do, I ask my talisman for help." She pulled a thin chain out from under her blouse. "A dear friend gave this to me many years ago, telling me that it had magic powers to guide me whenever I got confused or scared. I didn't quite believe him then, but it's been a great comfort to me."

Time stopped for Bud as she pulled the familiar pendant from her blouse. The outline of the rose had worn down but was still visible.

"Ellie?" His breath came out as a whisper.

She froze. Slowly, she raised her eyes and looked into his. He stared back.

Yes, it was her. How had he failed to recognize her? The eyes were the same bright blue, though they'd darkened with age and responsibility. They were the eyes he'd gazed into back at the orphanage. The ones that had first taught him the need to protect, to help.

"It's me, Vinnie. From the orphanage." He pulled his own pendant out from under his shirt.

The most beautiful smile he'd ever witnessed spread across her face. The smile he remembered.

"Vinnie?" She gasped. "It's really you? I thought you were so much like the boy I knew in New York, but I didn't dare ask. They put you on an orphan train, too, didn't they?"

He nodded. "I left a few weeks after you did."

She fingered the pendant. "I thought of you each time I touched this. It helped me so much over the years. I always thought you were the most generous person in the world. I never dreamed I'd see you again, to thank you." She came around the counter and reached out to take his hands. "All these years of fear and doubt, when the train brought me here, when Earl and Muriel brought me to their home, when I started school for the first time, twice as tall as the other girls in my class—this pendant got me through it. The string you gave me broke a few years ago, and I bought this chain to put it on so that it would be safe around my neck. It saved me, it truly did."

"Mine saved me too. When I had tough times, I thought about the brave little girl who needed this as much as me. I spent every day of the last twelve years hoping yours worked as well as mine." He gazed deep into the blue eyes he hoped to see every day for the rest of his life. "I know I'm not the brightest, and I don't have the money to help you buy the store if it comes to that, but I'll work hard so you'll never have to worry about a roof over your head or food on your table." His hand went to his wallet, securely tied to his belt. "I forgot to tell you—I found my wallet the other day. It was buried on the side of the store, where I put the new bench. If you marry me, there's enough here for me to build us a home. Or, if you'd rather, we can use it as a down payment toward purchasing the store, if the courts put it up for sale. Whatever you want."

She shook her head. "We don't need to use your money for the store. I found the signed adoption papers last night. I'm going to bring them to the constable right after the morning train."

"That's—that's great news. The store is yours." While he was happy for her, he couldn't stop the disappointment that she didn't need him quite as much as he needed her. But then she reached up to lay a hand on his cheek.

"I'm going to need help keeping the store profitable. And, I need even more help to make my life complete. If you can abide having a wife who's busy taking care of customers in addition to a family, I'd like to accept your offer."

It may have been his imagination, but Bud would swear that the sun shone brighter through the windows. His voice rasped as he vowed, "I'm here to help however I can. You make *my* life complete."

Before he knew it, her arms were wrapped around his neck and she was pressed against him. His arms circled her waist, and he held her close. He knew that wherever he was— New York, Nebraska, or Michigan—he could deal with whatever life brought him, if she was by his side.

"Excuse me," a female voice said.

They stepped away from each other, and he knew his cheeks were as pink as hers.

Nellie recovered first. "I'm sorry, Mrs. Waters. What can I do for you?"

"I wonder if you have any molasses. I'm baking this afternoon, and I don't see any."

"I apologize. I'll get some right away." Bud couldn't stop himself from watching her walk away from him. Twelve years ago, he'd watched her walk away, thinking he'd never see her again. But now—

"I hope you plan to make an honest woman of her." Mrs. Waters stood with her arms crossed, her frown tempered by the amusement in her eyes. He'd forgotten about the woman's presence.

Pasting on his most pleasant smile, he nodded in acknowledgement. "Yes, Ma'am. I wouldn't think of doing any less."

***

On a sunny afternoon in July, passengers on the Michigan Central Railway disembarking at Dowagiac found a sign propped up on the counter where they normally purchased their lunches:

> *"Miss Eleanor Cannon and Mr. Vincent Martinelli invite you to help them celebrate their wedding day by enjoying a free lunch. If you need anything in the store, please leave payment on the counter. Thank you for your patronage."*

When Ellie and Vinnie returned later that day, they found an envelope containing full payment for all the meals, along with several written messages of congratulations and well-wishes.

There was also a voucher for a train trip for two. The bridal couple considered using it to travel back to New York, to visit the orphanage where they'd first met. But eventually, they decided to go north, to the forests where a young woodworker had once dreamed of making his fortune. Perhaps they'd return to Dowagiac, and perhaps they'd sell the store and build their forever home in the northern woods. Whatever they decided, they both had their talismans to show them the way.

THE END

Introducing Rosanne Bittner

Trouble Rides a Fast Horse

Rosanne Bittner has built a reputation for writing gritty westerns with a hot heat level, about true love and high emotion, with subtle references to prayer and faith woven between the lines. "Trouble Rides a Fast Horse" is different because it's a modern-day Christian-themed story of a teenager and her beloved grandmother who is trying to discover why her granddaughter has been so moody lately. When Grandma learns it's about disappointment over a crush, she starts telling her own story of disappointment over a new boyfriend. Between the modern day and historical reveals, "Trouble Rides a Fast Horse" shows how a prayer isn't always answered in the way we desire. You can learn more about Rosanne and her 70-plus published historical books involving the 1800s American West at www.rosannebittner.com.

Heat Level: SWEET

TROUBLE RIDES A FAST HORSE
Rosanne Bittner

Mattie gently tapped at her granddaughter's bedroom door. The sixteen-year-old was sulking alone in her room over the fact that her best friend was dating a boy for whom she carried a secret crush—so secret that even her best friend didn't know about it.

Mattie was concerned, aware of how emotional teenage girls could be. "Can I come in, Jackie?"

She heard footsteps. The door opened, and there stood Mattie's dear, first grandchild with eyes slightly swollen from crying. "Jackie, can we talk? I'd like to tell you something about an experience I had similar to yours."

The young girl frowned, obviously wondering how a seventy-year-old woman would know anything about young love. Mattie smiled. "I *was* young once myself, you know. A teenage crush is something you never forget, sweetheart, and I had a bad one at your age."

Jackie shrugged. "Nothing you say will help, Grandma, but I would never tell you not to come into my room. I suppose Mom sent you up here."

"She certainly did not. She *is* concerned about you, but I came up here on my own."

"Where's Grandpa? I didn't even know you were here."

"Grandpa decided to spend the day fishing with a friend, and I got bored, so I drove over here for a visit. Your mom and I got to talking and of course she told me how you've been in here alone most of the weekend. I suppose you've been sharing your frustration with friends on Facebook."

Jackie shrugged. "No. I don't want anybody to know

because even Missy doesn't know I'm secretly in love with her boyfriend." The girl walked over and sat down in front of her computer. She deleted a game she'd been playing and turned to face her grandmother, who sat down on the edge of Jackie's bed.

"So, what's the boy's name?"

Jackie sighed. "Brady Hollister, and he's like…I don't know…just everything a girl could want. He's popular, plays football and basketball, gets good grades, works weekends at his father's hardware store, he's polite, and he even goes to church—not our church—but he does go, which most boys I know don't. I've prayed all school year that he would notice me. I've dropped hints, gone to events where I knew he'd be …then he up and asks Melissa out. I want to hate her for it, but she doesn't know how I feel about Brady, so it's not her fault. Besides, she's much more his type, prettier than me, more popular." She looked at her lap, pouting. "Do you know what I mean?"

Mattie reached out and patted Jackie's knee. "Believe it or not, I know exactly what you mean. And, I don't mean you aren't just as pretty as Melissa, because you *are*. I just mean that I went through something similar once, and I remember how it felt to think I wasn't good enough or pretty enough."

Jackie met her gaze. "I've even prayed about it, Grandma. I asked God to make Brady like me, but God apparently doesn't plan to answer that prayer."

Mattie scooted farther back on the bed. "Jackie, God doesn't always answer our prayers the way we want Him to. He just might have other plans for you, and usually they are far more wonderful than what we're expecting or asking for. In all my years of living, Jackie, through high school, marriage, children, and through all my moments of doubt, I will always remember a story my grandmother told me about prayer and

how God answered her own prayers once…in a totally round-
about way she never expected. After hearing her story, I
decided to give all my troubles over to God and trust Him to do
what is best for me and those I love. And, He ended up solving
my own problem after all."

Jackie leaned back in her swivel desk chair and folded
her arms. "Okay. I know you're going to tell me what this is all
about. I doubt it will help how I feel, Grandma, but I always
like talking to you and hearing your stories. What happened?"

Mattie thought how, in spite of how different the world
was now from when she was young, things in the matters of
love and life and youth and emotions never really changed
much. "Well, I was fifteen years old." Jackie rolled her eyes.
"Yes, a long, long time ago. I was sitting on our front porch
pining over a boy I was crazy about, but who didn't even know
I existed. I had the same problem you're having right now, and
it turns out my own grandmother went through the same thing,
or so I learned when she told me all about it. I called her
Grandma Bea, and she came out onto the porch that day and
caught me in tears."

Wonderful memories flooded through Mattie's mind and
heart. She could tell that Jackie doubted anything she said
would help, but she kept right on, not letting the girl try to stop
her.

"I was very close to my grandma, Jackie, just like you
and I are close. She and my Grandpa Clive were staying with us
because Grandma Bea was recovering from a heart attack and
Grandpa Clive was nervous about caring for her alone. My dad
let them stay with us, and back then most women didn't work,
so my mother was home all day to help out." She leaned closer.
"The strange thing was, I remember my father saying he *owed*
Grandpa Clive a return favor and that was why he didn't mind
helping out after Grandma Bea's heart attack. He said they

could stay with us because Grandma Bea and Grandpa Clive once cared for him at home for months as he recovered from a terrible swimming accident."

"Really?" Jackie moved over to the bed to sit down beside Mattie. "What happened?"

Mattie felt relieved that she was taking Jackie's mind off her boyfriend problems. "Well, at the time, I didn't understand the whole story, or how it affected my father's relationship with my grandparents…not until that day on the porch when Grandma Bea explained it. She was really teaching me about prayer and forgiveness, you know. And, through her story, I learned there was much more to the fact that my father had inherited a horse farm from my Grandpa. Up until then, I just took all that for granted. Grandpa Clive had a horse farm, and my father took it over when he was old enough. That seemed simple enough to me, but it wasn't. According to what Grandma Bea told me, God had a lot to do with all of it."

Jackie's eyes lit up. She scooted up to lean against the headboard of the bed and picked up a stuffed rabbit, enfolding it into her arms and reminding Mattie of when Jackie was younger. Mattie hated seeing her grow up, because growing up meant suffering the pains of what real life handed out, sometimes in cruel ways.

"So, what *happened* Grandma?"

"Well, as you already know, my Grandpa Clive had a horse farm once, a very fine one. My own father, Jess, took it over eventually, but that's part of my story. My brother, Cal, and I inherited the farm, and Cal eventually paid me for my share of it. When he got old, he sold out to Rainbow Stables, so that big horse farm on the other side of town stems in part from that original horse farm Grandpa Clive started when he was hardly more than a boy himself. That day on the porch, when Grandma Bea caught me crying, she sat down next to me on the porch swing and told me all about that farm and my own father and how their stories are a good example of answered prayer. I told Grandma Bea that a boy I was crazy about in school had asked another girl to be his partner at a school dance and Grandma Bea told me a story that made me feel better."

Jackie smiled. "Sorry, Grandma, but it's hard to picture you a young girl at a school dance."

Mattie laughed lightly. "Well, like I said, we are all young once." She toyed with a loose thread on the pillowcase. "Anyway, Grandma Bea was a great lady, very Christian, very loving. Because of that horse farm, she and Grandpa Clive ended up rather wealthy by most standards back then, although you never would have known it. Grandma remained a woman of simple taste who loved her family and homemaking and cooking and continued making a lot of her own clothes because she enjoyed sewing. It was always easy for me to talk to her. Most of the time I felt like she already knew what I was thinking before I even spoke. I felt silly telling her why I'd been crying, but I just knew she'd understand and wouldn't laugh at me. I told her God didn't care about my problem, but she told me that sometimes God takes the long way around when answering prayer, like with her and Grandpa Clive, and my father. She handed me a clean handkerchief to dry my tears with and proceeded to explain what she meant."

Mattie chuckled at more memories.

"That's another example of Grandma Bea's frugality. She always used real hankies, even after they came out with throw away tissues. She said it was silly to spend money on paper tissues when a handkerchief cost only a few cents and could be washed and used over and over." Mattie studied Jackie lovingly. "She always wore aprons, too," she added, but then waved away the memory. "I'm getting away from my story." She moved up beside Jackie, leaning against the headboard.

"Anyway, Grandma Bea told me that she once felt about Grandpa Clive the way I felt about the boy I was pining over, and the way you feel now about Brady Hollister."

"You mean she liked him but he didn't like her?" Jackie asked.

Mattie nodded. "Grandma told me that Grandpa Clive was a very handsome boy, very popular. She was plain and quiet and he hardly ever noticed her, even though they sat next to each other in the one-room school they attended. About the only time Grandpa Clive noticed her was when he snuck a look to the side and tried to cheat off her test papers. She liked him so much that she always made it easy for him to see the answers. She thought that would get his attention in other ways, but it didn't work."

Mattie and Jackie both smiled. "So, how did she finally get his attention?" Jackie asked.

Mattie grinned, arching her eyebrows. "She prayed."

Jackie lost her smile. "That's it? She didn't flirt with him or trick him into a date?"

Mattie shook her head. "No. Girls weren't quite so bold back then."

"Well, did he just start noticing her all on his own?"

"Oh, my, no!" Mattie frowned. "Just like you, she thought God was being mean by not answering her prayers right away. She thought maybe God just didn't care about a plain young girl who had a silly crush on a boy, but she later learned that God has ways of testing our faith before he gives us everything we want."

Jackie rolled her eyes. "Okay, so what happened?"

Mattie felt excited over her own story. "Well, Grandpa Clive always loved horses. Grandma Bea told me she figured he loved horses more than he loved his own ma and pa or anything else. He used to miss school sometimes – sneak back home to go riding. And, he liked to race them against other kids. He always had bets going. Back then, of course, pretty much everybody had horses if they lived in the country. Most even still used them for transportation. Automobiles were just beginning to be used by the average person. So, where young men today race cars, the young men in her day raced their horses. Grandma Bea said that Grandpa Clive and another boy were reprimanded one day for skipping school to race their horses. *Trouble rides a fast horse,* the teacher told them. Grandma Bea never forgot that saying, and neither have I, because it's so true. One little bit of trouble just leads to more trouble, and back then Grandpa Clive was always getting in trouble for racing, but that reckless nature of his was one of the things Grandma Bea loved about him. She said a lot of the kids used to all get together on Saturdays to watch boys race their horses, and Grandpa Clive usually won, but then one day something terrible happened."

Jackie sat up straighter. "What?"

Mattie sobered. "Someone dared Grandpa Clive to ride a wild mustang that nobody else could tame. He loved a dare, and so he took it. Grandma Bea just sat there quietly for a moment when she was telling me all this. Tears formed in her eyes. *Yes, trouble does ride a fast horse,* she told me. *That wild horse threw your grandpa, and he broke his neck.*

Jackie gasped. "He did? I never knew that!"

Mattie smiled sadly. "I didn't know that either, until Grandma Bea told me about it that day. Now that I think about it, I guess us old people need to do a better job of talking to you young people about what life was like when we were young."

"Was he crippled?"

"No, not for good anyway. But, he was laid up in a special brace for a long time." She leaned closer. "And *that's* how God answered Grandma Bea's prayer."

Jackie pursed her lips. "By hurting your Grandpa Clive? That's not a very nice way to answer a prayer. How did that make him like your grandmother?"

Mattie glanced down at the aged skin on the back of her hands. She'd always had trouble thinking of herself as an old woman. She was spry and healthy and energetic and never gave much thought to her age. Telling her story to Jackie made her realize she was behaving just like her own Grandma Bea did back then, trying to make a beloved granddaughter feel better, teaching a life lesson. She met Jackie's concerned gaze.

"The long way around—remember? God did something that meant Clive Howard had to stay put, and He knew that was the only way that boy would finally begin to notice Grandma Bea. His own pa's farm was just up the road from where Grandma Bea lived, so Bea's mother and Grandma Bea both took food to the family often because Clive's mother was busy taking care of Clive. They also helped with chores." She winked at Jackie. "Sometimes Grandma Bea's mother would ask her to sit with Clive and keep him company because he was feeling down and sorry for himself and bored and all the things a young man laid up like that would feel."

Jackie brightened. "And that way, your grandmother could finally spend time all alone with the boy she secretly loved and get him to notice her."

Mattie nodded. "That's right. She read to him, took him get-well cards from their friends and read those to him, too. They talked a lot, and Grandpa Clive began to see Grandma Bea as a real person. I guess he liked what he saw. He realized she was a caring person, and he sensed how she felt about him, even though she never let on to him. He was very grateful for the time she spent with him. Other kids would visit him, but none really helped him out like Grandma Bea did."

Jackie crossed her legs Indian style and leaned closer.

336

"That is so awesome, Grandma. God saw that in order for your Grandma Bea to get your grandpa's attention, something had to happen to make him sit still for a while."

Mattie nodded. "God made something happen that would let them spend time together and really get to know each other in a way they never did before. After that, Clive began paying a lot more attention to my grandmother. When he got well enough to walk and go back to school and all, and they were old enough to date, that handsome boy asked Grandma Bea to dances and hay rides and all such things, and they ended up marrying, a marriage that lasted fifty years, until Grandpa Clive died. How about that?"

"That's a great story, Grandma! Thanks for telling it to me."

Mattie arched her eyebrows. "Well, my girl, that wasn't the biggest test of prayer that came into Grandma Bea's life. The biggest test came years later, after their son, my own father, of course, was grown to about the age Clive was when his accident happened. Because of his love for horses, Grandpa Clive went on to raise horses on his own and to train racehorses. By the time my father was mostly grown, they were doing really well, making good money, but they weren't happy. No, Ma'am, they weren't happy at all—at least Grandma Bea wasn't. It was a very sad time for her, and again she was on her knees doing a lot of praying."

"But, she loved your grandpa and got to marry him, and they were rich! So, why wasn't she happy?"

Mattie reached over and touched her arm lightly. "Being rich doesn't always mean being happy, Jackie. Always remember that. Don't ever think that money is the answer to everything, because it isn't. Peace and harmony and love— those are the things that bring happiness. If the ones you love aren't happy, all the money in the world won't make things better."

"Why weren't they happy?"

"Well, according to my grandmother, my father and grandfather were exactly alike in personality. And, when that happens, there is a lot of friction when a young man hits the age where he thinks he's all grown up and knows more than his father. My father and grandpa began fighting—a *lot*. It was real hard on Grandma Bea, because she could see both viewpoints. She was always caught in the middle. My father would be mad at her if she agreed with grandpa, and grandpa was mad at her if she agreed with my father. It was a terrible time, and Grandma Bea cried a lot. My father was their only child, so he was the most precious thing in the world to her. Deep inside, he was precious to Grandpa Clive, too, but men have a different way of loving sometimes, and he had his own ideas of what my father should do with his life and how he should behave and all such things. My father, of course, didn't always do what his own father expected of him. He had his *own* ideas about life. They often argued about the horses and what to do about certain problems with them and such. My father became rebellious, and he ran with the wrong crowd and got into some trouble, and that made Grandpa Clive furious. He was disappointed in my father, and he told him so."

Mattie hugged the pillow closer. "Grandma Bea said that Grandpa Clive's harsh words hurt my father deeply. A mother aches for her child when she knows he or she is sad inside, and believe me, a grandmother aches even worse for her grandchildren." She reached over and put her arm around Jackie's shoulders, pulling her closer so the girl could rest her head on Mattie's shoulder. "Grandma Bea told me there were so many times when she just wanted to hold my father and tell him everything would be all right, but Grandpa Clive wouldn't let her. He said my father was grown and had to learn his own

lessons and that she shouldn't baby him. Well, that caused
problems between my grandparents, and in general, *nobody* was
happy."

Jackie straightened. "How did they get through all that?"

Mattie smiled softly. "Again, Grandma Bea turned to
prayer. And then one night, my dad and grandfather got into a
big fight over chores. My father fed the wrong grain to a horse
that had digestive problems and wasn't supposed to have that
particular feed. The horse got really sick and died." Mattie
stared at the blank computer screen as she continued.
"Grandma said that was a really bad night, the worst she could
remember in her life, because my dad and grandfather fought
so hard that she thought they might use their fists. Finally, my
father accused Grandpa Clive of loving his horses more than his
own son, and he stormed out."

"Wow." Jackie grasped a piece of her long, brown hair
and began twisting it. "Did they ever make up?"

"Grandma Bea did a *lot* of praying then, but again,
according to her, God didn't give her a quick, direct answer.
Again, He took the long way around. She said Grandpa Clive
went out to the barn for a while, then came back inside looking
sad and defeated. He went to bed without a word. Later that
night the phone rang, and they got the awful news. My dad had
gone to a wild party and drank too much. The party was at a
big pond kids went to back then, where there was a rope swing
kids took out over the water to dive from. My dad did just that,
but he landed wrong. When they dragged him out of the water,
he was lifeless but still breathing."

"Is that the accident that left Grampa with a limp?"
Jackie asked. "I used to ask him about it, but he said it was from
falling off a horse and hurting his hip."

"No. It was from that swimming accident."

"I never knew Grandpa and his father had a fight that

led to that."

Mattie shifted, becoming a bit uncomfortable with her position on the bed. "Neither my dad nor my grandfather liked to talk about it because it was such a sad time in their lives. They used to tell us not to talk about it either. They forgave each other and became much closer, so they wanted to put it all behind them. Grandma Bea told me that at first my grandfather felt guilty for my dad taking off that night and getting hurt. And, for a while, my dad did blame him. But, as time passed and my father recovered, they both came to realize that God caused that accident to give them time to pause and consider their blessings and how much they loved each other. Grandma Bea said my father lay in a coma for a long time. They didn't have insurance back then, so the hospital bills, they kept climbing, and finally Grandpa Clive sold every horse, except the foal of the horse that had died under my father's care, and sold most of his equipment to pay the bills. He rented a lot of his property out to farmers to keep money coming in. The whole matter nearly forced them into bankruptcy, but Grandpa Clive would have sold his own soul to help my dad get well if he could have. He was tortured over feeling responsible for the accident. When my dad came around and got better, and then learned what Grandpa Clive had done, he knew then how much his father loved him. He realized what a huge sacrifice it was for Clive to give up his horse farm. My Grandfather begged my father's forgiveness for him not being a better father, and the two of them knew their relationship with each other was more important than anything else. So again, God took the long way around to answer Grandma Bea's prayers for peace and harmony."

"Wow, I never knew any of that, Grandma." Jackie knitted her eyebrows in thought. "But, your father and grandfather ended up with a big horse farm again, the one your brother ended up selling to Rainbow Farms. How did they get back on their feet?"

Mattie smiled. "How do you think?"

Jackie thought a moment, then grinned. "They prayed?"

Mattie laughed. "Of course!"

"And did God take the long way around again?"

"Of course he did!"

Jackie reached over to a nightstand and pulled a piece of red licorice from a jar, sticking it into her mouth. "How did he answer this time?"

"At first, they survived by caring for other peoples' horses, especially race horses. My father took a new interest in horses because he knew how much they meant to my grandfather, and he'd found a new love for Grandpa Clive and wanted to help him rebuild the horse farm. He worked real hard helping take care of the horses they took in, and they began working with that one foal that Grandpa Clive had kept. Grandpa and my father both felt close to it because what had happened. It was during that time that my father realized he had Grandpa Clive's talent for reading a horse, judging its value and its heart. He saw something in that young colt. He worked with it and worked with it and got it so well trained—"

"The one called Trouble?" Jackie interrupted, suddenly putting it all together. "The one that won the Kentucky Derby way back before I was born?"

Mattie smiled elatedly. "Yes! That one! My father trained Trouble and worked with him and started entering him in races. Every time he won a race, they got more and more back on their feet, and when he won the Derby, they were able to totally rebuild the horse farm and start over!"

Jackie settled back against the headboard again. "That's a great story, Grandma."

"And now, please, tell me you feel better."

Jackie shrugged. "I guess I do. You made me forget my own troubles for a while, at least. I suppose that if God means for me to be with Brady, it will happen. I know that's what you're trying to tell me."

"Well, sometimes God doesn't give us the answers we want, Jackie. If he doesn't, it's usually for our own good, because nobody loves us as much as God loves us. Always remember that."

"I will." Jackie got up and went to sit in her desk chair again. "But, what about your own prayers—the boyfriend problem you were having?"

Mattie smiled slyly, having saved the best part of her story for last. "Well, Grandma Bea died just three years after she told me that story, and two years after that Grandpa Clive died. I used my grandmother's advice often in handling my own children, telling them that *trouble rides a fast horse.* They would look at me like I was crazy and say, *What does that mean, Mommy?* I would tell them it meant that one kind of trouble leads to another and another until it's like a race, and they have to stop it early before something bad happens and how God sometimes takes the long way around when answering our prayers. It happened twice to Grandma Bea, with Grandpa Clive and with her son...and it happened to me, too. Now when I look at a picture I have of my father and grandfather standing next to that beautiful, shiny black horse named Trouble, I think of Grandma Bea and those first prayers of hers for God to make Clive Howard notice her. I think about that boy I pined over that day, the boy who never did notice me...not until after he got back from serving in Vietnam. We were older then, more mature, and we noticed each other in all the right ways. And yes, God does sometimes take the long way around, Jackie. That man and I were married not long after that, and we're still married."

Jackie's face broke into a huge grin. "*Grandpa?*"

"The one and only. See what I mean? Some day you could end up with Brady Hollister, but if you don't, it will be best for you. You've hardly touched on what love really means, Jackie, and *no one* loves you more than God Himself. Trust Him and your prayers will always be answered."

Jackie jumped up and came over to give her a hug. "The best thing God ever did for me was give you to me," she told Mattie.

Mattie smiled knowing that hugs from grandchildren were one of the good things about growing old.

Just then, Jackie's mother walked into the room.

"Well, I came up here to see how things were going. I can see you're feeling better, Jackie."

Jackie straightened. "Grandma told me the story about the horse called Trouble, about her grandfather and her dad, and how she ended up with Grandpa Tom. Did you know all that?"

Sarah smiled, studying her own mother lovingly. "Oh, yes. Your grandma told me the story one day when I asked about Grandpa Cal's limp. I decided someday there would be a right time to tell you, and I see Grandma Mattie decided this was it. Somehow that story has gotten someone in each generation in this family through some kind of crisis."

Just then, Jackie's best friend Melissa shouted Jackie's name. As usual, she'd come into the house as though she lived there and bounded up the stairs, looking for Jackie. The slender blonde charged into Jackie's room. "Oh!" she exclaimed when she saw Jackie there with her mother and grandmother. "I'm sorry!"

"What are you doing here?" Jackie asked. "I thought you'd be home getting ready for another date with Brady Hollister."

Melissa made a face. "Him? We had just one date Friday night, Jackie, and he turned out to be such a jerk! Totally sold on himself, you know? We are so *over* already."

Jackie looked from her mother to her grandma, and then all three women burst out laughing.

"God *does* answer prayer in strange ways, Grandma!" Jackie said, giving the woman another hug.

"Are you guys crazy?" Melissa asked, looking confused.

"Come in, Missy!" Jackie told her, going over to drag her into the room. "I'll tell you all about it!"

Mattie and Jackie's mother left, closing the door behind them. Both women breathed deep sighs of relief and headed downstairs.

"Glad you came to visit, Mom," Sarah told Mattie.

"God sent me. Surely you know that, Sarah."

"Yeah. I know. Let's go have some coffee."

Both women smiled, enjoying the sound of screams and laughter coming from Jackie's room.

THE END

LOST & FOUND

Made in the USA
Monee, IL
01 April 2021